6/18

0 1 AUG 2018

S/C 01/20

→10/22

3/2/23

This book should be returned/renewed by the latest date shown above. Overdue items incur charges which prevent self-service renewals. Please contact the library.

Wandsworth Libraries
24 hour Renewal Hotline
01159 293388
www.wandsworth.gov.uk

Wandsworth

By the same author

The Strings of Murder
A Fever of the Blood
A Mask of Shadows

Loch of the Dead

OSCAR DE MURIEL

PENGUIN BOOKS

PENGUIN BOOKS

UK | USA | Canada | Ireland | Australia
India | New Zealand | South Africa

Penguin Books is part of the Penguin Random House group of companies
whose addresses can be found at global.penguinrandomhouse.com

First published 2018
001

Copyright © Oscar de Muriel, 2018

The moral right of the author has been asserted

Set in 12.5/14.75 pt Garamond MT Std
Typeset by Jouve (UK), Milton Keynes
Printed in Great Britain by Clays Ltd, St Ives plc

A CIP catalogue record for this book is available from the British Library

ISBN: 978–1–405–92624–9

www.greenpenguin.co.uk

Penguin Random House is committed to a
sustainable future for our business, our readers
and our planet. This book is made from Forest
Stewardship Council® certified paper.

The fourth one is for Doña Magda,
who's been (im)patiently waiting for it since 2016.

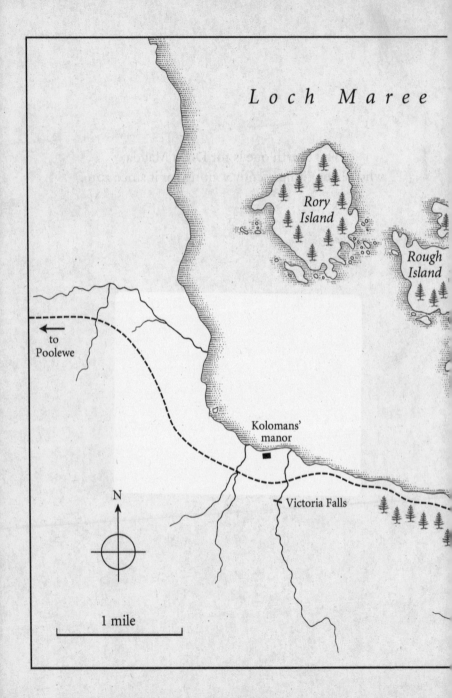

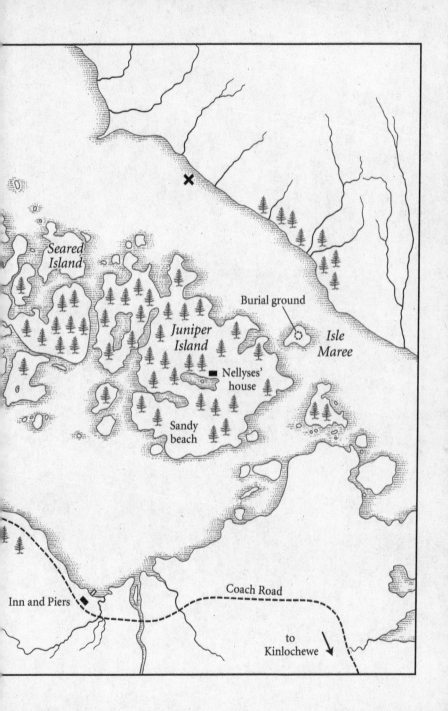

And whoso bathes therein his brow
With care or madness burning,
Feels once again his healthful thought
And sense of peace returning.

John Whittier, 1877,
on the occasion of Queen
Victoria's visit to Loch Maree

1873

28 May

I never wanted the wee brat, thought Millie, looking down at the round, smooth face of the infant. The sway of the boat had lulled him into sleep: his chest went up and down as if following the rhythm of the waves, his chubby little fingers clasped the ragged blanket.

I even held the herbal tea, Millie recalled. *I pressed my lips against the cup and smelled its poison. I wanted to purge you out of my body, as if you were an infection.*

A tear fell on the blanket, bursting without warning.

Millie wiped it at once. Nobody had ever seen her cry. Nobody except –

The child stirred in her arms and let out a soft moan, perhaps woken by her sudden movement, but Millie cuddled him more tightly, rocked him and lovingly whispered, 'There, there.'

Where had all that come from? She had never been tender, or gentle, or sentimental. She had never played with dolls. How was it that she knew exactly what to do now? How to hold him, how to get him to sleep. Why was she feeling that painful gulp and that tearing oppression in her chest?

'Don't get too attached, lassie,' said Mr Dailey, steering the boat in the dark. 'He'll be gone in a minute.'

'Mind your own business, you old twat.'

He could only laugh. 'Aye, that's our Millie . . .'

Mr Dailey rowed on, guided by nothing but the position of the blurry moon. A thick mist had set and the outline of the ancient burial ground appeared only when they were a dozen yards away: Isle Maree was just a greyish, almost perfect dome of oak canopies, barely brighter than the surrounding night. As they approached they saw a faint glimmer, amber and steady, coming from the heart of the small island – a lantern that announced the meeting would take place as agreed. Millie suddenly felt terrified.

The boat touched the shore softly. Mr Dailey plunged his boots into the water and pulled the rope until the prow sat firmly on the pebble beach. He offered Millie a hand she refused to take; the girl rose to her towering height and, despite her thumping heart, led the way towards the greenery. They walked past the outer line of oaks, whose thick trunks grew almost horizontally towards the water, like the stretched fingers of a pleading hand.

Millie followed the dim light and soon the ancient tombstones began to appear, dotted in between the gnarled oaks and hollies, their edges eroded by centuries of inclement weather.

'Here they come,' somebody said. It was a male voice Millie had never heard before, but she knew that was the clergyman, the man who was about to take her son away for ever. She recognized him at once, standing next to the two familiar figures: the sleazy Calcraft, who was holding the lantern, and the elegant Mrs Minerva Koloman, her pale face like silver underneath her crimson hood.

The priest raised his eyebrows when he saw Millie, and tilted his head slightly backward. Of course he did. Everyone reacted like that when they realized Millie was in fact a girl. Though she was inured to it, tonight the gesture made her falter.

'It is all right, child,' said the lady. 'Come closer.'

So she did, but Millie consciously planted herself behind a jutting gravestone, as if the moss-covered granite, which hardly reached her knees, could act as her battlement.

'So you are Millie,' said the priest. His voice was soft and friendly, but Millie hated everything about him: his kind smile, his carefully groomed hair, the relaxed fingers interlaced before his chest . . . the so familiar colour of his eyes.

'How many lasses with bastards were you waiting for?'

'Millie!'

'It's fine, Minerva,' said the clergyman, raising an appeasing hand. 'I wasn't expecting this to be easy on her. May I see the child, Millie?'

She recoiled out of instinct, clutching the little bundle closer to her. Calcraft sniggered, the lantern shaking in his hand and sending fleeting shadows all across the island.

Mrs Koloman approached. She was slender and almost a full foot shorter than Millie, but she shepherded her young maid around the tombs with no problem.

'Let us see his pretty face,' Mrs Koloman said when they were close to the priest. She pulled back the edge of the blanket with great care, and they all envied the baby's placid, careless sleep. Mrs Koloman sighed, looking at the surrounding graves. 'It is sad that you last see him here, in the land of the dead.'

'On the contrary,' said the priest, 'a child is life renewed.'

He stretched out his arms to receive the boy, but Millie took a decisive step back.

'*No!*' she cried, as if she'd been asked to toss the baby into the fire.

'What do you —'

'I'm keeping him, you hear me?'

Calcraft sniggered again, but Mr Dailey slapped him hard on the face. 'Show some respect, you idiot.'

Mrs Koloman reached for Millie's arm, but the girl pulled away. 'Millie, you know it cannot be.'

'Who says so?' she barked back, even though she knew it was useless to protest.

Mrs Koloman raised a hand and managed to seize Millie by the shoulder. 'He will be well cared for, educated; he'll want for nothing. It will be the best for him . . . Think of the alternative.'

Millie felt the streams of tears rolling down her cheeks and heard herself sob. It was an awful noise. It sounded like somebody else.

'Here,' said the priest, visibly intimidated as he warily slid his hand underneath the baby.

Millie felt the weight being lifted from her arms and again tried to step back, but Mrs Koloman held her in place with unexpected strength.

'Millie, let him go.'

The girl stooped to kiss her baby's forehead, but just as her lips were about to touch him she decided not to. She could not have surrendered him otherwise.

It felt as though they were tearing off a part of her body. Nothing had ever hurt like that. Not even when she was a young girl and the other children had thrown rotten things at her and called her names. She would have gone through all that a hundred times if it meant she could keep the boy.

'Love is hard, my child,' Mrs Koloman whispered, patting her on the back, about to burst into tears herself.

The priest rocked the baby with confident arms, and the way he tucked the blanket around the boy showed he'd probably taken care of dozens of 'orphans'.

He looked up. 'What shall we call him?'

The question took the edge off Millie's distress. She sniffed, realizing she'd never given it a thought.

'Benjamin,' she said soon enough, 'after my late father.'

The clergyman smiled. 'He does look like a Benjamin.'

Millie held on to that image. For years to come, whenever she doubted the fate of her son, she'd invoke the memory of the smiling priest and his kind words.

'Mr Dailey,' said Mrs Koloman, 'can you take Father Thomas to your inn? We've arranged for a carriage to pick him up tomorrow morning. Send us the bill as usual.'

'This one's on me, Mrs Koloman,' he answered. 'What about Millie?'

'She is coming with us. There is nothing to hide any more.'

Millie and Mr Dailey exchanged sorry looks. He had lodged her at his nearby inn for the past few months, keeping her out of view whilst her state was evident. Millie had helped the man's wife with what chores she could, and they'd spent many an evening exchanging stories by the fire. They realized now how much they'd miss each other.

Mrs Koloman noticed. 'We'll keep Millie in our service,' she said. 'She'll be able to visit you and Mrs Dailey often enough.'

Mr Dailey replied with only a manly grunt, blinking tears away as he showed the priest the way to his boat. The two men said their goodbyes and very soon they were gone, but Millie did not have the heart to watch them fade into the darkness. Instead she looked down at the two cracked slabs carved with crosses before her. They said they were the resting place of an ancient king and his beloved queen, sleeping side by side for ever.

'Calcraft,' said Mrs Koloman, 'go and prepare the boat. We'll meet you there.'

'Ma'am, there's nothing to pre—'

'Do as I say!'

Insolent as he was, the eighteen-year-old footman would not dare defy Mr Koloman's wife. He strode off to the northern side of the island, where the Kolomans' boat waited, taking the lantern with him.

As the light weakened, Millie stared at her now empty hands. Mrs Koloman took one in hers. The lady's skin was soft and immaculate, zealously guarded from the sunlight. Millie's hands were freckled and roughened by work.

Slowly, as if yielding under an immense weight, Millie bent down, rested her forehead on her lady's shoulder and wept in silence.

'I know, child, I know. I'm a mother too.'

She let Millie weep on, waiting patiently until the girl rose again, wiping her nose with her already mucky sleeve.

'Here,' said Mrs Koloman, offering an embroidered handkerchief. 'Millie, there is something else I need to ask of you.'

The girl just nodded, too drained to either think or object. The lady took a deep breath.

'There is someone who needs your milk.'

1889

17 August, 5:00 a.m.

Adolphus McGray slammed the main door open. The crack of the wood resounded in the hall like a thunderclap. Then just silence. The farmhouse was dark and deserted, like a grave.

Only then did Adolphus feel his heart pounding and the cold sweat dripping down his forehead.

'Father?' he called. 'Pansy?'

No reply.

The stillness of the place seemed jarring after his frantic ride. Adolphus walked on with faltering steps. Indeed, something was very wrong.

'Where's every—'

A cold shriek came from the library, the most anguished howl he'd ever heard. It was his sister.

'Pansy!' he shouted, running down the corridor as the shrieks grew louder, an insane voice that drilled into his ears.

Adolphus reached the library door and pulled the knob, but it was locked.

'Pansy!' he yelled again, banging on the door furiously. His sister let out a final, high-pitched cry, which went on and on: a shrilling, fixed note.

Adolphus thrust himself against the door. He hit it again – one, two, three times – until the frame gave way and the lock went flying.

Just as he entered the library Pansy's now rasping cry started to fade, her lungs depleted of air. It took Adolphus a second to distinguish anything in the dim light, but what he saw would be scarred into his memory for the rest of his life.

Pansy's white summer dress was stained; dark red splattered all over her. The fifteen-year-old was on her knees in the middle of the room, her slender body in a crouch. Adolphus at first thought her injured, but then he saw the two bleeding bodies lying next to her.

The old Mr McGray lay on the carpet, his arms bent awkwardly. The only movement around him was the blood pooling slowly from his chest.

Behind him, a female body lay face down. Although he could not see her face, Adolphus instantly recognized his mother, but there was something shiny apparently hovering over her . . . And then it struck him: a fire poker had pierced the woman's back and was sticking up like a fork in a joint of meat.

Adolphus let out a sickened gasp. His trembling legs failed him and he had to lean on the door frame.

Pansy started weeping, rocking backwards and forwards. Another shiny object was on her lap. It was the sharpest cleaver from the kitchen, the one that Betsy used to cut through bones. The wide blade was still dripping with his father's blood.

Adolphus also saw that Pansy was holding the knife with a firm grip, and then a terrible truth began to dawn on him.

'Oh, Pansy . . .' he whispered, tears rolling down his face. 'Wha . . . what've ye –'

'It was the Devil,' Pansy whispered, but in a voice that was not her own. It was a rough, poisoned sound, coming from the depths of her throat.

'Wha . . . what do you mean?'

Suddenly the girl rose, roaring like a beast, wielding the tainted cleaver, and hurled herself towards Adolphus.

A short step back barely saved him; the cleaver slashed the front of his coat and he felt the very tip of the blade cut his chest.

The girl came closer, tried to stab him, and all he could do was lift his hands to block the blade. He deflected the first blows, felt the cold steel, and tried to seize her wrists, suddenly aware of the blood he was spilling. Adolphus managed to grab her but she struggled like a wild animal.

'Pansy, stop it!'

He caught a glimpse of her bloodshot eyes, which locked on his, unrecognizable, her pupils like dark wells opening into a turbulent underworld. It was less than a second amidst the frenzied fight, but that stare would never leave his memory.

Then they heard voices.

People were approaching, shouting the names of all the McGrays. Among them were the servants, George and Betsy, their voices terrified screeches.

Pansy struck Adolphus hard in the stomach, bringing him to his knees, and a piercing pain in his hand forced him to let go of her. At once she stormed out of the room, shrieking as madly as before.

Adolphus heard the shocked screams of the men who'd just arrived, and his sister's voice echoing throughout the house as she ran haphazardly from room to room.

Pressing against the floor to stand up, Adolphus felt as if his hand were on fire, and when he looked down he could not contain a terrified squeal.

His fourth finger had been almost completely severed.

Adolphus lifted his hand at once, the pain suddenly searing, and the image sent stabs of fright throughout his body: his finger flailed about, hanging by a thin shred of torn skin, and he could see the white bones surrounded by bleeding flesh.

'He-help!' he panted, squeezing his wrist and desperately trying to rise, but no one could hear him over the shouting in the other rooms.

Still on his knees, Adolphus desperately dragged himself towards the door.

And then he saw it.

It was no more than a blurred look before he lost consciousness: a deformed, twisted figure moving spasmodically as it made its way towards the window.

The Devil, he thought, with large, twisted horns and charred flesh . . . and then he knew he was having the dream again.

McGray had dreamed of that ghastly night more times than he could remember, but every time it was as vivid as the real event. The sight of his dead parents, the maddening cries of his sister, the burning pain in his hand . . . nothing seemed to fade away, despite the years.

It was the dread of having that dream that kept him awake most nights, even if he denied that fact to himself. He'd do his best to stay up – read, write, smoke, drink a dram or two – and after six years he'd grown accustomed to it, but he could never relinquish sleep altogether.

Last night, for instance, he'd passed out from sheer exhaustion. He'd travelled all day in a steamer from Edinburgh to Aberdeen, and then on to the Orkney Islands, where Pansy was now secluded. He'd spent two full days travelling, eating nothing but salted herring, hard bread and thinned ale, and (something he had never confessed to anybody) putting up with unparalleled seasickness. Excellent swimmer though he was, he had never fared well on boats.

And when McGray had finally made it to the desolate, weather-beaten island, he was simply told he was not to see his sister.

'The very point of bringing the lass here is to keep her away from you!' were the blunt words of the very heavily built head nurse, one Mrs Jennings.

McGray – not exactly a model of restraint – had exploded in an outburst of rage and swearing which would have made the roughest tavern thugs wince. Mrs Jennings, however, held her ground. Even when McGray threatened to appeal to Dr Clouston, the nurse insisted the doctor would back her. After all, it had been *his* idea to bring Pansy here.

The 'good doctor', as most people here referred to him, ran Edinburgh's exemplary asylum: he had looked after Pansy for just over six years, and knew her medical history better than anybody else. Originally an Orkneys man, Dr Clouston had quickly prospered in the world of psychiatry, and if any person was capable of treating Pansy (and concerned about her welfare), it was him. He now sponsored this place, Manse Lodge, from his own pocket. It was a small retirement house for the islands' elderly, and Clouston thought it the ideal place to keep the girl safe. Though terribly upset, McGray had had to agree. Surrounded only by nurses and very senior folk, at least the girl would have some privacy.

It was just as he realized he was dreaming that McGray felt her presence.

She had approached delicately, emerging out of nowhere

and gradually intermingling with the nightmare he had just had. She was more of a feeling than an image, hovering over his bed like a ghost.

She whispered something to him. What was it? McGray could not make out the words, only the quivering little voice.

He even felt the gentlest touch on his forehead: a very slight caress, like a goodnight kiss from his late mother, only ten times fainter. It was that sensation, lingering on his skin, which made him believe it had perhaps not been a dream after all.

He lay in bed thinking about it, staring at the cracked ceiling. The yellowed curtains, paper thin, let in the already bright daylight, swaying slowly in the draught that came through the battered window. Mrs Jennings had let him spend the night, but under the strict condition that he left first thing in the morning. She'd given him a dingy, damp room on the top floor, with a bed far too small for him. He had slept with his boots on, his feet jutting out. The head nurse had mentioned that the room was free only because its elderly occupant had died the night before – as if such tales could scare away Nine-Nails McGray.

He finally sat up and caught a glimpse of himself in the room's tiny mirror. He did not care much for looks, but even he had to admit his appearance was rather bleak: his thick mane of black hair, specked with premature grey, was quite dishevelled, and his very square jaw, lean after years of constant strain, was covered in unkempt stubble. His eyes, wide and deep blue, were the one feature that still resembled the careless twenty-five-year-old who'd seen his sister go mad.

McGray heard a distressed voice coming from the storey below: a woman's voice, not one he recognized. There were thumping footsteps, followed by the angry yelling of Mrs Jennings.

'Och, that fat bitch is up already,' McGray grumbled, rubbing his eyes. The woman shouted again, a hint of despair in her voice this time. McGray let out a surly sigh, rose and donned his tartan trousers. As he stepped out of the room, wearing just the trousers and a half-unbuttoned shirt, he saw the wide woman herself hurrying towards him, followed by two younger nurses, all as pale as parchment.

'What is –'

'Your sister,' said Mrs Jennings. 'She's gone!'

Had she been a man, McGray would have seized her by the collar. 'What d'ye mean, she's gone?'

'Mary here was bringing her breakfast, but the lassie is gone!'

Mary was shaking from head to toe. 'I've looked everywhere, master. The other rooms, the corridors . . .'

'The kitchen and laundries,' added the second nurse, equally anxious.

McGray at once thought of his dream.

'Youse don't lock her room?'

'We never lock any rooms,' said Mrs Jennings with a note of pride. 'We don't keep prisoners here. And your sister has never done anything like this.' She took a short step forward. 'It is *you* who came and stirred the poor thing! She must have heard your shouting last night.'

McGray wanted to punch the woman right in her rounded nose but instead he darted along the corridor towards the stairs.

'I hope you are happy now!' Mrs Jennings shouted to his back, but by then McGray was scouring the first-floor rooms.

'No use, master,' said the nurse Mary, who'd run right behind him. 'We checked every room in the building before I even raised the alarm.'

'Outside . . .' McGray mumbled as he rushed to the main doors and on to the windy bay of Kirkwall. The chill of the morning hit him right in the bare chest, worsening the pang he felt as he scanned the open waters ahead of him.

Manse Lodge sat on a lonely road that hugged the small bay, only a few yards away from the wide sandy beach where the waves roared.

McGray unwillingly pictured Pansy running manically to the waters, perhaps hours ago, then plunging into the sea and getting forever lost in its immensity.

'*Pansy!*' he bellowed, looking in every direction. The smooth, treeless grassland rolled on and on as far as the eye could see, empty and barren, almost like another sea. The only features were the houses that clustered around the harbour, half a mile away, and beyond, barely visible, was the spike of Kirkwall's only church. But his sister was nowhere to be seen.

McGray called for Pansy again as he ran along the bay. It was midsummer but the sun never warmed those islands very much, and his panting breath steamed up before his face. He heard the nurses come out, their voices joining his, and he felt completely powerless.

'There!' somebody yelled from behind. McGray turned and saw a young nurse pointing to the water. His heart skipped a beat.

McGray strode in the direction the girl had signalled. The grass ended abruptly, the ground broken by the sea and descending steeply to a sandy path. The tide was low, exposing a flat beach which had been out of his sight. The wet sands glinted under the sun, the surface perfectly smooth. A loud wave had just broken, its waters rushing inland like a foamy carpet, and it was amongst that whiteness that McGray finally saw the tiny outline of Pansy.

He rushed down, staggering over rocks, sand and sea-weed, never taking his eyes from her. Pansy was utterly still, but McGray let out a long sigh of relief when he saw that at least she was standing.

As he approached, McGray saw that his sister was still wearing her white nightgown. She'd wrapped herself in only a thin blue shawl, but most of the garment was loose and it rippled about in the strong wind, as if it were the standard of a sunken ship and Pansy was all that remained afloat.

'Sister –' he began, but then felt a hand grasp his shoulder.

'She's in her nightie,' said Mrs Jennings, panting so hard McGray felt waves of her hot breath on his back. 'Let me get her.'

'Sod off, ye fat hag!'

It was her words more than her hand that planted him in the ground. 'Let her have some dignity.'

She said it with actual sorrow – the woman could not be entirely devoid of compassion – and she strode over the sheet of water that was now flowing back to the sea. Mary came running to help, lifting her hem and splattering all about.

As he stared at the women, both slightly shorter than his sister, McGray realized something. Time had passed for Pansy. She was not a girl any more; she was a tall, beautiful woman in her twenties, looking somehow dignified as she stared at the wild sea, her body as still as when she had stared at the gardens of the Edinburgh asylum. Seeing but not seeing.

For the first time, McGray felt a dark, terrible certainty: Pansy would keep on growing, life would keep on passing her by, she'd grow old – and her dark-brown eyes would remain forever vacant.

He stood on that same spot for a long while, feeling the gentle push of the water as it came and went around his feet.

Pansy had flinched when Mrs Jennings had touched her elbow, and for an awful moment McGray had feared she'd dart into the sea. But that was all, a fleeting, sharp flinch, and at once she'd gone still again. Then the nurses guided her, one on each side, back to the lodge.

They purposely avoided McGray, keeping Pansy as far from him as possible, and from that distance he could barely make out her features. After all his effort, after having travelled across Scotland, this was all he'd see of her.

And he would not press further. This episode clearly was his doing, and the guilt pressed his chest more than the cold wind. Dr Clouston had been right. The man clearly understood Pansy better than he did.

McGray dwelled on those thoughts for hours, planted firmly on the sand, his eyes lost in the sea. The sun was high in the white sky when a young man came to him. McGray had seen him come out from Manse Lodge but felt so drained he simply waited until the chap reached him.

'Are ye the peeler?' he asked.

'Aye.'

'There's a telegram for ye, sir. Hefty one too.' And he handed McGray a thick envelope.

It was a message from Ian Frey. Four entire pages of telegrammed text – something only the flippant Londoner would be willing to pay for.

McGray had read just the first lines when his pulse began to race:

Highland woman visited. Has case for you.
AND claims cure for Pansy.

PART I

Do not look at wine when it is red, when it sparkles in the cup and goes down smoothly.

In the end it bites like a serpent and stings like an adder.

Your eyes will see strange things, and your heart utter perverse things.

Proverbs 23:31–3

I

Edinburgh, 16 August, 6:45 p.m.

I must admit I had to blink twice before being irrefutably convinced that she was a woman.

Miss Millie Fletcher was vast: as tall as me, with even broader shoulders and hands so thick I as soon pictured her snapping rabbits' necks. She nonetheless had a delicate, almost childish face – wide blue eyes with long lashes, fine rosy lips and a pointy nose – but it was as if she consciously tried to conceal any hint of that daintiness. Her cheeks were densely freckled, her skin weather-beaten, and a deep fold in her brow hardened her countenance at all times. She wore her wavy blonde hair in a very simple plait, and no adornments, no jewellery, not a speck of colour in her attire. She wore a baggy man's jacket and plain woollen skirts, but something in her way of walking told me she was quite uncomfortable in them.

I first encountered her in the courtyard of Edinburgh's City Chambers, the headquarters of the Scottish police. I was keen to go home and celebrate that the long (and utterly useless) Irving-Terry-Stoker inquest was finally over. Furthermore, my dear uncle was in town, and I was eager to have a large brandy with him.

Alas, that would have to wait. McNair, a very efficient but equally scrawny constable, was having trouble containing the woman.

'I'm telling ye, he's not here!'

'Then where is he?' she answered in a firm voice and a rich Highlands accent. 'He's the only one who can help me!'

'For the third time, I cannae tell ye, hen. I'm sorry!'

I was tempted to walk round them hiding my face. That woman looked just like the sort of deranged character that gravitated towards McGray, a harbinger of calamity, hogwash or a mixture of the two. Nevertheless, she looked mortified, and that truly annoying conscience of mine again betrayed me.

'What is the matter, McNair?'

The young man was relieved to see me. 'Oh, Mr Frey, so good yer here. This lass, Millie Fletcher, wants to see Inspector McGray.'

'He is not in Edinburgh,' I said, consciously holding back that he'd gone to the Orkneys. I examined the tall woman, who rubbed her forehead in distress. 'What is the matter?'

'I'm leaving for the Highlands tomorrow first thing, but I need his help. I *need* to talk to him.'

Again I wished I could shrug and walk away, but the woman was about to shed tears of frustration.

'Inspector Ian Frey, madam,' I said with a resigned sigh. 'I am Inspector McGray's second in command. I will hear your case, if it is so important.'

She looked at me with suspicion. 'Would you . . . would you mind if we spoke in private, sir? It's a very delicate matter.' Despite her strong accent she had a well-modulated voice, with no trace of the unintelligible dialect or baffling slang.

'I was just heading home,' I said, looking at the coach that already waited for me. 'Would you care to join me?'

Again she hesitated, taking a deep breath before assenting.

She jumped on to the coach with the agility of a chimney-sweep and we set off at once.

The cab took us near the looming castle, which looked rather ghostly beneath the grey clouds. A light mist had set around its jagged mount, adding to the mythical appearance. It was still summer, but Scotland will be forever Scotland.

Miss Fletcher seemed confused (almost alarmed) when she realized we were heading to the more elegant streets of New Town, and she whistled at the Georgian mansions on Great King Street, where I had my not-so-humble abode.

We were received by Layton, my very thin, very English valet, who stared at Miss Fletcher with mystified eyes.

'Oh, Mr Frey, I did not know you'd bring company; your good uncle –'

'Please do not tell Uncle I am here. I need to discuss CID matters with this lady. Send us some drinks to my study. Tea, Miss Fletcher?'

'If you don't mind, sir, I'd prefer some whisky.'

Rather forward for a lady, but I nodded at Layton and led Miss Fletcher upstairs.

My private study was small but cosy, with a narrow fireplace, comfortable leather armchairs, a bearskin rug and a nice view of the sandstone mansions across the road.

'Not bad for a Scotch's den,' Uncle had said upon his arrival.

Layton came soon with a decanter and a few glasses on a tray. I dispatched him swiftly and closed the door, fearing Uncle Maurice would come and interrupt us in his very flamboyant way.

Miss Fletcher had already installed herself quite confidently in one of the armchairs, and was pouring herself a liberal measure of whisky. As I sat, she served me just as much, and I thought I could not possibly drink all that before my dinner. The woman, however, downed the full drink in one gulp and poured herself a second one.

I interlaced my fingers around the cut-glass tumbler, trying not to stare too quizzically at her. 'So, how can I help you, Miss Fletcher?'

'I'll be honest with you, sir. I've come because I was told about Mr McGray's . . . erm . . . interests.'

I nodded, ready to hear something most likely very silly. McGray's subdivision, after all, was devoted to investigating the 'odd and ghostly', and I cannot believe I have spent nearly a bloody year under his command, chasing witches and will-o'-the-wisps.

Miss Fletcher might well be bringing a case as absurd as that of the sly footman who claimed a goblin had killed and roasted his master's fattest pig. I did not want to appear disrespectful, mindful of both her apparent distress and the size of her fists, so I made my questions careful.

'May I ask how you came to hear about Inspector McGray?'

'Yes, sir. I – well, Mrs Koloman, the lady I serve, showed me an article in the *Scotsman*. It mentioned Mr McGray's involvement in that theatre affair last month.'

'The Henry Irving scandal,' I confirmed. 'Yes, that case was – how shall I put it? *Well covered* by the press.' In fact, had it not been for the murder of Clay Pipe Alice – the latest Whitechapel butchery – that case would still be monopolizing the headlines. 'Why do you think Inspector McGray's . . . unorthodox experience might help you?'

I made an effort not to add that even though I'd come to – somewhat – respect McGray's skills as a detective inspector I still thought him a reckless, deluded, loud and mentally damaged wreck.

'Oh, sir, I think *I* am the one who can help *him*.'

I tilted my head and took a small sip. '*Do you?* How?'

The woman shook her head. 'Well, I had better start at the beginning. I –' She stared at the ceiling, and her expression made me think of an inexperienced diver who's already jumped off the cliff: hesitant, fearful, but realizing it is too late to go back.

'Sir, the first thing I need to tell you is something very few people know about me. And it must be in strict confidence. Can I have your word?'

'Of course, miss. I am a CID inspector and a gentleman.'

She frowned a little as her words came out. 'I . . . well, I have a son. I had a son when I was very young, though I have never married.' The frown grew deeper. 'And the father was my employer's brother.'

I swirled my tumbler and sat back. 'Your secret is safe with me, rest assured.'

'Thank you, sir. That was sixteen years ago. I was barely a girl myself, a servant girl, with no money and no family to protect me. You can imagine the trouble I got myself into.' She gulped the rest of the drink and put the tumbler on the table with a loud thump. 'Maximilian Koloman was a wretched feller and told me to sod off. He said it wasn't his child; he didn't want anything to do with me or my son.'

I nodded. 'A dreadful situation. What did you do?'

'I was so desperate I had to appeal to his brother, that is my current master, Mr Konrad Koloman, of the Kolomans of Loch Maree. Have you heard of the family?'

'I am afraid I have not, but I have not spent much of my life in Scotland. How did your master take the news?'

'He was very kind to me. He and his wife, Mrs Minerva. They surely showed some mercy.'

23

'Forgive my indelicacy ... they did not doubt the parentage?'

The lady looked at me sideways. 'They knew Maximilian – and they knew me. They had no doubts. When I couldn't hide my state any more they sent me to a nearby inn and I gave birth in secret. They paid for the midwife, the inn, everything, and they let me go back to my job, but the Kolomans didn't want the entire region to know that Maximilian had fathered a bast–' She forced a deep breath. 'A love child.'

Miss Fletcher went silent for a moment, and I gave her time.

'Benjamin,' she said eventually, tears now pooling in her eyes. 'I named him Benjamin, after my late father. Mrs Koloman arranged he be sent north, to Thurso; a wee coastal town on the northernmost tip of Scotland. They knew a priest there through some family connections. My boy stayed in Thurso and was brought up in the parish. Dressed, fed, well educated. And Mr and Mrs Koloman again paid for everything.'

I rocked my glass gently. 'You said you were allowed to keep your job with the Kolomans. May I ask why you agreed to that? The prospect of working close to your son's estranged father must not have been very appealing.'

'It was part of the agreement, sir. They would pay for my child for as long as I worked for them and remained quiet.'

'I understand. So they bought your silence and kept a close eye on you.'

'Yes, Inspector, but it wasn't as bad as you're thinking. Maximilian never worked – the family is very wealthy – and he was always travelling in Europe, so I saw him only once or twice a year. And even then he avoided me, or the family sent me on errands to Glasgow or Edinburgh. They're not insensitive.

'And so the years passed ... In due course I became the Kolomans' housekeeper, while Maximilian spent his life

24

elsewhere, squandering his inheritance, and my own child grew happy and strong in the north, or so the priest's letters said. He told me my son was becoming a very clever young man.' There was a clear hint of satisfaction in her voice.

I shifted in my armchair. 'I suppose that something has marred the situation, to make you come here?'

'Why, many things have happened!' she said with a bitter laugh, and then, as confident as a pedlar in a tavern, Miss Fletcher helped herself to more whisky. 'First of all, Maximilian died about three months ago. He came back from one of his trips unexpectedly and very ill. My master, being his elder brother, fetched the best doctors money could afford, but it was no use. Maximilian just withered and died within weeks.'

'What was the malady?'

Miss Fletcher snorted. 'The family wouldn't tell, but all the other servants rumoured that it was a – gentleman's disease. Served him well, the buggering bastard.' She gulped the drink down in one go. 'Excuse my language, sir.'

'I have heard much worse,' I assured her whilst refilling her tumbler, which she welcomed. 'What happened then?'

'I was told that Maximilian, on his deathbed, asked Mr and Mrs Koloman to bring my Benjamin back into the family. He signed a statement recognizing him as his son and heir.'

Her tone left me puzzled; there had been a good deal of bitterness in those last phrases.

'Were you not happy with that outcome?' I asked.

Miss Fletcher brought the glass close to her lips but did not manage to drink this time.

'Maximilian also made his brother swear that Benjamin would be treated as part of the family, as an equal ... but I know better. You, Mr Frey, seem quite well off yourself, if you don't mind me saying. Do you think the boy has any chance of ever being treated as an equal in an upper-class family? Of course not! He'll always be the housekeeper's bastard!'

Again she banged her glass down on the table, spilling whisky all around, and sat back and crossed her legs in a very mannish way, visibly annoyed by the skirts.

I allowed her to take a few infuriated breaths before my next question.

'Miss Fletcher, I understand your distress, but I suppose it was something else that brought you here, was it not?'

The woman rubbed her face, struggling to keep her anger under control. She stared hard at the floor, and finally spoke after a very long pause.

'Something very strange happened a few days ago. I was in my rooms, at my master's house, ready to go to bed, when someone smashed my window with a brick. It nearly struck me in the face.'

'Oh?'

She drew a hand from her jacket's pocket. 'With a message tied to it.'

She handed me a crumpled piece of brown wrapping paper. I unfolded it and saw a scrawl in thick, black ink, the words smudged as if written in haste:

KEEP YOUR BASTARD AWAY
OR I SHALL KILL HIM

I leaned forward, grasping the note. 'Have you reported this to your local police?'

'I have, Mr Frey, but our constable is a lazy, irresponsible bloody fool. He laughed at me and sent me away. Said it was nothing.'

I shook my head. 'This could be a very serious threat.'

'I *know*, and nobody seems to care!' she shouted, but instantly covered her mouth and sat back again. 'Do . . . do excuse me, Mr Frey.'

'No need to apologize,' I said. 'Did you manage to see who threw this?'

'No, though I did look. It was a stormy evening, no moon or starlight.'

'Do you have any idea who could have done it? Any enemies?'

Her face became sombre. 'I know of a few who wouldn't want my son around Loch Maree. I could give you a list, but there is something more pressing at the moment.'

'More pressing? Tell me.'

'The Kolomans have already sent for my son. And I fear for him.'

'He still resides in Thurso, I suppose.'

'Yes.'

'Is he to travel on his own?'

'Not if I can help it, sir. That's why I came here.'

I meditated for a moment. 'I suppose you want the Edinburgh police to investigate this threat to your son and –'

'And someone to watch over him on his journey.'

Her request was rather problematic. 'I hear you, Miss Fletcher, and I do appreciate your distress, but you must understand we are CID, not private bodyguards.'

'I understand that.'

'And I can tell from your accent that you have come all the way from the Highlands?'

'Yes, the far north-west. Here, I brought this for you . . .'

She searched in her pockets and handed me one of those cheap travel books that are so in vogue these days.

I skimmed through the first pages, full of regional maps. 'Edinburgh is certainly a long way from your home. You could have requested anybody else's help. Why did you come specifically to us? What does Inspector McGray have to do with –'

'I can offer him something in return,' she interrupted, leaning forward, resting her elbows on her knees. There was a hint of a smirk on her face.

'Miss Fletcher, a police inspector will not bargain for services. We –'

'I can help his little sister,' she spluttered in a deep voice. 'I know how to cure Miss McGray.'

2

16 August (cont.)

'Never in my entire life have I seen such a titanic woman,' said Uncle Maurice, peering through the window and watching Miss Fletcher turn the corner. 'Not even on that horrid trip to Scandinavia. Do you remember?'

I looked at him in amusement, brandishing his large glass of cognac and an aromatic cigar, sporting a jacket of the finest wool money could afford. He reminded me of all the traits Scotland was slowly washing off me.

While my own father had been an absent, rather blurry character throughout my childhood, Uncle Maurice was my true paternal figure, and indeed he has passed many a quirk of his on to me – his taste for a good drink, fine clothes and expensive cigars are the most obvious ones. We also share the Gallic features of our émigré ancestors: the same dark-brown eyes and abundant dark hair. Uncle Maurice's once lean features have filled out a little of late, but he is still as restless and active as ever. He is now forty-six years old but has perennially lived as though he were twenty; he never married, never fathered children, and has an unquenchable zest for life I have come to envy. Had my own education not been so restrictive, I might well have turned out very much like him.

I had certainly laughed at his irreverent letter, announcing rather than requesting his visit:

*Your stepmother has been telling <u>everyone</u> in London that you live in
a pigsty without pavement or a decent roof over your head. Naturally,
I must come and see. And I believe it is now grousing season in the
Highlands . . .*

And when he arrived – his young footman dragging six
boxes of wine and cognac, a hundred Cuban cigars and
eight trunks full of fine suits and shirts and cufflinks – I
remembered why I am so fond of him.

'What did the lady want?'

I took a sip – I had still not finished the measure the
woman had poured me. 'It is police business, Uncle. I cannot tell you the details.'

Uncle smiled rather devilishly. 'Oh, so you are not going
to that Loch Maree?'

I nearly spat out my drink. 'Oh, for goodness' sake, Uncle!
Were you eavesdropping?'

He raised his palm, his cigar drawing swirls in the air. 'I
could not help it. I am sorry. I do not know how much Scotland has roughened you. I caught a glimpse of her and I
feared you might be about to propose!'

I massaged my temple. 'Is my career a joke to you all?
Some sort of idle hobby that warrants no respect?'

Uncle sat in front of me, ignoring my protests. 'I did not
quite catch that last part. When she spoke about a cure?'

I sighed. Concealing things from him would only pique
his curiosity even more. 'The woman believes in some wild
tales about miraculous waters.' I nodded at the travel book
that still sat on the little table. Uncle picked it up and began
leafing through it.

'The Highlands,' he said, a glow of excitement in his eyes.

'Yes, Loch Maree, as you heard.' I watched Uncle displaying

a foldable map. 'It is in the far north-west. Miss Fletcher works for a family, the Kolomans, who live just off its shores.'

'Yes, that part I heard, but then I had to run for a drink.'

'That loch apparently has many islands, and some of those islands themselves contain tiny lochs.'

Uncle smiled. 'Would that make them . . . water-locked lochs?'

'Technically, although the really curious thing is that in one of those islands there is a well. Its "miraculous" waters are supposed to cure madness.'

Uncle whistled, extending the map on the table. 'Water-falls, islands . . . It says here there are good stocks of salmon and grouse at this time of the year.'

'Uncle . . .'

He looked at the map's margin and frowned. 'Why do Scots always paint thistles as if they were bloody biblical wonders? They are weeds! Thorny dandelions at best.'

'Uncle, are you listening?'

'Magic well. Waters that cure madness. Yes.'

'And the woman wants to take McGray there and show him the so-called miracle. His sister, you might remember –'

'*Might* remember! That was the best story you have told me in years: the dead parents and the madness and the sev-ered finger . . . But what miracle was she talking about? Has she seen people cured?'

Again I sighed. 'So she claims. She says there is a rather strange family – the Nellyses, she called them – who live on those islands. According to her they arrived there several years ago, bringing a lunatic old man, who now has recov-ered all his faculties.'

Uncle ran his fingers over the streams and shorelines on the map. 'Will you mention all this to that Nine-Fingers man?'

I breathed out. 'I have to. That woman came asking for help, so it is my responsibility. Not that you would know the meaning of the word.'

Uncle chuckled, and for an instant I thought I saw a hint of bitterness in the way he looked at the map. He puffed at his cigar. 'What do you think he might say?'

I laughed openly. 'There is no need to guess, Uncle; I know it for certain. He will become mad with enthusiasm and do whatever this Miss Fletcher wants of him; he will go to those blasted lakes and get me into unimaginable trouble; he will eventually realize it is all another pathetic fishwives' tale, and before I know it he will be pursuing some other weird nonsense.'

'Do you not want to investigate? Help the damsel in distress? Bring more justice to our barbarous world, as you liked to preach when you worked in London?'

'Uncle, even if I wanted to, I cannot simply pack my cases and start an enquiry. There are police procedures that –'

'Did you not tell me the Scottish CID was still leaderless?'

Indeed, I had told him in detail. The hopeless Superintendent Campbell had been dismissed after his gross mishandling of the Irving scandal, and since then the general attitude of Edinburgh's CID had been of cheerful cluelessness: the ground officers did only what was strictly necessary to keep the city in order, whilst the higher-ranking officials fought like dogs over the vacant posts (not only the superintendent's, but all those that would result from the natural shifts in the authority ladder).

I said nothing. Instead I looked at Uncle Maurice, as he drank and smoked at leisure, perusing the book.

'Well,' he said at last, 'you also told me that this ... subdivision for the commiseration of the quack and the fool might be disbanded as soon as a new superintendent is elected.'

I had to drink when I heard that. The *Commission for the Elucidation of Unsolved Cases Presumably Related to the Odd and Ghostly* (a name in fact more ridiculous than Uncle's attempted parody) existed only because McGray had bribed the previous superintendent. Although anything is possible, I could not see a more corrupt rascal taking old Campbell's post, and any sensible man – myself included – would simply get rid of the department without a second thought and put the cellar which was our office to more useful purposes (like storing sacks of flour).

I could not believe I actually feared the prospect – despite all my moaning and my common sense.

I sighed, preferring not to think about it at the moment. 'Uncle, where are you going with this?'

He closed the atlas with a crisp thump. 'Ian, since you seem to be about to lose your job, would you not fancy a pleasant countryside holiday before going back to London?'

My jaw dropped. 'You must be joking!'

'Not at all. Think about it. Fresh air, exercise, breathtaking landscapes – do you think you will ever come back to Scotland when you no longer have a job here? You may never have a better chance to look at that scenery. And we can have a jolly good time a-shooting and a-drinking while your unhinged boss has a taste of those miraculous waters.'

'Uncle, please, do not say "jolly" again. You know how I detest the word.'

He only laughed. 'Besides, you just said that Miss Fletcher deserved a proper investigation. You might even be able to actually do some good.'

I sighed. 'I could do with some fresh air, I suppose . . . And it would certainly do me good to relax before I have to go back and face the upper-class vipers of London.' I took another sip of whisky. 'But no. I have surrendered under pressure in the past, and with dire consequences. It is my final word, Uncle: we are *not* going to Loch Maree.'

3

Loch Maree, 20 August, 2:50 p.m.

'Let me pull the boat closer, so the gentlemen don't get their boots wet.'

I was about to retort, but Miss Fletcher jumped into the water at once. Uncle Maurice, rather amused, watched her as she threw the rope over her shoulder and waded knee-deep towards the shore. Her breath did not even quicken, which was congruent with her looks. She was now wearing thick hunting gear, and seemed infinitely more comfortable in that than in the skirts she'd worn at our first meeting.

She lifted a rock the size of a flagon, secured the rope underneath and then looked up at me. 'Do you need a hand, Mr Frey?'

Again I was going to refuse, but Uncle hopped out rather abruptly, making the entire boat jerk and I nearly lost my balance. Miss Fletcher grasped me by the arm and did not let go until I had both feet firmly set on the gravelly beach.

I cleared my throat. 'Thank you, miss,' I said, a little flushed.

'Can't be too careful, sir,' she said, without a hint of mockery, as I adjusted my Norfolk jacket. The tweed was so new and pristine I felt rather embarrassed – Miss Fletcher's loose knickerbockers and high boots had clearly seen many a season in the countryside.

I threaded my way over the fine pebbles, still astonished at the speed with which events had been set in motion. I had telegrammed McGray the morning after my meeting with Miss Fletcher, and I had his reply before dinnertime. His answer had been everything I expected: he asked me to travel to Loch Maree immediately, but only after having consulted his blasted gypsy clairvoyant (Madame Katerina, a woman Oscar Wilde could only have envisioned after half a bottle of absinthe). I saw her, grudgingly, very early the following morning, only to be told some gruesome stories about the region – which I shall detail in due course. Not two hours later Uncle and I were already on the train. McGray had agreed to set off for Thurso and bring Miss Fletcher's son himself. If everything went well, he'd meet us here this evening – I had not heard from him since, so I could only hope things had gone well on his side.

Had it not been for a last-minute change of plans, we would have already met Mr and Mrs Koloman – apparently much admired in this corner of the Highlands. They had tele-grammed Miss Fletcher telling her they'd come to greet us at the loch's only inn, but had later sent their apologies due to an unexpected engagement. I would have preferred to wait for them at our lodgings, but Uncle Maurice insisted we go to the legendary islands, given the unusually fine weather. Miss Fletcher, who seemed increasingly nervous, had been only too eager to take us there in one of the inn's boats.

'So this is the famous Isle Maree,' said Uncle, looking around with pleasure and stretching his brawny limbs. He seemed so high-spirited nobody would have been able to guess his true age.

He lifted his binoculars and perused the northern shore. It was a fine August afternoon, with the blinding sun high in a cloudless sky – an oddity in those regions. The calm, dark waters extended six miles east and fourteen miles west, flanked on the north and south by steep mountains, as if Loch Maree were a deep gash in that craggy corner of the Highlands.

I remembered the map in the little guidebook, which Uncle had monopolized since that first evening. We were in the dramatic archipelago right in the centre of the loch. Isle Maree, one of the smaller islands, was also the one closest to the northern shore, lying a little apart from all the others, almost as if her sisters had cast her away – a reminder that the site was plagued with legends.

'I'd call it infamous,' said Miss Fletcher, as if reading my thoughts.

'What do you mean?' I asked her, but she simply scraped the sole of her boot on the gravel.

'Ian, do look at that,' Uncle said, pointing at a gnarly oak that grew right on the edge of the beach, with multiple trunks that grew almost horizontal, bent under the weight of their branches.

'People call that tree the pleading hand,' said Miss Fletcher as I approached. Her remark only added to my sudden shiver. Nailed to one of the knotty trunks there was a long, sun-bleached skull.

'A deer?' I said, looking at the mighty antlers, very much like the hunting trophies that hung on Maurice's walls in Gloucestershire.

'Yes. Red deer, I would say,' he replied. 'Just like those we have in the Forest of Dean. This one must have been a fantastic beast in life.'

I wrinkled my nose. The long, rusty nails were bent around the eye sockets, like hooks to keep it firmly in place. The cracked teeth and the sharp snout, pointing at the lake, made me think of a silent, portentous sentinel. I nearly whispered some of the words uttered by the mad gypsy, but I repressed them; I'd save those gruesome tales for McGray's ears.

'Is that pagan?' I asked, as I noticed dry wax dripping from the empty sockets. The skull must be a ghastly sight at night, its eyes lit with candles.

'Aye,' said Miss Fletcher, 'we still get pagan folk here. They come and do witchcraft from time to time.'

'Is it not the crazy man who does it?' asked Uncle.

'No, sir. Mr Nellys isn't up to this kind of thing.'

'How can you be so sure?' I asked. 'You told us the man was insane.'

'*Was*, Mr Frey. I told you, the waters cured him. And these skulls used to appear even before his family moved him here.'

'Why do you not remove them?' Uncle asked. 'It looks as though it has hung there for months. Years, even.'

Miss Fletcher shrugged. 'Mr Koloman's old gamekeeper, may he rest in peace, used to take them down all the time, but they always appeared again. We don't bother any more; they don't do any harm.'

I arched an eyebrow. 'Are you certain?'

'Yes, sir. People might come and do odd things, but nothing evil. This island has been sacred for thousands of years.'

'It certainly has a rather . . . eerie atmosphere,' said Uncle, climbing the soft slope that led to the burial ground. Indeed, I felt an odd tingling at the back of my neck, but I did not mention that out loud.

'It does not surprise me that it would be of interest to the Druids,' I said. 'You have a clear view of the sunrise and sunset: very useful for pagan rituals.'

Miss Fletcher pulled a waxy leaf from a nearby tree. 'And this is the only island where oak and holly grow. There must be something special in the soil.'

I looked over my shoulder. The greenery on Juniper Island, the closest neighbour and the largest land mass in the archipelago, looked completely different even from a distance: a clump of very tall pines.

'Not to ruin your theory, miss,' I said, 'but is it not a pagan tradition to plant acorns in people's graves?'

She suddenly looked down, grinding her teeth for some reason.

'Why so?' asked Uncle.

'Oak symbolizes eternal life. And holly is used in solstice and equinox ceremonies; it represents death and rebirth.'

Uncle whistled. 'Ian, you seem to have acquired an enviable knowledge of the pagan and the occult.'

'Most begrudgingly,' I mumbled.

We marched over the soft moss. Miss Fletcher did not need to guide us; Isle Maree was small enough for anyone to find his way. Uncle went straight to an incredibly large oak, its stump as wide as a millstone, its roots clasping the ground like meandering tentacles. The rugged bark was pierced with countless pieces of copper, all coated in verdigris.

By the foot of the oak, and surrounded by the thick roots, we found the little well. It was but an unassuming circle of stone, less than three feet in diameter, and the stones formed three concentric rings of steps, making it look like a tiny Roman amphitheatre. The opening itself was less than a foot wide, descending to thick darkness. I thought I heard a soft whistle, as if holding a seashell to my ear.

'Oh my! Is this the miraculous bloody well that –'

Thankfully he shut his mouth in time. Miss Fletcher, standing right behind him, did not seem to like his tone.

'Yes,' I said at once, 'precisely this.' I turned to Miss Fletcher. 'Can you show us Mr Nellys's . . . erm, residence?'

I thought it would be rude to use the word 'hut' (accurate though it might be, from Miss Fletcher's account).

'I told you we cannot call on him,' she said at once.

'Not without his family around,' I recalled her saying, 'I know. But I would like to have a quick look.'

Miss Fletcher grumbled, but in the end she pointed towards the centre of the island, where the holly seemed to take over. Even though I already knew the place was an ancient burial ground, the sight of the many tombstones made me feel a slight discomfort. Some were centuries old, battered, crooked and shapeless, their inscriptions eroded long ago. Others were as recent as 1885, with rich carvings of Celtic knots.

'This is as close as we should get, Mr Frey,' said Miss Fletcher, just as I saw a thin plume of white smoke. It came from the other side of the central mound, beyond the collection of graves, where a squat stone dome stood. Half covered in moss and the roots of trees, the little dwelling, barely four feet tall, looked more like a natural formation. Its crooked chimney was the only clear trace of human hand.

'That's where Saint Maelrubha lived when he came to preach,' said Miss Fletcher. 'According to legend.'

I was already convinced these were all fishwives' tales, but I still felt a twinge of curiosity. Inside those stone walls resided the old man who, *allegedly*, held the secret to curing McGray's sister. Miss Fletcher had claimed she'd 'witnessed the miracle', and her intimidating height was the only reason I refrained from laughing right in her face.

'And you said his family live on Juniper Island?' I asked.

'Yes, Mr Frey. Barely making ends meet. I'm close to them, but they don't like strangers, I'm afraid.'

'Inspector McGray has a way with . . . unfriendly people,'

I said, turning on my heel. 'I believe I have seen enough, miss. Thank you for the – Uncle, what are you doing?'

Uncle Maurice was kneeling by three very small gravestones. They were all plain rectangles of pale-pink granite, barely the size of my hand. There were no inscriptions or dates, but they had been polished to extraordinary smoothness, and their sharp edges told those were fairly recent interments.

'These must have been babies,' Uncle mumbled, taking his flat cap off as if we were in church. He placed a finger on one of the memorials, strangely mesmerized. For a moment he looked his age. 'At least they have a handsome place to rest . . .'

He stared at nothing for an instant, but then noticed my puzzled face and rose to his feet.

'Well, leafy and beautiful as it is, I cannot say this is the most remarkable spot I have ever been to.' He pulled a cigar from his breast pocket. 'I say we go back to the inn for a nice whisky. Eh, Ian?'

I looked at my pocket watch. 'We should still have time for that. Even if the Kolomans decide to be punctual this time.'

'I told you they had an emergency,' Miss Fletcher said immediately, a little indignant at my remark. 'Mr and Mrs Koloman *will* see you tonight.'

'They certainly missed the glorious weather,' said Uncle, squinting at the unusually bright sun and already making his way back to the boat. I had to hurry my pace to keep up with him.

Within a few minutes Miss Fletcher was rowing the boat southwards, taking us near the rocky edges of Juniper Island; not the most direct route back, but the one with the best views, she said.

Uncle Maurice, unable to wait until we made it back to the inn, produced his silver hip flask and had a couple of swigs.

He offered me a drink but I had to refuse. I wanted to be lucid when we met the Kolomans; I had many a question to ask them.

As we sailed around the island's northernmost promontory, very close to the craggy rocks on which nestled twisted pines and thick bushes, I thought I saw a couple of white figures jumping about. Their outlines came in and out of the foliage, and I squinted, trying to make out what they were.

'Uncle, can I borrow your binoculars?'

He handed them to me and I peered at the tall rocks. I saw the grey granite, the lilac heathers and the gnarly tree trunks, but the white shapes had –

'Dear Lord,' I mumbled.

I saw it for an instant: nothing but a flash in the greenery, yet clear enough to leave no doubt. It had been a snow-white goat frolicking on the rocks.

But there had been something else, something dark, coriaceous, fluttering amongst the shrubs and reflecting the sun like a lizard's skin.

I could have sworn I'd just seen the black wings of a rather large bat.

4

The eyes of the clergyman were not white but of a sickly, yellowish hue, and with winding veins clumping in the corners. McGray was glad the old man could not see him staring at them. He should know better – nine-fingered as he was.

'I'm sorry to break it to ye like this,' McGray said, receiving the tea the chubby maid was handing him. 'Ye'll understand the situation doesnae allow for delicacy.'

As if attempting to match his news, outside the weather was foul. The Thurso sky was overcast with such dark clouds it might as well be midnight, and the wind and rain still lashed Scotland's northern coast without mercy. From the sitting room's narrow window, McGray could barely make out the lines of the port: the grey stone houses, sad-looking and crammed to the very edge of the shore, seemed to cling to the land like scared cats that feared drowning.

The priest coughed and wiped the corners of his mouth with a handkerchief as murky as his pupils. 'The entire affair was never *delicate*, my boy.'

McGray smiled. The last person to call him 'my boy' had been his late mother.

'Aye, I ken all the details. My colleague had them directly from that Fletcher lass.'

'See, I'm reluctant to let the boy go. He still doesn't –' The maid put a cup in his hands. 'Grant, be a good lass and give us a minute.' The priest resumed when she had closed the parlour door. 'The lad doesn't know a thing about his parents. Mr and Mrs Koloman were adamant I never told him. He still believes he's a foundling, left at the gates of this house in the middle of the night.'

McGray downed his cup in a swift gulp – they'd given him more salted herring on the ferry from the Orkneys and there had been no ale to wash it down this time. 'Ye lied to him? That wisnae very priestly.'

The clergyman laughed. 'Oh, my boy, I've seen so many cases like this. Believe me, no good would have come from telling the truth. Benjamin was never supposed to see his relatives again. The Kolomans wanted to be rid of him, to keep his very existence a secret. And the mother agreed.'

'The mother was a sixteen-year-auld lassie back then.'

'Precisely. Too young and her whole life ahead of her. My sin of secrecy would at least give her a chance to pick up the pieces and build herself a future. It will be difficult to tell the boy, but I still don't regret a thing.'

'D'ye want to break the news to him, or shall I do it?'

'Of course I'll do it, silly boy! I owe it to him. Benjamin has been the kindest of all the children that have been handed to me. The smartest too. Some said I had a wee bit of a predilection for him and they were right; I wish I'd had a son like him.' He massaged the wrinkly skin between his wiry eyebrows. 'I was expecting him to carry on with the parish when he was old enough. Alas, that will no longer be possible.'

'So ye *will* let him go?'

The clergyman sighed, and then slurped his tea and smacked his lips. Frey would have remonstrated at his manners, but McGray smiled at the confidence of a man who did not care about appearances any more.

'What else can I do? If the Kolomans want him back, they're in their right. And they're the kind of people who always get what they want.'

'They say Benjamin must never be told who his mother is.'

The priest laughed with disdain, and the laugh became a throaty cough. 'Does she know of that condition? As far as I recall, she's not a woman to be trifled with.'

'I've nae met her yet, but aye, she kens. She told my colleague herself. And she agrees. She says she just wants the best for her son.'

'That's what we all want,' said the priest, wiping his mouth again. 'Will you take good care of him? Can I have your word?'

'Course. That's the reason I'm here. I won't take my eyes off him. It'll all end well.'

The priest let out another laugh mixed with expectoration. 'Oh, this shan't end well, my boy. Take my word.' He raised his blotchy hand, bidding McGray to approach. When he felt McGray's closeness he whispered, his breath reeking of diseased gums mixed with a whiff of vinegar. 'I've heard terrible things about that loch, my boy. *Terrible* stories about people travelling there and never coming back.'

McGray leaned forward. 'Now, have ye? What else?'

The priest raised his eyebrows, his forehead wrinkling like supple leather. For a moment McGray thought those milky irises were staring back at him. The man groped the air for McGray's hand. When he found it he instantly felt the stump of the missing finger.

He let out another weary sigh. 'We all carry our scars, don't we? Living in these rickety bodies that give in so quickly.'

McGray snorted. 'Och, don't ye beat round the fuckin' bush! What stories have ye heard? D'ye ken about the well? The healing waters?'

The priest squeezed McGray's hand. 'Those stories abound, my boy. Pagan tales I can't defend . . . as the priest I am.'

McGray heard the uncertainty in that last remark. 'And if ye werenae a priest?'

The milky pupils quivered, the old man gulped and shook his head. 'Please, *please* look after him,' he concluded. 'Better than you've looked after yourself.' And then the old man rose to his feet and called for the housemaid. 'I'll have a last supper with the boy and I'll tell him everything. In private, if you don't mind. And I want him to have a last quiet sleep here. You two can leave first thing in the morning.'

The maid came and helped the clergyman out of the parlour. He let himself be led away with the obedience of a young child, only to halt suddenly as they crossed the threshold. 'Oh, and I'm writing a letter for Mrs Koloman. I'll give you a sealed envelope tomorrow. It will be for her eyes and her eyes only. Don't you dare tamper with that letter, or I shall know.'

Grant, the stout housemaid, helped McGray find a room at the port's only inn. After a generous serving of potatoes and – yet *more* – salted herring, McGray settled himself in a surprisingly comfortable armchair in a lonely corner of the common room. Other than a couple of fishermen who'd already passed out from drunkenness, he had the place all to himself.

McGray savoured a cigar whilst pondering his best course of action.

I should have told the priest about the threat to the boy, he thought, puffing out smoke.

According to Frey's telegram, the note had been wrapped

around a brick thrown at Miss Fletcher's window. A clear warning:

KEEP YOUR BASTARD AWAY
OR I SHALL KILL HIM.

McGray himself would have suggested keeping the boy away until things became clearer. The fact that the local constable had mocked Miss Fletcher and refused to investigate was rather alarming; it could be simple incompetence, but there was also the possibility that someone had bribed the man – someone who did not want the affair investigated. Or it might be an empty threat, part of a typical family quarrel that would become evident after very little digging, but one could never be sure.

The one thing McGray knew for certain was the true source of his own motivation. He was helping these people only because of that miraculous well and the faint possibility that it might at last cure his sister. In his hurry, however, he might be putting an innocent boy in danger, and that little voice in his head would not go away.

His one consolation was that he knew very little about the mysterious Miss Fletcher. She too was following her own agenda, offering that alleged cure as blatant bait. For all McGray knew, she might be telling nothing but lies.

Once again, he'd have to take a leap of faith.

5

Loch Maree, 20 August, 5:20 p.m.

The innkeeper, one Mr Dailey, received us as warmly as when we'd first arrived. The man was round-bellied and rubicund, with a bushy moustache that more than made up for the utter absence of hair on his scalp. His wife was of such a similar height and girth one could have easily thought they were siblings, only she had an abundant mane of ginger curls, which had only begun to turn grey.

She led us to the well-appointed sitting room, whose wide windows offered a very pretty view of the loch and its islands.

'Can I get youse gentlemen a wee gillie to wet yer whistles?'

Uncle Maurice, a proud Gloucestershire dweller, was baffled. 'E-excuse me, ma'am?'

'Do you want anything to drink?' I translated, lounging in the nearest armchair.

'Oh, good woman, you have read my mind! I will have a measure of your best Scotch, please.'

'Och, if ye loo yer spirits ye must try the gin from Juniper Island. Ye'll sirple a whole tappit-hen. Bet youse.'

Uncle would have had more chance had she spoken Arabic or Japanese. He simply stared blankly at her.

'She says you should have the gin.'

'Did she?' Maurice shook his head. 'I . . . I shall follow your advice, madam.'

'Another gin for ye, Mr Frey?'

'Oh, no, I am not drinking tonight, Mrs Dailey. Just fetch me some claret, please.'

Uncle waited until she had left us. 'Why, Ian, you have become an expert in the lingo! I have not said it before, but' – he looked at me with scrutinizing eyes, as he'd been doing since his arrival in Edinburgh – 'I find you very much changed.'

I interlaced my fingers. 'Do you?'

'Indeed, and it has not been a very long time; I last saw you at Christmas, remember? That scar, for instance.' He pointed at my right hand as I reached for an ashtray. 'That must have been a nasty burn.'

'Chemical explosion.'

'Did it also reach your cheekbone?'

'Oh, no, that was another chemical explosion, a couple of days later.'

'And' – he tilted his head – 'I did not want to mention this, but I think your nose looks slightly, well, odd.'

I chuckled. 'Oh, that was a . . . I would call it an *involuntary* blow to my face.'

'Involuntary?'

'Erm . . . from Inspector McGray.'

'*What!* The man for whom you work?'

'Far too long to explain, Uncle. You should read my case notes some day.'

'Oh, Ian, you know perfectly well I am not that much of a *reader*. But I was not finished. I will risk sounding too much like my dear late sister, but you look alarmingly thin.'

I sighed. 'Well, I have only just been through a very difficult case and a five-week inquest.'

'Ian,' said Uncle, shifting in his chair, 'jokes aside, what do you think you will do when your ludicrous "ghostly" subdivision is no more? You said it might well happen very soon.'

I took a deep breath. 'Oh, Uncle, I have avoided thinking about it.'

'Would you go back to London?' he asked, rather innocently.

I snorted. 'I have considered it, but with the Laurence and Eugenia affair . . .'

Needless to say more: our circles in London were still scandalized by Eugenia breaking our engagement – jilting me to marry my loathsome elder brother instead. Their engagement was to last a few more months yet, and I refused to show my face in London whilst they made the most of it.

When had my life become so complicated? It seemed that both my personal and professional circumstances had joined forces to shackle me in the land my father abhorred like no other.

'You'd be more than welcome in Gloucestershire,' Maurice said with a grin. He had inherited a substantial country estate on the outskirts of the Forest of Dean. That inheritance partly explained why he had never married or had children; instead he had devoted his life to managing the land – and to smoking, drinking and chasing young ladies. No wonder he was always cheerful. 'It might be a good idea for you to spend some time there; you know it will all be yours when I am gone. Though it looks like you might beat me in that race!'

The innkeeper's wife arrived then with our drinks.

'Mrs Dailey,' I said as she put the glasses on the little table, 'we are expecting the local constable . . .'

'McYon?'

'No, no. I believe Miss Fletcher said his name was McEwan.'

'Aye. McYon.'

I blinked twice. 'The very man, yes. Could you send him to us as soon as he arrives?'

We did not have to wait for long. We'd barely had a few sips of the claret and gin (which Uncle described as *divine*) when the man came in.

The constable was everything I expected after hearing Miss Fletcher's statements: middle-aged, with rosy cheeks and a beard like a tangle of greasy wire. His plumpness suggested he'd not needed to run or even walk at a brisk pace in years. With his languid gait, half-open eyes and creased clothes, the man spread apathy like a contagious disease. And he was picking his nose as he stepped into the room. Thankfully he did not offer a hand to shake.

'Which one o' youse is Nine-Nails?'

'The man is rather famous,' Uncle whispered.

'Inspector McGray, if you will,' I said. 'And neither of us. We expect him to arrive this evening with the boy.'

McEwan sat in the last free armchair, sprawling lazily as if readying himself for a nap. 'Then who're youse?'

'Inspector Ian Frey. This other gentleman is not of your conce–'

'Youse are in my province. I say what's o' my concern.'

'Your province indeed,' I said. 'So you are the man who refused to investigate the death threat against Miss Fletcher's son.'

'What's that to ye, pretty boy?'

Uncle Maurice rose at once. 'I shall be in my room, Ian. Unlike you, I lack the tolerance to deal with thugs of this variety.'

McEwan followed him with his eyes. Even his pupils moved at a sluggish pace. 'He yer husband? A wee bit auld for ye.'

'Why did you refuse to investigate?'

He interlaced his fingers. 'Insufficient evidence.'

'Insufficient! The note was perfectly solid. Miss Fletcher's window was smashed and –'

'And the lass could've done it herself.'

I rolled my eyes. 'Why on earth would she do such a thing?'

McEwan simply shrugged, and then distractedly brought a finger back to his nostril. For once I wished Nine-Nails were around; he would have chastised this specimen swiftly.

'Do you realize there is a real possibility someone might try to harm that boy?'

With unexpected attention, McEwan inspected whatever matter he'd just pulled out of his nose. 'There's nae been a murder or a crime or a robbery in this land for almost seventeen years.' He tossed the thing on to the carpet. 'In fact, the last serious crime was reported by Miss Fletcher herself. The lass likes the limelight.'

'What crime was that?'

The man yawned so widely I could see his uvula and the broken lines of his back teeth. 'Alleged rape.'

I nearly knocked my claret over. '*Rape?*'

'Aye. She said Mr Koloman's brother had "taken advantage o' her" in one o' their wine cellars.'

'Was that rape –'

'Alleged rape.'

'Was that how she became pregnant?'

'Aye.'

I sat back, taking the information in. Miss Fletcher had not mentioned that point at all. Out of propriety, I had not asked her about the details of her liaison with the recently deceased Maximilian Koloman.

I looked up. 'You did say *alleged*. I suppose the man was never prosecuted.'

'Course he wisnae. Maximilian Koloman denied it all.'

'And was that all the evidence you needed?'

McEwan laughed. 'Lad, I know that type o' wench. Most o' the time they're asking for someone to do them a favour, pulling down their cleavages 'n' swaying their hips in front o' their masters. And then they moan 'n' cry when they finally get some attention.'

I felt fire in my stomach. 'I can see how . . . *thorough* your investigation must have been back then.'

'Och, don't look at me like that. Ye've met the lass. D'ye think it would be easy to pin down a mastodon like that? Nae, she must've wanted it.'

I needed a deep breath and a pretty long sip of claret, vinegary though it was. I would emphatically recommend the man's dismissal as soon as we had a new superintendent, but for the time being I needed to extract as much information from him as I could.

'What can you tell me about Miss Fletcher's employers, the Kolomans?'

'They're a very respectable family,' he rushed to say. 'Very good landlords, I always hear, and I've been constable here for nearly thirty years. Mr Koloman, uncle to the illegitimate brat, is a very elegant, very well-read man. His wife is too, and she is always helping the neighbours: every autumn she runs a wee school for the children in Poolewe, and gets them clothes 'n' toys. And she is good at medicine, always knows what's wrong with folk. Och, and the Kolomans' daughters are delicious things to behold – I only wish they went out more.'

My frown deepened. 'That is entirely at odds with the reputation of the late Maximilian.'

'That lad was an entirely different beast. He was abroad

all the time and came back only two, three times a year. We had to hide our lassies when that happened.'

I arched an eyebrow. 'But you still doubt he mistreated Miss Fletcher.'

'Och, aye! The man was what the lassies call handsome. Ye'll see when ye meet his brother; they looked very much alike. And besides his looks and his money, he knew how to seduce his women. Aye, I doubt he ever had to force anyone: if a lassie said nae, he only had to go on to the next one.'

'In my experience,' I said, 'such *charming* men usually find a refusal all the more alluring.'

McEwan's answer to that was a blank stare. I took a deep breath. I had no wish to hear another word from him, but Nine-Nails had given me specific instructions in his telegram: I should learn as much as possible about the people that lived in the archipelago.

'I must ask you: are you acquainted with the Nellys family?'

'The madwags on the islands? Of course. Michty ugly wretches.'

'And have you heard about that . . . miraculous cure of theirs?'

'Everyone round here has, but I think it's just an auld hags' tale. They say the manky water from that well has cured the man but that it only works as long as he stays on the island. The foolish lot!'

I recalled Madame Katerina stating the same. And there was also an alleged curse on anyone who took anything, be it an acorn, a pebble or a grain of sand, off the island. Ridiculous.

I heard a throat clearing and I saw Mr Dailey stepping in. Followed by Miss Fletcher.

She was already tense, as if she'd been preparing for this

encounter, but when she saw the constable she still changed colour. She made me think of a whistling kettle, her lips tensing as she exhaled noisily.

McEwan, the man who had laughed at her misfortunes and then done nothing, received her with a cynical smile.

'Miss Fletcher! Looking as ripe 'n' tempting as always.'

If I felt outraged, I can only wonder what went through Miss Fletcher's mind. Mr Dailey looked furious. He took a little step forward, as if to block the way in case Miss Fletcher decided to strike.

'The Kolomans sent their scullery maid with a message,' he said without any formalities. 'Inspector, they invite ye and yer good uncle to stay in the manor for as long as yer investigation may last. Youse will be well looked after; they have an impressive kitchen and an even better cellar. Much better than I could offer youse here.'

'I appreciate the gesture, but this is not a social visit.'

'They thought you might say that,' said Miss Fletcher, holding the note in her hand. 'But they insist you at least come to dine with them tonight. Their house is not two miles away, and I understand Inspector McGray will be going there directly.'

I checked the time. 'I am sorry. If we were to dine there tonight, we'd need to leave at once, and I still have a few questions to ask this . . . individual.'

'They have also thought of that, Mr Frey.' She had to take another deep breath. 'You might prefer to continue your questioning tomorrow morning –'

'Impossible!' McEwan jumped in. 'I need to go back to Poolewe. That's ten bloody miles away! It took me half the day to get here, and I won't wear out my good beast just to come back here 'n' talk about these dumb trifles.'

Miss Fletcher managed to keep herself composed, but only just. She was clenching both fists, her jaw was tense and she had slightly bared her teeth. When she spoke, her voice was low and throaty. 'Mrs Koloman apologizes for the inconvenience . . . sir, and says you can spend the night here. She'll pay for your accommodation. And anything you might consume.'

McEwan rubbed his hands together. 'Och, ye should've said so sooner, lass! Hey, ye, tell yer wifie to fetch me some ale. The good stuff, nae that watered shite youse give the Soothrons.'

'If you'll follow me to the dining room,' said the innkeeper, 'you can have it with your dinner. The stew is ready.'

'Even better!' And McEwan jumped to his feet and headed for the door. As he walked past Miss Fletcher he slowed down a little, casting her a lascivious look. Quite daring, for the man was at least six inches shorter.

As soon as he left, Miss Fletcher let out a quivering exhalation, shutting her eyes and throwing her head backward.

I stood up and went to her. 'I have no words to describe the way that despicable wretch has treated you. I will do *everything* I can to see him dismissed and then get a proper constable to oversee this area.'

'Thank you, sir, but my son is my main worry. Promise me he'll be your priority.'

I offered my hand to shake. 'You have my word, miss.'

And then, for the first time since I'd met her, I saw Miss Fletcher give the hint of a smile. She knew exactly what I'd just committed myself to – and I wish she had warned me.

6

'Fucking useless!' McGray snorted, jumping out of the hard bed. As he had predicted, he could not bring himself to sleep; in fact, he felt as wide awake as if it were mid-morning. If he'd been in his Edinburgh house, he would have given up long ago and gone to his cluttered library to read the night away. In this tiny, damp inn bedroom, however, there was little to distract him.

He had heard the rain slacken, and when he pulled back the moth-eaten curtain he saw that the night sky was surprisingly clear. The waning moon shed silver light all across the port of Thurso; McGray could make out the coast, the harbour and the road in plenty of detail. The place was deserted and, other than the dull murmur of the sea, as silent as a grave.

'Might as well,' he mumbled, reaching for his favourite overcoat – the one Frey described as 'jute-sack-couture' – and made his way downstairs. A midnight walk might soothe his mind, or at the very least occupy it.

As soon as he stepped out he felt the wind hit him in the face, laden with the salty smell of the sea, and cool but not uncomfortable.

He was tempted to light a cigarette, but the insistent wind would burn it away before he could take more than three puffs. He thought of following the road that went round the bay, towards the cliffs, from where he would have a nice view of Scrabster Pier, but as he glanced up at the church's bell tower something caught his eyes.

A small, black shape, of a darkness the moonlight could not penetrate, was fluttering around in that direction. McGray recalled the small bats he'd sometimes seen around his father's farmhouse in midsummer. He squinted, but then the erratic shape descended and became mixed with the shadows of the church.

McGray headed there. At a bend in the road he saw the familiar walls of the parish house. There was a solitary square of golden light coming from the upper level. He guessed that would be the window of the priest's bedroom; the old man was perhaps still dictating his letter for Mrs Koloman.

Then something blocked the light for an instant.

McGray could not tell whether it had been something inside the room or that same dark flying shape dancing around the house. Whichever, it had moved fast, come and gone in a blink.

He felt a sudden draught, chillier than the rest, and it was like an invisible hand pushing him forward, towards that lonely window.

McGray saw the low stone wall that enclosed the vegetable garden, lush with cabbages and carrots and plenty of garlic. He looked up at the window. From that distance he could make out the lace curtains, and through them a dark beam across the ceiling.

He saw it again: a fluttering shadow flashing behind the curtains, inside the room. There came a scream.

McGray's heart skipped a beat and he instantly leaped over the stone wall. As he ran to the porch he realized it was the clergyman's voice, anguished and piercing.

He tried to open the door but it was locked. The scream

had still not ended, and with no time to think McGray kicked at the wood with all his strength. The rusty lock gave in at once, and McGray rushed into the darkened house. The housemaid had just emerged from her back room, carrying a taper and looking deathly pale.

'*Stay here!*' McGray snapped, rushing to the stairs. As he climbed the steps he heard a last throaty moan, as if the priest were suffocating, and then the sound of glass shattering.

McGray reached the corridor and kicked the bedroom door open without even glancing at the latch. The cold wind met him, and he caught a glimpse of a black coat jumping through the smashed window. Right beneath the frame there was a solid desk, a disarray of paper being blown about. The little oil lamp had smashed on the floor and a small mat was catching fire. In front of the flames, lying on the floor, was the trembling priest.

His white nightgown was splattered in scarlet, and the old man covered his neck with both hands, retching and choking in his own blood.

McGray stamped on the fire and knelt by the old man. His milky eyes were wide open, his mouth welling with dark, viscous liquid.

'*Jesus!*' the maid screamed, kneeling on the other side. She'd ignored McGray's command, but he was glad of it now.

'Hold him!' he said, lifting the man's fragile torso and resting it on the woman's lap. 'Put pressure on the wound!'

And before she could say a word McGray jumped through the window and into the night.

He landed on the porch roof, skidding on the wet tiles, and then leaped down to the garden's muddy ground. The attacker was running down the deserted street, heading east at unnatural speed.

'*Stop!*' McGray darted forward, his eyes fixed on the dark figure until it turned a corner and vanished.

McGray cursed and sped up, his legs burning and his heart throbbing. When he reached that corner he looked desperately in every direction. He saw the low fence that surrounded the town's graveyard, the black shadows of the tombstones delineated sharply against the undulating terrain. Beyond them were fishermen's houses, and in between those, further away still, he saw the glinting reflection of the moon on the waters of the River Thurso. Everything was so infuriatingly dark.

McGray wished he'd carried his gun, or at least a lantern, but why would he? He'd gone out for a peaceful walk. As he cursed again, something seemed to move amongst the gravestones. McGray saw it from the corner of his eye, and when he looked down everything was still again. He approached the graveyard furtively, aware that the attacker might still be carrying whatever instrument he had used to slit the priest's throat. McGray's hands were empty.

He thought he heard something. It could have been the rustle of feet on dead leaves, or a rat, but it was the only trace he had, so he stepped forward slowly, his eyes combing the ground, peering into every nook and shadow, expecting to see the gleam of a bloodstained knife rise up from anywhere.

There was something there, McGray was certain. He could feel its presence, heavy in the air and creeping like a chill over the back of his neck.

There was a movement. McGray somehow felt it rather than saw it: a dark mass slithering soundlessly through the night.

'*Stop!*' he shouted again. The figure rose as if sprouting from the ground and rushed towards the river at a frantic pace.

McGray ran in pursuit, hearing nothing but his own

trampling and panting. How could anyone or anything move so silently? He saw the figure intermittently, losing it every now and then in the darkness of the narrow streets, each time thinking he'd lost it for good, and then seeing it flash against the silvery glow of the waters ahead.

Again he lost it for a moment. It must have been a matter of seconds but it felt like an eternity. McGray reached the fishermen's houses, halted for breath and looked around; the riverbank was crammed with boats, barrels and fishing nets. Not a soul was awake, all the tenants sleeping placidly while such horrors happened just outside their homes. McGray stepped swiftly towards the shore, his boots plunging into the mud, and turned his head in every direction. All he could hear was the boisterous current of the river, discharging its choppy waters into the North Sea.

McGray saw something there, drifting away on the current: a dark, almost undistinguishable shape, long enough to be a thin boat, but already so far out he could not tell for sure. And right above, clearly silhouetted against the dull sky, he saw once again the outline of a bat's wings.

McGray cursed on every step of the way back. There was no use chasing that shape on the river; he was not even sure of what he'd seen. And there was a man in dire need at the parish house.

He saw the front door wide open and flapping in the wind, but the entire place was otherwise as still as a grave. The priest's window was now only half lit. McGray rushed in at once, perfectly aware of what he'd find there.

As he climbed the stairs he heard desperate sobbing, a

male voice struggling to draw air in. McGray found the door ajar and slammed it open.

The splatter of red caught his eyes immediately, intensely dark as it spread across the old priest's nightgown. For an eerie second McGray thought Father Thomas had sat up to stare at him with his cloudy eyes, now fixed in a tormented gaze. He had to blink before he realized that the man was dead. His head had been lifted by the sixteen-year-old boy who was now cradling the clergyman's limp body.

It was the first time McGray met Benjamin, and for the rest of his life that would be the image he'd recall when people mentioned the name: a very thin, blond boy, his freckles like drops of blood on his ghastly pale face, his features distorted with grief and his bright-blue eyes reddened with tears. His trembling hands, drenched in blood, were both clasping the priest's neck keenly, as if his grasp could keep the old man with the living. The boy's guttural sobs seemed angst itself.

McGray looked around and found a clean towel on the ewer and basin, perhaps left ready for the morning. He took it and knelt by the corpse. He first closed the man's eyelids, as gently as his fingers allowed. Then he looked up at the boy.

'Benjamin?' As he expected, the boy was not able to reply. McGray carefully placed the towel on Benjamin's hands, whose entire body twitched at the contact. McGray wrapped the stained hands in the towel and held them firmly. 'He's resting now, laddie.'

McGray gave him a moment, feeling the intense tremor and the blood oozing through the cloth. After a while he lifted the boy's hands – not without resistance – and delicately rested the priest's head on the floorboards.

It was a sorry sight, but McGray had to steel himself.

From the moment he first saw the wound he'd known Father Thomas was beyond salvation. He reached for a blanket from the bed and covered the body, and then helped Benjamin wash his hands.

'Where's the lass? Is she bringing help?'

Benjamin nodded, his eyes fixed on the gore on his hands.

'Better ye don't look,' said McGray as the pristine porcelain basin became tainted. He was patting the boy's hands dry when they heard tumultuous footsteps on the staircase. The maid came back in, leading a middle-aged man who clearly was the town's doctor. The woman covered her mouth when she saw the now stained blanket over the body. Her own hands were still smeared with blood.

McGray approached her. 'I'm so sorry, Grant. I ken this is really hard on ye, but I need yer help right now.' He felt it was terribly unfair; the maid was distraught, but unlike Benjamin she seemed in control of her movements. 'Take the laddie downstairs 'n' youse both have a nice cup o' tea. Please look after him until I come to see youse. I'll deal with everything here.'

Grant nodded, and even in her sorrow she managed a hint of a smile. She must be glad she would not be facing it all on her own. She led Benjamin away, and as soon as they left the room McGray shut the door. The doctor was already lifting the sheet to examine the body; even he was unable to repress a gasp when he saw the gore beneath.

McGray allowed himself a deep breath. He had so much to do.

7

'We cannot lodge with them,' I repeated, as Uncle Maurice saw his trunks loaded on to the Kolomans' coach.

'They have very kindly offered, Ian. And I refuse to share a roof with that blasted, stinking, foul-mouthed, raucous-chewing constable. I swear I could hear his gobbling from the upper floor.'

Miss Fletcher was fastening the trunks on the carriage roof, so I drew a little closer and whispered in Uncle's ear. 'Do you understand the nature of my job? I need to investigate these people. For all I know, the Kolomans themselves could be behind the threat to the boy. I cannot fraternize with them.'

But Uncle Maurice was looking at his travel book. 'Oh, look, their manor is even mentioned here. "An awe-inspiring example of eclectic architecture, amalgamating elements of neo-Gothic and Continental –"'

'*I do not give a damn!*'

The driver started and Miss Fletcher nearly dropped the last trunk. My good uncle closed the book and squeezed my shoulder. 'Ian, I did not mean to upset you. It may not sound like it but I do appreciate how crucial your job is. *I* have never done anything for the betterment of humankind in my entire life.'

'Then how is it that –'

He lowered his voice. 'Give yourself some leeway. Accept their dinner, talk to them. Be suave. You might find more about them that way than by simply bursting in with a quizzical brow and a stiff lip.'

I snorted again; not because I disagreed but realizing that McGray might have said something along those same lines – though instead of 'stiff lip' he would have probably said 'shite-sniffing face'.

'Very well,' I said, following Uncle Maurice to the carriage. 'But I am coming back to the inn. And early. Do not expect me to linger until I have to spend the night there.' I was about to step into the carriage but then recalled . . . 'Uncle, wait. I need something.'

'What?'

I whispered, 'I left my gun in my room. I will not be long.'

'A *gu–*' I nearly slapped his face to silence him. He lowered his voice. 'A gun! Whatever for?'

'I'd much rather have it and not need it than –'

'Oh, as you wish. But you should relax. This is only a minor investigation, did you not say so yourself before we departed? It is not as if someone has died.'

The carriage took us along a very scenic path that followed the shores of the loch. To our left, opposite to the deep waters, there were thick pine forests and steep hills that reminded me of a Bavarian landscape. The still deep-blue sky, now dotted with clouds coming from the west, reinforced that impression. It was almost impossible to believe we were still in Scotland.

The trip was a brief one, for the Kolomans' manor was

indeed nearby. According to Uncle's guidebook, the family owned only a very small portion of land – hardly five acres – but extension was irrelevant, for the estate was situated on the most handsome point of Loch Maree's shore. From the map I predicted their house would have the best views of the islands and the hills beyond.

The road gradually separated from the shore, until the thick forest flanked the track on both sides. The pine trees were tall, dark and so dense I imagined the ground below them would be in utmost darkness throughout the year. These were the woods owned by the Kolomans, interrupted only by a granite arch with a small gatehouse beside it: the entry to a well-maintained path that meandered through the forest like a leafy tunnel. We could see little ahead, until the wild forest gave way to the manor's formal garden.

There the path was flanked by very tall rhododendrons in full bloom. The scarlet flowers were of a variety I had never seen, and the lower trunks were trimmed and evenly spaced, so that we had a good view of the smooth lawns, where perfectly shaped yews drew intricate geometric patterns. My eyes flickered from Greek-style statues to clumps of exotic flowers that Kew's Botanic Gardens would have envied.

The rhododendrons then opened up to reveal a majestic country house, built entirely of granite in various tones of grey: dark for the window frames, a little lighter for the walls and the stone steps, and almost white for the Dutch-style dormer windows lined up on the top storey. It was not a very large building, but it had elegant, solid lines, and a deceptively simple design. I'd gradually learn that every element was enriched with some detail, like the beautiful weathervane that crowned the centre of the façade, shaped as a pointing Hermes.

'Those columns remind me of Wallenstein Palace,' said

Uncle, looking at the rounded double pillars that supported arches all around the ground floor.

'They look more Austrian than Bohemian to me,' I said, just as we halted by the wide main door.

Miss Fletcher opened the carriage for us and Uncle Maurice jumped down with the eagerness of a youngster.

'Simply stunning,' he said, looking all around. 'And you nearly missed it all, Ian.'

I was beginning to share some of his enthusiasm (it was impossible not to feel uplifted under that bright sky and with the lush, immaculate foliage all around us) but I still hardened my countenance. 'I shan't be here for long, Uncle.'

The driver jumped from his seat.

'To the first guest room,' Miss Fletcher told him and then turned to Uncle. 'Smeaton will look after your luggage, sir. Please follow me.'

We climbed the flagstone steps to the main door. It was old oak with enormous wrought-iron hinges shaped as grapevines. It opened just as we approached, pulled by a young but muscly servant, and I saw that the door must be at least eight inches thick. We stepped into a small but impressive entrance hall, its grey stone walls decorated with only a few well-appointed tapestries. My eyes went to the imposing staircase: marble steps carpeted in burgundy, with simple straight lines and a square landing; it was a clear statement of strength and wealth. Underneath it, on the other side of the hall, there was an oak back door framed by a thick Gothic arch, which must lead to the shore right behind the manor.

'Boyde, are the master and mistress available now?' Miss Fletcher asked the young man.

'Not yet, missus,' he said, bowing to us. 'But they said the Miss Kolomans could receive the gentlemen.'

'Are they in the Shadows Room?'

'Aye.'

Miss Fletcher took us to the east wing on the right. The Gothic windows looked on to the gardens and the double columns. The latter I thought were entirely misplaced: that corridor, facing south, could have received plenty of daylight, particularly on a summer day like this, but the roofed portico right outside blocked most of it. The building must have been designed by a Continental architect, utterly ignorant of how gloomy the Highlands could be.

We soon reached a door that Miss Fletcher opened for us.

Why she'd called it the 'Shadows Room' became obvious as soon as we stepped in: the place was in almost absolute darkness. I had to blink a few times to realize we were entering a long gallery, its walls entirely covered with bookshelves, its large windows enveloped with thick velvet curtains. The only light was a bright, silver ray projected across the room. It came from a black wooden box to the left, the beam emanating from a hair-thin slit and expanding sharply like a solid cone in the air. At first I could not see what was projected on the opposite wall, for there was a Chinese folding screen, intricately painted and carved, blocking the view.

'Goodness, I am going to trip,' said Uncle.

'The darkness is to a purpose.'

The female voice came from behind the screen, and we saw emerge the face of a twenty-year-old woman.

I first thought I was looking at a ghost: her skin was as white as fresh snow, and under the silver light it glowed like mist. She wore a very dark dress that became lost in the shadows, momentarily making her appear as an ethereal head and shoulders floating in the air. Her golden hair, falling freely in pronounced waves, only enhanced the illusion.

I felt a shiver and drew breath sharply, and only then did I notice how beautiful the creature was. She had the most striking eyes I have ever seen: her irises were cobalt blue at the edges and turquoise in the centre, which made her pupils look as if they glowed from within. Amidst the prevalent black and white, for a moment those eyes seemed to be the only speck of colour left in the world.

'Good evening, sirs,' she said in a clean voice that cut the air like a knife, and just as I convinced myself she was not an apparition I saw an exact replica of that alabaster face emerge from behind the folding screen.

For a moment I thought I'd gone mad, but Miss Fletcher stepped in. 'May I introduce Miss Veronika and Miss Natalja? They're Mr and Mrs Koloman's twin daughters.'

Uncle Maurice moved forward at once, grinning. 'Maurice Plantard, your very humble servant for the rest of my days. Why, you are the most beautiful gems in God's creation!'

The second girl, standing at the back, frowned a little, but her sister, the one with the darker dress, showed a cunning smile and offered her hand. She must be quite used to flattery.

'It is a pleasure to meet you, sirs,' she said as Uncle kissed her very fine hand. 'Can you guess which one of us is Miss Veronika?'

Uncle raised a brow, not letting go of her hand. 'Miss, you undoubtedly look like a Veronika to me.'

The girl squinted slightly, casting him a sly look. 'Is that the professional verdict of a police inspector?'

'He obviously is not the inspector,' the second girl said, approaching me and offering me a hand – clearly to shake, not to kiss. 'Natalja Koloman, pleased to meet you.'

'Oh, Nat, you always spoil the fun,' said Miss Veronika, her hand still wrapped in Uncle's.

'You *must* be Inspector Frey,' said Miss Natalja; the tone of her voice was a touch lower than her sister's. In the future I'd recognize them first by their voices rather than their looks.

'How could you tell –' I did not finish the sentence; instead I touched the faint yet noticeable scar on my cheekbone. 'Oh.'

'And that and that,' she said, pointing at my burned hand and my now slightly bent nose.

Uncle laughed. 'I keep telling him the job is eating him alive.' He looked around. 'Would you young ladies mind it terribly if I opened the curtains?'

'Oh, I'd much rather tell you about our work, Mr Plantard,' said Veronika at once, pulling Uncle's hand. 'That requires this very nice penumbra.'

Miss Fletcher cleared her throat. I thought she'd push Maurice away from Veronika, but she simply said, 'I shall call for some refreshments. Brandy, sirs? Gin?'

'Gin?' Veronika cried. 'Never mind that horrid stuff. I am sure Mr Plantard and Mr Frey will want to try some of the wine from our vineyards.'

Before I could object, Miss Fletcher had already gone and Miss Veronika was leading Uncle to the folding screen. I did not even have a chance to ask whether someone shouldn't chaperone us. Everyone in that house seemed to move a smidgen more quickly than I could react.

'Are you at all interested in the principles of spectrography?' asked Miss Veronika.

'I have never heard the word in my life,' declared Uncle. 'But coming from your sweet lips it sounds like the most fascinating topic.'

Miss Natalja and I shook our heads in almost perfect synchrony.

I saw there were in fact two folding screens, as identical as the girls, and between them two cushioned sofas, a little table and a tea set. And scattered all around there was a disarray of books, notes, quills, pencils, instruments (three thermometers of varying lengths, a compass, measuring tapes . . .) and all manner of drawing tools (rulers, protractors and right-triangles).

Against the wall there was a white canvas mounted on a mahogany frame, on to which the light was projected. Only it did not look white but was diffracted into a perfectly square rainbow.

'That is incredibly pretty,' said Uncle, although I could tell he was merely being polite. 'Is that one of those new colour slides?'

I spoke before Uncle showed the full extent of his upper-class ignorance. 'These young ladies seem to be experimenting with light. I assume you have a crystal prism inside that box?' I pointed at the source of the light. 'It separates a beam into its compounds, just like rain droplets do in the sky. I saw a few demonstrations in Oxford but never such a perfect separation of colours.'

'We use Bohemian crystal commissioned expressly for us,' said Miss Natalja. She went into the darkness and brought out a small chest made of polished ebony. It was lined with green velvet and divided into compartments, each one containing a prism of slightly different dimensions. She handed me one. 'These are not only different in shape but also in composition. We've found that the spectra changes depending on how much lead the crystals contain. Before you arrived we were in the process of measuring the width of each band of colour.'

'It is not only lead we look at,' Miss Veronika added. 'Any substance will produce its own unique . . . rainbow, if you will. And it also depends on the light; the spectra of candlelight will be very different from that of the sun. We are particularly interested in the latter.'

'That sounds fascinating indeed,' said Uncle, although his eyes were drifting towards Miss Veronika's neckline.

'Are you measuring temperature as well?' I asked, nodding at the thermometers.

'We are reproducing William Herschel's experiments,' answered Miss Natalja. 'Have you read his work, Inspector?'

'I am afraid not. I know the name because he discovered the planet Uranus, the only planet not sighted in ancient times.'

'I cannot blame you,' said she, picking up one of the thermometers. 'His work on light was overshadowed by that discovery. Look closer – you will find this *fascinating indeed*.'

As Natalja cast Uncle a reproachful stare she drew the thermometer close to the canvas, to the centre of the violet band.

'You will notice a slight increase in temperature.'

I looked intently for a moment – Uncle Maurice yawned very discreetly – and just as I thought nothing was going to happen, the mercury in the thermometer rose but a fraction of a degree.

'Did you see it?'

'Indeed,' I said.

'What do you think will happen if I move the thermometer to the red band?'

'Well, the same, I'd assume.'

Miss Natalja did so, and sooner than before the temperature rose, this time by almost twice as much.

I was impressed. 'Different colours give you different amounts of heat! Who would have thought?'

'Most remarkable,' said Uncle, but again his eyes were otherwise engaged.

'There is something far more remarkable,' said Veronika,

noticing my uncle's stare but shamelessly enjoying the attention. 'Show them, Nat.'

Natalja moved the thermometer *beyond* the red band, to the margins of the canvas where there was no light. I was of course expecting the temperature to drop – but it rose instead!

She nodded. 'There you have it. Lord Herschel called them "heat rays". Warmth, it seems, is just a form of light that our eyes cannot see.'

'Light we cannot see?' Uncle asked, finally curious.

'Yes. And nobody knows why we cannot see it,' said Veronika.

I was speechless, but again Natalja went on before I could react. 'Inspector, what do you think happens on the other end of the spectra? Beyond the violet?'

I shook my head. 'Does the spectra go on beyond that as well?'

'Indeed, but what happens there is far more intriguing than heat. Temperature seems to increase only towards the red band. If I try the thermometer beyond the violet, it will take a long while for us to detect even the slightest increase – if any.'

'So nothing is happening there,' said Uncle, but Miss Veronika was reaching for a leather file, from which she produced a long strip of paper.

'I don't suppose you gentlemen are familiar with the work of Johann Wilhelm Ritter?'

Uncle looked at me. 'Ian, you are the one with the German blood.'

Again I shook my head. 'I have never heard the name.'

'Few people have,' said Natalja, 'which is truly unfair. The poor man was a genius. He could have been a new Da Vinci, if only he had lived longer.'

'He performed horrid experiments on himself,' her sister

intervened, wrinkling her nose in disgust. 'Applied electric current to his ears, mouth, eyes . . .'

'No wonder he died young,' I said.

'He read Herschel's work and inferred that the light spectra must also continue at the other end – he had some exotic ideas about symmetry and polarity in nature.'

'*Naturphilosophie*,' Veronika added with a perfect German accent, 'a dangerous tradition of thought. Well, nothing good can come from that batch of German philosophers who claim –'

'Sister, let's not digress . . .' Natalja said. She held one end of the paper strip and with the aid of her sister placed it against the projected rainbow. 'Herr Ritter did find something beyond the violet band, so at least in this instance his philosophies were . . . somewhat right. See, like he did, we asked Papa to soak this strip of paper in a solution of silver chloride –'

'What's that?' Uncle asked.

I volunteered, 'It is one of the chemicals used in photography. The CID has it in store at all times these days.'

'Indeed,' Natalja went on. 'So you must know it is sensitive to light. Now, look at the stains on this strip.'

The paper went progressively darker as it approached the violet band. Veronika unrolled her end of the paper, and the stain went darker even beyond the violet light.

'And *that* is the main difference between sunlight and candlelight,' she said.

'We are using a candle right now,' said Natalja. 'But for this strip we used sunlight, which gives us the most noticeable stain. We hardly see any change of colour with a candle or a gaslight.'

Veronika smiled coquettishly at Uncle. 'Mr Plantard, you look a very strong, active man. Do you like hunting?'

'I certainly do, miss.'

'Have you ever wondered, whilst out in the open, why you get a tan from the sun but not from a candle or a hearth?'

'My stepmother surely has,' I said. 'She never sits near a window unless it faces north.'

'Very much like our mother and ourselves,' said Veronika. 'And we think the difference is there; whatever it is in sunlight that blemishes our skins, it *must* be beyond that violet band.'

'Herr Ritter called them "chemical rays",' Natalja concluded.

I assented in silence. These girls were brilliant experimentalists – nothing like those amateur botanists who fill notebooks with useless sketches of sweet peas or those aristocratic ladies who pin common moths to frames and fancy themselves taxonomists. These girls appeared even more insightful than many scholars I'd had the chance to meet at the English universities.

And their parents would not disappoint either.

Miss Fletcher came back then, bringing us news rather than drinks.

'Gentlemen, Mr and Mrs Koloman have just arrived,' she said, opening the curtains with one powerful pull. 'They will receive you in the main drawing room. I hope the girls have kept you entertained?'

'Exceedingly,' said Uncle in a silky tone.

I saw that the long day was finally drawing to a close, the sky turning from bright blue to a deep indigo. As the dying daylight filled the gallery, I noticed that the Miss Kolomans were in fact wearing very odd dresses. They looked rather like those Regency engravings from the start of the century, or like the ancient Greek robes one could see carved in marble at the British Museum . . . only even simpler: plain garments of soft, flowing material, which followed the shapes of the girls' bodies. No corsets.

'Your father says you had better change into your dinner gowns while he talks to Inspector Frey,' said Miss Fletcher.

'That sounds more like he wants us out of the way,' Veronika muttered, placing the paper strip back into the file.

'As if we didn't know what brought these gentlemen here,' her sister added, and then, for the first time, she showed me a little smile. 'We shall see you at dinner, then.'

The girls curtsied and left, and as Miss Fletcher led us through a wide corridor Uncle whispered to me: 'Gorgeous gals, Ian. Do you not think so? And . . .' he lowered his voice further, 'lovely shaped even without any corsets.'

'Rather indecent, if I may say. They looked as though they were in their nightgowns! If I had a daughter, I'd never let her receive visitors looking like that.'

Uncle winked. 'Thank goodness you have not fathered all the girls in the world.'

Miss Fletcher showed us the way to a large drawing room in the opposite wing of the manor. Before she opened the door she leaned towards me to whisper something.

'Inspector, someone came from the telegraph office in Poolewe with a message for Mr Koloman. My . . . my master wouldn't tell me anything about it. He said "not yet" . . . but I could see it in his eyes.' She gulped. 'I think something terrible has happened.'

8

It had been a sleepless night through and through, but at least McGray had not faced the ordeal on his own. The doctor and the local constable had been incredibly solicitous: the body had been inspected, respectfully taken to the constabulary for further investigation, and the doctor had even summoned one of his apprentices to clean the room.

Constable McLachlan had arrived promptly, asked the proper questions and fetched a couple of officers to search the streets, in case the attacker had lingered. He'd also realized that Benjamin and the maid would give more useful statements in the morning, once their nerves had settled a little. McGray had agreed to meet him at the parish house at seven o'clock, but since he'd been unable to sleep he'd set off to inspect the surroundings as soon as the sky had begun to brighten, a little before six in the morning.

McGray found the vegetable patch trampled in places, a few cabbages ripped from the ground by strong feet, and then traces of soil on the low stone wall. It proved useless to look for marks on the road, for it had rained in the small hours and the parish house stood in one of the busiest spots of the town. Right now the road was packed with carts carrying all manner of goods to and from the piers. McGray had not expected Thurso to be such a bustling place, and it would be at its busiest in the mornings, when most of the cargo and ships departed.

Something McGray did find, however, were soil marks on the walls: someone had climbed to the priest's window; the traces were all too clear. McGray bent down to look at a smear of mud, scraped on the edge of a jutting brick. There were similar marks all across the wall, made by a very skilled climber who could use even the slightest crack or bump as support.

'Found anything, Inspector?'

He rose to see the tired face of Constable McLachlan. He was a thin, middle-aged man with pale, perceptive eyes and very bushy mutton chops. He conducted himself with an utter lack of humour, not interested in making friends and speaking only when it was strictly needed, but his intelligence was evident.

'The attacker climbed up this wall,' said McGray. 'See? There and there.'

'You said the window looked untouched last night, right before the murder?'

'Indeedy. So Father Thomas –'

'Father Thomas let his attacker in through the window willingly?' The constable arched one grey eyebrow to an unthinkable height.

'Aye, and very quietly. I don't think the maid or the boy had heard a thing until the old man yelled, which was just when I arrived. But we should verify that with them.'

McLachlan produced a small notebook and took copious notes. He also inspected the prints on the wall and the trampled vegetables, before knocking at the door.

'I hope they are fit enough for questioning.'

He had to knock again before the maid came. Her eyes

looked terribly red, and from her creased clothes McGray could tell she'd spent all night on a chair. She let them in and they found Benjamin standing at the centre of the parlour, the same room where Father Thomas had received McGray not a full day ago. The boy looked as though he'd been waiting for them on that very spot for hours.

'Did you find anybody?' he said at once. McGray noticed how dry the boy's lips were.

'Not yet,' said McLachlan. 'We need to ask you a few questions.'

'I'll bring youse some tea,' said Grant, scurrying out of the room before anyone could even say whether they wanted any.

It was McGray who had to offer the boy a seat.

Benjamin 'Smith' – now Koloman – was a bashful fellow, quite tall but spindly, and he walked slightly hunched, as if his own height embarrassed him. He spoke with the exact same accent as poor Father Thomas, the soft, untraceable sort that McGray's late father would have called 'sheepish Scot'. Benjamin sat down and folded his long hands on his knees, unable to look them in the eye.

McGray assumed that McLachlan would interrogate the boy with the same lack of tact typical of Frey, so he took the lead.

'We're sorry we have to ask this so soon, laddie. Are ye all right?' Benjamin nodded, his eyes fixed on his own hands. 'Did Father Thomas tell you why I came here in the first place?'

Again Benjamin nodded, but soon he had to press his eyelids and there were tears slipping through his fingers. McGray guessed the attack must have happened shortly after that conversation.

'What were ye doing when . . . when it all happened?'

Benjamin was still covering his eyes. 'P-packing. I . . . I

79

didn't take the news calmly. I locked myself in my room and started packing. If I had known . . .'

McGray gave him a moment. He could only imagine the turmoil in the boy's head: the sudden revelation about his origins, the prospect of leaving the only home he'd known, and then witnessing the gory death of his one protector.

'Did ye hear anything? Someone enter the house?'

The boy drew in deep breaths, rubbed his eyes and then forced himself to show his face. 'I heard a window open and close, but Grant does that all the time to ventilate the rooms. Then I heard Father Thomas talking to someone, but I thought he must be dictating a letter to Grant. He does it almost every day.'

'So there was nothing to make ye think he might be in danger?'

'Nothing, sir. Everything was perfectly normal. Again, if I had known . . .'

He looked away, as if about to retch. McLachlan was jotting down notes at full speed.

'Did he see any visitors other than me yesterday?' McGray asked, but Benjamin shook his head. 'Is there anyone ye think might want to do him harm?'

'Who could possibly wish that?' Benjamin snapped, a sudden fire in his eyes.

'Even I knew of Father Thomas,' the constable muttered. 'Everyone in Thurso did. He was very pious, very generous. He helped raise many children too.'

That last sentence disturbed Benjamin a good deal, and McGray had to go to him, pat him on the back.

'Sorry, laddie. Just one more question before we let ye go. Father Thomas said he'd send a letter to Mrs Koloman, yer aunt. Ye just said ye thought ye heard him dictating something.'

'Yes. I did think so, but Grant told me Father Thomas didn't ask her to write anything last night.'

McGray raised an eyebrow. 'That's odd. Did ye make out any of his words? Anything at all?'

Benjamin shook his head. 'No. He was mumbling. He always does –' He looked down. 'He always *did*, when dictating.'

The boy was on the verge of tears, so McGray told him he could go now. He would try to ask more questions later.

Just after he left, the maid came in. She faltered as soon as she saw that Benjamin was not there, and McGray had to stand and lead her gently to a seat. Grant had done a very poor job with the tea, but McGray could hardly blame her (and he drank it gladly, still thirsty from all the salted herring of the previous days).

McGray asked the same questions he'd asked Benjamin, and Grant's statement matched his:

'I went to bed early, sir,' she said, her hands shaking. 'I . . . I must confess I did eavesdrop a wee bit . . . I heard what Father Thomas told Benjamin about his family. I'm sorry, I –'

'All right, all right,' said McGray. 'We're all human. Benjamin says . . .' McGray stopped, thinking he should not volunteer anything just yet. 'Did ye go to yer room straight away?'

'Yes, sir. Yesterday was a long day. I still had a few chores to do, but I left them for today.'

'Nae letters?'

'No, sir. Father Thomas did mention something about a message, but in the end he just said I could go to bed.'

'Did ye hear anything after that?'

She instantly frowned and tears rolled down her cheeks. 'Oh, sir, no! I fell asleep like a log. To think I was dozing like a baby while –'

Grant sobbed and wiped her tears with the edge of her apron. McGray poured *her* some tea. She seemed to be telling the truth.

The most immediate facts covered, McGray could now focus on his own troubles.

He was not sure he should ask his final question with McLachlan present, but McGray was past caring about perplexed looks. 'Lass, did ye ... ever hear him talk about madness or miraculous cures?'

Grant shook her head and McLachlan stopped taking notes. 'What is all that about?'

'I'll explain later,' said McGray, but with no intention of doing so.

Grant could not provide any further help and seemed only too glad when they stood up to leave.

McGray took a deep breath as he put his coat back on, feeling utterly frustrated. A cruel crime had been committed right under his nose and he'd not been able to do anything about it. His one comfort was that had he not been around the attacker might have gone on to slaughter Benjamin too. Perhaps the boy had been the main target, and the poor priest had simply been in the way.

Outside the daylight was dull, the sky entirely covered with a uniform layer of clouds. They found Benjamin kneeling down by the flattened vegetables, looking rather intently at a sorry cabbage.

'He liked it pickled,' he mumbled, rising slowly to face them again. He folded his hands by his chest in a very priestly manner. 'Grant and I were going to harvest them next week.'

The boy's eyes were full of sorrow, but at least those moments on his own had taken the edge off his grief.

'I've lost very dear folk too,' said McGray. 'And it was just as awful as last night. Believe me, I ken how ye feel – and I think yer handling it brilliantly.'

He squeezed Benjamin's shoulder. The boy gulped with difficulty, but then looked at him and nodded, a little reassured.

'Father Thomas said you'd take me away today. This morning, in fact.'

'Aye, but –'

'Will that still happen?'

McGray was not expecting him to recall the logistics of the trip. 'Laddie, d'ye really want to leave right now?'

Benjamin looked up at the open window and shuddered. 'I couldn't spend another night here.'

It was McGray's turn to assent. He'd not once revisited the farmhouse where his parents had died, and that had happened six years ago.

'Well, we were s'posed to take this morning's ferry, but –'

'I am afraid you've missed that, gentlemen!'

The rich, clear voice came from the road, and McGray saw two tall figures approach. One was an elegant blond man of around twenty-five, wearing a light-grey velvet coat and waving a top hat in a lively manner. An older chap, rather rough-looking with prickly stubble and a quarrelsome expression, followed him closely.

'Dominik Koloman,' the young man said effusively, offering his hand to shake. McGray and McLachlan introduced themselves mechanically. 'And you must be my cousin!'

He saluted Benjamin with an unexpected embrace, patting his back vigorously and then placing the top hat on the boy's head. He then grasped Benjamin's shoulders and shook him with affection. 'Good Lord, you *do* look a Koloman!'

The resemblance was all too clear. They both had the exact same shade of blond hair, the same shape of the jaw, the same brow; but Dominik also looked entirely different. His raised chin, proud chest and perfectly groomed hair were in stark contrast with Benjamin's freckles and frayed woollen jumper. And Benjamin looked bedazzled, clearly wishing to push his new-found cousin away. At once he took off the hat and handed it back.

McLachlan asked the question in everybody's mind. 'Mr Koloman, what are you doing here?'

'I had a telegram from my mother, my good man.' He winked at McGray with condescension. 'That would be Mrs Minerva Koloman to you. She wrote to tell me the news about my cousin. I was spending the summer in Stavanger' – another wink – 'that's in Norway.' He turned to Benjamin. 'I must take you there some day, cousin. Astonishing port. Outstanding landscapes.' Then he turned back to McLachlan. 'My mother told me Benjamin lived in Thurso and might be in need of transportation, so I thought I would shorten my trip and take him home with me.'

McGray was studying the man and his rough servant with an arched brow.

'When did youse arrive?'

'Why, *minutes* ago,' Dominik replied with a grin. 'That's how I know the ferry to Poolewe has just left. The man who runs them is a very old friend of the family. He supplies my parents with all manner of goods. He recognized my humble vessel and came to greet us – quite hurriedly, for he was already delayed.' He squeezed Benjamin's shoulders again.

'We heard what happened, cousin. This entire town is talking of nothing else. I am so sorry, Ben.'

But there was something in his tone that made the condolences sound silly, a cheerfulness and nonchalance the young man could not fully repress. McGray had heard that careless note many times from Edinburgh's young gentry.

He stared at Dominik for a second, recalling the dark shape he'd seen the night before on the river, rushing towards the sea.

'Laddie,' he said to Benjamin, 'do ye mind giving us a minute?'

The boy did not reply; he simply stepped back and went into the house, a little too eager to get out of view.

Dominik gave him a rather condescending look. 'Oh, my poor young cousin must be utterly –'

'When did ye hear about him?' McGray interrupted.

Dominik looked McGray up and down, still smiling, but it seemed as though his jaw had frozen. 'I believe I received the telegram about a week ago.'

'I need ye to tell me the exact date.'

Dominik widened his smile. 'Might I know why?'

'Nae, just answer.'

'I do not recall the exact day but I still have my mother's telegram. You are welcome to look at it if you need to.'

'Yer mother tells you about the laddie, and then ye jump on yer boat here to pick him up?'

'You are an extraordinary listener, sir! Indeed, that is precisely what I have just said.'

'A week is very quick to travel from Norway.'

'Oh, Calcraft here moves across the North Sea as if it were a walk in Les Tuileries. That's in France.'

Calcraft simply nodded, casting McGray a look of derision. He had all the appearance of a sailor coarsened by the sea and the elements, and all the arrogance of a captain who can't stand talking to his petty passengers.

'Is that true?' McGray asked him.

Calcraft sneered. 'Are you doubting my skills or my master's word?'

McGray's chest swelled and Dominik had to raise a conciliatory hand. 'Oh, do, do excuse my man. His excellent skills more than compensate for his curtness.'

As he spoke, Dominik produced a small pocket Bible and opened it. McGray thought he was about to recite a psalm, but instead Dominik tore out a page, produced a little pouch of tobacco and began rolling himself a cigarette. He noticed the men's befuddled look.

'Why, where are my manners? Do you want one?'

'Nae. Thanks, laddie. I spoke to the priest yesterday. He kent nothing about –'

'I beg your pardon – he what?'

McGray snorted. 'He *knew* nothing about yer arrival.'

'Oh, of course not! I told nobody. I simply realized Thurso was on my way and thought it would be a jolly good surprise to meet my cousin and take him home myself.'

'Aye, a *jolly good* surprise,' McGray mocked. 'Are ye in the habit of throwing bricks?'

Dominik looked totally confused. 'I . . . well, I don't really know what you mean. I enjoyed skimming pebbles as a child, if that helps you.'

And he smiled as widely as possible, his Bible-paper cigarette between his teeth.

McLachlan made just one discreet note.

'May I ask you,' Dominik said, 'how long you intend to stay in Thurso? Are you to take care of the investigations?'

'I might,' said McGray.

'Well, we are planning to sail this afternoon. I have my own paddle steamer, you see. I could take my cousin with me . . . whilst you investigate?'

McGray chuckled. He'd never leave Benjamin alone with this arrogant bag of slime.

'Thanks, but nae. He's been entrusted to me. Can ye wait a couple o' days?'

Dominik shook his head. 'I know you have your work to do here, but I have a cargo that will spoil. I must set off today.'

'Then I'll wait 'til the next ferry.'

'They only run once a week,' Dominik warned.

'Shite! Is that true?'

'That is true,' said McLachlan.

'And I'm afraid the railways don't go that far west,' Dominik added. 'You might try a stagecoach but the roads in this part of Scotland are shockingly medieval. The journey would take you three or four days – that is, assuming everything goes smoothly. Your best choice is to wait a week for the boat.'

McGray snorted in frustration. 'What time are ye leaving?'

'Five o'clock, at the latest. So that we can be home tomorrow afternoon.'

'All right. Ye'll see us at the dock if I decide we go with youse. Now sod off.'

'If you don't mind, I would like to introduce myself properly to my cousin. We barely exchanged two words just now and my mother and father have always told me –'

McGray cast him a murderous stare, and Dominik simply bowed and left.

McLachlan came closer. 'Do you suspect that man?'

'A conceited, condescending, possibly jealous relative? Of course I suspect him. I can picture the rascal rubbing his sissy hands, anticipating his childless uncle would leave him tons o' gold – and now this wee chap is in his way.'

'Are you not speculating a little too far?'

'Oh, I've dealt a fair bit with those upper classes. I ken how they think.'

'And regarding the logistics of the murder . . .'

'He could've kept his steamship offshore, sent someone here on a wee boat to do his dirty work and then pretended he's just arrived.'

'Cumbersome but plausible. Will you take his offer and go with him?'

'I'd rather not; there's something dubious about him. Then again, a week's a bloody long wait. I have other businesses to attend in Loch Maree, and my colleague's likely to be there by tomorrow noon.'

'It is not absolutely essential that you stay around. I will carry on the investigations here; after all, this is my jurisdiction, and I have the resources.'

'Ye sure?'

McLachlan nodded. 'In all honesty, I'd rather you took the boy away as soon as possible. If he was the ultimate target and the killer is still at large, the last thing we want is to keep him here.'

McGray bit his lip. McLachlan had told him exactly what he wanted to hear; he could not wait to reach Loch Maree and talk to that Miss Fletcher. But that was *his* wish, and in the past he had dragged innocent people into deadly situations because of his personal crusades. He would not allow himself to make that mistake again.

'If the attacker is still here, we'll find him,' McLachlan assured him. 'This is not a big town, and everyone here was fond of Father Thomas. People will help us. And you might find crucial details in Loch Maree.'

McGray sighed. He must make up his mind, and very soon. He ended up kicking a few crushed carrots.

'I'll need ye to telegram any progress,' he told McLachlan reluctantly. 'Frequent updates if possible. That place is as remote as the seventh gate o' hell. Like that brat said, there arenae railways, and it's a ten-mile journey to the nearest settlement in either direction.'

'Rest assured, Inspector. And I'll ask you to take good care of that boy. Everyone in Thurso who appreciated Father Thomas will thank you.' It was all too clear that McLachlan, dispassionate though he was, counted himself amongst them.

McGray smiled jadedly. 'Youse might end up cursing my name for evermore.'

9

'Promise you will tell me everything, Mr Frey,' Miss Fletcher pressed, her thick hand still grasping the door's handle. 'Please.'

'If there is anything in that telegram that you have the right to know, I shall make sure you do,' was my diplomatic answer, and we stepped into the Kolomans' most lavish room. I could devote pages and pages to it – in fact I could have spent weeks in there, discovering its secrets one by one. It was a long gallery with domed ceilings and wrought-iron chandeliers, and it was crammed with all manner of scientific artefacts, musical instruments and works of art. The walls were almost entirely lined with books, and the few spaces between the shelves were filled with either tapestries or oil paintings – no family portraits, I noticed. I must simply mention that there was a grand piano, a brass barometer, several red velvet seats, and that the wide fireplace was the most imposing feature in the room. Its mantelpiece was of solid granite with no carvings, and the hearth was loaded with coal and ready to be lit. Above it there was a strange artefact that resembled a clock, but it had sixteen marks instead of twelve, and only one hand, whose position was not even close to the present hour.

As I had predicted, the windows offered a breathtaking view of Loch Maree (unlike in the Shadows Room, here the heavy damask curtains were open). I recognized the lines of pine trees growing on Juniper Island, and the imposing mountains further away. Their craggy granite rocks, perhaps of the same stone used to build the manor, contrasted with the smooth grass that coated their slopes. The tops of the mountains were now crowned by grey clouds that had crawled in swiftly from the west; only a few small dots of blue sky were still visible.

By the window there was a thin brass telescope on a polished tripod. It was not the instrument itself that fixed my attention, but the hand that rested on it, boasting a thick golden ring with a large ruby.

There was Mr Koloman, staring at the landscape with dreamy eyes. He was not particularly tall, but his thin figure and long legs made him appear so. His blond hair was abundant with only a few white strands, just like his perfectly trimmed goatee. With his immaculately fitting black suit and his elegant pose, he much reminded me of an old portrait of the Austrian emperor.

'Good evening, Inspector Frey.'

It was not he who spoke but his wife, who had just emerged from behind the grand piano. I guessed she'd not been playing music but reading the telegram that still was in her hand. I saw she had crumpled the paper.

In the now dim sunlight, the first I saw of her was the twinkle of her jewellery: the dark red of garnet beads and silver around her slender neck. Unlike the twins, she did wear a corset, her hourglass figure hugged by a long fitted jacket worn over matching silk skirts. I'd seen my stepmother wearing a similar attire last month, which meant Mrs Koloman was dressed in London's latest fashion. I recognized in her the beautiful blue eyes of the daughters, only her features were not as soft: her jaw was a little more angular, her nose a little sharper. And with very thin wrinkles around her eyes and mouth, her general countenance was rather stern.

We bowed to her and I made the introductions.

'We are so glad you accepted our invitation,' said Mr Koloman as we shook hands. 'It is a shame we could not meet under more peaceful circumstances.'

'Indeed,' I said and then looked at the message. 'Have you just received bad news?'

Mrs Koloman nodded. 'Yes. I suggested we conceal it from Millie – Miss Fletcher. Though I know she must be told soon. You see, we've been told that Father Thomas, the priest who raised my nephew, has died.'

My eyes opened wider.

'In "very alarming circumstances", according to the telegram,' said her husband. 'Please, gentlemen, join us for a glass of wine. I took the liberty of having your drinks brought here.'

Uncle Maurice and I sat on velvet armchairs, Mr and Mrs Koloman on a long sofa, and the lady poured us a very dark wine. The smell, strong and perfumed, really tempted me, but there was so much to discuss I would not touch my glass for a while.

'My colleague might have heard about it,' I said. 'Inspector McGray telegrammed me saying he intended to arrive in Thurso on the eighteenth.'

'Inspector McGray apparently witnessed the entire affair,' said Mr Koloman, 'and was partly involved in the investigations. He is to tell us the details when he arrives. All we know for sure is that Father Thomas, sadly, was murdered.'

Uncle choked on the wine, and I was glad I'd not picked mine up or I'd have spilled it on the Persian rugs.

'Miss Fletcher receives a death threat against the boy,' I said, 'and now his guardian has been murdered! Do you realize how serious this is?'

Mrs Koloman reached for her husband's hand. 'We do. And I am terribly frightened.'

I leaned forward. 'Mr and Mrs Koloman –'

'Please, call us Konrad and Minerva,' said the lady.

I bit my lip. 'I'd rather we keep a certain degree of formality between us, given the job I must do. I need to look at these happenings from every angle and consider every possibility, no matter how remote. Do you understand?'

They were sharp enough. 'You think the threat might have come from within our family,' said Mr Koloman. 'It is natural you should suspect that, but I can assure you that that is impossible. Absolutely impossible.'

'So it might be, but I need you to tell me everything about your family. And I do mean everything.'

'You need but ask,' said Mrs Koloman.

I looked at her husband. 'I understand the late Maximilian Koloman, Benjamin's father, was your younger brother.'

'Indeed,' he said.

'And as such I assume he owned a share of this estate.'

'Yes, and of the family vineyard in Bohemia.'

'You should definitely try our wine,' said Mrs Koloman. 'Our Moravian grapes are excellent.'

'She is not lying,' said Uncle, swirling his glass and basking in the bouquet.

'Thank you,' I said impatiently. 'I will in a minute. Now, tell me, who would have inherited his share? If Benjamin had not been in line, of course.'

Mr Koloman allowed himself a sip of wine. 'My poor brother was not of a fastidious nature. He had not made a will. It was only a few days before his death that he made us fetch a solicitor and put things in order.'

'And I heard he had no wife or . . . legitimate offspring,' I said.

'That is correct.'

'So, legally, in the absence of a formal will, his estate would have gone to his nearest kin – that is *you*, Mr Koloman.'

His nod was almost imperceptible. 'Yes.'

A tense hush fell upon us, and I let it go on. The first person to speak can be very telling sometimes.

'Oh, this is excellent!' said Uncle Maurice, his nose stuck into his glass. 'Full-bodied yet very easy on the palate. It reminds me a little of a Bordeaux, or a very strong Italian.'

I rolled my eyes. 'Uncle, do you mind?' But he was too entranced to care. I looked back at the Kolomans. 'You would have inherited that share. Would you have liked that?'

He clearly understood what I meant. 'I already managed his share of the estates. I have for years, since our father passed away. I managed Maximilian's lands, his three townhouses on the Continent, his taxes, his income – everything.'

'So you might have felt as though it was . . . already yours?'

'Inspector, I'll be direct. I have no interest in increasing my own personal wealth. You might have noticed that I am by no means short of capital.'

'So you welcomed your brother's rushed will?'

'Of course I did! And Minerva too. Our own children are not likely to take charge of the business. Dominik, our eldest, very much took after his uncle. He travels all around Europe all the time. He is incredibly smart, but responsibility is not his strongest suit, and he cannot stand more than a few weeks in the same surroundings. And our daughters, clever and keen as they are, are still women, and unfortunately this is not a woman's world.'

'Not in business anyway,' Mrs Koloman said with clear bitterness.

'I'd always assumed they'd hire an overseer to manage the estates when I'm gone. Now I hear that Benjamin is a very accomplished young man, well read and good with numbers.

We even heard that the late Father Thomas wanted him to take over his parochial duties. He seems perfect to continue my work. I told Maximilian so, just as he signed the new will favouring Benjamin.'

'How did your children receive the news?' I asked.

'Veronika and Natalja were thrilled,' said Mrs Koloman. 'At some point they had considered taking care of things themselves, silly as it sounds. Veronika even told me once that she might marry someone who could look after the vineyards. To keep it all within the family, as it has always been.' She placed a hand on her husband's knee. 'I'm sorry, Konrad, I never told you this.'

His frown was deep. 'I told the girls I did not want to parade them for marriage as if they were cattle in a market! When was that?'

'About a year ago.'

'Minerva, Minerva, you should have told me. I would have talked to her.'

'Perhaps, but it doesn't matter any more, does it? Now that Benjamin will be here?'

I thought she was far too hasty in assuming the boy would be capable – or willing – to take charge, but I said nothing.

Mr Koloman took a deep breath. 'We can talk about that later, Minerva. Mr Frey, do you have any more questions? Dinner must be nearly ready. I hope you will join us. We can resume our conversation then.'

'Oh, Ian will be glad,' said Uncle Maurice, and then went on babbling nonsense about the wine, which I did not care to listen to. I was mulling over the situation.

'Mr Koloman,' I interrupted, 'do you have more brothers and sisters?'

'I had a younger sister, but she sadly died many years ago.'

I nodded. 'So I suppose Benjamin is to inherit half of everything I can see?'

'Well, yes . . .'

'And your half of the estate will ultimately have to be divided between your three children? So they'll each own a sixth, while Benjamin, effectively a stranger, will own half?'

The Kolomans went silent, looking terribly uncomfortable, as if suddenly sitting on thorns rather than velvet. The lady seemed particularly affected, gripping her glass so tightly I thought she might crush it.

'I have reason to doubt your children are as happy to welcome Benjamin to the family as you might think,' I said, not really expecting a reply. I finally picked up my glass and had a little taste.

Uncle Maurice was right. It was smooth, yet rich in flavour and scent: one of those wines one can drink and drink and only realize one's had too much when it is too late. I felt a wave of warmth as I savoured the liquor, like a boost to my mood.

'What about your eldest son?' I asked. 'What is his name again?'

'Dominik,' said Mrs Koloman.

'How did *he* take the news?'

The woman became sombre. 'I . . . I do not know. He is in Norway now. I telegrammed him but he never replied.' She saw my expression and her brow rose. 'Which is not at all unusual for him. As my husband told you –'

The door opened and Miss Fletcher came in. She was pale and her hands trembled.

'Sir, ma'am, they're here! Inspector McGray, and . . . Benjamin.' She swallowed. 'And they've come with Master Dominik.'

IO

'*More* sodding herrings!' McGray had cried the previous night, when the deck boy put the plate on the table. He had soaked them in milk and added spices, which only worsened McGray's seasickness. As he gulped them down he pledged never to eat the blasted fish again.

Dominik made the trip all the worse. He was simply insufferable, forever smoking, sipping his 'family wine', and telling jokes and stories with a good humour that nobody on board, except that Calcraft rogue, shared. Benjamin had not laughed or smiled, or even pretended to pay attention to his cousin; he simply ate his meal quickly and excused himself. McGray followed, and they went to a shared cabin. Thankfully Benjamin slept most of the trip (or pretended to) and Dominik did not come around to nag, so McGray was free to nurse his queasiness.

He was only too glad to see the small port of Poolewe appear in the distance, and he was the first man to jump to the ground as soon as the steamer had docked. He shut his eyes and pinched the bridge of his nose, still feeling the sway of the water.

When McGray looked again Dominik had planted himself right in front of him, a sardonic smile on his face.

'That is a nasty Achilles heel,' he said, pulling out his little Bible to roll himself a cigarette.

'Och, go f—'

'Mr Dominik!' somebody shouted in the distance. It was a very beefy sailor, bald and shiny with perspiration. 'Welcome back, sir! How lucky you are. You missed the sun.'

He laughed and pointed at the sky, covered with clumps of dark cloud that seemed to have clustered only around the port.

'It was quite miserable where I last docked too,' said Dominik, lighting up his cigarette. 'Foul weather seems to follow me.'

The man laughed far more loudly than the comment merited. He nodded at the hired coach that was being speedily loaded with trunks, crates and barrels from Dominik's ship. 'Sir, we have quite a few parcels for your parents and sisters, but I'm afraid Miss Fletcher hasn't come for a while.'

'The dainty *miss* is busy,' said Calcraft, dragging a hefty trunk.

Dominik looked around, perhaps to see if Benjamin had heard, and then giggled.

'We'll see she comes soon,' said Dominik. 'We don't want to clog up your storerooms.'

'That's no problem, sir,' said the sailor. 'I only thought there might be things that could, you know, go bad.'

'Oh, no, I am taking care of that,' said Dominik, and just as he spoke a small barrel rolled from the roof of the coach and crashed on to the pebbled street. Its lid went flying and hundreds of bright lemons spilled all around.

'Watch those barrels, you stupid brats!' Dominik shouted, suddenly red with anger, and he tossed his barely smoked cigarette into the water.

The young footmen could not have apologized more fervently.

'Let me help them,' the sailor said, rushing over. 'We're all waiting eagerly for Mrs Plunket's famous curd.'

As they meticulously gathered up every single piece of fruit, Dominik stood proudly, his hands on his lapels, looking every inch the lord of Poolewe.

The locals were certainly dazzled by his presence. Another two men approached to greet him, a few others waved from the distance, and anyone who walked past either bowed or asked him to give their regards to his parents.

'Youse are popular,' McGray had to admit.

'Indeed. We have brought good business to this port for decades. You will understand when we get home. My grandfather imported tons of granite to build our manor. My father is partial to exotic woods and plants; ten years ago or so he had thirty-five giant rhododendrons brought from Nepal. And my mother is the closest these people have to a decent physician; she runs a little school too, in the autumn months, when the children are not needed in the fields.'

Benjamin disembarked then, clutching his meagre luggage and refusing Calcraft's help.

His cousin grinned. 'Ben, you are going to adore this little port. Would you like me to introduce you to –'

But Benjamin didn't stop. He simply took his seat in the carriage, looking grim. Dominik chuckled, tearing another page from his Bible.

McGray sighed. 'Give him time. He's been through a lot.'

Dominik ran his tongue in a leisurely way along the paper, and rolled the tobacco with utmost care. 'Haven't we all?'

McGray had to laugh at that. What hardships could that arrogant, spoiled, rich chap have had to endure?

'And,' McGray spoke loud enough for Calcraft to hear, 'ye should make sure yer servants show some respect. Things seem to have changed.'

Dominik turned on McGray the most annoying smile,

his eyes challenging. 'A few things will never change. Mark my words.'

And without waiting for a reply he jumped into the coach, smiling sardonically at his cousin. McGray could not help thinking of a marauding wolf, salivating just before jumping on its prey.

PART 2

... as surely as I live, declares the Lord God, I will prepare you for blood, and blood shall pursue you ...

Ezekiel 35:6

Miss Fletcher could not stop wringing her leather gloves as we waited in the entrance hall. I'd agreed to keep quiet about the priest's death, at least momentarily, but only because she was already overwhelmed. The poor woman was about to meet her son for the first time in years, perfectly aware that the boy was never to know the truth. I thought it a silly charade, but there was nothing I could do; it was a family matter.

Mr and Mrs Koloman had told Miss Fletcher she did not need to be present, but she had, at least for now, ignored the suggestion.

'Sixteen years is a long time,' I whispered.

'It feels like a century,' she said, and Mrs Koloman held her hand.

'We saw the carriages coming!' said Veronika, rushing down the stairs with her sister. They *had* changed, but these dresses were even more indecent than before: again they were made of very thin, flowing silk, which followed the natural shapes of the girls' bodies; the garments were held by straps as fine as threads, leaving bare shoulders and a licentious amount of bosom. Veronika wore dark red and Natalja a bottle green that looked nearly black.

Uncle Maurice rushed to the stairs and again kissed Miss Veronika's hand. Natalja quickened her pace, albeit with a sideways smile. I could tell she was leaving the coast clear for her sister.

'Do you like my dress, Mr Plantard?' Veronika asked. 'I designed it myself.'

'It is absolutely ravishing,' he said, his eyes nowhere near the fabric. 'You are very talented.'

Natalja stood next to me, her eyes fixed on the main door. I knew I ought to say something but I was paralysed like an anxious child; I could not help feeling as if she were walking around in the nude.

'Very . . .' I gulped, 'very unusual style, I must admit.'

'We believe the dress should not outshine what lies underneath,' said Veronika, now arm in arm with Uncle.

Outshine? I echoed in my head. I looked at Mr and Mrs Koloman, who did not seem to notice my discomfort and definitely did not give a second thought to their daughters' impudence.

Boyde, the solid manservant, opened the door then, letting in a draught of cool air from the gardens (modesty forbids me to say how, but I knew the twins felt a little too cold).

A large carriage had just halted, followed by a cart loaded with a mountain of trunks and barrels of all sizes.

I instantly recognized Dominik, who had the same height and general poise of his father, and then McGray jumped off the carriage with a sluggishness that was very rare for him.

In fact, Nine-Nails looked ghastly (not that he is ever a model of elegance). His stubble was particularly scruffy, his eyes quite reddened, and his skin had a sickly hint of green. He helped a spindly boy down, and Natalja at once brought a hand to her mouth.

'Gosh, it's as though Uncle Maximilian has come back to life!'

She was the first one to step forward, smiling, and waited just a few feet from the threshold. It was McGray, rather than Dominik, who gently pushed the boy's back to guide him in.

Natalja reached for her cousin's hand, and placed the other on his cheek. Benjamin blushed intensely, but then also smiled and they embraced. It was an instant connection; words were not needed.

Mr and Mrs Koloman whispered to each other and they also approached the boy.

'Welcome, Benjamin!' said Mr Koloman, shaking the boy's hand so effusively Benjamin's entire body quaked.

Only then did Dominik approach, and I watched his every move without blinking.

'Ben, this is my father, your Uncle Konrad. And your Aunt Minerva.' He smiled and seemed courteous enough, but his entire countenance had an air of falseness I have seen countless times at the London ballrooms. He poked Benjamin on the shoulder. 'And I see you have already met your cousin Natalja. That's spelled with a j.'

The very instant Dominik touched Benjamin, Miss Fletcher jolted. I noticed even though she had retreated to a corner of the hall, and my eyes went alternately from her to Benjamin. Seeing them in the same room, it was obvious that he was her son. He might look like the Kolomans, but he also had her freckles, her height and her bright-blue eyes. This was not something they could keep quiet for long, and was likely to become one of those open secrets so common amongst the upper classes. I went to her, feeling her sorrow.

'Are you all right?' I asked her. She tried to assent, but could not even do that, and simply turned on her heel and quit the hall. I looked back at Benjamin, who'd not noticed her presence at all. My eyes then fell on Dominik's man-servant, who was bringing in a large trunk. The man, clearly a weather-beaten sailor, was staring at Miss Fletcher as she walked away. He chuckled without shame.

'Go, go and greet your cousin,' Uncle Maurice told Veronika, whose eyes were also following Miss Fletcher. The girl answered something in French I did not catch, and then joined her family as they clustered around Benjamin.

'They look like a happy lot,' Uncle said. Veronika was just standing on tiptoes to kiss Benjamin on the cheek, and Mr Koloman was joking about the boy's remarkable height.

'Indeed,' I muttered. 'They *look* happy.'

'Oh, Ian, is this your boss?'

McGray had walked around the family and was approaching us. Uncle had recognized the four-fingered hand I'd mentioned in so many letters.

'We've loads o' work to do, Percy,' McGray told me joylessly. His frown deepened when he saw Uncle Maurice. Nine-Nails was about to say something but Uncle went first, drawing back his torso as if dodging a blow.

'Ian, what in the good name of God is this man wearing?'

McGray went a little greener. 'Och, what d'ye –'

Uncle winced. 'He looks as though he was gobbled up by a bagpipe that then exploded from the indigestion!'

'I'll make *ye* gobble yer –'

'Or as if he'd attempted to dress as the jester to Mary Queen of Scots but could not be bothered to go all the way through with it.'

McGray closed his right fist. I took a step aside.

'It could be worse, I suppose,' Uncle concluded. 'For instance, he could be Welsh.'

McGray threw a mighty blow, but Uncle Maurice, who had devoted his life to nothing but hunting and fencing, dodged it with enviable reflexes. McGray threw a second punch, this time stumbling forward, but Uncle ducked it just as easily.

Nine-Nails looked befuddled like never before, and I did a very poor job of concealing my amusement.

'Och, fuck off! Both o' youse!'

I cleared my throat to drown a snigger. 'McGray, my uncle, Maurice Plantard. Uncle, Adolphus Nine-Nails McGray.' They did not shake hands. 'McGray, are you ill? You look like you just swallowed a mouthful of curdled milk.'

'Seasickness,' said Dominik from afar. 'One of the worst cases I have seen.'

Mrs Koloman came over to us. 'Is that so? Poor Mr McGray! Let me offer you an aperitif. That always settles my husband's stomach.'

Nine-Nails nodded. 'Thanks, missus. Could ye also show us somewhere quiet? I've a lot to discuss with my measly colleague. In private.'

'Of course. Millie will –' She realized Miss Fletcher had vanished. 'Oh, I am so sorry.'

The muscly young man who had opened the door came up immediately. He had a childlike face and seemed very solicitous, but he brought with him an odd smell, a mixture of chemicals and strong body odour. 'May I help you, ma'am?'

Mrs Koloman smiled. 'Yes, Boyde, show the inspectors to the astronomy parlour. And ask Mrs Glenister to bring them some ginger liqueur.'

'Right away, ma'am,' he said, before giving a deep bow.

'I suppose you do not need me now,' said Uncle, sliding across the room to rejoin Miss Veronika. I heard her introduce him to Benjamin like one does an old family friend.

Boyde approached and bade us to follow him, but I hesitated, realizing we'd be leaving Benjamin unsupervised. I saw the family encircling him, all of them smiling and welcoming, but there was something in that picture I did not like. I could not tell what, however.

'I don't think the laddie's under threat,' said McGray, noticing my concern. 'At least, not right now.'

I did not take my sight from the group as we ascended. The only eyes that met mine were Natalja's.

If one wanted to have a private conversation, the astronomy parlour was the ideal place. It was a wide room on the top floor at the easternmost end of the manor, running right across the building and with three dormer windows, so that one could look at the skies to the south, north and east without obstruction. I paced nervously as McGray recounted the priest's death in detail.

He'd just finished the tale when Boyde returned, bringing a silver tray. He made to pour the drinks but I took the decanter from him. 'We can manage ourselves, thank you very much.'

'Or course, sir. Mrs Plunket, our cook, sent you some savoury biscuits. She says they're good for seasickness too.'

He bowed and left. McGray ignored the biscuits and went straight to the liquor, though he looked at the tiny cut-glass tumbler with a wrinkled nose. In his hands it looked like a thimble.

'Are you sure that man, Constable McLachlan, was reliable?' I asked him.

'As reliable as they come. I'm sure he'll keep us well informed.'

'Good. We should keep an eye on the correspondence.'

I then told McGray how the family's estate would be divided. It was just as he had guessed.

'So we both suspect the lad Dominik?' he asked.

'Indeed. As much as I'd like to keep my mind open, he is the natural suspect. And this tale of him returning from Norway at the right time to pick up Benjamin seems a little too convenient to me.' I placed a hand on one of four shining telescopes. 'If he orchestrated the murder – as you said, leaving his ship offshore – then his manservant, that Calcraft man, is his accomplice.'

'He might have even done the dirty work for his master,' said McGray. 'We really must keep an eye on the laddie. What do ye think o' the parents? Konrad and . . . ?'

'Minerva.' I savoured the spicy drink as I pondered the question. 'They seem clever. I need to question them further, but I can tell you that the mother looked rather nervous, more so than Mr Koloman, even though I practically accused him directly at one point.'

'The missus cannae be too happy with these events. The frolics of her brother-in-law are taking a bloody good chunk from her children's inheritance.' McGray downed the drink in one go, but rather than pour another measure he took a swig straight from the decanter. 'Did ye meet the idiotic constable?'

I told him all about that meeting, and we agreed the man must be dismissed. Having covered all the aspects of Benjamin's case, I thought of the other matter that had brought us here. I stared into my drink for a moment, unsure whether I should ask this. 'How did you find your sister?'

McGray hissed, turned and went to the window that overlooked the loch. 'I only saw her for a minute. She was doing very well . . . up until I came round.'

'I am sorry,' I said.

McGray stared out at the tranquil waters. The sky had begun to show the shades of the night. 'Did ye go to the wee island?'

'I did, and I saw the well. I also saw the ruinous little hovel where the man lives, but we are not to disturb him without his family's consent. They all live on that big island. Apparently they manufacture gin but barely make ends meet.'

'And ye talked to Madame Katerina?'

I blew inside my cheeks, recalling that nasty Sunday morning in the gypsy's divination room. I'd caught the woman freshly out of bed (most likely after a night of heavy drinking at her side brewery) and I still flinched at the memory. 'I wish you had not sent me to her. She is as crazy as ever.'

'What did she tell you?'

'She knew a good deal about the loch and its islands, as you expected. She told me about that ancient saint. He had an impossible name . . .'

'Maelrubha.'

'Correct. I looked into your books and found that some Scots call him St Rufus. I shall use that name, if you do not mind.'

'Go on.'

'St Rufus founded a little chapel on that island, back when the early Christians were attempting to convert the Celts. Apparently he dug the well – it is a nondescript hole in the ground, with some stones around it. It is possible that *he* made up the legend about the waters.'

'Dammit, I told ye to be less Frey-like when ye looked into this! It's my sister who's at stake here.'

'Yes, and I was! But even your beloved gypsy clairvoyant is of that opinion. Now, here is the disturbing part . . .'

'Disturbing?'

'Yes. Katerina says St Rufus probably fabricated that tale to discourage the more ... *savage* practices of the Druids. Apparently the Celts were convinced that the island was sacred and that people could be cured there, but not with water from a well.'

I had McGray's undivided attention. 'Tell me.'

I went to the east window and looked out at the dim stars that had only just begun to appear. The shadows in between the islands' trees looked much darker now, and I imagined the horrid happenings that those woods might have witnessed. 'In their rituals the Druids sacrificed bulls ... and then bathed people in their blood.'

I felt a sudden chill as I turned back to Nine-Nails. It could have been a draught coming through the windows, or the disquieting expression in McGray's eyes, which seemed to twinkle in the growing darkness.

He whispered, 'Does it work?'

'Drinking the waters or bathing in blood?'

'Either!'

I snorted. 'Katerina has heard of many people coming here and drinking from the well. Some even do this stupid ritual of sailing three times around the island. Katerina has never heard of it working for anybody.'

'And the ritual with the blood?'

I shook my head. 'You are not thinking of taking your sister there and ... well, doing *that*, are you?'

'Answer the sodding question, Frey.'

I had no choice but to tell him exactly what the gypsy had said.

'She has not heard of the ritual being attempted – not in living memory at least.' I saw the twinkle again in McGray's eyes and rushed to go on. 'Before you get any twisted ideas, Miss Fletcher says it is *the waters* that cured Mr Nellys. The waters that not even your clairvoyant believes might work.'

McGray sighed deeply. 'I'll go there tomorrow.'

'What about Benjamin?'

'Ye can keep an eye on him while I do what I need to.'

'You are not intending to drop the case now because of those cretinous legends, are you?'

'O' course nae, Percy! I saw that poor auld priest die. And how that affected the laddie. I ken he's in dangerous territory.'

'Yet you are the one who brought him here. Even if I had insisted otherwise, I know you are so bloody stubborn you would not have –'

'Aye, aye, save yer fucking claret breath. I hate the shite-sniffing face ye pull when yer preaching. I did bring him here. Ye might nae believe it but I do feel it's my responsibility to make sure the laddie –'

A tap at the door interrupted him. It was Uncle Maurice.

'Ian, Mr Koloman sent me in case you two were discussing delicate matters. Dinner is ready. Mrs Koloman says she hopes you both have an appetite.'

McGray looked forlornly at the loch one last time, gathering his strength. 'As long as they're nae serving salted fucking herring!'

The main drawing room looked like a Christmas scene. The large trunk I'd seen Calcraft bring in was at the centre of the room, and there were smaller boxes and shreds of wrapping paper scattered all around. Everybody was laughing and cheering.

Veronika and her mother sat on cushions on the floor surrounded by fine materials, bobbins of lace and books of patterns. Uncle Maurice stood by them, a hand on his hip and in the other a glass of wine.

'*La Mode Illustrée*,' he said. 'I did not think you followed their guidelines, Miss Veronika.'

'But *I* do,' answered Mrs Koloman. 'And Veronika likes to read it to mock me.'

'Mama, I would *never*!' the girl said jokingly, her smiles always directed at my uncle.

'Inspectors!' said Mr Koloman, all welcoming. 'Do join us. My dear son likes to spoil us with presents whenever he visits home.'

We followed him in and he put glasses of wine in our hands before we could object.

Dominik was pacing around, drinking liberally from his glass, but the wine did not seem to affect him at all – not yet, at least. He gave us a rather petulant nod.

Natalja was seated in one of the armchairs, opening a small parcel cushioned with straw. She pulled out a bell glass set on a mahogany base. Inside there was a perfect prism like those she used in the Shadows Room. I have seen less excitement in girls presented with diamonds – my former fiancée included.

'A sodium chloride prism!' she cried.

'Of course, Nat! This chap in Norway made it for me. It cost me a bloody fortune.'

Natalja jumped from her seat and hugged her brother. Dominik stumbled and spilled some of his wine on the rugs.

'You must keep it under the glass lid whenever you're not using it,' Dominik warned, half choked by his sister.

'Because of the humidity?' asked Mr Koloman, and his son assented.

Natalja hugged the container. 'I will try it now.'

Her mother rose and tugged at her arm. 'Tomorrow, Natalja. We have visitors tonight.'

The girl twisted her mouth, her reproachful stare directed at McGray and me, and I understood her frustration – finding herself perhaps at the brink of a scientific discovery yet being told she must attend some unwanted guests.

I suddenly realized something, and so did McGray.

'Where's Benjamin?' he asked.

'Changing and refreshing,' said Mr Koloman. He saw our instant alarm. 'Oh, don't worry, Inspectors. Boyde and Calcraft are with him.'

The young man who stank of chemicals and Dominik's devious-looking sailor . . . I nearly spat out my wine, and McGray and I were about to storm out of the room, but the doors opened right then.

Benjamin himself came in, wearing a black suit and looking quite uncomfortable in it. The trousers and sleeves were a little short for him, but his burgundy ascot tie had been done in a perfect knot.

He was still nervous, and the compliments from Dominik

and Mrs Koloman seemed only to increase his stress. It was Natalja who broke his rigidity, if only partially. She took him by the arm and showed him around the bookshelves. After a moment we even heard his very shy laugh.

Mr Koloman approached me while his wife and other daughter resumed the unwrapping. Dominik had just presented Veronika with a collection of German books.

'We are a tightly knit family, as you can see,' he said proudly and then grasped my forearm. 'We *will* take good care of the boy. I swear.'

He clinked our glasses and I had to take a sip out of good manners, only the blasted wine was so delectable I could not help rolling it around in my mouth (and I can imagine the sort of face I must have been pulling).

Mr Koloman smiled at my reluctant appreciation. 'I hope you find our table as impressive as you do our cellars. Have you ever tasted kid's meat?'

'I – I beg your pardon?'

He laughed. 'By *kid* I mean a young goat, Inspector. We do not kill younglings here, I can assure you!'

The meat fell off the bone, as soft as butter and so juicy it melted in the mouth. They'd marinated the tiny joints in spices and wine, and roasted them to perfection. And the excellent wine was a heavenly match: I'd had two glasses already and was tempted to ask for a third.

McGray too was delighted, devouring the meat and the roast potatoes with remarkable gusto. From time to time I winced at the loud squelching, but none of the Kolomans seemed to care and Uncle's attention was far more pleasantly engaged.

'I do feel sorry for eating the darling things,' said Veronika, who had rushed to sit next to Maurice. 'I wish they weren't so delicious.'

Uncle whispered something in her ear, and they exchanged a complicit look.

'They would die anyway,' said Dominik in a monotone.

'How so?' Uncle asked.

'They come from Juniper Island,' Mr Koloman answered, and I instantly looked up. I *had* seen a goat there . . . and I still believed I'd seen a bat fluttering around. 'The Nellyses keep goats and make some wonderful cheeses,' Konrad went on. 'We will offer you some for dessert. The female kids are kept for more milk, of course, but the males have no use. If we didn't buy them for meat, the Nellyses would have to sacrifice them.'

'I need to talk to that family,' said McGray, his mouth full. 'What can youse tell me about them? This miraculous cure?'

There was palpable tension in the room. The twins rushed to put food in their mouths, Dominik pretended to wipe his lips far too thoroughly, and Mr Koloman turned to Boyde to have his glass refilled.

It was Mrs Koloman who spoke, though she looked grim. 'I meet them regularly. Mr Nellys is very frail these days.'

'Have ye seen him improve?' McGray prompted.

Mrs Koloman took a moment to answer. 'His mind certainly has, and I cannot explain it. He used to have horrid hallucinations about monsters and diseases corroding his insides, but he hasn't had a single episode in years . . . apparently ever since his family brought him here.'

She looked down, moving the food around her plate, suddenly unable to take another mouthful.

'Then why d'ye look so gloomy?' McGray asked.

'His mind may have improved; his body, on the other hand . . . It is so sad.' She breathed deeply. 'I'll see that Millie takes you there tomorrow morning, if you please.'

'I was told you have medical training, madam,' I said.

'You heard well, Inspector. I help whenever I can. I aid pretty much everyone in the vicinity, if it is in my hands.'

'But you spend far too much time with the Nellyses,' said Dominik, a clear reproach.

'His wife gets weaker every day, Dominik,' his mother said promptly. 'She has a very hard life, looking after the goats, and making their gin and their cheese.'

'Don't they have any children?' McGray asked.

'Yes, a grown son and a younger daughter. She must be around Benjamin's age.' Mrs Koloman smiled at her nephew, who simply shifted uncomfortably on his seat. She picked up her wine, looking sombre. 'I'm afraid they'll end up just like their parents, broken by the work and the elements.'

'Wasting their lives away only to look after that sickly old man,' Dominik grumbled. 'The entire family devoted to bringing him back from madness – what a bunch of deluded fools.'

McGray clenched his fists around his cutlery so hard I thought he'd bend the silver.

'He was losing his mind, getting worse and worse,' Mrs Koloman told him. 'They couldn't just let him fade away in a lunatics' asylum.'

Benjamin was the only one who seemed to notice McGray's tense jaw. I realized the twins and Mr Koloman had remained deliberately silent.

'This obsession with looking after the sick and infirm,' Dominik said after clicking his tongue. He looked at Veronika. 'I brought you a new book by this German chap, Nietzsche. He has some compelling ideas on the matter.'

I opened my mouth to speak but McGray kicked me under the table. His gesture was clear enough: we would not take part in their debate. We would let it unfold naturally.

'Oh, Dominik, you know I don't like those German philosophers,' said Mrs Koloman, somewhat echoing what her daughter had said in the Shadows Room.

'But think about it, Mama,' Dominik pressed, leaning forward. 'The Romans and the ancient Greeks valued strength, beauty, health. Common sense would tell you one should aspire to those virtues, but instead we are moral, *compassionate*.'

Benjamin opened his mouth, but his cousin continued. 'The poor, the weak, the illiterate, they of course have resented their masters from the beginning of time, and they made up this silly fantasy of an afterlife reward to console themselves.'

Benjamin hesitated for a second longer, and Mrs Koloman intervened, not even seeing that her nephew wanted to speak. 'Those are very dangerous ideas, and I think it's wrong to publish them so carelessly. If that sort of book were to fall in the wrong hands ... I can see it inspiring wars, massacres —'

Dominik and the twins all interjected, but then Mr Koloman raised a hand and there was instant silence. He smiled at his nephew. 'Benjamin, you seem to have something to say. Go ahead.'

All eyes turned to the boy, who blushed and slowly put his cutlery down (he'd barely touched his food and wine). 'Does this man Niet—'

'Nietzsche,' Dominik said. 'That's German.'

I saw the tendons in Benjamin's neck pop out when his cousin winked at him. 'Does he discuss the origin of that resentment?'

Dominik sat back, looking utterly amused, and swirled the wine in his glass. 'What do you mean – cousin?'

'That resentment exists only because some masters like to crush and humiliate their servants. *That* is an animal vice: enjoying the suffering of the defenceless, enjoying pinning them down and subjugating them.'

Benjamin's hands were shaking, and for the first time he lifted his glass and took a long drink. 'In fact, I take that back. Even animals don't torment each other just for pleasure . . . like some high-born men who torture unprotected women.'

Mrs Koloman let out a soft gasp, but that was the only sound that followed.

So Benjamin knew. He knew everything about his father's sins. Whether the priest had told him or the boy had deduced it all by himself, I could not tell. Did he also know already that his mother was Miss Fletcher?

Benjamin gulped down more wine, and it was as if the kick of the drink brought out the best in him. 'Also, what does this Nietzsche call *weak*? Does he provide a good definition? After all, the *weak* Jews managed to free themselves from Egypt. The *weak* French servants managed to crush their filthy aristocrats. I think the masters are only strong for as long as the so-called *weak* ones allow it.'

A deep hush fell on the room, and when Benjamin put his glass down it made a loud thud. 'May I be excused?'

He left the room at once, before anyone could reply. So much for the meek boy the Kolomans might have expected.

13

McGray found Benjamin at the foot of the staircase, covering his face with his clenched fists. It looked like the situation had finally overwhelmed him.

'Ye all right, laddie?' The boy could not reply, so McGray simply patted him on the back. 'It's all right. Give yerself some time.' He let the boy be for a moment, before whispering, 'What were ye trying to tell yer cousin? Did Father Thomas tell ye that yer mum –'

'Was abused by my father?' Benjamin barked. 'Of course he did. He also said she might still live around this loch; he told me to keep my eyes open.'

McGray nodded. So the priest had managed to keep his word and yet plant doubt in Benjamin's mind.

Should he tell Benjamin that his mother was still a servant in that house? Would that be completely out of place?

Fortunately, the answer showed itself. He saw someone stirring in the shadows: Miss Fletcher. She started, and squeezed the two light shawls she had in her hands. McGray raised his hand, bidding her to come closer. This was a good time; she might give her son some comfort.

Miss Fletcher lost all colour. She took a step forward, looking at her son with so much affection it was painful to behold. But then, just before Benjamin lifted his face, she faltered and hurried into the dining room, moving as silently as a ghost.

McGray shook his head, but he knew this was something he couldn't force.

'I'm going to my room,' said Benjamin, too drained to speak further.

'I'll see ye get there safely,' McGray replied, only too late realizing he'd said too much.

'Safely?' Benjamin repeated, and McGray knew he couldn't keep the truth from him any longer. It might be a lot for him to take in, but he needed to know.

'Benjamin, laddie . . .' McGray took a deep breath, 'we think yer in danger.'

'More wine, Mr Frey?'

'Why, thank you, Mr Koloman, but I really do not – oh, you are pouring already; well, perhaps just a drop or – oh, no, there is no need to fill my –'

'There you are, the best red wine to come out of Moravia this decade. It would be a shame to waste it!'

'Shame indeed,' said Uncle Maurice, pushing his own glass forward. Mr Koloman filled it almost to the brim.

The door opened then and I saw Miss Fletcher come in, bringing two light shawls. She looked as pale as a spectre.

'Will the Miss Kolomans go for their daily walk?'

Natalja stood up almost at once and grabbed a shawl. She also placed a hand on Miss Fletcher's, perfectly aware of the woman's agitation. 'Of course we will. Sister?'

Veronika was giggling with Uncle Maurice. 'One night without will not kill me.'

Mrs Koloman went for the shawl and put it around her daughter's shoulders. 'Discipline, my dear. That has always been your downfall.'

Her tone did not admit objections. Veronika stood up,

her mouth twisted, but Uncle rose as well and led her by the hand towards Miss Fletcher. 'Do listen to your good mother. Discipline and exercise make gorgeous young ladies.'

Veronika smiled. 'We shan't be long, shall we?'

'The usual walk,' said Miss Fletcher, impassive.

'Is it not a little late for a walk?' I asked.

'Oh, I'd never send my girls out under a blazing sun, Inspector,' said Mrs Koloman. 'I want them to keep their skins pristine for as long as possible. And there is still enough light out there to walk at leisure.' She pointed at the window; the sun had set and the stars had come out, but there was a band of cyan sky just above the mountains.

'That's why I love these lands in midsummer,' said Mr Koloman, 'the drawn-out twilights.'

'Is it not dangerous?'

'Not at all, Mr Frey,' said Natalja. 'There is not a soul for miles. What danger could we face?'

'Well, I suppose –'

'Besides,' she interrupted, 'as Mama said, the air and exercise are good for us. We intend to lead very long lives; we had better take good care of our casings.'

She'd directed those last words to her sister, whose hand she was now grasping.

'I could always join you,' Uncle offered. 'I do like a walk.' But Miss Fletcher was already taking the girls away, for some reason eager to leave at once.

'Oh, it's a very dull affair, sir. Very dull indeed.'

And she shut the door on him. He was about to protest at her rudeness, but Dominik spoke then.

'The inspectors will have to excuse me as well. I need to check on some of my cargo.'

He emptied his glass and left through the door that led to the kitchens. Rather odd for someone as arrogant as him.

Mr Koloman was the last one to rise. 'Gentlemen, might we leave you on your own for a little while? My wife and I have one or two matters to discuss. We shall join you in the main drawing room in no time.'

Boyde took us there, and then brought us yet more wine and a tray with that goat's cheese Mr Koloman had mentioned. The fire had already been lit, as if by invisible hands. The fleeting flames projected sharp shadows all across the room, making it look as if the sculptures and the scientific artefacts were dancing to an erratic rhythm.

Uncle went to the window and looked out at the lake. I joined him, and as soon as I saw the darkened landscape I realized how isolated we truly were. There was nothing but an expanse of dark water ahead of us, and beyond barren mountains crowned with thick clouds; the nearest towns were ten miles to the east and ten to the west; and to the south, at our backs, the maps showed a chain of unconquerable peaks.

I followed Uncle's eyes and caught a last glimpse of the three females, just before they became lost in the woods. The twins were arm in arm, talking to each other, while Miss Fletcher followed at a prudent distance. Her gait was tired, and she distractedly beat the ground with a fir branch.

Maurice sighed and I finally lost my temper.

'Uncle, that girl is twenty!'

He took an unhurried sip of wine, his eyes still on the last spot where we'd seen the twins. He looked at me with feigned innocence. 'Sorry, was that the end of your sentence?'

'Yes! You are more than twenty years her senior.'

'Ian, your own father is twenty-three years older than that Catherine woman he married.'

'Precisely. Do you want to end up like them?'

He cackled. 'Oh, my, Ian, that could not possibly happen! Your stepmother is a crow from the seventh hell. Do *not* tell your brother Elgie I ever said that.'

Uncle Maurice was the one person in the world who despised my stepmother more than I did. He still grieved the death of his sister, and Catherine – sour, malicious, self-righteous Catherine – would never be anything other than a usurper. He usually won my sympathy by saying horrible things about her, or at least distracted me enough from the current argument, but not this time.

'Uncle, there is also the issue of –'

'Of Miss Natalja having her eyes on you?'

I nearly spat out my wine. '*What?*'

'She plays the unsympathetic part, but she definitely has a soft spot for you. Did you not notice?'

I heard McGray's unmistakable laughter as he entered the room. 'Notice? This saintly dandy wouldnae notice if the lassie showed up 'n' took off her shimmy.'

Uncle grinned. 'I know precisely what you mean. That comes from his father's side of the family. English *and* German blood there!' They both shuddered.

I rolled my eyes and forced a deep breath. 'Where is Benjamin?'

McGray shook his head, pouring himself a good amount of wine. 'I had to tell him about the death threat.'

'Did you? Why?'

'All this secrecy was getting ridiculous, Frey. And he needs to take care o' himself too. Did ye want him to be caught off guard?'

'I suppose not. How did he take it?'

'Nae very well, as expected. He wanted to be on his own.' I was ready to protest but McGray raised his hand. 'I made sure he's safe. His room can be locked from the inside, and it's on the upper floor, lake side. I'd challenge the best o' climbers to get to his window.'

I lowered my voice. 'What if there is another key? What if someone tricks him into coming out? I do not trust these people.'

'Your presence might deter any attack,' said Uncle, for once speaking good sense. 'I think you should stay for the night.'

'Oh, of course you should!' said Mr Koloman, apparently in renewed good spirits. We all started; he and his wife had come in so stealthily I could not tell how much of our conversation they might have heard.

'I shall ask Mrs Glenister to get another chamber ready,' Mrs Koloman offered.

'We must have rooms adjacent to Benjamin's,' McGray told her before I could protest.

'Of course, Inspector, I had that in mind already.' She pulled the rope of a bell and not a minute later a woman in her sixties appeared. She was terribly thin, with skin as wrinkled as a prune, all clad in black and with her grey hair done in a very tall beehive.

'Glenister, Inspector Frey will be staying with us after all. Give him and Inspector McGray the rooms we had discussed.'

That Glenister woman looked at us with suspicion, her eyes mere slits. She made me think of the unforgiving governesses described in *Jane Eyre*.

'As you wish, madam. I'll set my girl to work on it right away. Should Mrs Plunket prepare them breakfast as well?'

Her tone was rather insolent, as if scolding her mistress for having unexpected visitors.

'Yes, Glenister. Leave us now.'

The woman curtsied and left.

I put my glass on one of the little tables. 'I would like to go to bed as soon as the rooms are ready, if you do not mind.' In fact I wanted to be near Benjamin's room as soon as possible, just in case. 'And I would like to question the members of your staff tomorrow morning.'

'We shall arrange that, Inspector,' said Mr Koloman. 'It should not be long before your chamber is ready. Shall I entertain you with a game of backgammon in the meantime?'

'Thank you, Mr Koloman, but I do not have the head for board games tonight.'

'Oh, you do look agitated,' said Mrs Koloman. 'Would you like a little more wine?'

'No, thank you, ma'am,' I said at once. I was already feeling the drink creeping to my head. 'In fact I'd appreciate some water, please.'

'Of course,' and she went to a small but well-stocked drinks cabinet.

'A little story then?' Mr Koloman asked, and he glanced up at the thick clouds that now blocked half the western sky. 'The evening certainly suits itself for some gore around the fire. Just as I predicted.'

'As ye predicted?' McGray wondered.

'Indeed. I have an interest in meteorology. You might have noticed my barometer and thermometers.' He pointed at the instruments on the wall. I had not noticed the thermometers until then. 'And I am particularly proud of that.' He signalled the strange clock-like artefact over the mantelpiece.

'Indeed,' I said, just as Mrs Koloman handed me a pewter glass. 'Thank you, ma'am. I was wondering what that might be.'

'A little contraption I designed. Did you notice the Hermes statue at the centre of our façade?'

Uncle and McGray shook their heads.

'The weathervane?' I asked.

'Indeed. You are very observant, Mr Frey. I designed a cog mechanism that connects my Hermes with this compass here. As you can see, the wind now comes from the west-south-west. And given the air pressure, I can tell you tomorrow will be a dull day.'

Uncle was lounging on the red sofa and yawning. 'Mr Koloman, you did promise us a story.'

'Oh, but of course!'

Mrs Koloman was refilling glasses with wine. I looked down at my own. 'Mrs Koloman, this water is brown!'

'Oh, I am so sorry, Inspector. We get it from our own well; it is pure enough.'

'Well, I think –'

'But here, have some more wine instead.' And she put a full glass in my hand before I had any say in the matter. I sat back in one of the armchairs, next to McGray, as Mr Koloman passed around a box of Cubans.

'Once upon a time,' he was saying, 'in a land far, far away, there was a very powerful lord living in a brooding castle. The lord was so rich and powerful he fancied himself in command of the universe. He was a tyrant, ruling his peasants with an iron hand, having his every whim fulfilled and punishing anyone who dared challenge him.

'When the time came for him to choose a wife, he snatched the most beautiful girl from the neighbouring nobility. The maiden's mother knew the lord well; she was aware of the ghastly

future that lay before her daughter, so she opposed the marriage –
only to die soon afterwards in very mysterious circumstances.'

'It is already becoming spooky,' Uncle said, puffing on his
cigar quite merrily.

'The marriage thus took place,' Mr Koloman continued.
'The lord's wife was a healthy, fertile creature, but she gave
him only daughters. Girl after girl after girl. All fair, all
beautiful, all accomplished – but still all girls.

'One day the angry lord stepped into his lady's chamber
and found her crying, desolate. He asked her what was
wrong, though in his heart he already knew.' Mr Koloman
lowered his voice, pacing amongst the shadows. 'The lady
was no longer fertile. Her womb had given all it was meant
to give. There would be no heir.'

He paused for a sip of wine.

'The lord was shocked. He struck his wife again and again
until he killed her, and then he went on to rape all his daughters, one by one. The screams that night were heard all across
the country. "I shall have a son!" he roared again and again.
He knew no mercy; he had become a fiend.

'One of the girls was cursed with a pregnancy. She tried
to keep it secret; she even tried to be rid of the baby, but the
lord found out just in time and prevented it. He tied her to
her bed and made the servants watch her day and night until
the child was born.'

My eyelids felt heavy. The wine I'd not been able to resist
was working its wonders.

Konrad refilled my glass, though it was still three-quarters
full. 'To the lord's delight she gave him – a boy. The boy he'd
yearned for. The lord had apparently lost his wits by then; he
was blinded by eerie happiness, so much so he didn't notice
the boy was terribly deformed.'

McGray leaned forward, enthralled.

'The poor girl, at once the child's mother and his sister, could stand it no more. She freed herself in the middle of the night and went to the child's room. She picked up her baby from the cradle, wrapped him in her arms and took him out of the castle. It was a dark, stormy night and nobody saw her take the child to the nearby brook – or they pretended not to see. She said goodbye to the sleeping creature, kissed his ugly forehead . . . and then plunged him into the water. She wept and wept as she held the little body against the bottom of the stream. She could not behold her own doing. She simply looked up, at the thunderous sky, while she waited for the life to desert her deformed baby.'

Mr Koloman went to the mantelpiece and stared into the flames. I struggled to keep my eyes open, but even with blurred vision I could see the intensity in his face.

'When the child stirred no more she rose and shrieked, appalled at what she had done. Her hands were so cold they'd turned blue and purple. She did not dare look down, look at the face of her son, which by now must be the colour of her hands.

'Nobody knows exactly what happened then, only that the girl and the lord were found in the morning, both hanged by the neck, not far from the brook. Some say they hanged themselves; some say it was the other daughters; some say it was the villagers, sick of the terror and the depravity that reigned in the castle.'

He gave a wry smirk. 'It doesn't really matter, does it? The land had finally seen justice . . . of a sort. The lord had been punished, his poor daughter was finally at peace.'

'Not really at peace,' Mrs Koloman added, looking grim. 'Her soul could not have found peace.'

'That is precisely what some people think, my dear. Some say the shrieks of the poor mother and the roars of the dark lord could be heard in the castle every night henceforth, until the place was abandoned and became derelict, and that the country folk, to this day, are still afraid to meander through the ruins. I agree, Minerva. There are wounds that even death cannot assuage.'

'What a ghastly end,' Uncle mumbled.

'Oh, but that's not the end,' said Mr Koloman. 'Some say that the child did not perish. That his little body survived the icy water and drifted away until a merciful hand picked him up and raised him. Others say that his body *did* die – how could a frail, deformed little creature withstand such an ordeal? – but that his soul endured. In his short life the baby had known only pain and hatred, his tiny heart a well of dark, vicious feelings. That hatred kept his soul in the land of men, lingering for all time in those woods, envious of the joy and the love he never had. Abhorring happy children, above anything else.

'Some say he still haunts that brook, that only little children can see him. That he ensnares them, invites them to play in the water. "Come and play," he tells them. "Come and see these little pebbles!" And when the children bend to pick them up he drowns them, like his own mother drowned him. And then the parents hear his sharp, wicked laughter echoing across the woods, and they don't need to see their children's bodies to know what has just happened.'

The silence was absolute, broken only by the occasional crackle of the fire. I was barely managing to keep myself awake, feeling a pleasant sway, as if sitting in a boat on that gentle loch outside.

McGray picked up his glass, but then halted. He stirred in his seat and then rose like a spring.

'What is it?' asked Mrs Koloman as McGray strode to the window.

Mr Koloman and Uncle Maurice followed. I joined them clumsily, my four limbs slightly numb, but I too saw plainly what was happening out there.

It was Natalja, dragging half her shawl as she ran desperately across the lawn.

She was screaming.

14

We all ran to the entrance hall. Boyde had also heard the screaming and was already opening the back door under the stairs.

Natalja came stumbling across the gardens, her face distorted and covered in tears. Her father went to her, embracing her tightly as soon as she set foot on the granite steps.

We hurried outside and the chill of the evening awoke my senses a little more.

'What happened?' asked Mr Koloman, grasping the girl's arms. 'Where is your sister?'

Her mother came closer and placed a gentle hand on the back of Natalja's neck. The girl instantly exhaled and, though still crying, managed to speak.

'Veronika . . . She's having . . . some sort of fit. She fell after we saw –' The girl shuddered.

'Tell Glenister to fetch my case,' Mrs Koloman barked at Boyde.

'Is Fletcher with her?' Konrad asked, and Natalja nodded.

McGray approached them. 'What did ye see?'

Natalja buried her face in her father's shoulder and we barely understood her muffled voice. 'A dead man.'

We all seemed to take a step back, as though she'd pushed us away with invisible hands.

'In the woods?' McGray pressed. She nodded, unable to face us. 'Who?'

All she could utter was: 'Horrid!'

'We'll need some lanterns,' McGray said, pulling out a gun. I drew mine too, glad of having brought it. Mr and Mrs Koloman were clearly not expecting that, for they both started at the sight.

Mrs Glenister appeared with a doctor's bag and heard McGray's request. 'Shall I tell Boyde and Calcraft to go with the inspectors?'

'Yes,' said Mr Koloman. 'Tell Smeaton to send the carriage behind us. And look after Natalja.'

'I want to go!' Natalja protested, but Mr Koloman pushed her firmly into Mrs Glenister's arms. 'Sorry, dear, you have seen enough. Where are they? On your usual path?' Again she nodded. 'Good. Try to calm down. Glenister, give her something for the nerves.'

'Come here, miss,' the bony woman said, leading the girl in. Her motherly tone was entirely at odds with her sour face.

The lanterns came soon enough. Boyde was lighting them as he approached. I took one and was about to ask where the man Calcraft was when Nine-Nails took my arm. 'Ye sure yer coming? Ye look a wee bit drunk.'

'I am perfectly fit!' I squealed, although I could hear the stubbornness of the slightly inebriated.

'Come on,' Uncle urged, seizing a lantern and leading the way. 'We are wasting time.'

Mr and Mrs Koloman joined him and we strode briskly across the back gardens, which were as sumptuous as those at the front. The servants had lit torches at every corner of the intricate yew patterns, casting golden light all around, but as soon as we entered the woods, on the eastern side of the manor, our lanterns became the only source of light.

I offered my arm to Mrs Koloman, but as we advanced

over the uneven footpath, stumbling on stones and roots and branches, it was rather *her* leading me.

We followed the resolute leaders, Maurice and Mr Koloman, McGray right at their heels, and Boyde came behind us. Our beams of light flickered across the forest, letting us see the countless trees, as thick and straight as Greek columns.

Then we heard her. Deep, desperate grunts tore the air, travelling fast through the otherwise deserted woods.

Mr Koloman quickened his pace. He was a very fit man – we all struggled to keep up – but he was also the most anxious, even more so than his wife.

'There!' he cried, shedding light ahead. The first thing I saw was a blur of dark red on very pale skin, and my heart skipped a beat at the thought of blood. Mr Koloman must have guessed the same, for he went silent. After a few agonizing strides we realized it was Veronika's dark-red dress. But that would be poor consolation.

The girl was prostrated on the ground, howling. With one hand she pressed her abdomen, while the other was held by a very distressed Miss Fletcher.

'My darling!' Mr Koloman shouted. He flung himself on his knees just as his daughter let out a piercing, guttural scream. Mrs Koloman also knelt beside her, gasping, but then opened the leather case, in full command of herself.

'This dandy also studied some medicine,' McGray said, pushing me forward.

'Are you wounded?' I asked, bending down, but she did not look it. She was simply in excruciating pain, rocking from side to side, her teeth bared as she growled. I gently lifted her pale hand from her stomach but found no obvious sign of injury.

'Has this happened to her before?' I asked the parents. The poor girl was in no state to talk.

'Never,' Mrs Koloman said at once, taking Veronika's hand to kiss.

'It might be poison,' I said. At once I remembered the poor nurse I'd seen die of strychnine poisoning, not that long ago.

Mrs Koloman was already rummaging through her instruments. She pulled out a small vial labelled as laudanum. 'Be brave, my dear,' she muttered. 'This will help with the pain.'

'You cannot give her that!' I protested. 'We have no idea what she might have ingested; if you give her yet more narcotics —'

'She's my daughter!' the woman barked at me. 'I know what I'm doing.'

I tried to snatch the vial but Miss Fletcher held my arm. She was unnervingly strong. 'She said she knows what she is doing!'

'I will not see my girl like this,' mumbled Mrs Koloman.

I would have objected further, but then we heard Boyde let out a scared yelp. I looked up and saw, black against the silver beam of McGray's lantern, the figure of a man suspended in mid-air.

I felt a nasty chill as I stood up. The man's body was upside-down, and I had to blink a few times before I realized what had happened: his feet had been tied to a thick rope and he'd been hung up like a sacrificed chicken. Even his arms had been tied behind his back, like cooks do with the wings of poultry.

Veronika's cries of pain in the background made the image all the more unsettling. McGray, usually as hard as nails, was aghast.

I walked round the body, recognizing the tattered navy jacket, and then I saw the lifeless face of –

'Constable McEwan,' Boyde said with a dry mouth.

'So this is that poor sod,' said Nine-Nails. This was the first time he had seen the man.

'Good Lord,' I murmured, feeling a sudden nausea. McEwan's head looked simply horrendous: there was a wide gash right across his throat, the blood still liquid, trickling sluggishly. It was a straight, clean cut, done with the precision and confidence of a surgeon.

Above the gash the skin was pale, almost sickly grey; below, his face looked blushed. It made me think of the dark dregs of wine, settled and caked in the bottom of a glass. McEwan had bled almost to the last drop. I pointed my lantern to the ground, expecting to see a mighty pool of gore.

There was none.

'He must have been killed elsewhere and then hung here,' I said, my mind already working. Nine-Nails had a much more ominous expression.

'Blood baths,' he mouthed when our eyes met, and I felt yet another chill.

The rattle of hooves startled me. I looked back and saw the carriage approach. Smeaton, the very thin, very short driver, halted a mere yard from the Kolomans. He was about to jump down, but Mr Koloman raised a hand.

'No! Take her back at once.'

Uncle Maurice and Miss Fletcher lifted the screaming girl. Again she was pressing her abdomen with both hands, the pain only slightly relieved by the laudanum.

I noticed tears in her eyes as she looked pleadingly at my uncle.

'*Stop!*' McGray roared right then, but not at us. I saw him dart into the black forest at full speed. I ran after him, completely sober by now.

I pointed my lantern as steadily as possible, for McGray was shaking his lamp manically as he rushed ahead. I followed his shadow until he halted abruptly in a small clearing. I nearly collided with him as he looked down, shedding light on the bed of dry pine needles.

'What was it?' I asked.

'A wee light. There's someone here. Some—'

He ran again, this time to the left, towards the loch. We moved downhill as we approached the shore, my momentum keeping me on my feet as I thrust myself forwards. I clashed against a tree, saw stars, and then moved on. McGray had run uninterrupted to the edge of the forest. The pine trees gave way to a narrow shore, barely a couple of yards of mud, reeds and pebbles. The water pulsed in between the rounded rocks with an incongruous calmness.

And then I saw it – barely a glint in the distance, hovering over the water, halfway between us and the dark, thorny shadows that were the islands.

McGray shouted again, and then pointed his gun and shot twice.

The light went out then, and under the advancing clouds the loch became a blotch of darkness.

I swallowed, struggling to catch my breath. My words came out as a laboured murmur. 'Did you hit that?'

McGray shook his head. 'Cannae tell.'

15

McGray shot one last time for good measure, and then we both looked around for marks in the ground.

'It looks like someone pushed a small boat ashore here,' I said, lighting the muddy bank. The marks were deep and clear, but the waters, though calm, would soon erase them.

'I don't like this,' said McGray, his eyes now fixed on the gloomy island. 'The Nellys family 'n' the auld man live over there.'

'Do you think they might have done this?' I asked.

McGray laughed. 'Nae, I was thinking they might be in danger, but yer perverse thoughts for once seem logical.'

We realized we could do no more with only the light of lanterns, so we walked back to McEwan's grisly corpse. Everyone except Boyde had gone. The young man – I saw he could not be more than nineteen – was shaking, and for some reason he would not look us in the eye. 'The master said they couldn't wait. They'll send the carriage back as soon as Miss Veronika gets to the house.'

'Good,' said McGray. 'We cannae leave the corpse here, dangling like a joint o' ham.'

I sighed and forced myself to look at the hanging body. It was not the most dreadful thing I'd ever seen but still a most unwelcome sight. Every detail spoke of a neat job: the constable's face was clean, only a few specks of red on the collar of his already grubby shirt, and the knots around his feet and wrists were expertly tied. The rope had been thrown over the lower branches of the nearest fir; I followed it down with the light and saw it had been secured to the base of that same tree.

'Ye'd need a very good arm to do that,' said Nine-Nails, for even the lower branches were at least fifteen feet high. He stepped closer and examined the rope around the wrists. He arched an eyebrow, in the way he usually does when taking a mental note.

I did not have a chance to ask what he was thinking; the carriage arrived then and Uncle Maurice stepped down. His face was covered in perspiration.

'Did she get back all right?' I asked.

He kicked dead branches as he spoke. 'If you can call that all right. The mother locked herself in the girl's room and almost threw me out of the house. The father snarled at me to come and "help" you' – he cast a baleful stare at the body – 'with *that*.'

The knot looked terribly tight, but McGray had only to pull the rope's end and it immediately came undone. The body fell a couple of feet before Nine-Nails seized the cord again, and when the corpse bounced it spilled droplets of blood all around.

I wiped it from my face with stoic resignation but Uncle Maurice, a novice to this sort of ordeal, squealed like a child.

Nine-Nails laughed. 'Och, he's worse than ye, Frey! Is he the queen bee in yer hive?'

'Excuse me, I may hunt, but I am *not* in the habit of smearing human blood all over my finery.'

McGray was about to give him some of his wit but I interjected. 'Uncle, do not, do *not* argue with him. The last thing we need right now is a battle of buffoonery.'

We lowered the body very carefully. McGray looked for

something to wrap around the still-oozing neck, but all he found was his tartan waistcoat (hardly a loss to the world). Once wrapped, we placed the body in the carriage, and in order to make room for us, Nine-Nails had to prop the corpse up as if it were sitting.

'I'd rather walk,' said Uncle. 'That is not a travel companion I relish.'

'D'ye really want to walk?' McGray snapped. 'With the chance of a bloody murderer on the loose?'

Uncle grunted, pulled a cigar from his breast pocket and jumped in. Though only a few minutes long, that eerie ride would give me recurrent nightmares for years to come.

🌿🌿🌿

'The wine cellar?' Uncle protested.

'I cannot think of another room,' I said as we watched Boyde and McGray carry Constable McEwan down the stone steps. 'We need to keep the body from rotting until it can be examined; other than the food stores this is the coolest spot in the house.'

I cleared a wide table used to decant wine and they placed the corpse there. Uncle went to the racks and grabbed a few bottles.

'Before the foul humours hit these,' he said, and then quit the room.

'Leave us, laddie,' Nine-Nails told Boyde, who was all too glad to get away.

McGray sat on top of a wine barrel. 'What can ye tell me from that?'

We'd need a proper forensic man to do a thorough examination, but I did a very quick inspection nonetheless. As I ran a finger along the mush of sliced muscle I remembered why I had not finished my degree in medicine.

'I cannot tell the exact time of death, but it was very recently. No rigor mortis yet, and' – I felt his armpit – 'he is even warm in spots. It *must* have happened while we had dinner . . . or even more recently, while Mr Koloman told us that story.' I had a quick look under the man's shirt and trousers. He stank of ale. 'No other injury or signs of violence.'

McGray did not look happy. 'What now? If we were in Edinburgh, I'd send a few peelers to look around, and another few to make sure nobody left this house.'

'If we were in Edinburgh, we'd have Dr Reed to examine the body while we investigated.' I rubbed my face as the gargantuan task took full shape in my head. 'And the person who'd be investigating a local murder is the very man who has been killed.'

'How fuckin' selfish.'

'We need to question everyone in the manor; we need to make sure everyone can be accounted for at the time of the death –'

'And that boat we saw. We need to check those islands.'

I snorted. 'There is so much to do and only you and I to do it. We need to call for reinforcements, perhaps send a telegram either from Poolewe or Kin . . . Kinloo . . .'

'Kinlochewe. Both are at least three or four hours away. We'd lose half a day or more just going there 'n' back.'

I thought about it. 'Indeed. I suppose I could ask my uncle to do that for us. In fact, I will ask him to leave before dawn. If the telegram gets sent tomorrow morning, we might have officers here the day after.'

McGray stroked his stubble. 'Aye, do that. But we cannae

rest on our laurels. We need to secure the house 'n' make sure any suspects stay within our grasp.'

I sensed the tone in his voice. 'Do you have someone in mind already?'

'Aye. See.' He went to the corpse, which lay on one side, and pointed at the rope around McEwan's wrists. 'That's very neat, Frey. And the knot around the tree was a sailor's knot; that's why it kept the body firmly in place but was also very easy to undo.'

'A sailor's . . .' I arched an eyebrow. 'Dominik?'

'Aye. Him or Calcraft. Dominik left the table early 'n' I've not seen Calcraft since he brought in all that luggage.'

I nodded. 'I do not like that Dominik. Not one bit.'

'Come on, let's gather everyone together and the alibis will emerge. And if Dominik 'n' Calcraft cannae give us one, I'll have them locked up until the peelers arrive.'

I shook my head. 'The Kolomans are not going to like that.'

'Sod them. Unlike yer pretty uncle, I'm nae here to pluck up flowers.'

'No,' I said, rather gloomily. 'We both know why you came here.'

16

The long drawing room filled quickly. We watched the entire household arrive one by one, each servant introduced by Mr Koloman. They were all bleary-eyed, all nervous.

As I waited, I stared out of the window. The horizon should still be deep blue in a perpetual dusk, but by now thick clouds had covered it all and the only feature I could make out was the shore of the islands, where the thin layer of mist over the water seemed to glow. In my mind I pictured a lonely, silent killer, running across the desolate immensity of the Highlands – and in the meantime all I could do was wait for a band of scared servants to line up so we could ask them useless questions.

We already knew some of the staff: the young and brawny Boyde, formally introduced as a footman but who seemed to help with anything that required strength, including the gardening; the small and scrawny Smeaton, who drove the carriage and was in charge of the horses and stables; the thin and dry Mrs Glenister, who acted as Mrs Koloman's chambermaid but seemed to be everyone's despotic mother; and of course Miss Fletcher, who was the head of the staff – the Kolomans, quite unusually, had no butler.

There were only a few new faces: the fantastically wide Mrs Plunket, who was in charge of the kitchens; a teenage girl called Tamlyn, who was chambermaid for the Miss Kolomans; and a young scullery maid called Ellie, who could barely keep herself awake. Mr Koloman, quite strangely for a man of his stature, kept no valet. Their staff, it appeared, was quite lean. And they all spoke with the same soft, almost plain acquired accent, as if educated in the same school.

Once I had taken note of their names (on very fine paper provided by Mr Koloman) they all lined up in front of the red sofas and chairs, which were reserved for the family. The only family member present, however, was Mr Koloman: his wife was still tending to their daughter, Natalja was apparently too distressed to leave her bedroom, and McGray deemed Benjamin had had too much for one day (Nine-Nails had simply knocked at his door, made sure he was all right and then let him sleep). Everyone knew there was no trace of Dominik or Calcraft but nobody seemed willing to mention it out loud.

Mr Koloman requested to be the one who announced the murder, and he did so with the tact and frankness of a good landlord. There were gasps, cries of distress, and Ellie, merely twelve years old, even burst into tears.

'Inspectors Frey and McGray here will be doing everything they can to keep us safe and find the culprit. For that, I need you all to cooperate and answer their every question.' There were more gasps and Mr Koloman raised both hands. 'None of you is under suspicion, of course. Answer truthfully and you shall be all right.'

'We will question you individually,' I began. 'Firstly, I would like to talk to –'

We heard a shrill, out-of-tune song. The discordant voices grew louder and then the drawing-room door burst open. The singing resumed, brasher and clearer. It was Dominik and Calcraft.

They were both drunk, staggering and holding on to each other as they swayed about the room.

'Why, a family reunion!' cried Dominik, his words slurred. 'Shouldda told me!'

I was going to suggest somebody led them to another room to question them in private, but McGray had no such scruples. He stood up and grabbed Dominik by the collar. 'Where have youse been?'

Dominik blinked and looked at McGray's hand as if it were an alien thing. 'You . . . you're missing a finger. Did you know that?'

'Answer me, ye twat!'

Calcraft did, after a loud hiccup. 'Out.'

'Out where?'

'Just out.'

McGray made to punch him but I managed to stop him in time.

'You will not get anything meaningful out of them right now. We need them sober. A statement from a couple of dribbling drunks will not be acceptable in court.'

McGray sighed in frustration and thrust Dominik away. The young man nearly fell on his back, but Boyde jumped closer and held him up.

'I want them locked up 'til the morning,' said McGray. 'We'll question them then.'

Dominik grinned stupidly and lifted his chin. 'You'll do no such thing.'

McGray produced his gun and there was a general cry. 'The fuck I will, ye pretty boy. Consider yerself under arrest.'

'This is an outrage!' Mr Koloman roared. 'You have no right to do this!'

'Course I do! I'm bloody CID.'

'My son could not possibly –'

'Yer pretty son came round Thurso at the worst of times.

And he was out there just as that sorry constable got murdered. D'ye see my point?' Mr Koloman simply gulped, red with rage, and McGray turned to Miss Fletcher. 'Yer the housekeeper. Take me to suitable rooms to lock up these blootered bastards. And I want all the keys.'

I saw the hint of a smile on Miss Fletcher's face. She rose to her full height and when she shoved Dominik and Calcraft out of the room she did it with a little more force than was strictly necessary.

Everyone in the drawing room went mute. All eyes fell on me, ranging from the scared to the amused to the inexplicably indignant. I felt a throbbing in my temples and was tempted to send everyone away, grab a carafe of wine and drink myself to sleep.

I took a deep breath instead. 'Now, we all need to calm down. As I said, I will question you one by one.' *Before you have time to concoct alibis*, I thought. 'Until I am finished, I want everyone to wait here.'

Plunket, the astoundingly wide cook, raised a shy hand as though she were in school.

'Yes?' I said, feeling like a cantankerous schoolmaster.

'May I fetch some tea? For the nerves, you see.' She was rubbing the back of the crying scullery maid.

I sighed. 'Very well. But do *not* wander.'

17

It was still remarkably early, but the sky was already lightening.

McGray and I sat in a small yet charming breakfast parlour, overlooking Loch Maree. Mrs Plunket left us a large pot of strong coffee and then excused herself. Like us, she had not slept, yet she still had to prepare the breakfasts for the family.

I spread my notes on the table. 'This wide woman was in the kitchens sorting the servants' supper and preparing some sort of marinade for tonight's dinner. The scullery maid was serving supper for the other servants; most of them were gathered in their below-stairs dining room. They have all vouched for each other and the details they told us match. Mrs Glenister and the girl Tamlyn left the table early to prepare Mrs Koloman's and the girls' chambers and clothes. Glenister left the girl alone when Mrs Koloman called her, as you might remember. Boyde also left early; he says he went to the cellar to decant some more wine and then leave fresh carafes in the drawing room and bedrooms. We both saw him open the door when Miss Natalja came back crying for help; I am satisfied he would not have had time to leave the house, slaughter McEwan and then return.' I shook my head. 'So everyone has an alibi, except for Calcraft and Dominik, who are still to answer to us.'

McGray looked at the notes intently, rearranging the sheets as he muttered to himself.

'I ken Calcraft 'n' Dominik are our main suspects . . . but . . .'

'Oh, for the love of God, say it.'

McGray raised an eyebrow. 'What if . . . the twins did it?'

I did not blink. I simply lounged in my seat. 'Do you mean . . . aided by Miss Fletcher?'

McGray nodded. 'Aye. The gal's like a weathered battleaxe; she looks strong enough to lift a man and hang him like that.'

'And she must know about knots,' I said. 'She took my uncle and me to the islands on a boat; she seemed quite experienced.'

'And she had a good motive, from what ye've told me.'

'Of course she had. But why would the girls be willing to assist a murder? Or to witness it and say nothing about it? Why cover for Miss Fletcher?' I rubbed my temples, feeling my head throbbing again. 'Perhaps Miss Veronika was not ill at all. It might all have been an act to get herself taken away.'

'If that's the case, maybe even the parents knew . . . They were very reluctant to let ye treat the lassie.'

I poured myself some coffee. 'That *was* strange, yes, and the mother's insistence on injecting her with laudanum. Then again . . .' I took a sip of the excellent Colombian brew and shook my head. 'Let's not read too much between the lines. That entire theory seems . . . disjointed, illogical. If I had daughters, I would not casually send them out to slaughter men. Also, McEwan had been working here for years; they could have killed him any other time – *without* CID inspectors nearby.' I stood up and paced. 'However, I should definitely examine Miss Veronika; she might need further medical attention. And we must also question the people at the inn; that is the nearest dwelling and almost certainly the last place where McEwan was seen alive.'

'And we should also inspect the islands. Don't forget the wee light and the boat we saw last night.' McGray lounged back, gulping down his coffee. 'Ye'd think that a case like this, in the middle o' bloody nowhere with just a handful o' folk around, would be simpler.'

I smirked. 'I do not expect anything to be simple any more. It saves me a good deal of disenchantment.'

Nine-Nails agreed, and I suddenly realized this was a momentous event: we were discussing the intricacies of a case without calling each other names, without arguing, and giving good thought to each other's theories. It had only taken eight or nine months and four *very* serious cases. I preferred not to bring attention to the fact.

McGray pressed his fingertips together, the stump of the missing one sticking out. 'I'll go to the inn and then to the islands 'n' see what I can find out. I'll take Miss Fletcher with me.'

'Are you sure you want to do that?'

McGray chuckled. 'Why? D'ye think she'll beat me up if I ask blunt questions? She might do so if it were someone as lanky 'n' lily-livered as ye.'

'I meant are you sure you can stand another trip over water?'

'Och, shut up! It's a proper ailment.'

'Well, it is ironic that the man who has just called me lily—'

'I said shut it, dammit! In the meantime ye can stay here, examine the sick lassie and question the two drunken sods. Ye adore —'

'I do *not* adore questioning people,' I retorted, though well aware it was close to a blatant lie.

McGray laughed as he pushed his chair back. 'Aye, right. And go to sleep a wee while, Frey. As usual, ye look fuckin' hideous. I'll go to the inn right now; if the people that work there are involved in some way, we'd better find out soon.'

'Are you going there right now? Will you not sleep?'

'I bloody rarely sleep, remember?'

I'd not realized how tired I felt until McGray mentioned sleep, and I was very tempted to go to the guest room the Kolomans had arranged for me. I peeped inside and saw the four-poster bed bursting with pillows, the Gothic window that overlooked the loch, and the ancient-looking tapestry that decked the main wall. I sighed, closed the door and walked on to Miss Veronika's chamber. The other interrogations could wait until I had rested; the ill girl could not.

Tamlyn, the young maid, was stepping out of Miss Veronika's chamber carrying a sponge and a basin of lavender-scented water. When she saw me she started, spilling some of the contents on the floor. She curtsied and hurried away before I could say a word.

I knocked at the door. 'Mrs Koloman?' No answer. 'I have come to check on your daughter.'

I was about to knock again when she replied, 'Come in, Inspector.'

I opened the door and walked in cautiously, as if stepping on a tightrope. The curtains were shut and the only light came from a small oil lamp. The room was pretty much what I'd expected: crammed with books on science alongside fashion patterns, hand-drawn designs scattered everywhere, and cuts of silk, muslin and linen.

Mrs Koloman sat by the four-poster bed, looking terribly pale and red-eyed. Her distress struck me as genuine, unless the woman was a very good actress – and God knows I've had enough of actresses.

'How is she faring?' I asked, approaching as one might a scared deer. Veronika lay quietly, wrapped in heavy blankets embroidered in red and gold. Her snow-white nightgown, and her skin almost as colourless, again made me think of a ghost. At least she appeared to be sleeping peacefully.

'Much better,' said her mother. 'The laudanum helped.'

I had to contain a disapproving grunt. 'May I examine her? I had some medical training at Oxford.'

'There is nothing to examine. The worst of the pain is gone.'

'I insist, ma'am,' and I added a white lie, 'for my own peace of mind.'

Mrs Koloman took her time to reply. 'Do it, if you have to. But you'll understand I must be present, for the girl's decorum, you see.'

'Of course,' I said, though thinking she had not objected to her daughter's unabashed flirting or her scandalous clothes. In fact, in her long-sleeved nightdress, buttoned up to the neck, Veronika was wearing more clothes in bed than she had at dinner.

'Inspector, do you have instruments, or should I supply them?' Though delivered with courtesy, the question was a clear challenge.

'I was not expecting an emergency such as this. If you have instruments, I would appreciate the use of them.'

Mrs Koloman picked up her small leather case and put it on the bed. She simply opened it and waited. More challenge.

I rummaged through the shiny, well-kept instruments and the tiny vials. 'You keep an enviable assortment of medicines.'

'I do. It is a necessity, if you spend a good deal of the year in a place as remote as this.'

I pulled out a fine stethoscope and listened to the girl's heartbeat. 'Would you prefer to live in town? Your husband can certainly afford it. I am surprised your name is not widely known in London circles.'

She did not reply, her arms crossed tightly, so I proceeded to examine Miss Veronika. I could feel the vigilance of the mother, so I made a conscious effort not to touch the girl's skin with anything other than the stainless-steel chest piece. Veronika stirred slightly at the touch of the cool metal, but then was calm again. Her heartbeats were rapid but normal, and her airways sounded clear.

'Was abdominal pain the only symptom?'

'Yes. She complained of nothing else.'

'No rashes or swelling?'

'No,' she said. 'And her ablutions were normal, if you need to know as much.' I blushed. 'Do you still think she was poisoned?'

'That is one possibility.' I felt the girl's forehead: no fever. 'And you only gave her laudanum?'

'Yes.'

I mused, folding the stethoscope and putting it back in place, exactly as I'd found it. Miss Veronika had no obvious symptoms. The pain could well have been entirely neural . . . or feigned, but I could not be sure until I examined her properly or had the chance to talk to her, lest she'd not mentioned all her ailments to her mother.

'Ma'am, would you mind if I spoke to your daughter? May we wake her up?'

Mrs Koloman gathered breath and very consciously avoided my question. 'I hear you locked up my son.'

'We did what was necessary. Your son was present in Thurso right after the clergyman died. He also was outside at the exact time the constable was being murdered. You must understand –'

'I know my son!'

'Madam, you will excuse my curtness, but I have seen many sentenced men whose mothers swore they *knew* their children.'

'Why would he want to murder a poor priest in a godforsaken port? Or a good-for-nothing constable?'

It was my turn to gather breath. 'Ma'am, let me remind you that your son has not been sentenced yet. If he and his footman, Calcraft, are innocent, I can assure you –'

'Please, don't condescend to me.'

'Very well,' I said, tired of acting the conciliator. 'I need to ask you a few questions too. Shall we go to another room? I can see you do not want your daughter disturbed.'

Mrs Koloman did not reply, but she stood up, kissed Miss Veronika's forehead and extinguished the lamp's flame. We went to the corridor, which was as silent as a grave, and Mrs Koloman led me to her own room. She had a small personal parlour adjacent to her bedchamber – as in most wealthy families, she and Mr Koloman had separate bedrooms. In her parlour, which must be her solitary haven, there were only two armchairs and a little table with a basket of needlework. She picked it up and began working on a very intricate design, sulking as she waited for my questions.

'Ma'am, the first thing I wanted to ask you is how is your other girl faring?'

'I hardly know. The poor thing was far too distressed to talk.'

'Have you talked to Miss Fletcher?'

Her hands went still.

She tried to do a new stitch but in the end had to put the embroidery aside. 'I . . . I feel guilty even mentioning this . . .'

I leaned forward. 'Go on.'

'I think I saw Millie sort of . . . I cannot say *smiling* but she certainly wasn't overridden with shock. I can't blame her, though. She wouldn't be human if she didn't feel some joy after that man's death. What that wretch did to her was abominable. He should have brought her justice but instead he laughed at her disgrace.'

I interlaced my fingers. Was she simply trying to throw the scent away from her son? I could tell any direct questions about Dominik would only upset the lady. I should lead my questioning there as if treading on eggshells. 'Miss Fletcher's disgrace was, I am afraid, caused by your late brother-in-law.'

Mrs Koloman looked away, gnashing her teeth. I gave her time; she eventually spoke. 'My husband was far too patient with his brother. I can tell you this now that he is dead: Maximilian was a fiend. He had mistresses on every shore, impregnated girls and then paid them to have the *problem* removed. Millie nearly did. *I* was the one who persuaded her otherwise. I arranged everything with the priest.'

'Some would say your son took after his uncle –'

Too abrupt, I thought, but it was too late already.

She pointed a finger at me. 'My son is nothing like that monster!'

'He certainly leads a very similar lifestyle.'

She took a deep breath, returned the basket to the table and stood up. 'I need some sleep. You should get some too.'

And she raised a hand, showing me the way out.

She closed the door with a thump, and in the corridor I found McGray and Uncle Maurice. They were both ready to depart.

Uncle stared at the door as if trying to see through. 'Did the mother talk to you? Did you manage to see Miss Veronika?'

I walked a few yards, asking them to follow me, before I answered. 'Yes. It is a really odd condition. I cannot even speculate –'

'Is she in pain?' Uncle cut in.

'She doesn't seem to be, but again, I cannot tell if that is because of the opiates or because the pain has truly receded.'

'Keep an eye on her,' said McGray, handing me a jingling set of keys. 'And everyone else we've locked up. Please, *don't* mess things up while we're away.'

'When have I – Oh, never mind.'

'That wee silver one is for the chest in Mr Koloman's room where I locked all the other duplicates. Only *we* have access to those places.'

I shoved the bulky set in my breast pocket. 'And we have been here for only one night. I hope things do not continue at this rate, or even in this manor we will run out of rooms to lock suspects in!'

18

McGray and Maurice walked down the granite steps just as Smeaton and Miss Fletcher got the carriage ready.

'The weather today is decidedly Scottish,' Maurice remarked, looking at the gloomy, grey sky. In the dull light the neat gardens, with their moss-covered sculptures and their symmetric yew borders, looked more like a sad, misty graveyard.

'Aye, as if fucking England was a bloody Mediterranean paradise.'

'I happen to be French.'

'*French!* Yer a tenth-generation sodding émigré, are ye nae?'

Maurice shook his head. 'I beg your pardon. I hardly understand half the words you say – and the half I *do* understand makes even less sense.'

They jumped into the carriage and not a word was said until they reached the inn. McGray handed Maurice a piece of paper with the message and the addressee. 'Now, I'll say this slowly enough so even ye can understand: Pleeeaaasse, haaaave thiiiis . . . deeeliveeerrrred . . . aaaas . . . diiiisscuuuu . . .'

'Oh, so you are not only vulgar but also mildly retarded!'

McGray brought a hand to his forehead. 'Och, ye . . . bloody . . . fro–'

'Do step out, my good man, before you give me more ammunition.'

McGray snorted, kicked the door open and jumped out, along with Miss Fletcher. He pointed at Smeaton. 'Make sure that pseudo-Froggie gets to the telegraph and sends that message. And then get 'im straight back to yer master's house. Did ye get it?'

'Aye, I'll –'

'And as much as I cannae stand the miserable sod, if I hear he's missing even one o' his bloody Frenchie hairs, ye'll have to deal with this.' He raised a fist and Smeaton simply nodded, driving the carriage away.

'If you don't want to walk back,' said Miss Fletcher, 'I am sure Mr Dailey, the innkeeper, can lend us one of his boats.'

'He *will* lend us one, lass. After I've talked to him I want ye to take me to the islands, as we had agreed before the death.'

Miss Fletcher's lips parted but she didn't say a word; she simply nodded.

McGray turned to the building, its grey stones a perfect match to the surrounding fog. 'So Queen Vicky stayed here?'

'Aye, she did!' said a man's coarse voice. McGray saw the milky silhouette of a broad-shouldered, broad-bellied man with a bushy moustache. 'Twelve years ago. The wretched woman was wider than she was tall. And miserable. She was here for twelve days but spent nine locked in her room with a "headache" – that wee window over there.' The man offered a hand to shake. 'George Dailey, at yer service. Millie, is this the policeman who wanted to talk to the Nellyses?'

'Aye, that's me,' said McGray. 'But before that I need to talk to ye and everyone else in yer inn. Constable McEwan is dead.'

Mr Dailey at once staggered, went pale and dropped the sack of spuds he was carrying. '*What?*'

'Sorry, I've been told I can be blunt sometimes.'

'Are ye sure? There must be a mistake. I thought he'd still be in his room!'

Miss Fletcher picked up the bag for him. 'The inspector is telling the truth. I found him myself. There's no doubt.'

Mr Dailey took a few panting breaths. 'My, my! I saw him just last night; his horse is still in the stables. How . . . how did it –'

'D'ye mind if I look at his room right away? The lass here can tell ye all the details in the meantime.'

Miss Fletcher winced, perhaps at the memory of the dead body, perhaps because of something else.

'O-of course!' said Mr Dailey. 'Do come in.'

He led McGray and Miss Fletcher to a large dining room, where his wife was setting the tables for breakfast. Her husband whispered in her ear and the woman dropped the cutlery she'd been handling.

'Can I look at the room now?' McGray asked. 'That'll give youse a moment to take it in.'

'Och, I don't need a moment,' said the woman. 'The lad was a useless pile o' dung. But for my life, no such thing had ever happened here in living memory!'

'D'ye have the keys to his room?' McGray insisted. 'I'm in a wee bit of a hurry.'

'Our guests rarely lock their doors; there is hardly a soul in the vicinity. But here's the master key, just in case he did. It's the second door on the left.'

Mrs Dailey looked up. 'I don't think ye'll find much. The constable just went up there for a nap right after dinner.'

McGray simply thanked them with a nod and went upstairs. Contrary to Mr Dailey's expectation, McEwan's door *was* locked. McGray turned the key and entered a generous, very clean room. The window overlooked not the lake but the road. McEwan would have been able to see anybody coming and going. However, there were scant signs of the room having been occupied: the bed was still made, with faint marks on the linen, where McEwan had lain. A chair had been pulled towards the window and there were some ashes on the sill.

'So ye were having a wee smoke, looking out,' McGray mumbled to himself.

That was all he found. McEwan had not even carried any luggage, which was to be expected; the man had not intended to spend the night there when he first set out from Poolewe.

McGray went back to the dining room and found the Daileys and Miss Fletcher breaking bread and sharing a large pot of tea. He had a cup himself and listened to their remarks on the death before asking his questions. 'Can youse tell me what McEwan was up to while he was here? Everything. Doesnae matter how trivial.'

Man and wife looked at each other, a little tense. It was she who spoke. 'He did very little, really. He gobbled up his dinner – two servings of my stew – drank a few pints, then went upstairs for a nap.'

Mr Dailey joined in. 'He told us not to disappear, cause he'd need more beer after his sleep. After an hour or so he came downstairs, but he wouldnae drink straight away. He . . . did something very odd.'

'Did he?'

'Aye. He went outside to smoke. Can ye believe it?'

McGray frowned deeply. *He went outside to smoke?* Why on earth would anyone do that?'

'We found it very strange too, but that's what he did. He stayed out there for a while 'n' then came back in demanding a pint.'

'How long was a while?' McGray asked.

'Oh, dunno, sir. Ten, fifteen minutes?'

'What did McEwan do after that?'

Mrs Dailey shrugged. 'Just drank. Spilled quite a bit on

himself – and then went out without saying a word. He seemed in a hurry.'

Mr Dailey shook his head. 'I remember we joked he needed to kick up a stink.'

McGray half smiled.

Then Mrs Dailey opened her eyes wide. 'Oh, and I did see him then, through the kitchen's window – I was doing the last dishes o' the day. He took the footpath that goes into the woods.' She pointed west, in the direction of the Kolomans' manor. 'I lost sight o' him when he went into the forest. I remember he was smoking; the light o' his cigar was the last of him I saw.'

'What time was this?' McGray asked.

'Oh, *that* I remember,' said the woman. 'It must have been a quarter past nine. I checked the clock after I did the dishes.'

McGray sat back, interlacing his fingers. 'From what we've gathered, the murder must've happened merely minutes after that.'

Mrs Dailey put a hand to her chest.

'We heard nothing,' Mr Dailey said immediately, 'and we went to bed soon after. As I told ye, we thought he'd come back late 'n' was still in his room. Ye and yer English colleague were s'posed to meet him here today.'

McGray pondered for a moment. Why would McEwan go out to smoke if he'd been doing so in his room? Had he been waiting for someone? If so, he had probably gone out to meet that person. His killer, perhaps?

'Do youse have any other guests?'

'No, sir,' said Mrs Dailey. 'It's been awfully quiet this past fortnight.'

McGray nodded. 'Thanks, youse have been very helpful. All I've left to do is go to that island. The boat –'

Miss Fletcher rose. 'I'll go and get it ready, sir.' She bowed and left, looking rather nervous. Perhaps she feared what McGray might ask her whilst they were alone in the boat.

Mr and Mrs Dailey also excused themselves and went to the back rooms, leaving McGray momentarily alone.

He went to the large bay window and saw Miss Fletcher walk to the inn's small piers, where a few boats, surely for guests, swayed gently. He looked up and let out a sigh at the mesmerizing landscape. The islands' pine trees, tall and straight above the mist, suddenly looked like the bars of a cage full of secrets.

19

I rose naturally a few minutes before nine o'clock. I had slept for only about three hours but I felt a new man, and quite hungry. Instead of ringing the bell I decided to wash, dress and go downstairs directly. I already had a plan of action.

The first thing I did was check on Benjamin. Unlike McGray, I was not happy merely hearing his voice; I wanted to *see* him.

As soon as he opened the door I realized the boy had not rested at all. His eyes were reddened, as if he'd cried most of the night, and his skin looked pale and dry.

His small oil lamp was still by the windowsill, and next to it I saw a big book. I noticed a corner of its leather cover was slightly scorched, and I pictured Benjamin trying to read with shaking hands, so nervous he'd not noticed the tome was singeing.

'Is everything all right?' I asked him.

He shook his head shyly, barely meeting my eyes. 'I . . . I heard a lot of rattle last night, sir. Something bad happened?'

I felt so sorry to break yet more bad news to him, but it had to be done. And I could not think of a soft way to put it.

'I am afraid so. The local constable has been murdered.'

Benjamin sat on the edge of the bed, folded his long hands together and looked at me with a very puzzling face. His frown deepened a little, but I could not tell what his actual sentiment was. Shock, perhaps.

'It happened last night,' I added, since he remained silent. 'While your twin cousins were outside and the rest of us . . .'

Something struck me then.

Benjamin had not been accounted for either. He'd been locked in this room – allegedly. He'd had the keys and would have been able to go out if he wished. The bed sheets were a tangle, suggesting he'd spent hours tossing and turning, but it would take seconds to mess a few layers of linen. He did not look at all like a murderer, but in my experience that meant nothing.

'. . . the rest of us were here in the house,' I went on, concealing my sudden suspicions for the time being.

Benjamin lowered his face and stared hard at his hands. 'Was that the constable who refused to investigate the threat against me? The one who also refused to help my mother years ago?'

So McGray had told him absolutely everything.

'Yes. Constable McEwan.'

After another moment of silence he asked, 'Do you think he found out something about that threat? Something that put him in danger?'

'I have thought of that, but recalling the man's unmitigated apathy I find it extremely unlikely.' I saw him twist his mouth, unconvinced. 'We will be investigating, and my good uncle is on his way to Kin . . . Kinloo . . .'

'Kinlochewe.'

'Yes, to send a telegram calling for reinforcements. As soon as they arrive I will suggest you leave the manor, given the circumstances, until we shed light on these deaths.'

Benjamin rubbed his face, trying to fend off tears. 'What do you want me to do in the meantime? Should I stay here, locked up all day?'

I sighed. 'I know it is difficult, but I would strongly suggest so.' He was now a suspect too (he even had a clear motive, being aware of how McEwan had mistreated Miss Fletcher), so I needed him close at hand. 'Open that door only for Inspector McGray or myself. Understood?'

'Yes.'

'I will come back in a few moments with some food –'

'Thank you, sir, but don't bother. I couldn't eat anything.'

'I can imagine, but I will still bring you something. You should keep up your strength.'

I left then, and walked away only after I heard him turn the key.

The house was deserted, every corridor and room downstairs. For a moment I thought every soul in the manor had fled, until I walked into the dining room and heard faint voices. They came from the kitchen.

I descended the narrow stairs that led there, and found the spacious room bustling with life.

The impossibly wide cook was by the fire, peeling potatoes with a tiny blade that was almost lost in her chubby fingers. The maid Tamlyn was having some porridge, talking worriedly to Mrs Glenister. The latter was preparing a silver tray with bread, tea and jams, perhaps for Mrs Koloman. Boyde was in the centre of the room, turning the lever of a butter-maker as quickly as if his life depended on it; the young man was sweating like a mule, his body odour overpowering all other scents in the kitchen – even though Mrs Plunket was simmering some sort of pungent curry.

Everyone went quiet as soon as I walked in, and even though I have met my share of uncomfortable silences, this one was particularly caustic. They all stared at me, except for

Tamlyn, who lowered her face so far she nearly dunked her nose in the porridge.

'Keep turning that,' Mrs Plunket said, pointing at Boyde with her shiny knife.

'How may we help you?' Mrs Glenister asked, standing upright and looking very tall with her enormous beehive.

'I would like some breakfast. And prepare trays for Benjamin, Mr Dominik and Calcraft. I will unlock their doors for you.'

'Tamlyn will see to that,' said old Glenister as she picked up the tray. 'My mistress cannot wait.'

I simply stepped aside. She was one of those maids who fancied themselves in command of their masters.

Tamlyn hurriedly arranged pots, jars and trays. The scrutinizing eyes of the other servants and the noise of the butter-maker made me edgy, so I decided to wait in the breakfast parlour. When my food came I ate at full speed, hardly tasting what I had, and then Tamlyn took me to Dominik's bedroom. I knocked at the door with little delicacy, and even before I heard him reply I unlocked and opened the door.

'Breakfast is served,' I said, inexpressive.

The room stank of tobacco, a thin cloud of smoke hovering about the ceiling. Dominik sat by the window, a cigarette in his hand, staring at Loch Maree. He was wrapped in a purple brocade dressing gown, the collar and cuffs trimmed with black fur. That and his brooding pose made him look very much the lord of the manor.

Not yet, I thought, as Tamlyn arranged the tray and the coffee pot. She did her job silently and left the room in a hurry.

'Have a seat, Inspector,' Dominik said with a mocking smile. 'Would you like some coffee? A cigar? Tyrannical control over my parents' home?'

I did take a seat, but there was no time for petty games. 'Dominik, and excuse me if I use your Christian name' – I did not want him to think he inspired too much reverence – 'you are not a simple-minded man. You know why we had to lock you away.' He simply sipped his coffee and I took his silence as assent. 'Now, I will give you a fair chance to redeem yourself. Tell me what you and Calcraft were doing out there last night. Tell me nothing but the truth, and give me convincing evidence if you can.'

I waited while Dominik helped himself to food and more coffee. Just as I was about to stand up and leave he spoke.

'I went to the cellar to check that the wines had been properly stored. I also brought an important cargo of Sicilian lemons –'

I tilted my head. 'I thought you travelled from Norway.'

'Indeed. I had them shipped especially. My mother and sisters are very fond of their lemon curd and I like to pamper them, as you have seen. Mrs Plunket has a secret recipe and –'

'Do not distract me with those lemons. Get to the point.'

'Calcraft helped me take them to the coolest pantry. He did a very good job throughout this trip – he always does – so I took a couple of bottles and we went to have a drink outside.'

'Because . . . you could not drink indoors?'

Dominik smiled. 'I believe I am free to drink wherever I want in my father's estate.'

'Dominik, you know what I mean. Would you please –'

He raised his voice. 'My mother is not fond of Calcraft, if you must know.'

'Is she not? May I ask why?'

Dominik shrugged. 'Women. Apparently, Calcraft made a few *insensitive* remarks at the height of Miss Fletcher's . . .

troubles. My mother did not like it so she sent him away with my uncle. As you know, he travelled a good deal, just as I do now. Calcraft became a proficient sailor very quickly, and Uncle Maximilian told me he was very loyal, so I put him in charge of my own ship when I was old enough to travel on my own.'

I nodded. 'So you two went to have a drink outside, away from the disapproving eyes of your mother.'

'Yes.'

'Nobody in your household saw you. They would have told me by now.'

Dominik shrugged again. 'I had no idea any of this was about to happen. I did not care to leave witnesses.'

'Where exactly did you go?'

'We went across the front gardens and then to a tiny bay on the westernmost part of our lands.'

'You both became very intoxicated very quickly.'

'Inspector, again, I am free to drink at whatever speed I like.'

I took a deep breath. If Dominik was telling the truth, he and Calcraft had been at the opposite end of the Kolomans' grounds, as far as possible from the crime scene as they could reasonably have been. *If* he was telling the truth.

'You cannot prove any of that,' I said.

Dominik pushed his cigarette into a heaving ashtray. I noticed small print on the singed paper, and recognized biblical lines. 'The only evidence you might find are a few empty bottles we left on the spot and a few cigarette ends. You'll know they are mine because I use this paper,' and he pulled the little Bible from his pocket. Even with it still unopened I could see pages had been torn out indiscriminately. 'We have good servants, but I doubt they sweep and mop every square inch of the grounds.'

I nodded. 'Good. I shall look for those bottles.'

'And let me out?'

'Let us hope so, Dominik.' I shifted in my seat. 'One more thing.'

'Yes?'

'I noticed you showing a certain hostility towards your cousin.'

'Hostility! I received the boy as warmly as possible. Ask your gaudy, tartan-clad clown of a colleague. Whenever I tried to talk or joke the silly boy just stood there all taut, as if I spoke bloody Cantonese.'

'He had witnessed a murder a few hours earlier. The murder of not just any person but the man who raised him.'

'Is that supposed to be my fault?'

I nearly smiled, thinking it might be. 'Can you tell me the exact time your steamer docked in Thurso?'

He tossed his head back and cackled. 'Oh, this is bloody unbelievable! Will you tell me now I also killed the stupid priest?' He noticed I was studying his face, for he became serious. 'Can you tell me why I'd want to murder two lowly, inconsequential men?'

I could not, but I decided not to answer that directly. 'There is another matter, something that must be in your mind. All of a sudden, your inheritance will go from one third to one sixth of your family's estate. Benjamin is to receive half. Does that not bother you?'

Dominik raised both arms, showing off his broad sleeves and looking around at the richly carved furnishings. 'Does it look like we are short of money, Inspector?'

I sighed. 'In my experience, the more riches people gather, the more they seem to want.'

Dominik let out another cackle. 'Thank you for your

insight, sir. You are doubtless a worldwide authority on the intricacies of the human condition.'

I stood up. I would take no more of his insolence. 'Thank you, Dominik. That will be all. You have made many, many things clear to me – more than you think.' I went to the door and manifestly produced the set of keys. 'If I find the remains of your moonlight drinks with your servant, I shall let you know.'

I slammed the door and locked it as noisily as the key permitted. At the moment I did not have the temper to question Calcraft, whom I expected to be even more brazen, so I decided I'd look at the grounds and –

I started. Tamlyn stood in the corridor, silent and terribly pale. She was staring at me, her mouth opening and closing, but no sound came out.

'Are you all right, girl?'

She looked in every direction and came closer. 'Sir, there's something I need to tell you.'

'Go ahead.'

Tamlyn cast a fearful look at Dominik's door. I asked her to follow me and we went to the end of the corridor, away from any of the rooms. 'Speak freely.'

She gulped, her eyes on the wide windows that looked over the gardens. 'Promise me –'

'I will tell no one you spoke to me. You have my word. Now, tell me.'

Tamlyn took a deep breath, her hands at her chest. 'I gave Miss Veronika a sponge bath just before you saw her. Do you remember?' I nodded. I had seen her walk out of the girl's bedroom with a basin full of scented water. 'Well . . . I saw . . . something . . .'

Her eyes pooled with tears and she pressed the back of her hand to her forehead.

'Tell me,' I encouraged her, as soothingly as possible. 'You saw something . . . What was it?'

Another deep breath. 'Something . . . had bit her.'

'*Bit* her!'

She nodded frantically, tears now rolling freely. 'Something bit her belly. I saw marks all over.'

20

McGray felt queasy almost as soon as he set foot on the boat, but it would not be as bad as the paralysing sickness he'd felt on the sea. Despite the gloomy weather, the loch was calm; the mist had thickened and then settled stubbornly, the lack of wind keeping it in place. And Miss Fletcher seemed to recognize his discomfort, so she rowed carefully.

'We need to see the Nellys family on Juniper Island first,' she said. 'They will take us to the old Mr Nellys; he doesn't like strangers.'

'All righty,' McGray answered, discreetly assessing the tall woman's countenance. Her eyes were red; she'd probably not slept at all, like most in the manor. Still, she rowed with steadfast strokes and kept a straight face. That woman was a sturdy oak.

'How are ye, lass?'

She looked at McGray without expression. 'What do you mean, sir?'

'Cannae be easy, having yer son back and ye've not even talked to him.'

Miss Fletcher pulled the oars with sudden strength. McGray instantly felt a wave of nausea and had to grasp the gunwale.

'He's not mine any more. That was the deal.'

'Aye, I ken that, but last night ye ran like the wind when ye saw him.'

Miss Fletcher glared at him, only just managing to blink

her tears away. Sorrow and anger were bursting out together. 'I can't face him! I thought I could, but I was fooling myself. As soon as I saw him walk in I wanted to run to him, tell him that –' She let go of the oars and took a deep breath. 'He looks just like my late father . . . Their eyes . . .'

The woman gulped, shook her head and put her severe face back on.

'Ye cannae hide for ever, hen. Yer son will eventually see ye, and when that happens –'

Miss Fletcher resumed the rowing, nearly capsizing the boat. 'Sir, I'd rather we didn't talk about that any more. With all due respect, you won't hear me asking you how difficult it's been dealing with your sister's ailment.'

McGray gagged just then, unable to give her a proper reply. Miss Fletcher looked away, pretending her full attention was now on the waters. She rowed faster, which did not help McGray's nausea. He thought he perhaps should have started with the more crucial questions.

'Tell me what . . .' He repressed a retch. 'Tell me what . . .' Another one. Miss Fletcher had to halt. McGray shut his eyes, waiting for the boat to stop swaying. 'Damn, this must be what Percy feels like whenever he sets foot in the Ensign Ewart pub!'

Miss Fletcher made no comment. She rested her arms on her knees and waited.

McGray cleared his throat. 'Tell me what happened last night, when ye and the lassies found the constable.'

She looked back at him with evaluating eyes. 'We just found him. Well, the girls were the first ones to see him; they were walking ahead of me.'

'Did ye –' McGray covered his mouth with a clenched fist, not quite recovered yet.

'If you don't mind, I am going to guess your questions,' she said, resuming the rowing, albeit at a much slower pace. 'Did we see anyone? No, we thought we were all alone in the woodland. Did we notice anything out of place? No, we did not. Did we touch or move or' – she gave McGray the sternest of looks – '*do* anything? No.'

She sped up after that, and McGray found it impossible to speak again. He breathed deeply and fixed his eyes on the mist ahead. He could see the outlines of all the mountains and the islands, moving closer at a seemingly sluggish pace. Everything looked grey, indistinct, and this, combined with his dizziness, made McGray feel as if they were entering a land of ghosts.

They reached the craggy edge of Juniper Island: imposing rocks jutting up like walls, eroded by wind and rain, with the hardy roots of pine trees growing into every crack and crevice.

Miss Fletcher turned the boat and guided it in between the rocky shore and a small islet. The fog was thicker there, and it took McGray a moment to see they were heading towards a small sandy beach.

'They're waiting for us,' said Miss Fletcher, but McGray had to blink before he could make anything out.

As if materializing slowly from thin air, three figures became darker and clearer. McGray recognized two females of similar height, standing on either side of a very tall, lanky man. They all wore hoods, their faces obscured further by the fog.

The wind began to blow and McGray felt a sudden chill. He was momentarily surprised by those ghostly figures standing there, expecting their arrival, before he remembered that this meeting had been agreed a few days earlier. The Nellyses would not even know about the death of the constable – unless they were involved. McGray could not stop thinking of that fleeting light he'd seen disappear over the dark waters the night before.

The soft touch of the boat against the sandy beach and the ensuing stillness were a welcome relief. Miss Fletcher jumped out and offered McGray a hand. He was in no state to refuse help. Even when his boots sank in the wet sand and the figures approached, he still could not make out their faces with any clarity. He could see only noses and cheekbones, all very pale.

The woman on the right, thinner than the other, came closer and removed her hood. McGray had to repress a gasp.

The woman's skin had been ravaged by the elements: it was leathery, dry, wrinkled and blotchy, as if it had withstood years of rashes and burns. Her hair, though arranged in an elegant chignon, was grey and brittle, and her eyes were framed by almost black rings. Those eyes, of a blue so pale they appeared nearly white, caught McGray's attention; their expression was of sheer exhaustion, as if she'd lived for thousands of years knowing nothing but misery.

She offered a gloved hand. 'Amanda Nellys. Welcome to our island.' Even through the glove, her hand felt bony and fragile. 'These are my children, Lazarus and Helena.'

The tall man pulled his hood back, but the face McGray saw looked more like the woman's brother. His skin was only a little less wrinkled but his cheeks were, if possible, even more hollow. He had the same pale-blue eyes, but instead of tiredness, his glowed with resentment. McGray could but guess his age.

The daughter, to his surprise, looked fifteen or sixteen. She shared the clear eyes and the general features of the other two, but her cheeks were rounded and her skin, though almost as pale, was smooth and unblemished.

'Pleased to meet you,' she whispered in a shy voice. Her brother neither spoke nor offered a hand; he simply stared at McGray, as if gauging him.

'Pleased to meet youse too,' said McGray, not quite able to smile at them. 'Mrs Nellys, can we have a wee chat? There's been a . . . development.'

'Of course. Please follow us. And mind where you tread; the ground is quite marshy here.'

Miss Fletcher tied up the boat, pulled out a sack of provisions she'd brought from the Kolomans' manor, and hailed the eerie family with a fondness McGray found surprising. The plump girl even ran to her and embraced her, and they whispered and giggled until they noticed McGray's confounded stare. Miss Fletcher cleared her throat and they set off.

McGray followed the family up a steep hill. The squishy ground gave under his boots, and very soon the grass, heathers and juniper bushes were as tall as his waist – no wonder the place was called Juniper Island.

When they reached the top of the hill he had a full view. The woods were not as dense as they were on the southern shore; instead, the terrain looked like alpine grassland. The craggy mountains on the other side of the lake enhanced that illusion.

Mrs Nellys walked on to a footpath and led the way to a flimsy-looking fence. Behind it the grass was much shorter than on the rest of the island, and McGray soon understood why.

The fenced land was home to a herd of snow-white goats, which seemed to graze happily as far as the eye could see. The Nellyses went through a little gate, and when McGray followed, he again had to contain a gasp.

All the goats had at least one bat clinging to their bodies.

Some were simply perched on the goats' backs, standing straight and almost proudly, wrapped in their own wings. Others crawled furtively to the animals' necks and joints, looking for veins they could bite. McGray shuddered when he saw a goat carrying three bats, all clustered around a red spot on its neck.

McGray gulped. 'Yer beasts . . .'

'Never mind them,' said Mrs Nellys with a dismissive wave. 'We're taking care of that pest.'

Ahead of them there was a small loch – a loch within the island – and in the centre of that loch there was a tiny islet, no more than ten feet wide and bursting with heathers and young pines.

'The Celts said the queen of the faeries had her castle there,' said Helena.

Lazarus pulled her by the arm. 'Leave the man alone. Policemen don't believe in all that nonsense.'

McGray smiled and winked at the girl, who blushed.

Beyond the loch-within-a-loch there was a small dwelling of whitewashed stone and slate roofs. It had a crooked chimney emitting a trickle of smoke, and it was surrounded by a neat vegetable patch. On all the windowsills there were pots of bushy herbs. McGray found it rather charming; Frey, on the other hand, would have called it 'a picturesque slum'.

Mrs Nellys led them into a cavernous room that was at once kitchen, workshop, dining and living room. The central table was crammed with tools, vegetables and dried herbs; a pot was bubbling over the fire, and next to it there were several baskets and demijohns disposed around a low stool.

It was a humble dwelling, and the interior was quite cold despite the crackling fire. McGray assumed it would be a warm place in winter, but in summer the thick stones refused to let the heat in.

'Have a seat,' Mrs Nellys offered, going to the fire to stir the pot. She was curdling milk to make cheese.

'You've not finished with that gin,' Lazarus told his sister, who sat by one of the baskets of juniper berries. The girl patiently pierced them with a needle one by one before putting them in a demijohn full of clear spirit.

Miss Fletcher showed them the sack of provisions. 'Mrs Koloman sends you this. There's flour, eggs, honey and some lard.'

'We've told her we need nothing,' Lazarus snapped.

His mother ignored him. 'Thank you, Millie. Just leave it in the cupboard.'

So she did, pulling out a small parcel wrapped with creased, probably reused brown paper. 'And this is from me.'

After carefully placing the little parcel on the shelf she sat with McGray at the main table.

'Would you like something to drink?' Mrs Nellys offered. McGray wanted to refuse, but Lazarus was already pouring him a small measure of gin.

'We'll take you to our father in a moment,' he said, picking up a long knife he'd been sharpening. 'I just need to finish off a few things.'

'Just as well,' said McGray, sniffing the drink. The scent was excellent: crisp and herbal. 'I'm afraid we have to give youse some bad news.' All three faces looked at him. McGray breathed in, not knowing what to expect. 'Constable McEwan died last night.'

Mrs Nellys's jaw dropped, as did the wooden spoon into the pot. The woman's eyes immediately went to her son. She was about to tell him something, but covered her mouth in time. Slightly flushed, she looked at McGray. 'He *died*? How?'

McGray did not blink. 'Murdered.'

Lazarus was motionless, his fingers tense on the knife. His voice went down an octave. 'Helena, collect the guano.'

'But I just started –'

'*Go!*'

Miss Fletcher looked at the girl with a reassuring smile. 'Do as your brother says, darling. I'll come and see you in a minute.'

Helena had no choice and banged out of the house, stamping her feet. Mrs Nellys took the pot off the fire and sat at the table, whilst McGray told them briefly what had happened.

Lazarus grimaced, looking quite stressed, and his mother shook her head, but neither seemed saddened in the slightest.

'We probably met the man less than five times in twenty years,' was the first thing Mrs Nellys could say.

'You were the lucky ones,' Miss Fletcher said bitterly.

McGray took his time to savour one last sip of that outstanding gin. He knew the pleasantries would end as soon as he spoke.

'My colleague 'n' me saw the body last night . . .' McGray kept an eye on Lazarus's hand, which was popping veins as he clenched the knife harder and harder. 'We saw – nae, we *chased* someone. Someone was in the woods around the time the constable was murdered – someone who took a wee boat 'n' sailed on to the loch.'

Mrs Nellys held her breath. The knife caught a glimmer from the fire.

McGray concluded: 'This is the closest dwelling to the scene – by boat.'

Lazarus stared at the blade, feeling the edge with his fingertip. The silence was absolute; even the fire seemed to have halted its crackling.

The man looked at McGray. He must have been in his late twenties but he appeared twice that age. An inexplicable anger was boiling in his eyes.

And then he attacked.

21

With a swift push Lazarus lifted the table and all its contents rained down on to McGray, who barely had time to cover his face with his forearms. The mother yelped. As McGray pushed the battered table away he had a glimpse of Lazarus crossing the threshold.

'Stay here!' he shouted at the women, unsheathing his gun and sprinting across the vegetable garden.

A frightened Helena was crouching on the ground, picking up whitish bat droppings.

'Where did he go?' McGray yelled.

The girl pointed to the grassland, northwards, and McGray saw Lazarus running like the wind through the herd of goats. He followed.

'*Stop!*' McGray roared, but Lazarus wove between the animals with an agility McGray had not expected, familiar with every mound and dent in the terrain. 'I'm armed!' McGray shouted, and as a warning he shot into the air.

A mistake.

A cloud of scared bats rose up, their dark wings filling the sky and flapping madly all around him. McGray ran on, protecting his face and trying to keep his eyes on Lazarus. Through the mess of fluttering wings he saw the man's long legs, much further away than he'd –

McGray let out a squeal. One of the bats clung to his raised arm and McGray had a disturbing view of its beady eyes, hog-like nose and muzzle smeared with blood and dribble.

He jerked his arm as he ran, never slowing down, and when the bat finally let go McGray looked ahead. Lazarus had gone.

The terrain rose in a steep slope and McGray ran until his legs burned. He reached the top and looked in every direction. Another bat flew towards him, but he threw it a sideways punch and the animal spun in the air.

McGray looked back at the house and saw Miss Fletcher running after him, scaring the bats away with her brawny arms. He saw the goats dotted all over the field, and then looked ahead again, where the ground descended rapidly towards a narrow bay. That side of the island was rocky and dense with conifers. McGray squinted, managed to make out a dilapidated boat tied to a tree and, not waiting to spot Lazarus, he rushed in that direction.

He stumbled between sharp rocks and thorny pine trees, his feet struggling to find footholds. At least the bats didn't venture here. His boot sank into a crack in the rocks, his foot twisted and before he knew it his entire body was falling forward, only to be stopped abruptly by a thick dead trunk.

McGray felt the impact throughout his body. He saw stars and his gun rolling down the hill. And then his eyes found Lazarus. The dark figure was leaping expertly from rock to rock, getting closer and closer to the boat.

Grunting, McGray pushed himself from the trunk and thrust himself onward recklessly, not looking where he stepped or paying attention to the searing pain in his ankle. Lazarus had already reached the shore.

'*Stop!*' McGray hollered, covering the distance as fast as he could. Lazarus looked back and nearly lost his balance. His long arms twirled and his torso swayed, but his feet remained firmly in place.

'Get away!' He brandished the long knife he'd been sharpening and jumped into the boat, which was tethered to a jutting stone. Lazarus gave the rope a swift pull and the knot came undone at once.

McGray pictured the knot that had held McEwan's corpse, and right then lost his footing. He stumbled, fell on his knees, grunted in frustration and then dragged himself on all fours over the rocks. Lazarus was but a few yards ahead now, the boat slowly drifting away. McGray could see his bony hands, one clasping the knife and the other pulling the rope. The frayed end was still on the rock, sliding quickly towards the water. It fell into the loch.

McGray flung himself forward, plunged his hand into the cold water, and his heart skipped a beat as his fingers touched the fibres. He got hold of a few threads, pulled them up and then used his left hand to seize the rope firmly.

'*No!*' Lazarus shrieked, falling on his rump when McGray pulled the boat back. He rubbed the knife against his end of the rope, the strands snapping one by one as McGray pulled the boat towards himself, grunting with all his might.

The boat hit the rocks and McGray stretched out a hand, but Lazarus stabbed at it.

McGray wound the rope around his wrist, locking it firmly. 'Don't do something even more stupid, laddie.'

Lazarus bared his yellowed teeth and kept the knife up high. 'I'm not the stupid one right now!'

McGray took a step towards him just as Lazarus made another stab. McGray pulled the rope in one swift move, and Lazarus nearly fell again. As he wildly tried to stab at Nine-Nails he completely lost his balance. McGray leaned forward and grabbed the man's collar, but then Lazarus clutched him by the wrist, plunging both men into the water.

It was as cold as McGray expected, and he heard himself panting desperately.

He saw the knife, merely inches from his face. He had a fleeting memory of another blade: the one wielded by his own sister years ago.

A wave of fire grew from within his chest. With more dexterity than he knew himself capable of, he seized Lazarus's wrist and banged it against the rock. The man howled in pain and the knife slid from his grip.

McGray saw Lazarus's scared face, wrinkled and pale, and threw a punch for good measure. The man's limbs went lax. McGray seized him by the collar and swam to a flat, smooth stone, pushing the whimpering Lazarus out of the water, before struggling out himself. He lay on the stone, taking glorious deep breaths.

At last McGray rose, wiped the water off his face and said: 'Consider yerself under arrest.'

McGray and Miss Fletcher dragged Lazarus back to the house. Nine-Nails had used a length of the man's own rope to tie him up, and although Miss Fletcher had helped, she'd done so with reluctance. As they walked across the grassland, where the bats were slowly returning to their living perches, she tenderly wiped the blood from Lazarus's nose. McGray gave her a quizzical look; he'd never imagined she'd be capable of such delicate movements – then again, people made similar assumptions about him.

She noticed his expression and blushed. 'I don't want his mother to see him like this.'

But a clean face was little consolation. Mrs Nellys ran out

of her little house, lifting her hem and trampling her own garden.

'He did nothing!' was her anguished shout, her face smothered in tears. Helena came close behind, her face red, crying, 'No, don't take him!'

McGray felt terribly sorry for them. He spoke as calmly as his own racing heart allowed.

'Missus, a man who's done nothing wouldnae run away like that.'

'He's done nothing!' Mrs Nellys whimpered again, cradling her son's face in her hands. 'Tell them, Lazarus! *Tell them* you've done nothing wrong!'

Lazarus gave her the saddest, most devastated look but didn't speak.

'He went out last night, didnae he?'

That silenced the women's cries. They lived together in that tiny place; they knew he had. McGray felt wretched.

'There'll be an inquest in due course,' he said. 'We've telegrammed our superiors. Yer son will have a chance to defend himself then.'

'What will you do to him in the meantime?' the distraught mother asked.

'I'm afraid we need to keep him in custody. There are two other suspects, missus. We're keeping them at the Kolomans' manor.'

Mrs Nellys lifted her chin, going from devastated to indignant in a blink. 'You're *not* taking my son there!'

'I'm sorry, missus. I must.'

She was about to protest again, but forced a deep breath. Her face furrowed even more as she struggled to compose herself. McGray partly understood why her face was so ravaged.

'Who are the other suspects?' she asked.

McGray didn't want to answer, but decided they had the right to know.

'Dominik Koloman and a servant o' his. One Calcraft.'

The wrinkles deepened further, her indignation growing. 'They'll deceive you all. They'll make you think my son is guilty. Promise me you'll tread carefully. *Promise me!*'

Helena cried louder than before. Miss Fletcher went to her and put her arm around the girl's shoulders, whispering something in her ear.

Mrs Nellys had the most drilling eyes, so McGray had to steel himself.

'I'll promise ye it will be a fair inquest.'

The woman closed her eyes and turned her face away.

'I'll keep you up to date,' said Miss Fletcher. She kissed Helena's forehead gently and patted Mrs Nellys on the back. 'And I'll see Lazarus is well looked after. You know I will.'

As soon as they moved, Mrs Nellys stepped up to her son, kissed his hand and mouthed, 'You'll be fine.' And then she turned on her heel, unable to watch them go.

McGray held on to Lazarus firmly and they headed back to the beach.

'Ye did well to keep silent,' said McGray as soon as the Nellyses' dwelling was out of sight. 'Yer mum 'n' sis don't need to ken the details.'

Lazarus kept his face down, staring at the uneven ground. 'I didn't kill him.'

'We'll find out, laddie. Right now I need to ask ye other questions. About a completely different matter.'

Lazarus looked at him with confusion. 'My father?'

'Aye. We'll do a small detour.' McGray could almost hear Frey tearing his robes because he was about to take a freshly arrested man on a boat trip. He turned to Miss Fletcher, who was already pushing the boat into the water. 'Lass, take us to Isle Maree.'

Again, she looked hesitant, but she said nothing. Lazarus didn't protest either when McGray pushed him into the boat. Nine-Nails felt queasy as soon as he set a boot in the swaying vessel, and it became worse when Miss Fletcher began to row.

'Wait!' they heard someone shout in the distance. McGray turned and saw Helena running down the hill. Like her brother, she knew every inch of the terrain by heart.

The girl reached them quickly, water up to her knees.

'You dropped this, sir.'

And she handed McGray his gun. He received it, disconcerted. 'Thanks, lassie.'

'You will need it,' she said, and she followed them with her eyes as they sailed away, until the fog between them turned her into a blurry, milky ghost.

22

Miss Fletcher took all her frustration out on the loch, rowing fitfully and grunting with each pull.

McGray pressed a fist to his mouth, struggling to keep his breakfast in his stomach. He was only glad Lazarus faced the other way.

The fog had not dissipated at all. If anything, McGray thought, it had become thicker, and when Isle Maree came into view it was but a grey dome of trees in the distance.

'They've done it again,' said Miss Fletcher.

It took McGray a moment to see what she meant. After they had advanced a dozen yards or so, two tiny specks of golden light became visible. The fuzzy lights appeared to be suspended in the air, completely still, like ominous eyes expecting their arrival. Lazarus gasped.

McGray thought he saw a pale face emerge around the lights. Only when Miss Fletcher secured the boat on the pebbly beach did he realize what it really was: a deer skull, nailed to the trunk of an oak. The lights were two candles ensconced in the otherwise empty sockets. Somehow – perhaps combined with his queasiness – the sight made him shiver, and as soon as he set foot on the ground he felt a stabbing oppression in his chest. The discomfort did not fade for as long as he stayed on that island.

'I wouldnae like to live in this place.'

Miss Fletcher helped Lazarus out of the boat.

'So you feel it too?' he said. 'Not everybody does.'

Miss Fletcher scowled. Of the three, she looked the most affected.

McGray held Lazarus by the thick knot around his wrists. 'Now take me to the well, lad.' And he let the gaunt man lead the way. McGray had never imagined that his visit to Isle Maree would be guided by a tied-up murder suspect.

They reached the well, which was just as Frey had described it: an ordinary hole in the ground lined with grey stone. Even McGray couldn't help finding it disappointing.

'This is it,' whispered Lazarus. 'The waters that cured my father.'

McGray pushed Lazarus towards Miss Fletcher. 'Watch over him.' He felt in his breast pocket. He'd taken a little vial from the Orkney nurses and was happy to find it, even after the skirmish in the water. McGray pulled it out and knelt next to the well.

Lazarus took a step forward. 'You can't take anything off this island! You'll be cursed.'

'I'm already cursed, laddie.' And McGray plunged his arm into the well. He felt the cool water, as still as a pond, and waited until the vial stopped bubbling.

'I'm talking about a terrible curse,' Lazarus insisted. 'Real tragedies. Madness. Death.'

McGray smiled with bitterness. He sealed the vial and shoved it back into the same pocket. 'Told ye, lad. I'm already cursed.'

As he said that he thought of Frey's words about the blood baths, those baths that might be the actual cure for madness. The idea had been haunting him since he'd first seen the constable's body, drained of almost all its blood: Could these people be doing something different? Using human blood? Could that be the reason the ritual had worked only for them?

McGray cast Lazarus an evaluating look, debating whether or not to ask him those questions directly. He stepped closer to him and lowered his voice. 'Have ye heard about animal sacrifices? And blood baths?'

Lazarus kept his expression neutral, but when he spoke every muscle on his face looked tense. 'I don't know what you are talking about.'

McGray raised his eyebrows. 'Ye don't?'

They stared at each other in silence, a battle of wills. McGray finally gave in, thinking he'd better talk to the old man first. He would have plenty of time to question Lazarus later. 'Very well, now take me to yer dad.' Lazarus objected, but McGray unsheathed his gun and pressed it against his back.

'I'll mention this at the inquest,' said Lazarus as he led them through the island's small graveyard. 'You're abusing your powers.'

McGray pushed the gun a little harder. 'Do what ye want. And I can tell them I suspect yer dad took a wee boat 'n' did the deed himself.'

He'd not said it seriously, but as he spoke he realized that was also a possibility.

They reached a dwelling that again looked just as Frey had described. However, unlike the well, Frey had made it sound much worse than it really was; the foppish Englishman had obviously not seen how precarious some rural dwellings could be. This hut at least had a working chimney and, given the trickle of smoke, a good fire.

'Is this where St Rufus lived?' McGray asked.

'Yes, but only his foundations are left,' said Miss Fletcher. 'The Nellyses built the top half and the flue.'

'Let me talk to him first,' Lazarus pleaded. 'He doesn't like strangers. This might upset him.'

McGray agreed. After all, he wasn't there to torture people.

Lazarus went to the low, tatty door, and spoke with his cheek pressed against it. 'Father? Are you all right?' No response. 'I've come to see you. Millie's here too.'

McGray heard someone stir inside, and then a latch being pulled. The door, swollen and cracked after years of damp weather, opened a couple of inches. McGray took a step forward but Lazarus threw him a begging look.

'Wait outside for a moment, please. If he becomes upset, he won't be of any help.'

Miss Fletcher wore the same anxious expression.

McGray peered through the gap, but could see only eroded stones lit dimly by a quivering fire. He knew it would take Lazarus but a few seconds to warn his father or instruct him what to say. Then again, there was no use questioning a troubled man. McGray exhaled in frustration.

'Very well, but don't try anything youse might regret. I'll stay right by the door 'n' I'll hear everything youse say.'

'That is fair,' Lazarus said, and then he and Miss Fletcher entered the hut.

McGray watched fragments of their shadows, making out little of what was happening, and heard only murmurs. Lazarus sounded soothing, so did Miss Fletcher, and then came the cries of a husky, muddled voice. All McGray could catch was 'tied'.

Sooner than he expected, Miss Fletcher opened the door. 'Mr Nellys says you may come in, but only if you swear you'll treat his son with dignity.'

'All right, all right. I'm nae beast.'

He had to stoop to pass over the threshold, but then descended a few steps. Almost half the abode was below ground, so that even McGray and Miss Fletcher were able to stand upright. The place stank of mould.

McGray looked around. It was a small, almost cave-like dome that looked more like an oversized kiln. There were no windows; the only light came from the fire and through the cracks in the door. The slabs on the floor were covered with woven mats and blankets, for there were no furnishings. The only contents were a heap of provisions (a sack of potatoes, a block of cheese and old loaves of bread) and a pile of ancient-looking books. The leather of their covers was cracked and eroded, and the pages of the open volumes were crumpled by dampness.

And then he saw Mr Nellys: curled up by the fire, wrapped in at least three ragged blankets and with a heavy book on his lap.

McGray felt almost physical pain at the sight of him. The man's skin was grey, blotchy, as dry as the covers of his books and as pale as that of larvae. There were scant strands of hair left on his head, all white and brittle. He looked frail, broken, and when he shifted his legs – the smallest of movements – his joints cracked. The old man's eyes, on the other hand, were sharp and alert, evaluating McGray from head to toe.

This was the man Miss Fletcher alleged had been brought back from incurable madness, the man who every day drank from the miraculous well.

'Is this the chap?' the old man asked Lazarus, who nodded. Mr Nellys's voice was coarse and throaty but he enunciated clearly. And his stare was so acute even McGray felt slightly daunted.

'Adolphus McGray,' he said, sitting on the floor by the fire. Again he looked around, thinking how to ease his way to the important questions. 'I see ye like reading? What are yer books about?'

Mr Nellys closed the book with a thump. 'Your time here is precious, young man. Don't waste it with small talk. What do you want?'

That might have offended others, but McGray smiled, happy he could be direct. 'I heard ye were ill beyond hope – mental illness – but ye came back. I want to know how.'

Mr Nellys half closed his eyes. McGray felt the man was looking through him.

'Who do you want to help? Someone you love very much, I suppose, if you've come this far.'

McGray saw no reason to lie. 'My sister. She was fifteen when she lost her wits. She . . .' he barely managed to finish the sentence, 'did this.' And he showed his mutilated hand.

Mr Nellys stretched out his own, bony and veiny, and felt McGray's scarred stump, looking at it with stern eyes. 'I'm very sorry.'

'She's nae violent any more, but she has nae spoken in six years. Unless someone stirs her she won't walk or even move. She simply – exists . . .'

He felt a painful lump in his throat.

Mr Nellys nodded, the loose skin on his neck quivering. His eyes were full of understanding. 'Amazing, what one is willing to do for those one loves.' He looked at Lazarus, whose lip was trembling, and then the ancient eyes fixed on McGray again. 'I can see the hope in you. You'll never give up. You'll never accept what's happened. Your brain tells you that you should, but your heart won't let you.'

McGray had to bite his lip, blinking tears away. Nobody had ever described his feelings more accurately, not even himself.

Mr Nellys sighed. He extended a quivering hand, held McGray's and brought it close to his eyes. The man examined the stump, the remaining fingers, the skin on the palm and the back, and then let go. 'I'm sorry for your sister,' he said, and then his voice dropped to a low, gloomy tone. 'But these waters are not for her.'

McGray almost snapped his neck as he looked up. 'What?'

'I'm sorry, son.'

'How . . . how can ye tell?'

'I just can. I am cursed, my son. That's what these waters cured me of.'

'What sort o' curse?'

Lazarus breathed out noisily at this.

'That's my concern, young man,' said Mr Nellys.

'My sister said it was the Devil's work. And I –' McGray swallowed. 'I *saw* the Devil. Don't ye think she might be cursed too?'

The fire crackled and a few sparks fluttered above the hearth, as if the flames themselves reacted at the mention of their master. McGray could almost feel the mystified stares of Lazarus and Miss Fletcher, while the blue eyes of Mr Nellys, as pale as his son's, moved slowly from side to side, visibly confused.

When he looked at McGray his face was again composed. 'Cursed she might be, but that changes nothing. I'm looking at you and I can tell your sister's cross is nothing like mine. This cure is not for her.'

McGray wanted to grab him by his soiled shirt, lift him and shake him until the old man told him what he wanted to hear. He rubbed his stubble until his skin went red. 'Is it because the cure only works on this island? Would she need to live here, just like ye?'

The despair in his voice was evident.

'Listen to my words. Even if you tried, even if you brought her here and fed her the waters and made her live as miserably as I do, it would not work for her.'

'I think yer lying. Ye must be lying!'

'He's telling the truth.' Lazarus intervened. 'We've seen many others come here and try the waters, even a few so-called witches. So far the waters have worked only for my father. I swear on my life.' Lazarus bent to whisper in McGray's ear. 'It might result from the nature of his . . . curse.'

'They might still work on my sister.' Even McGray was aware of the obstinacy in his voice. There was no reply, but all the faces were grim. McGray looked at Miss Fletcher, suddenly feeling a rush of blood to his head. 'Did ye ken this? Had they told ye this, and ye brought me here with lies, just to get a bloody bodyguard for yer son?'

Miss Fletcher went white. 'N-no, sir. I had no idea –'

'Och, *shut up!* I think youse all are a bunch o' bloody liars!' He looked at Lazarus with anger. 'Maybe even murderers.' McGray jumped to his feet, nearly bumping his head against the ceiling and startling everyone. 'Baths in bull's blood. Does that mean anything to youse?'

'We do *not* do that,' said Lazarus through gritted teeth.

'Nae? Cause ye use human blood instead? Is that why ye killed the constable?'

Mr Nellys, the very person they had all feared might go berserk, was the one who raised an appeasing hand. 'Calm down, calm down, young man. What are you talking about?'

Miss Fletcher explained all that had happened, and Mr Nellys, to McGray's astonishment, smiled. 'So that useless ball of slime is finally dead.' He exchanged a meaningful look with Miss Fletcher, and then his eyes went back to

McGray. 'So that's what you're implying? That I bathed in his blood?'

McGray looked at Mr Nellys's limbs, bony and stiff. It was clear he could not have conducted the murder himself, but he might still be the brains behind it all. 'Aye, precisely that. And yer son supplied it.'

The old man's stare became dark, his eyes as piercing as an eagle's. 'Do you really believe that? Or are you lashing out at me because you don't like the answer I gave you? Don't let your own troubles disgrace my family.'

'*My own –*'

'Tell me . . . you and your sister, did you two have happy times?'

McGray clenched his fists, felt the fire in his chest and stomach, and finally forced himself to breathe deeply.

He thought of the lazy summer evenings at their farm-house, the Christmas Eves around the fire, the mornings teaching his sister how to ride and how she had refused to learn side-saddle, how Pansy had been the only person able to make their grumpy father smile –

His voice quivered. 'Aye. Many.'

Mr Nellys spoke warmly. 'Embrace them. Think of them fondly . . . And then move on.'

McGray looked away, wanting to punch the walls until his knuckles bled. He could not move on. Not yet. Perhaps not ever.

Mr Nellys shook his head, looking down. 'I'm sorry you had to come all this way to hear that.'

'*Fuck yerself!*'

His roar made everyone jump. McGray turned to face the wall and covered his eyes.

It had all been useless. As ever.

He felt the vial in his pocket. He would still try it. He would ask Dr Clouston to send it to the Orkneys so that Pansy could drink it. There was nothing to lose. McGray once again forced a deep, calming breath.

'I might come later, see if ye change yer mind and tell me the truth. In the meantime I need to take yer son to the Kolomans' manor.'

Mr Nellys opened his eyes wide. 'You can't take him there. Those people hate us. That damn Konrad in particular –'

'A shame,' McGray snapped, too drained to argue, and he pushed Lazarus to the door. 'Move, ye sod.'

Mr Nellys again raised a hand, rather hesitantly. 'There is one thing . . .' Then he covered his mouth, as if regretting his words, but it was too late. 'There is one thing . . . I do need to tell you.'

McGray looked at the old man. Those pale eyes were full of concern.

'Go on.'

Mr Nellys looked at his son. 'Lazarus, go out, go out.'

McGray nodded at Miss Fletcher and she took Lazarus away. Before she closed the door McGray whispered to her: 'If I come out 'n' see that ye've slipped away with him –'

She pulled away. 'Oh, who do you think I am?' And she nearly smashed the door as she slammed it closed. Suddenly, with the irregular stones and the trembling shadows projected by the fire, the hut looked like the entrance to the underworld.

Mr Nellys waved his hand, asking McGray to lean closer. So he did, just as the man's breathing became more and more agitated.

'What is it?' McGray asked.

Mr Nellys could not look at him. He watched the fire, his

veined eyes glinting. 'The bats . . .' he hissed from his stomach, as if the words refused to be spoken. 'It's . . . it's the bats.'

'What about them?'

McGray was still expecting the man would reveal something about the secret cure. It would not be so. It would be something horrifying.

Mr Nellys gulped. 'They come at night . . . They . . . they come at night sometimes, and . . .'

He could not go on. McGray had to place a hand on the bony shoulder. 'Tell me. It's all right.'

After a pause that felt endless, Mr Nellys spoke.

'They bite me. They come here. They bite me . . . and they drink my blood.'

23

Calcraft sank his teeth into the meat and devoured it with an eagerness that made my stomach churn. A trickle of light from the cellar's window cast banded shadows on his face, which made me think I'd been transported to a mucky jail.

The man's story had corroborated Dominik's point by point, and Calcraft had a prodigious memory; he recalled exactly which bottles they'd taken, which shelves they'd checked, the precise spot in the pantry where they'd placed the barrel with the Sicilian lemons — all of which, without witnesses, was hardly conclusive: they could easily have staged their tracks in advance.

'How long have you worked for the family?'

'Twenty years. More.'

'I have been told Mrs Koloman is not too happy with you.' He simply shrugged, which set my teeth on edge. 'A shrug is not an answer.'

'Perhaps, but she's not my mistress so I don't really care. I work for Master Dominik.'

'I hear you might have made inappropriate comments regarding Miss Fletcher's . . . troubles.'

'I might have. But so did everyone round here. Just go to the pub in Kinlochewe and you'll see.'

'What did you say that made Mrs Koloman so angry?'

Again he shrugged, but this time he added some words. 'Can't really remember. That was years ago.'

I blew out my cheeks in frustration. The man was set to

volunteer nothing. He seemed to be what my florid father calls a *war dog* – a man with no goals or aspirations of his own but loyal to his master beyond any doubt or question.

'Very well, that is all for now. Tamlyn, take that tray away.'

The girl, who had stood in silence, her back against the wall, did so.

'You won't let me out yet?' Calcraft asked. That was his first proactive sentence.

'No,' I said plainly.

'I have to use the privy.'

I was tempted to ignore him and leave, but then thought again. I had enough problems as it was.

I had a quick look out of the window. The day was still overcast and foggy, the islands barely visible from where I stood. I wondered what McGray might have found over there.

I breathed out, thinking I'd better focus on my side of the loch. I felt caged in that manor, completely cut off from the world and surrounded by a handful of people who resented or mistrusted me – and with a lot of pressing work ahead of me. I needed to look at Veronika again (the maid's statement was quite disturbing), examine the corpse in more detail and also inspect the woods. After a quick think I decided to begin with the latter; McEwan's body was safely locked in the cellar and any marks Veronika might have would not disappear in an hour or two. The surroundings, on the other hand, could easily be tampered with.

Boyde offered to fetch my overcoat when he saw me walk to the back door, and also to come with me, which I declined.

I did not need another Koloman war dog looking over my shoulder.

I first went west, to the small bay where Dominik and Calcraft had allegedly got drunk. It was indeed a stunning landscape, with a dramatic view of the islands and the imposing Mount Slioch. Everything around me looked wild, ancient and undisturbed by the hungers of industrialization.

I took a deep breath and enjoyed the peaceful silence for a moment. After all the noise my head had endured for the past couple of days, those few minutes were like a heavenly balm. Dominik at least knew the best of his lands; if I wanted to have a quiet drink with a cigar, I thought, this would definitely be the spot I'd choose. A small stream discharged its waters into the lake, its soft trickle adding to the relaxing quality of the place, which marked the edge of the Kolomans' property.

I kicked at the damp grass and very soon found the exact items listed by the two men: two bottles of wine (a Bordeaux and a Moravian red, as specified by Calcraft), the leftovers of a loaf of bread and the ends of a couple of cigarettes (rolled from Deuteronomy and an unidentified psalm). There were marks on the mud as well: of feet walking round and round the same small area.

That place told me nothing new, nor did it erase any of my existing suspicions, so I did not linger there for long.

I took a different route to the east, following the shore as closely as the terrain allowed. I passed woods and then the northern side of the manor. There was a smooth lawn between the back gardens and the shoreline, and a small pier. I saw no boats there, so perhaps the Kolomans only used it for visitors, or to receive supplies from the two nearby villages.

I recognized the clay footpath I'd seen from the drawing-room window, the path taken last night by Miss Fletcher and the sisters. I walked to the edge of the woods, where Uncle and I had seen them disappear, but before entering the dense forest I looked back at the house.

The windows of the Shadows Room and the main drawing room were perfectly black rectangles, the heavy curtains shut behind them. On the upper level I counted the windows, spotted my own chamber, McGray's, Benjamin's and those of the family. On the top level, behind the dormer window of the astronomical observatory, I saw a whitish figure. As soon as my eyes fell on it the shape disappeared. I could not tell who it had been – a servant, perhaps? – or whether they'd been spying on me.

I shook my head, thinking I did not need more puzzles, and made my way to the small clearing where we'd found McEwan.

I'd not walked more than a few yards when I heard a rustle of clothes, and then a soft, childish voice humming an eerie song. I must have been very tense, for it startled me. The noises, I realized, came from the very direction I was heading.

I rushed forward, and upon passing a thick cluster of trees I found Ellie, the scullery maid. The young girl was on her knees, scrutinizing the ground, her nose mere inches from the dead needles.

My voice came out as a roar. 'What do you think you are doing?'

The girl let out a squeal and jumped to her feet, blushing like a cherry.

I looked at the ground. She had disturbed all the earth and fallen foliage around. It would be useless to look for marks or footprints now.

'*Answer me!*'

My shout made her jump, and only after a long pause did

the girl stammer, 'L-looking for cones, sir. They're good for kindling.'

I looked at her empty hands and then at the mat of needles, peppered with countless pine cones. 'You have very little hands, young lady. How did you intend to take them away?'

Ellie was dumbstruck.

'Who sent you here?' I asked. 'Was it Mr or Mrs Koloman?' She didn't reply. 'Was it Master Dominik?' The young girl began to cry and I lost my temper. 'Good Lord, go back to the manor right now!' She darted away before I'd uttered half the sentence. 'And tell your masters Inspector Frey says nobody is to tamper with these grounds!'

I tried to calm myself as I watched her run. I'd have some very harsh words with the Kolomans.

24

'Would you mind looking at me while we talk?'

Mr Koloman was having his beard groomed. Boyde had trimmed it neatly, and had just wrapped his master's face with a hot towel. For a moment I envied Konrad's bliss, sitting on his bedroom's balcony with a tumbler of gin in one hand, basking in the towel's warmth and scent.

It was a while before he replied. '*Mr* Frey' – so I was not an inspector for him any more – 'I know enough about the law. You and your colleague have no right to carry out these investigations here. I am in no way obliged to answer to you.'

'Mr Koloman –'

'Having said that . . .' He waved a hand to have the towel removed, and again he did not continue until Boyde had thoroughly groomed him. I tapped my foot on the floor throughout. 'Having said that, I am a gentleman, and when the inquest takes place I do not want you to claim I obstructed your work.' He rose, buttoned up his shirt and patted his upper cheeks, now shaven to perfect smoothness, the beard underneath flawless. 'I can assure you I did not send that girl to *tamper* with your precious evidence.'

'Then who did?'

Mr Koloman evaluated himself in the mirror. 'Boyde, the white tie.' He looked at my reflection. 'Have you not asked the girl yourself?'

'I tried. Out there and just now in the kitchen. She is

scared out of her wits. All she says is that nobody asked her to go for the pine cones, that it is part of her duties.'

'And do you believe she lies?'

'Indeed. I have described the scene to you. Her intention was clear.'

Konrad took his time to knot his tie and I pictured myself setting his Austrian-styled moustache on fire.

'Mr Koloman –'

'I will see what I can find out for you. But it will not be a priority.'

'Very well. Freeing your son will not be mine either.'

And I stormed out of the room, still half convinced I'd just talked to the very person who had sent the girl out. What they'd intended to tamper with or conceal, I could not tell.

For the first time that day, as I walked to the main staircase, I heard noises in the manor. Someone was playing the piano, the echoes travelling along the corridor as if the house had been designed for that purpose.

I walked down the steps, suddenly mesmerized by the music. It was the saddest, most melancholic melody, very low chords supporting a sweet, mellow theme, like the trickle of a fountain.

It came from the main drawing room, and when I opened the door I heard the notes in all their richness. The piano's lid was open, and through that gap I saw the troubled face of Natalja. The girl was so focused on her music she did not notice my arrival, and I approached slowly, my steps muffled on the Persian rugs.

The curtains were all open, but the grey landscape, dull and blurry, was a perfect complement to the tune.

As I walked around the piano I noticed the lid had concealed a second person, seated on the stool, right next to her.

It was Benjamin.

'What are you doing here?' I blurted out. Natalja's fingers froze and Benjamin stammered helplessly.

'It's my fault, Mr Frey,' Natalja said, standing up and squeezing her cousin's shoulder. 'I was very lonely. I didn't have anyone else to talk to. I knocked at his door –'

Benjamin rose too. 'I'll go now, Nat. We can chat later.'

He barely met my eyes and almost trotted away. I was about to follow but Natalja snapped at me.

'He can look after himself, you know. Nobody in this house wants to harm him.'

I sneered. 'There is a death threat against your cousin, miss. And a man was slaughtered in your family's grounds. Does that mean nothing to you?'

She threw me a murderous stare, her eyes growing misty, and she sat back down so abruptly the stool nearly tipped backward.

I put a hand to my brow, realizing I'd been a little too harsh. This girl too was going through quite an ordeal – she had seen a slain man last night, her sister was mysteriously ill and her brother was suspected of murder. Not to mention that, isolated as we were, nobody had any place to run.

'I do apologize, miss. I am only doing my job. All I want –'

'All you want is our safety and all that,' she spluttered, fighting back tears. I felt an annoying wave of compassion and brought myself closer. I was about to pat her back but that would have been most improper, so I simply sat on the stool. Too late I realized the seat was barely wide enough for the two of us – Benjamin was very skinny. So close to me, Natalja seemed very small.

I desperately searched for something to say. The first thing I saw was the empty music rack. 'I see you play from memory.'

'I was improvising. Benjamin seemed quite entertained.'

'Improvising? That sounded . . . wonderful.'

She hinted a smile. 'Do you know much about music?'

'A little. My youngest brother is a violin player. I only learned a few chords on the piano, many years ago.'

'Can you play a C minor chord?'

'I . . .'

'Here.' She took my hand. Her touch was so unexpected I jolted. She noticed, but only widened her smile as she placed my fingers on the right keys. 'Play a G, then an E flat, and the higher note is –'

'C, of course.'

'Exactly. Can you play an F minor?'

'Yes, that one I know.'

'Now alternate three Cs and three Fs. Do you like the six-eight tempo?'

'I . . . could not possibly tell.'

She placed her hand on mine and pressed in the right rhythm. It already sounded like a tune. 'It is my favourite tempo. It feels like the swell of the sea.'

Natalja took my other hand, the one closer to her, and placed it on the second chord. When she let go, the back of my hand felt suddenly cold.

'Keep like that, Mr Frey,' she whispered, then looked out of the window with dreamy eyes, her head swaying gently in time with the chords, and then she brought her fingers to the higher notes and filled the room with an enchanting melody I had never heard.

She nodded expressively, indicating me to slow down, and she brought the melody to a sharp, sweet conclusion. The last note lingered in the air for a while and my ear chased it, not wanting it to end.

There was a seemingly endless moment of silence, but Natalja appeared to embrace it.

'I have a very busy mind,' she said at last. 'Music is the only thing that can placate my thoughts.' She looked at me. 'Have you ever felt overwhelmed like that? Your mind so full you can't believe your skull doesn't explode?'

I laughed. 'Have I felt it!'

She smiled and then looked back down at the keyboard, playing what I recognized as one of Mozart's mellow sonatas.

I did not want to ruin this fleeting peace, but I thought there would not be a better moment. 'Miss Natalja, I am . . . worried about your sister.'

She missed a note but resumed immediately. 'So am I. So are we all. But Mama told me she's much better today.'

'I understand this has never happened to her before.'

'No,' she answered quickly. 'It hasn't. She is a very healthy girl – as your uncle may have noticed.'

I sighed. 'My good uncle can be –'

'You don't need to apologize for him. Veronika, for some reason, was glowing in his attention. If she is happy, I am happy.'

'It is your sister's good health that makes her fit of pain all the more perplexing. From her symptoms, unless she is only just now developing some sort of neural condition, I think she might have been poisoned.'

Natalja's fingers went still. 'She *cannot* have been. Who would want to do that?'

'I cannot tell, but that is my strongest theory.' I chose not to mention the possibility Veronika might have faked it all.

'I can see why you'd guess that,' said Natalja, 'but there were only family members here last night, and servants who've worked for us for years.'

'Years?'

'Yes, decades even.'

I moved a little closer, oblivious that the distance between us was quite scandalous already. 'What about the younger staff? Say . . . Ellie and Tamlyn?'

She looked up, a sudden spark in her eyes.

'Well, Ellie has been here around a year. My late grandfather hired his servants at around that age – as children, so he could train and educate them; you may have noticed they all have very good diction. My father has done the same. Some people leave, of course, but others, like Plunket and Glenister, have stayed on and will probably work here for the rest of their lives.'

'I see. And . . .' I tried to drop the name as casually as possible, 'Tamlyn?'

Natalja looked up, perhaps trying to remember. 'Our chambermaid left earlier this year. She met a tradesman from Gairloch and went off to marry him, so Tamlyn had to be hired quickly. She came with very good references, from a large household in Aberdeenshire, but Mama didn't have time to check all her details properly.'

I was still struggling to contain my astonishment. Ellie, whom I'd found disturbing evidence, and Tamlyn, who'd told me about those mysterious scars . . . those girls also happened to be the newest servants, those who would owe the least loyalty to the Kolomans. I felt a pattern begin to emerge, like one of those silhouettes in the mist – clearly there, but still too hazy to be identified.

I must have been silent for a while, for Natalja began closing the keyboard's cover.

'There is one more thing,' I said. 'I . . . I cannot tell you how I came to know this, but I have heard' – I lowered my voice to a murmur – 'your sister was bitten by some sort of creature.'

Natalja dropped the cover and a loud boom filled the room.

She looked at me with fear, puzzlement and a full range of other emotions I could not read.

Natalja leaned closer, so close I could see every streak and speck of cerulean in her eyes. 'Bitten? *How?*'

'I do not know. You were with her last night at all times. I thought you might tell me.'

'Indeed. And I am absolutely sure nothing bit her . . . Not that I saw.' She looked sideways. 'What . . . what sort of injuries are you talking about?'

'I have not seen them myself. I was not able to examine her properly – your good mother, you see.'

She nodded. 'If she was curt, I apologize for her. Mama was so distressed.'

'No need, miss, but I must examine your sister, and ask her about her symptoms. If I am wrong and she was not poisoned, those bites might well be the cause of her seizure. You may be present, of course, but . . .' I felt terribly guilty, as if taking advantage of this young creature. 'It would be best if we kept this between us. Your mother and father, caring as they are, might . . .'

Her eyes widened, and for an instant I feared she'd jump to her feet and scream that I was proposing the most licentious scheme. But she surprised me.

'I can arrange it if you think it's necessary. I'm terribly worried too, and Papa and Mama may not be cooperative . . . considering Dominik is locked away.'

I was about to apologize for that, but Natalja did not seem unduly bothered by it. She went on. 'I can tell you I didn't see anything – or anyone – approach Veronika last night . . . but as soon as I saw poor Constable McEwan hanging like that . . .' She trembled and placed a hand on my knee, startling me. Newlyweds are less demonstrative. 'I did not see things with clarity after that, I must admit. A pack of wolves could have passed in front of me and I would have hardly noticed.'

For a second I simply stared into her eyes. She was truly worried, but that was not what kept me from looking away.

Then she said something strange. 'You've frowned more than you've smiled, Mr Frey.' And she was about to touch the creased skin between my eyebrows.

Right then the door burst open and I snapped an involuntary '*What?*'

Uncle Maurice came in, looking exhausted after the long ride. Smeaton, the coachman, came behind him, his thin face soiled from the road.

'Fetch me some of that wine we had last night,' Uncle said to him. 'And I will *really* appreciate your expediency.'

'E-excuse me, sir. My expe-what?'

'Hurry up, my good man.'

The little man bowed and left, and only then did Uncle realize how closely Miss Natalja and I were sitting. It was not she but I who rose swiftly, clearing my throat.

'Uncle! Did you . . . did you . . .'

Natalja stood up, utterly entertained. She squeezed my forearm and smiled. 'I'll let you know when we can perform . . . the study you requested. Mr Plantard, I hope you had a pleasant journey.'

She curtsied, wearing a wicked smile, and left. I was blushing so much I felt the waves of heat emanating from my cheeks.

'I most definitely need a drink right now!' said Uncle, grinning from ear to ear and looking for a decanter of any sort of liquor, unable to wait for the servant. 'Tell me absolutely everything; spare no detail.'

'There is nothing to tell!'

'Oh, nephew, nephew. Can you imagine how sweet that would be? You and I marrying twin sisters!'

'Sweet! Did you not mean *twisted*?'

Smeaton came in then – I was surprised *and* relieved by his speed – bringing a decanter and two glasses.

I snatched the tray from him. 'Leave us.' I filled the first glass nearly to the brim, looking daggers at my uncle. 'I am the one who needs to ask *you* some questions. Did you deliver the telegram?'

'Ian, will you not humour me for a little while?'

'*Did you deliver the telegram?*' I hissed, and I handed him the full glass so abruptly I spilled some wine on the rug.

Uncle took it and had a leisurely sip. 'Very well, I shall not tease. Yes, I delivered the telegram. What a waste of a morning! Abysmal roads – so bumpy I could not even read a word of my pocketbook.' He drank again, probably thinking I'd be happy with that account.

'What else?'

'Well, there is hardly anything further to say. The bloody telegraphist was an utterly rustic little chap who could barely read. And that Smeaton kept gossiping and asking about the gals in town. Most vulgar, coarse talk I heard. If you and your nine-nailed boss had not made it so clear I had to see every single word delivered –'

'But it *was* delivered?'

'Of course. Would you doubt me?'

I poured myself only half a glass. I felt I'd need my full senses for as long as I stayed next to this ill-omened loch. '*You* I trust. It is everyone else around here I worry about.'

As I brought the glass to my lips and sniffed the bouquet my eyes drifted to the windows, towards Loch Maree. I saw a boat docking at the Kolomans' small pier.

A swaying Nine-Nails jumped on to the jetty. Even from a distance I could see the greenish hue of his face, but that was not what caught our attention.

'What in the name of God is that crazy Scotch doing?' Uncle asked, squinting. 'Why is he dragging that rachitic old man?'

I held my breath, scrutinizing the pale, lanky figure. 'That is not an old man . . .' I whispered, and I could say no more. The sight of that man's face made me shiver.

25

Uncle and I rushed to the entrance hall. There we found Boyde, running to the oaken back door. Natalja and her mother were at the staircase, their feet hammering down the steps as quickly as their skirts allowed.

'*Konrad!*' Mrs Koloman was shouting. 'Konrad, come quick!'

I saw young Tamlyn emerge from the east wing, and Mrs Glenister right behind her, still grasping some needlework.

Uncle and I reached Boyde as he began to unlock the door. I felt an icy hand rest on my arm and saw it was Natalja's. I realized she would have used this very door to go out for her walk last night.

As soon as Boyde opened it Uncle and I ran to the pier.

'Is this the man?' I asked before anybody else had a chance to speak. 'Is he the one we saw in the woods last night?'

'He won't deny it,' said McGray. His face was green indeed, and his feet quite unsteady on the ground.

'*Lazarus?*' Mrs Koloman shrieked from behind us. She came running with the agility of a young girl, her face in utter distress.

I looked at McGray. 'Is he one of the Nellyses? The family who live on the island?'

'Aye, the mad auld man's son.'

No wonder Uncle had thought him an elderly person; blemishes and grey hairs had ravaged the features of a man well under thirty.

McGray could say no more, for Mrs Koloman reached us and pushed me aside.

She grabbed Lazarus by the collar. I thought she'd shout accusations, but her voice came out full of worry. 'Why have they brought you here? What have you done?'

Lazarus looked down and Mrs Koloman pressed a motherly hand against his cheek; the contrast between their skins, one leathery and blotchy, the other one white and smooth, could not have been greater. She looked at him pleadingly, her eyes pooling tears.

Mr Koloman strode up, demanding explanations too.

'I saw a man in a boat last night,' said McGray. 'Lurking around the spot where we found McEwan. It was this lad. He's not denied it.' There was a hint of guilt in his voice. 'His mother and sister knew about his absence, and they have a wee boat at hand.'

'He could not have done it!' Mrs Koloman insisted.

McGray looked stern. 'He tried to flee in his wreck of a boat when I confronted him. He nearly killed me.'

Mrs Koloman covered her mouth. Her husband turned to Lazarus. 'Is that true?' he asked him, not a hint of compassion in his voice. His reaction could not have been more different from that of his wife, who stared at him with fuming eyes. Lazarus neither spoke nor moved.

Miss Fletcher came up too, with slumped shoulders and a grim face.

'Is that true?' Mrs Koloman appealed to her. Miss Fletcher struggled to nod, as if her neck had gone numb.

Mrs Koloman could not contain her tears any longer. Miss Fletcher gently moved her away so we could pass, and Natalja joined her mother, consoling her with a tender hand. And I'd thought that girl could not look any paler . . .

Mr Koloman poked Lazarus on the shoulder as we advanced, but he was looking at McGray and me. 'You will lock him up as well, will you not?'

'Aye. 'Til the inquest takes place.'

Mr Koloman looked at the weather-beaten man with contempt, but also with a trace of satisfaction; he must be thinking that Lazarus could well be Dominik's salvation.

'Take him to the pantry,' he said. 'The likes of him don't deserve our last empty guest room. *Tamlyn!*' The girl jumped and then came to us on trembling legs. 'Guide them there.'

Tamlyn curtsied and mumbled something unintelligible, pointing at the door.

McGray pushed Lazarus, who, hunched and tired, dragged his feet forward. I have seen that beaten walk only in men on their way to the gallows.

As we stepped in I was shocked to see the state of Mrs Glenister. The woman was crying copiously and wringing the needlework as if set to tear it to pieces.

I would have asked her why, but then I saw someone prowling in the semi-darkness of the hall.

Benjamin.

'What do you think you are doing here?' I snapped.

He did not answer. He was staring at Lazarus, thunderstruck, his lips parted.

Lazarus looked back at him, and I thought I heard him let out the faintest of sighs. Then Natalja went to her cousin, put her arm around him and moved him sideways.

'Take Benjamin to his room,' I told her. 'No detours, please.'

McGray and I waited only until those two reached the stairs, and then resumed our way to the west wing. I peeped back and had a glimpse of the flustered Mrs Koloman, her face buried in her husband's shoulder – he himself looked quite self-assured. Further back, a dark silhouette on the door's threshold, was Miss Fletcher, as still as a stone. I wondered if she had seen her son.

I wondered if he had seen her.

26

The pantry was a large room right underneath the kitchen, very cold and full of the smells of spices, root vegetables and cured meats. I found those scents very pleasant, but McGray, still a funny colour from the moving boat, had to bring a clenched fist to his nose. Lazarus, if possible, looked even worse, as though the mere sight of meat sickened him.

McGray made him sit on a pile of sacks of caustic soda, lifting a little cloud of the white powder.

'Well?' I said, wasting no time. 'Did you do it? Did you kill the constable?'

Lazarus said nothing. He simply slouched, as if trying to bury his heart deep inside his chest.

'You are not doing yourself any favours with your silence. From where we stand, it is as damning as an open confession.'

He looked up, his very pale eyes full of thick, bright-red veins. His lips were dry and cracked, and his entire face was covered in blotches ranging from dull brown to bright pink, layer upon layer of skin damage, some of it clearly years old.

'What is wrong with your skin?' I asked, in as conciliatory a tone as possible. In the semi-darkness of the pantry I could not see it properly. 'Is it some sort of allergy?'

'None of your business,' were his first words to me.

'I've tried, Frey,' McGray said, his patience gone. 'The lad won't speak. And he *did* attack me.' He made his way to the door. 'Perhaps a few nights in the quiet will persuade him to talk.'

I gave Lazarus one last look, and as I glanced at his stained cheeks a creeping chill took hold of me.

There we left him. I turned the key and shoved it into my pocket, along with all the keys to the other restricted rooms.

The corridor was dark and completely deserted, so I took the chance to whisper the uncomfortable questions.

'Did you see the old Mr Nellys?' McGray nodded. 'Is he sane?'

McGray pressed a hand to his forearm, opened his mouth, but then hesitated.

'It's complicated, Frey.'

I whispered as softly as I could, 'If this man Lazarus killed the constable, do you realize what that implies? That he drained his blood and –'

'*I see that!*'

The echo boomed around the corridor. Nine-Nails rubbed his jaw and then lowered his voice. 'I see that, Frey, and . . .' He gnashed his teeth. 'Let's discuss it later.'

I did not want to press further. McGray's mind must be in turmoil. If those absurd legends were true – and that was a big *if* – that meant that Pansy's cure would involve . . . bathing her in human blood. I felt a nasty tingle at the back of my neck. Would McGray be willing to perform such a gruesome deed? I decided I did not want to know the answer – not yet.

'So what do we do now?' McGray asked, bringing us back to our more immediate troubles. 'Are we done for the day?'

'Almost. I would like to check on the corpse. Just to make sure it is not rotting yet.'

McGray let out a wry little laugh, perhaps predicting what we'd see.

The cellar already smelled of death. A nuanced note but sickly nonetheless, and I felt a wave of nausea when I saw McEwan's face. I forced myself to prod the neck and cheek, and when I did the latter a ghastly yellowish liquid leaked out of the dead man's nostrils.

'It will not last much longer,' I grumbled, wrinkling my nose and barely containing a retch.

'Look a' that!' Nine-Nails said, looking utterly fresh all of a sudden. 'I've never seen a dead body do that.'

'How on earth can you stomach this, yet the shortest trip over water turns you the colour of this man's bile?'

'Och, don't be so sensitive, Percy. How long d'ye think he'll last?'

'I am at a loss. This place is cool enough; I thought it would be longer.' I shook my head. 'At this rate it will not be more than a couple of days before we must dispose of him.'

'We should have reinforcements here very soon, including a forensic man. Maybe tomorrow morning. Is there anything ye can do to preserve him 'til then?'

I took a step back, remembering my first conversation with the Miss Kolomans. They'd mentioned their father had given them silver chloride for their diffraction experiments.

'Perhaps Mr Koloman has the right chemicals . . .'

Konrad Koloman had a small yet excellently well-appointed laboratory. It was also in a basement, this one on the opposite wing of the manor, directly underneath the girls' Shadows Room.

The shelves and benches were crammed with vials, flasks

and beakers, all glinting in the dim light that filtered through the barred windows. On the central bench there was a large distillation set – two large flasks connected by a long condenser. It was empty at the moment, but its convoluted glass tubing was stained a nice shade of purple.

Boyde was the only soul around. He was sitting on a low stool, meticulously dusting a handful of sealed test tubes. I remembered that the first time I'd met him he'd given off a hint of a chemical whiff. The young man seemed unusually excited by the dull job, looking intently at the colourful crystals and liquids contained in the vials.

'I need some light,' said Mr Koloman, feeling for a switch on the wall. 'My eyes are not as good as this young chap's.' And suddenly the place was inundated by golden light from incandescent bulbs on the ceiling.

'Are those electric?' I asked.

'Indeed,' said Mr Koloman with an air of pride.

'How do you generate –'

'Sodium batteries. I learned how to synthesize them after I read Verne's *Vingt mille lieues sous les mers.*'

'Whah?' cried McGray.

'Some stupid Frenchman who has written a good deal of dull-witted nonsense,' I said. 'Why, you might like his books!'

'Why don't ye use candles?' Nine-Nails asked. 'Like . . . *normal* folk.'

Mr Koloman took this as a compliment. 'Oh, we are far from normal, Mr McGray. And I have a keen interest in chemistry. Purely recreational, of course.'

I took a step closer to Boyde and had a look at the chemicals. Some labels read *copper sulphate*, *mercuric cyanide* and *aqua regia* – hardly the sort of materials I'd leave in the hands of a seemingly illiterate young servant.

I frowned, and McGray knew exactly what was going through my head.

'Aye,' Nine-Nails said, 'purely recreational.'

'I do not have formaldehyde,' Mr Koloman was saying as he went through his shelves. 'Would ethanol help?' And he showed me an amber bottle that contained scarcely a few ounces.

'Is this all you have?'

'Indeed. Natalja uses a lot to clean her lenses and prisms. Very versatile, ethanol. If I was told I could keep only *one* chemical . . .'

I could not care less about his digressions. 'In a manor like this you must have ice.'

'Yes, we usually do,' explained Mr Koloman. 'To cool down champagne and oysters, you see. Every winter we bury a good deal to last us the year, but it is late summer now and we did throw a large party. I'm afraid we've depleted our reserves.'

I grunted, pondering my choices. 'Mr Koloman, I know this is too stupid a question, but given your affluence . . . do you happen to own a photographic camera? At least I could document the state of the body, in case our reinforcements arrive too late.'

Mr Koloman winced. 'I did buy a Gandolfi for Veronika a few years ago – that's why I still keep some of that silver chloride. Alas, she lost interest very soon. Natalja dismantled it and used the components for her diffraction experiments.'

I cursed inwardly. 'Would she be able to reassemble it?'

'Maybe. I can ask her. And we do have a few plaques left. You wouldn't need more than that; you could take them with you and have them developed by the police elsewhere.'

'Indeed. That will be very useful, Mr Koloman. Thank you very much.'

We rushed back to the cellar-turned-mortuary, where a very nasty job awaited.

I dabbed the body with ethanol as best as I could, especially around the wound on the neck. I knew the organs would go on decomposing at the same rate, but at least the forensic man would be able to assess the most crucial elements of the crime. And since we still did not know whether Natalja would be able to rebuild the camera (she was doing her best in the Shadows Room at that moment) I decided to undertake a more thorough inspection of the body before it was too late. McGray took notes as I dictated.

'Ye've checked that bloody toe three times already!' he finally protested, after two hours of work.

'I need to be absolutely thorough, Nine-Nails.'

'If ye missed something – which doesnae seem likely – ye've missed it. Come on, let's discuss all this mess o' shite over some nice spirit.' He sneered at the amber bottle. 'Nicer than that.'

Uncle Maurice found us on our way back to the astronomy room and followed us, even though nobody had invited him. We only let him join our discussion because he was carrying two bottles of red wine under his arm. McGray triple-checked nobody was eavesdropping before locking the door behind us.

'Very well,' I said. 'We need a plan of action in case the CID fail to arrive, and if Miss Natalja cannot –'

'Calm down, calm down!' Uncle interrupted, pouring

glasses for us all – there seemed to be Bohemian goblets at the ready in every room of the manor. 'Have you two considered it might be time you stepped down?'

'Step down!' I repeated. 'Are you truly suggesting we should simply sit back and do nothing?'

'Ian, you two have done far more than was required. This is neither your jurisdiction nor did you come here on an assignment to investigate the local atrocities.'

'Uncle, has Mr Koloman been washing your brain?'

'He might have said those very words over luncheon, but I was of the same opinion even before we spoke. Ian, you and Mr ... Nine-Fingers here have done all that could be expected of you. You have examined the corpse and preserved it as well as the circumstances allow. You have chased, captured and isolated the most likely suspects. You have questioned every single soul in this house and recorded their statements. Nobody in the police force could ever accuse you of dormancy. You have behaved admirably.' As he concluded he put a glass in my hand. 'Both of you,' and he gave McGray the other drink. 'Let the bloody constables come and do their job. Let the inquest follow its due course. *Drink up*, for goodness' sake!'

McGray and I did so, as if reprimanded by a grumpy father.

'Uncle,' I said after a moment, 'what would the world be if we all refrained from action simply because it is not *our duty*?'

Uncle shook his head. 'Ian, that very attitude is going to take you to an early grave. That is why you ended up in Scotland, and with a broken nose and a burned –'

'Nae,' McGray jumped in, 'those wounds were just ineptitude.'

223

'At least come and have dinner,' said Uncle. 'And a quiet sleep. You do seem to need it.'

I was more tired than I cared to admit, so I agreed and followed Uncle to the door.

'McGray, are you staying here?'

'Aye, let me finish this one on my own,' he said, raising his glass and turning to the window. I did not insist he follow us; I knew he had a lot to ponder on.

27

Dinner was a tense affair.

Mrs Koloman had changed into an exquisite grey dress, her skirts an intricate work I can only describe as origami in silk. Her husband boasted that Veronika had designed and made the garment herself, for they could not find a seamstress skilled enough. The lady looked refreshed and as beautiful as her daughters, yet more sombre than ever before. And her mood only worsened when I told her Benjamin had refused to dine with them.

Mr Koloman's spirits, on the other hand, had lifted, and he was almost as enthusiastic a host as he had been before the murder. He announced a first course of smoked oysters (he'd been saving the tins for a special occasion but said he'd begun to crave them after mentioning them in his laboratory) and was magnanimous with the wine as the servants cleared our plates.

'It will all be all right now,' he told his wife after a rather long swig. 'It is obvious Lazarus did it.'

She did not reply but chewed on with a tenser jaw.

Natalja placed an assuaging hand on her mother's arm, her sharp eyes ensuring her father did not notice. The girl then looked at me furtively, but when our eyes met she said nothing.

Again they served us kid meat as a main course, only this time curried. I noticed everyone ate with distrust – even McGray. We all seemed to be thinking the same: these goats had all come from Juniper Island, bred and slaughtered by a murder suspect. Natalja could not finish hers.

'May I be excused?' she asked at last, clenching her cutlery.

'Of course, darling,' said her mother. 'I am sure the gentlemen will understand.'

'But of course,' said Uncle. 'It has been a long couple of days.'

The girl stood up and we all rose. She came straight to me and offered a hand to shake. 'Good night, Mr Frey . . .' And I felt how she dexterously placed a piece of paper between my fingers. I put it in my pocket whilst she shook hands with McGray and Uncle – the latter tried to kiss her but Natalja pulled her hand away and walked out briskly, never looking back. I waited until Mr Koloman and Uncle Maurice were deep in earnest conversation, their eyes off me, before discreetly looking at the note:

Meet me at the door to V's bedroom at 12:00. Not a minute later.

'Terrible!' said Mr Koloman, making me jump. 'Simply terrible!'

I shoved the note in my pocket. 'Wha . . . What?'

'What an ordeal we've all been through,' he answered, again pouring wine most liberally. It seemed to be going to his head. 'My daughters are strong girls, but this has been a little too much.' He saw the tension in my face. 'I am sure Natalja will restore that camera tomorrow morning, Mr Frey. She did her best before dinner, but I'm afraid she needs some rest now.'

I nodded rather than spoke, fearing that my voice might betray my nerves. It probably made me appear resentful, for Mrs Koloman leaned forward. 'Mr Frey, I would like to apologize for my behaviour.'

'Excuse me?'

'You are too polite to make any remarks, but I know I have been curt and disrespectful, while you simply were doing your job. The things I said to you when you were attempting to help my child!'

'It is of no consequence, ma'am,' I said, feeling rather awkward. Given the apology, I was tempted to ask her permission to examine Veronika again, but something in the way she looked at me told me this would in fact be the worst moment.

I looked away, realizing how intently I'd been staring at her.

'My apology was sincere, Mr Frey,' she reiterated. 'If there's anything I can do . . .'

'Course there is,' McGray jumped in, and then he also jumped from his seat. He walked around the table and whispered something in Mrs Koloman's ear.

She frowned. 'I . . . I beg your pardon?'

'Just ask 'im that,' McGray insisted.

Mrs Koloman looked at me with utter befuddlement. 'Would you . . . would you like a lavender bath?'

Boyde was pouring the last bucket of boiling water into the copper tub. Tamlyn had already added a cupful of scented oil, so my entire bedroom was full of the perfume.

'You did not have to do this,' I said for the hundredth time. All the servants were now giggling at my expense, yet I could not refuse lest Mrs Koloman should feel offended.

Boyde at least attempted to keep a straight face. 'Served, sir. Ring the bell when you want me to take the stuff away.' He bowed and left.

I was wearing one of Dominik's brocade dressing gowns. The inner lining was of the softest merino wool, so warm and comfortable I cursed the entire Koloman family. I cursed them again as I plunged into the deliciously hot water, and cursed all their ancestry as I dunked a butter biscuit in the aged brandy they had left within easy reach.

My muscles took in the heat, my entire body unwinding. I inhaled the scent and let my mind wander. I could easily forget I was in the middle of the Scottish wilderness, miles and miles away from the bustle and the smoke of the towns and cities, and yet basking in the most luxurious comforts our civilization has to offer. No wonder the Kolomans retreated here and seemed so content locked up in their very own microcosm: eating, drinking, walking, and devoting their time to their books, their artistic clothes and their scientific experiments. I might do the same one day.

I could have fallen asleep in the water, so I forced myself to open my eyes. I looked at the ceiling and its carved beams. I had not realized how Gothic that room was: with its four-poster bed, its rugs and its heavy tapestries it looked like one of those oil paintings that were so in vogue, depicting romanticized scenes of the Middle Ages.

The tapestry hanging right in front of me was the most convincing element. It was either very old or had been aged on purpose: its dark red weaving was embroidered with a small hunting scene, right at the foot of a majestic oak that filled most of the surface. Amidst lobed leaves and acorns I espied little faces framed in shields, expertly integrated into the branches. It looked like a faded family tree.

'I adore that too,' someone said behind me.

My heart jumped as I looked back, nearly twisting my neck. It was Miss Natalja.

I drew in air, but the noise I made was akin to a piglet's squeal. 'Miss, what on *earth* are you –'

She put a finger to her lips, bidding silence as she walked around the bath. She moved as stealthily as everyone else in this house. I realized with horror that there was nothing to hand I could use to cover myself – not even bubbles in the water.

'Miss, get out, *now*!' I hissed.

She walked quite casually towards the tapestry, neither peering at the bath nor avoiding it.

'Would you like to peruse our family tree? Our lineage goes back the best part of a thousand years, to the rise of the Ottoman Empire and beyond. I can recite all the names.'

I have faced murderous lunatics, poisoning, blizzards without shelter, vicious witches, Scottish food – yet never, *never* has my heart thumped as frantically as then.

'Miss, this is entirely inappropriate!'

Natalja frowned, looking if anything more angelic. 'What do you mean?'

She dropped her shawl. She was still wearing one of those indecent dresses of fine material. No stays. From where I sat I could even see the fabric hugging her ribs and narrow hips, an elegant Greek sculpture that could have belonged to any age but mine.

'Miss, I cannot fathom what you are doing here.'

'Can you really not? Shall I tell you how it all works?'

I grunted. 'Miss, I have nothing against these newfangled notions of female independence, but I shall not be the one to muddle your reputation!'

She let out a soft, musical laugh. 'Oh, Mr Frey, how delightfully Victorian you are.'

'What . . . what did you call me?'

'Why should I need a reputation? I have ample money, no hypocritical society to answer to, and no wish to ever marry.'

'You . . . y-you are very vulnerable at this moment . . .'

'Are you implying I don't know what I'm doing? Why, you insult me, Mr Frey.'

She knelt by the bath and I recoiled like a frightened child, ashamed of my irrepressible movements. I strived to cover as much of myself as I could – which was in fact very little.

Natalja's hand rested on my temple. Her skin was cold but soft, and she smelled as beautifully as the bathwater. 'You studied some medicine, did you not?'

'What does that have to do with –'

She ran her fingers along my eyebrows with the most delicate touch. 'So you've studied God's marvels. You know how our eyes turn lifeless light into colour and beauty.' Her hand went to my nose and mouth, where she felt my agitated breath. 'You know how our lungs use mundane air to refresh, and nurture, and purify.' Her hand went to my neck, and it was as though her touch sent electric sparks through my skin. She went on, placing her small hand on my chest, my warmth swiftly seeping into her skin. 'You know how your heart pumps life-giving blood to the furthest corners of your body, every minute of every day, until you die . . .'

I gulped. 'Miss, you had better leave now . . .' I began, but I only half meant it.

'What a masterpiece these bodies are,' she whispered, smiling. 'What *miracles* we all are . . . even more precious because our bodies last for such a little while. Why let them go cold? Or hungry? Why keep them in the dark?'

And her hand slid down my torso, reached the surface of the perfumed water, and then went further . . . and then –

I jumped to my feet with dazzling speed. Natalja fell backward as half the water spilled out of the bath. I groped about, found a hand towel and desperately covered my most intimate miracles.

'Miss Koloman –' I squawked as I pointed at the door, and then cleared my throat and managed to roar, *'Get out!* Or I'll drag you out!'

The girl was curled up on the floor, trembling and unable to meet my gaze. She made me feel terribly guilty.

I tried to speak. 'I . . . I –' I realized how poorly I was covering myself. I reached for the thick dressing gown, wrapped it tightly around me and stepped out of the bath. Miss Koloman was shaking, and I offered her a hand. 'Miss Koloman, please . . .'

She would not accept my help. She stood up on her own and pulled strands of blonde hair from her face. Her eyes were on fire: anger, shame, frustration, all of them boiled in her striking irises, about to burst into raging tears. Had I just made a terrible mistake?

Before I could entertain any more doubts I went to the door and opened it as quietly as possible – convinced as I was that half the manor had already heard my outburst.

Natalja, still breathing agitatedly, grabbed her crumpled shawl and made her way out.

'I shall never speak of this,' I said as she passed the threshold.

I thought she'd leave without a reply, but then she stopped and mumbled, 'Meet me as agreed. My sister should not have to suffer because of my . . .'

She did not bother to complete the sentence but simply scurried along the corridor. My eyes followed her until her white gown disappeared in the shadows, and then I peered in the other direction to make sure nobody had –

My heart skipped a beat.

Nine-Nails was standing there. God knows since when.

We looked at each other in utter silence, and after a

moment his mouth formed slowly into a grin so wide I could see every single tooth. 'First time ever?'

'Oh, shush! Come in!'

'Hey-hey-hey! Don't ye need a wee rest before –'

'*Nine-Nails!*'

My screech echoed along the corridor and McGray hurried in.

He saw the drenched rug and let out a whistle. 'My, oh, my! Youse were busy!'

'Oh, do shut up! I had to fend her off. It was the most appalling behaviour.' McGray made a few very crude jokes before I interrupted him. 'Why are you here?'

'Nae to be *fended off*, if that's worrying ye.'

'Either speak or take your puerile gibberish –'

'All right, all right. Frey, I was gonna wait 'til the morning, but . . .' He pressed his forearm like he'd done earlier and he sighed. 'I didnae tell ye what I found in Juniper Island.'

I reached for my brandy. 'I feel like I am going to need this. Go on.'

McGray helped himself from the decanter before he answered.

'The island is full of bats.'

Suddenly, despite the thick dressing gown, the heat from the bath and the shame of my previous encounter, I felt very cold.

'*Bats?*'

'Aye. They're like a plague, sucking the blood o' the Nellyses' goats.'

'Sucking blood? McGray, are you sure?'

'As sure as I'm looking at yer constipated face right now.' He rubbed his stubble in frustration. 'Go on, Percy. Mock me. Tell me I'm a hare-brained –'

'No, no,' I interrupted. 'I . . . I saw them too . . . Or at least I thought I saw them.'

'Really? When?'

'On my first day here, when Miss Fletcher took us to Isle Maree. She rowed very close to Juniper Island and I thought I'd seen a bat. It was but a glimpse; I thought I was imagining things. Did the Nellyses say anything about the creatures?'

'Nae. The missus just told me to *ignore them.*'

I paced. 'I assume you had a good look at them?'

'Aye. These are nae the sort o' wee bats I used to see at my dad's farmhouse. I remember Pansy and I used to sit in the dusk 'n' watch them flutter around. The things here are much bigger.'

'Like the one we saw months ago at –'

'Och, nae! *That* one was a true monster. Nae, these ones' wingspan must be about a foot long, maybe a wee bit more.'

My eyes flickered as I thought. I pulled up a chair and sat down. 'I vaguely remember reading, years ago, that blood-sucking bats live only in tropical climates. Mexico and the South Americas.'

'How can yer head be so full o' so much useless shite?'

'Said by the man who can recite the names of all the Wiccans' sacred hobgoblins!'

He looked at me, very still. 'Aye, ye win this round. Ye sure these things don't live in Scotland?'

'Not entirely sure; I read that years ago. But the Kolomans might have a zoology book on their shelves. I'll check in the morning. I find all this truly disturbing.'

McGray chuckled. 'And there's more. I spoke to Mr Nellys.'

'About your sister's –'

'Never mind that right now. The auld man said – and he didnae want his son to hear this – that the bats come at night and bite him.'

'Bite him?'

'Aye. And he had marks on his belly. He showed me.'

I felt as though a chilly draught filled the room. 'Like Veronika . . .'

'What about her?'

I told him about Tamlyn's story, Natalja's note and our meeting at midnight. McGray looked quite stern when I mentioned the possible bites on the girl.

'This lassie . . . d'ye think it was the bites that made her so ill?'

I raised an eyebrow. 'Yes, that is entirely possible. Why do you look so concerned?'

'Well, that's why I couldnae wait 'til the morning to come and see ye . . .'

He pulled up his sleeve and showed me his forearm. There was a long, deep scratch from his wrist to his elbow.

'The bastards got me.'

28

'Good Lord, when did that happen? While you were chasing Lazarus?'

'Aye. One o' the wee beasts clung to my arm.'

'You must have that cleaned.'

'I fuckin' did that, Percy. I washed before dinner, but it didnae help. This won't scar.'

'I see. Let me clean it again.'

'What for? If I'm to catch anything, it's too late now.'

'Let me do it nonetheless. I still have a little of that ethanol. It might work better than just soap.'

I went to the small chest of drawers, where I'd left Mr Koloman's bottle. There was just enough left to dab McGray's wound.

I took his arm and looked at the scratch more closely. Only very little blood had managed to clot around the wound, but it dissolved as soon as I touched it with the towel dampened in spirit.

'What on earth?' I let out with a gasp.

'Is that normal?' McGray asked.

'Not at all. Perhaps –' I looked up. 'What time is it?'

'It was close to eleven when I left my room,' said McGray.

'Good. I think we should go and check the Kolomans' books now, never mind the morning. I will help you until midnight, and then I will go and meet Miss Natalja. If you might be infected with something, there is no time to lose.'

I bandaged his arm and donned some clothes. McGray grabbed an oil lamp and we both headed to the drawing room. The manor had again gone utterly silent, our footsteps the only sign of life.

'Why are we moving as if treading on bloody eggshells?' McGray grunted as we descended the stairs. Until then I had not realized how tense we both were, like petty thieves lurking about the corridors of a prison. Perhaps it was because of the sharp shadows our lamp projected on the stone of the neo-Gothic walls; perhaps we both intuited something frightful might be about to happen.

McGray pushed open the door to the drawing room and I could have sworn I caught the glimpse of a light dying out. Nine-Nails must have seen it too, for he stood still for a moment, his eyes going from side to side.

There were the outlines of the books and the grand piano, the twinkle of the brass meteorology instruments, the unsettling shapes of the stuffed animals and the antlers on the walls. The long room struck me as a little colder than the rest of the house.

'Very well,' said Nine-Nails, placing the lamp on a central table, from where it shed just enough light on the endless bookshelves. 'D'ye think there's any order in these books?'

'I would expect so,' I said, walking along the lines of tomes, 'unless they manage their books like you, in which case we might as well go to sleep.'

Luckily that was not the case. There were no tags or labels, but I soon realized that the books were grouped by subject: meteorology, history, chemistry, physics, medicine . . .

'Cannae see any book that might talk about bats,' said McGray. 'Zoology? Biology?'

'Look at that, they have James Blundell's treatise on blood

transfusion,' I said. I pulled the book out, clicking my tongue. 'Risky, dubious procedure. Works in a third of cases and kills half. Nobody knows why.'

'Ye sure? I've heard they do it at Edinburgh's Infirmary all the time.'

I laughed. 'I rest my case. Only the Scots could be so barbaric!'

I was about to put the book back on the shelf but then I froze.

'What is it?' McGray asked.

I tilted my head, staring at the gilded name of Blundell. 'I do not know . . .' I mumbled, conscious of how deeply I was frowning. 'I feel . . . as if all this were terribly . . . familiar.'

'Familiar?'

I shook my head, looking for the right words. I kept my fingers on the book, as if any movement might scare away what little enlightenment I had achieved. 'I can only compare it to . . . my brother Elgie playing fragments of a violin piece I've not heard in years. Something I feel I recognize but do not quite remember until he plays the entire piece.'

We remained in silence for a moment, McGray allowing me to think. But when I finally shrugged and pushed the book back into place, Nine-Nails turned on his heel, nearly knocking me over.

'What was that?' he asked.

My eyes followed him as he looked about the room. 'What was what?'

'There's . . . I heard something.'

'What?'

He raised a hand, bidding me be silent, and even held his breath as he listened out.

The hush was absolute, not even broken by the wind from

outside, but I would not be deceived: McGray's hearing has always been better than mine.

After a seemingly endless moment I thought I *felt* something rather than heard it. Something in the air. There was somebody else in the room.

Just as I realized it McGray darted forward, to the grand piano, and I saw a shadow lurking underneath.

McGray stretched out an arm and pulled somebody out. There was a whimper and I instantly recognized Benjamin's lanky frame.

The boy covered his face as if fearing we'd attack him. An oil lamp rolled away, its glass shade making a racket when it hit the foot of one of the sofas. That was the light I thought I'd seen.

'What the hell are ye doing here?' McGray shrieked, lifting the boy and making him sit on the nearest armchair.

'How many times do we have to tell you not to lurk around?' I said, even more annoyed than Nine-Nails.

Benjamin stammered and his babbling made no sense. McGray had to pat him on the shoulder. 'All right, all right, we're nae gonna impale ye. Why are ye here? Ye should be upstairs!'

'I . . . I was looking for a book,' Benjamin muttered.

McGray laughed. 'A wee bit late for a read, don't ye think?'

'I couldn't sleep, sir. And you've just . . .' He looked down. 'You've arrested that other man . . . I thought there wouldn't be any more danger.'

My face must have contorted in utter incredulity. I would have asked him a good deal of questions, but right then McGray's wound was my topmost priority. 'We will have to seize your key. This has been one too many times you –'

The boy lost all colour. 'No! *Please!* I promise I won't go out again.'

'We should have never allowed you to keep a copy,' I added, extending a hand for the key. I felt as though I were scolding a naughty son of mine. I saw Benjamin's lip quiver as he cast a pleading look at McGray.

'I am waiting,' I said.

McGray shook his head. 'Ye heard him, laddie. We cannae leave ye to wander, especially at night.'

Benjamin pulled the key out of his pocket, as slowly as if it took a Herculean effort. I snatched it only to put it in McGray's hand. 'Lock him up, please. I will keep searching.'

McGray nudged the boy and Benjamin made his way out, crestfallen. Just as he crossed the threshold he looked over his shoulder.

'Mr Frey . . .'

'Yes?'

'I think I saw a taxonomy book in the Shadows Room.'

If the room was dark during the day, at night it was pitch-black. The oil lamp I'd found in the drawing room had only a little flame and the light did not reach far. As I stepped in I felt as if I were surrounded by a small bubble of light, everything beyond it a dreadful mystery. I would have felt a little uneasy with McGray by my side, but now, on my own, my footsteps and the rustle of my clothes were enough to make my hair stand on end.

I felt silly, like a frightened child seeing monsters in his nursery. I tried to focus all my senses on the search, but that relieved only some of my anxiety.

I walked along the lines of books, many of them very old, their leather bindings flaking off. The titles seemed to move progressively from physics to biology, and I soon found what I needed.

It was a thick, blackened volume, dated 1860: *Phylogeny of Mammalia: Chiroptera*. It struck me as a very specialized book; then again, the Kolomans had hundreds of tomes in each room.

I took it to the table between the two Chinese screens, the very spot where Natalja and Veronika had explained their diffraction experiments, and put the lamp down.

I thought the flame trembled, but how could it? There were no draughts in the room and the lamp had a glass shade.

'Your imagination, Ian,' I told myself. I opened the book and immediately perceived the woody, musky scent of old paper. The book had no index per se, so it took me a while to find the relevant chapter. When I did, the first thing I saw was a ghastly engraving depicting a black bat clinging to the neck of a horse.

'Hematophagous bats,' I read, skimming through lines. 'Three known species . . . all tropical.'

The next page was a fold-out diagram of a dissected bat, showing all the organs and the pig-like muzzle in so much detail I felt my stomach churn.

'You are not beautiful creatures,' I murmured, turning the page swiftly. 'Usually target large birds and mammals . . . any warm-blooded animal may be subject to attack . . . The spread of disease amongst cattle and poultry is common in these warm regions . . . Cases of rabies and anomalous fevers have been documented' – I turned the page and again felt a shiver – 'in farmers and young children . . .'

The door slammed open and I dropped the book, which fell on the lamp and knocked it over. The shade shattered on the table.

It was only McGray, carrying the other lamp. And he read my expression right away.

29

My pocket watch marked five minutes to midnight when McGray and I left the Shadows Room. He took the book with him to read at leisure, and left me to go and meet Natalja on my own. If the girl was to take me into her sister's chamber secretly, it would be best we made as little noise as possible.

As I turned the corridor's corner I stumbled upon Boyde, who crashed against me, dropping the small candle he'd been carrying.

'Good Lord!' I cried, my heart thumping.

'Sir, I am so sorry!' he said, picking up the taper. I gave him light from my lamp. 'I just went to your room. It was late – I . . . I thought you'd want me to take the bath away. Did you have an accident? I found water all over –'

'Yes, yes, I did. Could you leave now, please? I want to rest.'

'What about the bath and the –'

'Clear it in the morning!' I snapped, and the chap finally understood I wanted him away.

He obliged, though he looked over his shoulder until he reached the stairs. I waited there, in case the young man decided to come back, but after a minute or so he had not. I turned on my heel – only to be startled again.

Natalja was already there, surrounded by darkness, her pale skin almost glowing in the lamplight. The light did not quite reach the hem of her nightgown, so, very much like the first time I saw her sister, Natalja looked like a floating ghost.

'Are you –'

She hushed me, her eyes as full of anger as before, not quite meeting mine. I noticed she smelled of wine and her lips were slightly stained; she had probably needed a drink after our shameful episode.

With a movement of her head – her hair was still damp from the lavender water – she bade me follow, and I walked a couple of yards behind her, as if an invisible shield stood between us. I realized there could be nothing but awkwardness between us now.

We reached Veronika's chamber. Natalja opened the door so silently I could have sworn she'd not touched it, and she led the way in. The room smelled of lavender, like the night before, and there we found the twin.

The girl was fast asleep, her chest going up and down with her deep breaths. I wondered if her mother had given her more laudanum. She did not smell of it though.

Natalja stood by me like a soldier as I lifted the blankets. Her sister did not stir. Thankfully her white nightgown buttoned at the front, and it was easy to undo it around her abdomen. Very carefully, almost fearing to touch her skin with Natalja guarding me, I pulled the soft material aside. Veronika's skin, tight around her waist, was so pale her veins shone blue.

And there were no marks at all.

30

And that was supposed to be my quiet night.

I stepped into my bedroom, my mind swirling with ideas. I managed to wade through the noise and reduce the matter of the murder to the two most likely theories: either Dominik and Calcraft had murdered the priest and the constable (for some reason related to the inheritance issue), or Lazarus had been behind it all for some obscure reason he refused to reveal – his use of human blood struck me as a very real possibility.

Then again, what if Benjamin or Miss Fletcher had –

I shook my head, thinking I did not need to overcomplicate things.

To my surprise I fell into a deep sleep as soon as I rested my head on the pillow. I was so exhausted after the last two days' commotion I did not even dream, and woke up only when someone called at my door. It was a soft, hesitant knocking, but it would not go away. I stumbled up, unlocked the door and saw it was Boyde, bringing me a tray with breakfast.

'Sorry, master. I wouldn't have disturbed you, but your door was locked.'

'Why do you wake me up so early?' I moaned, and as I spoke I realized that Boyde's sleep would have been far shorter.

He replied shyly, 'It is half past ten, sir. You missed breakfast with the masters.'

'*Half past* –' I went to the side table and grabbed my pocket watch. The young man was right. 'For goodness' sake!'

I wrapped myself in Dominik's dressing gown (I made a mental note to ask Mr Koloman who the tailor was) and attacked the strong coffee and toast. However, I managed only a couple of quiet bites before the parade began.

First it was McGray, who wasted ten full minutes with tasteless jokes about my laziness (he used a much fouler word, of course). At the first opportunity I told him what I had seen in Veronika's bedroom.

'Did ye look at her legs? Arms?'

I blushed. 'Of course I did not. Her sister was guarding me like a bloody beefeater.'

McGray chuckled. 'Aye, she must've been very jealous Veronika got all the touching.'

'Nine-Nails!'

'All right, all right. There's another thing. Mrs Koloman's asking if we'll ever feed her pretty son. And remember now Benjamin's locked up too, and that Lazarus lad. Fuck, and that Calcraft too. It's like we're running a damn hotel here.'

I sighed. 'Not quite a hotel, McGray. This bloody manor has become a makeshift police station, complete with cells and a stinking morgue.'

'And a lazy sodding dandy for a gaoler.'

'*I* am having my breakfast. You can go and feed them if you want; the keys are in that drawer. Otherwise they can bloody wait.'

McGray grabbed the keys. 'I'd usually tell ye to sod it and do yer job. But I'm feeling kind today.'

'My, those bats *must* have infected you badly!'

He left then, but mere moments later the second visitor arrived: Mr Koloman.

'I hope you are enjoying our coffee,' he said with a wide

smile. 'Your good uncle told us you were partial to Colombian beans.'

'How may I help you?'

He sat at the table and I grumbled, thinking this would take far longer than I could endure.

'I wanted to ask you if I could take Benjamin out of his room. I want to show him the house and the grounds. This will be his third day with us and I've not had the chance to do so. It will be good for his spirits too.'

'Mr Koloman, do you think it is safe to take him out for *walks*?'

'I think it is perfectly safe now, yes. Lazarus is obviously the murderer.'

I shook my head at his self-assurance, but preferred to focus on the more immediate matter. 'What about the threatening note? Are you forgetting that not one but two murders have happened near Benjamin in the past few days? Quite frankly, I think your untroubled attitude is astounding. If I were in your place, I'd be worried sick for the boy.'

He clenched a fist and drew breath sharply, very nearly losing his temper. He managed to compose himself, however. 'Inspector Frey' – so I was *Inspector* again – 'the boy has been under my roof for a while now. If anybody here wanted to harm him, they would have already found an opportunity. Do you not think so?'

I chewed my toast. It was my turn to be uncooperative.

'Your uncle will join us,' Mr Koloman went on. 'I should have told you from the very start. He would also like a tour of our estate. *Him* you trust . . . I hope?'

I sighed. 'Most of the time I do.' I smiled sideways. 'Inspector McGray has the key to Benjamin's room.'

'Oh! I thought Benjamin was free to –'

'We had to seize it. We found him wandering around the house last night.'

Mr Koloman went a shade paler. 'Wandering? Where? At what time?'

I did not want him to know we'd been looking through his books (or about my other nocturnal misadventures) so I simply waved a dismissive hand. 'Minor details. We thought it was not safe, given the death threat, so we took the key from him.'

Mr Koloman sat back in his chair, his gaze lost.

'Does that bother you?' I asked.

He only shifted in his seat, his lips tense. He clearly wanted to spit out how much our interventions irritated him, but he would not confront me openly – not yet.

'You can go to Inspector McGray and ask if he is happy for Benjamin to make a tour of the grounds.' I knew very well how McGray would respond.

He nodded, forced a smile and made his way out.

'Oh, Mr Koloman,' I said, before he closed the door. 'Can you send the girl Tamlyn here? I want to ask her something.'

'Tamlyn? I believe she is running some errand in the gardens, but I'll tell Mrs Plunket to come and –'

'I am afraid I need Tamlyn.'

He frowned a little. 'Very well, if you please. I will see that Mrs Glenister sends her to you as soon as she can spare her.'

'Thank you.'

He nodded and left. I sighed and took a leisurely sip, but by then my coffee had gone lukewarm. I was debating whether to drink it or ask for a fresh brew when somebody knocked again.

'Oh, good Lord, who is it now?'

Natalja came in.

She must have slept very little, for her eyes were circled by sharp rings. As usual, she was wearing one of her indecent dresses, but she'd also covered herself with a long overcoat. And she brought two very thick books.

Without a word she dropped them next to my breakfast tray, and opened the first book – an ancient-history tome – at a marked page. There was a large engraving, almost aboriginal-looking, depicting an aberrant creature: a human-like body with a bat's head, and with skinny, sinuous arms attached to black wings. It was exhaling what looked like fire and fumes from its muzzle.

'What is this?' I asked her, but Natalja did not reply. She simply went back to the door.

I jumped to my feet. 'Wait. *Wait!* How did you know we were looking for this?'

The girl looked at me with scorn but finally broke her silence. 'I went to see my cousin before breakfast. We had to talk through the door. He told me you locked him in.'

'Miss, we had to. He was exposing himself to –'

'He said he overheard you and your colleague in the drawing room. That you were looking for books about bats and that it seemed important. I remembered reading these a while ago, but I knew you would never look at a history book. Let alone a medical one.' She nodded at the second tome.

I glanced at the engraving. 'Do you think that this might . . .' When I looked up she was gone.

I groaned and turned back to the book. The illustration's footnote stated that the creature was called Camazotz and was a deity of the ancient Mayans.

The book told a legend about twin brothers. They travelled across the Mayan underworld, Xibalbá and, much like

Dante, they visited its many 'houses'. The fourth one was The House of the Bats: 'for there are none but bats inside. In this house they squeak. They shriek as they fly about, for they are captive bats and cannot come out.'

The hero twins (whose names I found unpronounceable) had to spend a night in there, hiding from the 'death bats'. 'These were great beasts with snouts like blades that they used as murderous weapons.'

In the morning one of the twins crawled out, wanting to see the dawn. But one of the death bats saw him and cut his head off, and then took it to the gods of the underworld, who used it to play ball.

I closed the book at once. Twins ... bats ... I did not want to poison my mind with similarities that must be purely coincidental. Surely.

No wonder the story had left its mark on Natalja's memory. She was a clever creature; she too had noticed the parallels, and might even be frightened by them. I should have a word with her – as soon as her temper improved. And I should tell McGray, who would probably love this nonsense.

I put the book aside and focused on the medical one, which was much older. The spine was gilded with some initials, but the leather was so cracked and faded it was almost impossible to read them, or the title. I saw the latter on the first page though; it was a collection of essays on leech treatment. I winced at the very word.

I opened the book at the ribbon marker, to a page full of dense text without a single paragraph break. Natalja had circled a few lines in pencil: 'Lacerations in livestock raided by blood-drinking bats do not immediately scar. This result is similar to the effect seen after applying leeches to an open wound.'

The thought of a slimy little monster clinging to human skin has always made me shiver. Though bloodletting with leeches was no longer considered the prodigious, universal cure it once was thought to be, it was still recommended in very particular cases (when the composition of blood needed to be rebalanced, or when there was no alternative available to induce syncope). I myself had been lectured on how to apply them – not a month before I decided to quit the faculty in Oxford.

I could not face another bite of my toast, so I dressed and went to the Shadows Room. The prospect of facing Natalja yet one more time was not tempting at all, but I remembered I needed to see how she was faring with the Gandolfi camera. I only hoped we were still in time to photograph the decaying body.

Unfortunately she was not there when I stepped in. The curtains were wide open, letting in the dull morning light. The previous day's fog had finally lifted, so I had a clean view of the loch and islands. The sky, however, was still a uniform shade of light grey. I could not even tell where the sun was.

I'd not inspected the room the night before – not with the pathetic lamp I'd had with me at the time – but now I could see the heap of parts and tools spread over a corner desk. I recognized the camera's bellows, now looking like a disembowelled accordion. The main case had been cut at unlikely angles, as if to mount it on to some other device, and there was the lens too, cut into a funny shape. Even a novice in photography could tell the apparatus was beyond repair.

'My daughter tried her best,' said Mrs Koloman, startling me so much I dropped the lens. 'Oh, sorry, I didn't mean to . . .'

I rushed to pick it up. 'It is all right. I am simply looking at your daughter's work. This seems hopeless.'

'I'm afraid so. You should have seen her at breakfast, sleepy and irascible. The poor thing surely spent most of the night here.'

'Indeed,' was my laconic answer.

Mrs Koloman looked distractedly at the loose pieces. 'I was a little worried when I didn't see you at breakfast. I heard you had an accident with the bath?'

I arched an eyebrow. Did this woman know something or was she merely being polite?

'Yes, ma'am, but I managed to contain things. Thank you for asking.'

'Good. I'll be very happy when all this is over.'

'As shall I, Mrs Koloman, and I hope the police get here very soon. I am surprised nobody has arrived yet. By the way, have you not received any telegrams from Thurso? That constable, McLachlan, was supposed to keep us informed of his investigation into Father Thomas's death.'

Mrs Koloman covered her face. 'Oh Lord, there's that dreadful affair too . . . No, we haven't had any telegrams. What do you think that might mean?'

She looked terribly upset, so I forced a smile and a lie. 'Most likely that he has nothing to report yet. Do not worry, ma'am. I am certain there will be constables joining us at some point during the day and this whole nightmare will be over before you know it.'

'I hope you are right. The very thought of that poor man lying dead in our –'

There was an ear-splitting crash against a window. It startled us both, but when I looked I caught only a fleeting glimpse of something dark and blurry, which disappeared before I could even register its shape.

I dashed to the window. 'What was that?'

I looked in every direction, but all I managed to see was a dark form moving upwards swiftly, clinging to the walls of the manor above the window. It could only have been a bat.

Mrs Koloman came up behind me and pointed at the waters. 'Look!'

There was a boat there, moving towards the manor's pier. It jerked and swayed madly, almost capsizing at times.

An ancient woman was rowing on the right-hand side – or rather splashing about with one paddle, her movements desperate. The other paddle, held more steady, was in the hands of a plump teenage girl.

'What are they doing here?' Mrs Koloman hissed, her chest swelling.

'Are they –'

'Mrs Nellys and her daughter, yes.'

Even from this distance and through the glass I could hear it. The old woman was screaming.

31

'*Give me back my son, Minerva!*'

I could hear that shrill voice as I ran downstairs, Mrs Koloman by my side, but the only souls around were –

'Veronika!' Mrs Koloman cried. Her daughter was at the foot of the staircase, Mrs Plunket helping her ascend. They were both pale, looking for the source of the scream. 'What are you –'

'*I want my son back!*'

The screech now resounded throughout the hall, and I saw that the old hag had already made her way in through the back door. She made me think of a witch, with her brittle hair, her cadaverous cheekbones and her ravaged skin. She wore a stained apron over a ragged dress, whose original colour had faded to a murky shade of brown. Her boots and half her skirts were soaking wet, and she left a trail of muddy footprints across the floor.

Her eyes chilled me, for she had the most desperate gaze, her pale pupils flickering about. My first thought was that she must be mad.

'Tell them he couldn't have done it! *Tell them!*' she roared at Mrs Koloman, still holding the paddle and jerking it around in the air. She looked at me. 'Is this the other inspector? Tell him my son didn't do it!'

'Take the girl to her room,' I said as I descended swiftly, but the cook and Veronika remained frozen at the bottom step. 'Madam, your son is perfectly safe.'

Just as Mrs Koloman and I reached the hall, Miss Fletcher came through the back door. She was dripping sweat. 'I'm sorry, ma'am. I spotted the boat in the distance but I was quite far away, looking at that broken fence –'

And then she saw Mrs Nellys, who went to her, nearly on her knees as she begged. 'Millie, you know my family. Tell the inspector my Lazarus couldn't have done it.'

Miss Fletcher held her up, a sudden terror growing in her eyes.

'*Tell them!*' Mrs Nellys repeated. Her daughter arrived then, a plump, rather meek creature. I recognized in her the features of the mother, the pale eyes in particular, which were reddened with tears.

'Give me that, Mother,' she pleaded in the softest voice, reaching for the paddle. She was just as drenched, and her hands trembled with cold. 'You said we were here to talk.'

Miss Fletcher, to my surprise, went straight to the girl and embraced her like a mother would. The poor thing broke into uncontrollable tears, resting her head on Miss Fletcher's shoulder.

Mrs Nellys took a few deep breaths, lowered the paddle and finally dropped it on the floor. She looked at Mrs Koloman with eerie intensity; all the hatred in the world was distilled into that gaze.

'You know Lazarus didn't do it,' she said through her teeth, her voice an octave lower. 'You *know*!'

Mrs Koloman was frozen – we all were – but she stood her ground, a tall, stately matriarch facing the stooped, bony crone dripping water and mud. Still she gulped, and when she spoke her voice quivered. 'Sabina, the other suspect is my own son.'

It was as if she'd thrown cold water over Mrs Nellys. The woman's chest swelled and she even took a step back.

'*You witch from hell!*' she hissed, her eyes pooling tears. Then she appealed to me, addressing me with surprising deference. 'Don't let them deceive you, sir. You have to free him.'

I felt so sorry for her, begging for aid in her patched-up clothes, soaked to the bone and trembling in distress – and her poor daughter, who looked just as broken, being consoled by Miss Fletcher. Yet I could not tell them lies.

'That is not for me to decide, madam. The constables should arrive this very day. There will be a formal inquest.'

The woman sneered. 'And you will own that, Minerva. Won't you? You and Konrad will bribe everyone involved! All you want is his ruin. *Our* ruin. You won't rest until you see him hang!'

Mrs Koloman half raised a hand, as if barely containing the impulse to slap that woman. 'How dare you say that, Sabina? Lazarus would be dead if it weren't for me.' She looked at the plump girl. 'So would Helena. And for years we've sent you food, and bought your meat and your gin . . . and the three meagre blocks of cheese you manage to make each month. You would all have starved and be rotting on those islands if I had turned my back on you.'

'We can do without you. Mr Dailey at the inn also –'

'Mr Dailey only buys your produce because I *beg* him to. He doesn't like you very much, did you know that? His wife is afraid of your tribe.'

Mrs Nellys's eyes nearly fell from their sockets. She covered her mouth and let out a fleeting whimper, before making a pathetic attempt at a dignified silence. Her daughter tried to embrace her, but then Mrs Nellys stumbled, as if stricken by sudden vertigo, and nearly fell. Miss Fletcher ran to her and held her.

'She hasn't eaten since yesterday!' Helena cried. 'I told her she shouldn't row all the way here, but –'

'That's fine, my girl,' said Mrs Koloman, putting her arm around Helena's shoulders. Her sudden maternal tone was entirely at odds with her earlier rant. 'I'll give her something for –'

'I don't want your remedies!' Mrs Nellys managed to groan.

'But you do need to lie down, missus,' said Miss Fletcher as she lifted the woman in her arms. 'Ma'am, may I take her to the last guest room?'

Mrs Koloman looked at the frail woman, her eyes still on fire, but then her gaze went to the mortified Helena, and to Miss Fletcher, and her features softened a little.

Miss Fletcher attempted to smile at the girl. 'Helena, you had better stay here. I'll take good care of your mother, I promise.'

Helena stretched her arms towards her mother, but Mrs Koloman held her in place.

Veronika and Mrs Plunket still stood like statues at the bottom of the stairs, and their eyes followed Mrs Nellys as Miss Fletcher carried her right in front of them. Veronika's expression was striking: she stared at the poor woman in sheer, indescribable terror, unable either to blink or to breathe. She only remained on her feet because Mrs Plunket held her firmly.

The cook whispered something in the girl's ear and Veronika shuddered, suddenly coming back to her senses, and she managed to look away.

'My dear, you're freezing!' I heard Mrs Koloman say. She

was holding Helena's hands. 'Mrs Plunket, take my daughter to her room, and then bring a blanket and some hot soup for Helena. And for the love of God, find any of the girls and tell them to set a fire in the drawing room.'

'At once, ma'am,' said Mrs Plunket; she and Veronika were already on their way upstairs.

'Come, my dear,' said Mrs Koloman. 'I need to get you out of those drenched clothes. I might have something you can wear.'

'Mrs Koloman,' I said as softly as I could manage, 'please let me know when the child and the mother are fit to talk. I have several questions I'd like to –'

And then we all heard a gunshot outside.

32

'Go upstairs!' I urged, running to the back door. As I unsheathed my gun I took one last glance at the staircase. As soon as the women disappeared I kicked the door open. I strode out, my heart thumping and my hand ready to shoot. I would soon feel slightly ridiculous.

'Nothing to worry about!' McGray yelled from the distance, but I did not lower my gun until I saw him appear. He came from the west end of the manor, snorting and stamping on the ground with fury.

'What happened?'

He shook his head, pointing over his shoulder with his thumb. I saw Mr Koloman emerge around the same corner, and behind him came Benjamin and Natalja. And Uncle Maurice.

I nearly gasped, for all the men were armed with either rifles or slimmer shotguns. Even Benjamin, though he held the weapon as far from his body as he could, as if it were a skunk.

Mr Koloman was grinning, oblivious to his nephew's discomfort. He pranced forward in a manner that very much reminded me of his son, with the rifle over his shoulder, and in the other hand he brandished what I thought at first was the world's most famished grouse. The daylight was dull indeed, for I did not recognize the animal until Mr Koloman stood three yards from me. It was, of course, a bat, most likely the one I'd seen minutes ago.

'We found this thing flapping around the house,' he announced.

I winced, for the animal was a very ugly sight: black, hairy and dripping blood. However, that was not what surprised me the most.

'Why did you never tell us you had all these guns?'

McGray was red with anger. 'Aye, I was as shocked as ye. They have a room full o' them, guns and ammunition. I told them they could take the laddie out for a wee while, and before I knew it they were all armed and strolling about the garden.' He looked at Uncle Maurice with indignation. 'And yer soddin' Frog of an uncle told them to never mind the "*Aber-bloody-deener*". I'm from Dundee, ye cretin!'

Uncle Maurice looked rather pleased with himself, which only worsened my mood. 'Ian, these are hunting grounds. Of course they keep guns. *I* keep even more on my estate. You have seen them.'

'This is ridiculous!' I cried, both to him and Mr Koloman. 'Do you not grasp the situation? You should have told us you had firearms within everybody's reach!'

'They won't for much longer,' said McGray, patting his breast pocket, where the keys jingled. 'I'm locking these in the gun room right away.'

Mr Koloman's smile had not faded. 'Inspectors, I have told you plenty of times already, Benjamin is perfectly safe here. If anyone in the family had the slightest –'

'Och, shut that hole in yer face!' McGray snatched the dead bat.

'Where did you find that thing?' I asked.

Mr Koloman used the rifle to point. 'On the west wing, close to the kitchen . . . By the pantry, in fact, where you are keeping Lazarus.'

'That's true,' said McGray, staring at the dead bat. 'I was the first one to see the poor devil.'

'Give the weapons to my uncle,' I told them. 'We are locking them up ourselves. And do go inside. Your wife has some news for you.'

Benjamin seemed only too glad to be rid of his gun. Mr Koloman, still in high spirits, put his arm around the boy's narrow shoulders. 'We must do as we are told, mustn't we? Come, you look like you could use some red wine.'

'Sir, it's not yet eleven . . .'

'Do not call me sir, for the love of God!' and their voices became lost as they went inside. Natalja rushed away without even glancing at me.

'She's been furious all morning,' Uncle whispered in my ear. 'What have you done to her?'

McGray chuckled. 'Ye should ask what has he *nae* done —'

'Oh, that is the least of my worries right now. Uncle, what the heck did you think you were doing, encouraging them to go shooting at a time like this? *Gosh*, you are worse than Elgie, and he has only just turned nineteen!'

McGray was sombre. 'Percy's right. Don't mingle with these people like that. And don't ye dare mock or question our authority again.'

'In fact,' I said, all bleakness, 'you should go back to the inn.'

Uncle smiled, but for once he seemed uneasy. 'Oh, Ian, you cannot be serious.'

He did not stop smiling, as if my words could not sink in.

'I am,' I said, 'and the sooner you leave the better. There will be constables here soon and I cannot bear the thought of you passing them drinks and cigars while they question people and inspect the corpse.'

Uncle Maurice faltered for an instant. He attempted to widen his already fading grin, but I was glaring at him.

'Very well,' he said in the end, his voice graver than I'd ever heard it. 'I shall just say farewell to the family. Basic manners, Ian.'

He dropped the rifles in my arms and went inside.

'I hope he is not too offended,' I mumbled.

McGray shrugged. 'Mnah, buy him a bloody crate o' fancy Frogs' wine and it'll all be forgotten. We do need him out o' the way.'

I sighed. 'In that you are right. Things are getting more and more convoluted: Mrs Nellys is here with her daughter. She is demanding we free Lazarus.'

'*What?* She's here? How did she manage to row all the way from the island?'

'By nearly killing herself. Miss Fletcher had to take her to a bed. The last one in the house, I believe.'

McGray whistled. 'At least we still outnumber the dead ones.'

I sighed at that thought, and for some reason a little voice in my head whispered: *For now.*

'It is an old specimen. See, the fangs are eroded.'

The little jaw, oozing blood and saliva, looked exactly like the engraving in Natalja's book, so at least the repulsive image was not a complete surprise.

McGray and I were both leaning over the unfortunate animal. We had spread its wings on a small table in the astronomy room – the only place where we seemed to have some privacy.

'That book said they could live for almost ten years,' said McGray. 'So this wee lad has seen his share o' Scottish winters.'

'Yes, this species don't hibernate. In winter they must have a place to roost. A . . .' I remembered the chilling lines in that history book. 'A cave, perhaps.'

McGray straightened his back. 'And if they cannae withstand the cold . . . they'd also need to be fed in the coldest months.'

My eyes opened wide. 'Are you suggesting that the Nellyses in fact *breed* these things?'

'And feed them with their goats' blood. Aye.'

I looked sideways. 'I just heard Mrs Koloman say that the Nellyses manage to produce only a meagre amount of cheese.'

'Really? That makes nae sense. They have a lot o' goats, Frey. And remember I saw a bat the night the priest was murdered. These things seem to follow that family like hungry pets.'

'Breeding bats,' I muttered. 'Why would anybody do that?' Once again I felt I was looking at the loose pieces of a dark, disturbing puzzle. 'Blood is at the core of everything,' I mumbled, completing my thought.

'Aye. The bull's blood baths; the constable appearing without a drop o' blood in his body; these bloodsucking flying beasts; and then –'

I saw the buoyancy in his eyes. I was about to ask what he was thinking but there was a gentle knock at the door.

'Yes?'

Mrs Glenister stepped in, looking, if possible, more irritated than ever before: her hands were interlaced tightly, her lips a mere slit across her face.

'Inspector Frey, Mr Plantard says he wishes to have a

word with you before he leaves. I'm afraid he is already at the main entrance.'

McGray went to the south dormer window. 'Aye, yer uncle seems to be taking his goodbyes very seriously.'

I had a look too. The Kolomans' main carriage was there, already loaded with most of my uncle's trunks. The entire family – including Veronika, of course – had gathered around him.

'What did he give 'em to drink?' McGray asked scornfully. 'They only met him a couple o' bloody days ago, yet they're all melting on him like butter on a fat hag's arse.'

Mrs Glenister cleared her throat very loudly. 'Shall I show you the way – *gentlemen*?'

I breathed out. 'Very well. The sooner he can leave the better.'

And I laid out a handkerchief to cover the bat, but very poorly. Mrs Glenister raised an eyebrow, looking intently at the leathery wings that still stuck out. 'When I was younger,' she said, 'there was not one such creature in these lands.'

McGray and I both turned our heads towards her. Our movement was so sudden she took a step back.

'Could you elaborate, please?' I asked, and Mrs Glenister gulped.

'Mr Plantard appears to be in a hurry, sir.'

'That soddin' imp can wait,' said McGray. 'Tell us, how long ago was that?'

The wrinkles between the woman's eyes had deepened and extended almost to her hairline. 'Twenty-five . . . no, nearly thirty years ago. Not a single one of them in sight.'

'And then?'

Another gulp, and then she burst out, as if she'd longed to say those words for a very long time, 'They all arrived with the Nellyses. Only a few at first, but then more and more . . . And now we see them every summer, fluttering about whenever it's warm. It seems every year they dare come a little closer to the house. We would never have seen them on the mainland five years ago, but now my master shoots at least a couple every summer. This is the third one this year.' She trembled and rubbed her arms, as if stricken by a sudden draught. 'I had a nightmare once. I saw thousands of them flapping through the manor, in every hall and every room.' She took a breath, perhaps about to say more, but then closed her mouth tightly and looked away.

'Why do you think the Nellyses brought them?' I said.

'God only knows. The ghastly things just seem to follow that family wherever they go.'

Like this one did today, I thought.

I shook my head and hurried to the door. When we arrived at the manor's main entrance Smeaton was already in the driver's seat, looking quite bored as the Kolomans said their goodbyes. Boyde had just loaded the last trunk.

Veronika seemed quite sad, supporting herself on Natalja's arm as Uncle Maurice kissed her hand.

'I do hope we can meet again,' the girl was saying. Either she had recovered some colour or she was flushed at my uncle's presence. 'Under more pleasant circumstances, of course.'

'I shall write as soon as this sad affair is over,' he replied with his most charming smile. 'You would all be welcome to visit my estate in Gloucestershire.'

'Perhaps this very winter,' Mr Koloman jumped in, giving Uncle a hearty handshake.

I watched the scene from a distance, my arms crossed, perfectly aware of how bitter I looked.

Uncle saw me and his smile faded immediately. He

excused himself, came over to me and we walked to a quieter corner of the sumptuous garden. Bushy lavenders bloomed all around, and Ellie was gathering the flowers in a basket, perhaps for more baths. As soon as she saw me she ran away.

'I know I have been disturbing things,' Uncle said as soon as the girl had gone. 'I am sorry.'

'There is something about this family I do not like,' I mumbled, but when I looked over at them I found the twins pointing at the roses and rhododendrons, while their parents, arm in arm, whispered and smiled at each other. In their flourishing gardens, the solid manor behind them, they were the very image of plenty.

'Oh, my, they are dreadful indeed,' said Uncle, all sarcasm. He did not let me protest. 'Ian, Konrad seems to adore Benjamin. So do Minerva and the cousins. They have all told me so: they see Benjamin as a blessing. Konrad now has someone to manage the estate; Dominik can go on world-trotting; the girls can now marry for love . . .' He glanced at Veronika with dreamy eyes, and then looked at Natalja. 'Or not at all, if they so wish. If anyone around here will look after Benjamin, it is them.'

Uncle might be irresponsible, immature, hedonistic and decadent, but he is decidedly good at judging people. I took a deep breath.

'Let's assume you are right. Then who sent the death threat?'

He gave me a weary smile. 'Sometimes we need a little help to see the obvious.'

He rested a hand on my shoulder and made me look back at the house. I saw an ashen face looking out from one of the upstairs' windows: Mrs Nellys was staring at us without shame, her mouth downturned.

'Uncle, why –'

'There is something clearly wrong with that family. Many things, in fact. I cannot tell why they would not want Benjamin around, but I am sure you will be able to find that out. You are right; I am far too irresponsible for this sort of affair. I –' He gulped painfully, and then looked down. 'I have never told you this . . .'

He stooped over the nearest lavender, plucked a bloom and brought it to his nose.

'What?' I said softly.

'I once got a girl . . . a sweet girl in trouble.'

I felt my heart rushing. 'Oh, Uncle, there is no need –'

'Yes, Ian, there is every need. Only a handful of people ever knew. Your mother included.' He sighed. 'She took care of everything for me. She assured the family that their daughter would be well looked after. She made sure your grandfather promised an income for the child . . . Dear, dear Cecilia. She was the best sister and the best woman in the world. I wish you'd spent more time with her.'

I wanted to say *I do so too*, but the words stuck in my throat.

'And what did I do?' he continued, tossing the flower aside. 'I went away to spend three months between Paris and the Swiss Alps, and spared no other thought for the matter. I even refused to see the girl again, and when I returned I learned that she had died. Her family had sent her off to give birth in secret, somewhere very remote in Cornwall, and she did not survive. Neither did the child. Perhaps because of the poor conditions there.' Uncle Maurice swallowed again, tightening his entire body to hold back tears. 'People whispered it had been a boy.'

I remembered the melancholy in his eyes when he had stared at the tiny graves on Isle Maree. Now I understood.

After a moment of deep silence he nodded at the Kolomans. 'This family reminds me too much of that year, Ian. I see a lot of myself in Konrad, attempting to undo at least some of the harm that was done in the past.' Uncle smiled wryly. 'He still can. I, on the other hand . . .' He smirked, his face full of regret. 'I have not even learned the lesson, it would seem. I simply cannot confront hardship with a straight face.' He squeezed my arm affectionately. 'You are far better at that than me, Ian, and I admire you for it. I really do.'

A light breeze came then, stirring the scents of the lavenders and the nearby pines.

I did not know what to say, and Uncle read it in my face, for he just squeezed my arm a little tighter, smiled and went away.

All the things I could have told him then . . .

33

'I just know!' Mrs Nellys said for the tenth time.

There was a tray full of cold meats, wine and succulent fruits by her side, but she had refused to eat or drink at all.

'You do realize that will not help your son at the inquest?' I asked, replacing the stethoscope in Mrs Koloman's instrument case. Mrs Nellys had firmly refused to be examined by the lady, so I'd had to step in. 'And before you blame Dominik Koloman one more time, I must tell you that he at least has given some explanation of his whereabouts at the time of the death. A statement impossible to verify, yes, but your son has offered none.'

She crossed her arms and looked away. I knew I would not get anything from her.

McGray had been standing by the window throughout my interrogation, staring at the gardens. At last he spoke.

'What can ye tell us about yer bats?'

'They're not *my* bats,' she retorted at once.

'Do youse breed them?'

'Why would we breed those monsters?' she almost shrieked. 'They besiege our goats and bleed them to death if we're not careful. We make hardly any profit because of them.'

'We heard they arrived here at around the same time you and your husband's family moved to Juniper Island,' I said.

Mrs Nellys finally said something useful. 'We had the goats brought here not long after we moved – they were shipped here in cages. We think the bats might have come along in that shipment, clinging to the goats, or perhaps hidden in the straw.'

'Where were the goats shipped from?'

She shook her head. 'Cuba? Argentina? One of those places. They were supposed to be a very good breed: tame, hardy, excellent for milking. My father had taken ill and I had to look after my husband. We needed a source of income, and we were told goats would be a good business. Not too demanding.' She smiled bitterly. 'What a bunch of lies. To think of the money we paid for them!'

'Where did youse live before?'

'Everywhere. My father and I moved all around, looking for a cure for my husband. We lived in Germany, Boston, Norway . . .'

McGray whistled. 'Sounds like youse were quite wealthy.'

'*Were!* If my poor mother could see us now . . . I ended up selling her most precious jewellery for pennies. Most of it went to charlatan medics, all of them claiming to have a cure for my husband.'

McGray looked sombre. How much of himself was he seeing in that woman? Very much like him, she had squandered all her time, effort and resources looking for that one elusive cure, never giving up, never coming to terms with her reality.

'And youse finally moved here because of the healing waters,' McGray pointed out.

'Yes.'

'Ma'am,' I intervened, 'I have trouble believing those –'

She could not have sounded more resolute. 'The waters cured him. Of that I'm sure.'

'Are you?'

'Your colleague has seen my house. You can imagine how

hard it is to get by in these lands, how lonely it can be. Do you think I'd subject my children to all this for nothing?'

'They were born here, right?' McGray asked.

'Yes. This is the only life they've ever known.'

McGray could not look her in the eye as he spoke. 'Ye've sacrificed so much . . . Ye . . . must love Mr Nellys a good deal.'

Her only reply was a long, tired sigh.

'Yer husband says he's cursed,' McGray said.

Mrs Nellys covered her brow. 'My husband sometimes has . . . well, episodes.'

McGray dragged a chair closer to the bed, sat down and spoke slowly, as if fearing he was about to rouse a dormant beast. 'Has he ever told ye . . . he thinks the bats bite him?'

Mrs Nellys did not blink for an abnormally long time. It was chilling to behold. 'He said what?'

McGray did his best to sound conciliatory. 'That they bite him. That they come in at night and bite him. He told me so himself.'

The poor woman was flabbergasted. 'I told you he still has episodes. Very rare, but he still does. He must be hallucinating again. That was one of his worst symptoms before we found the cure.'

McGray opened his mouth, probably about to tell her he'd seen scars on the man's body, but he held back; the woman seemed quite mortified already. Before he could change his mind I moved the conversation to a different topic.

'Ma'am, you and Lazarus seem to have a severe skin condition.'

She instantly began scratching the back of her hand, as if my mere words had brought a nasty itch to life. 'It's the goats, I think. We must have developed an allergy to them.'

'The goats?' I echoed. 'May I see?'

Hesitantly, she extended her hand, now red after the intense scratching. Very much like her son's, Mrs Nellys's skin was blotched with overlapping marks of disease, the newer patches tender pink, the older ones brown and calloused.

'Helena has not developed this condition,' I pointed out.

'No. The Lord has spared her.'

I looked closer. 'I am not an expert in skin diseases, but I'd be more inclined to believe this has been caused by the bats.'

'I told you, we don't breed the beasts!' she snapped, withdrawing her hand at once.

'I was not suggesting that,' I said, albeit untruthfully. 'The bats might have passed something on to your goats, and those you *do* handle constantly. That might be the actual source of the allergy. As soon as the constables arrive I will make sure that a specialist comes to see you. I still have a few contacts in Oxford.' I did not mention that some of them would dance in glee at the chance of looking at a possibly undocumented malady.

Mrs Nellys was already casting me the most distrustful look. 'When can I go home?'

'You are very weak, ma'am,' I said, standing up. 'I recommend you spend the night here.'

'I will never sleep under the roof of –'

'*Ma'am.*' I raised my voice. 'I said *I recommend* out of politeness. I do not want you to faint – or worse – and leave your daughter stranded on that island all alone. If I find you are better in the morning, we will see that you and Helena are taken back to your home. Otherwise you will have to remain here for as long as I see fit.' I nodded at the tray. 'So you had better eat.'

And as we left the room I saw her stretch a hesitant hand towards a large piece of her own cheese.

'I hope those bloody constables arrive soon,' I grumbled as we walked along the corridor.

Nine-Nails sounded exhausted. 'Aye. I'll be glad to go home.'

I arched an eyebrow. 'Will you? I thought you'd want to investigate those "miraculous waters" some more.'

'I have what I need, Percy,' he muttered, and he hurried into his bedroom before I could ask what he meant.

34

An eerie silence took hold of the manor.

We had nothing left to do but wait, and how galling it was. I must have spent the best part of an hour standing by one of the windows of the astronomy room, expecting at any moment to see a carriage or a handful of riders coming to our aid. My heart skipped a beat every time the wind moved the firs or some bird glided from branch to branch. I was unaware of the time until the sky turned dull and lifeless, my patience wearing out as the dusk crept upon us.

McGray joined me just as the last rays of sunlight were dying on the horizon. He was pressing his arm.

'How is that wound?' I asked him.

'It's healing pretty quickly now. Looks like that clean-up with the spirit really helped.'

He rolled up his sleeve to show me the scar. He had removed the bandages already, and his blood appeared to have clotted as normal. Nevertheless . . .

'D'ye think the worst's passed?'

There was no way I could assure him of that. After seeing Mrs Nellys I was almost convinced those bats were transmitting some odd disease; not rabies, like the cases mentioned in Natalja's books, but something I had never encountered before. However, I saw no point in alarming him just then.

'Yes, I think so.'

He smiled. 'Yer a fucking terrible liar, Percy.'

After reluctantly allowing Boyde to prepare a hot bath for Benjamin – Mr Koloman had kindly pointed out there was no need for us to watch over his nephew 'as the boy refreshed his unmentionables' – McGray and I again found ourselves taking meals to the three suspects, like unwitting gaolers on an evening round.

Tamlyn emerged from the kitchen with the trays. As soon as she saw me her lips and hands began to tremble, nearly spilling Dominik's carafe of wine.

'I checked what you said,' I told her in a whisper as we walked along the corridors.

'What's that, sir?'

'Miss Veronika's wounds. Please, do *not* pretend you cannot –'

Nine-Nails pushed in between us. 'There, there, Percy. What's the need for torturing the lassie? Tamlyn, the dandy here says . . .' – he looked around to make sure there were no eavesdroppers – 'he says he found nothing. *Nothing*. D'ye understand?'

She nodded vehemently. 'Then I must've been mistaken.'

I raised my eyebrows. 'You seemed quite convinced when you first said it. And scars do not vanish in . . .'

I looked down, realizing something I ought to have deduced long ago. McGray's eyes widened. He knew too.

'What d'ye think the –'

It was my turn to raise a hand. 'I will deal with this, McGray. Tamlyn, you have done well.' And I smiled at her.

The trembling of her hands diminished ever so slightly, and we resumed our way to the locked rooms.

We found the men increasingly impatient. Calcraft grunted like a hungry dog, and Dominik, as I had expected, was on edge. He pleaded for more tobacco – we saw no reason to deny him – and we left him pacing to and fro, looking grim and, surprisingly, quite pale.

In contrast, Lazarus had given in to an unnerving lethargy, as if his own fate did not bother him at all. He'd not touched the food we had left in the morning, and he lifted his face only when we told him about the arrival of his mother and sister.

'What are they doing here?' he snapped.

'They came to plead for you,' I said. 'Your mother in particular is very poorly. She has not eaten since yesterday, according to your sister.'

Lazarus had no colour left, but the premature lines around his eyes deepened. 'She hasn't eaten?'

'She's worried sick,' said McGray. 'Don't ye think ye should tell us what's really going on? Where did ye go that night? Did ye have anything to do with the constable's death?'

Lazarus simply tensed his lips and stared at the floor.

I took a deep breath. I thought I'd better take a different approach, rather than repeat the same question like a parrot. 'She told us about that skin condition you caught from the goats. It is curious that your sister seems quite healthy.'

Lazarus put a hand to his brow. 'I only got it when I was seventeen or eighteen. Helena might be yet to show symptoms. I fear the day she does. Our family seems to be withering and dying . . . very slowly . . .'

I leaned closer. 'I know people who might help, medics

and scientists I met in Oxford. If you help us, if you tell us what really happened, perhaps I could bring them here to –'

He looked up so quickly he nearly cracked his neck. *'Don't! Leave us alone! We've managed so far. We will continue to manage.'*

'With all due respect,' I said, doing my best to provoke him to talk, 'you do not seem to be managing particularly well at the moment. Do you want your mother and sister to go back to their island? Do you want them to be cut off from the world, left to fend for themselves when the police come and take you to jail? To leave your father secluded for ever in that little shack?'

Lazarus began to breathe more and more anxiously, until his chest heaved and he burst into a furious growl, jumping to his feet and throwing the tray of food against the wall.

'Go to hell! Leave me alone!'

His voice was booming, and he glared at us with blood-shot eyes, the red in deep contrast with his almost white pupils. The only sounds were his snorting breath and the trickle of soup dripping from the shelves.

I merely nodded. 'As you wish,' I said, and walked to the door. Tamlyn came in and began picking up the shattered china and crockery. 'Leave that. You can clean up in the morning.'

We left the pantry and McGray locked the door. He dispatched the girl and on our way to the main parlour we passed through the raucous kitchen. Mrs Glenister, Boyde, young Ellie and the alarmingly wide Mrs Plunket were in a frantic race to prepare dinner. I saw piles of summer berries and blue cheese, five ten-year-old bottles of wine being decanted, and I perceived the tasty aroma of boeuf en croûte. My mouth watered and my empty stomach growled.

We heard chatter and laughter in the drawing room. As

we walked in, the first thing to catch my eye was a tall, spindly man dressed in an immaculate black suit. I had to blink twice before I realized it was Benjamin.

Mr Koloman was adjusting his nephew's bowtie with one hand, holding a large glass of wine in the other. He noticed us and his smile grew to an impossible width.

'Inspectors, I bet you wouldn't recognize him if you saw him in Mayfair!'

I spotted the old-fashioned cut of the jacket, and that the sleeves and trousers were a little too short for the boy, but other than that Benjamin looked quite the gentleman, with a snow-white shirt, shining shoes and a neat haircut. The faltering hint of a smile suggested he liked the change but was too shy to admit it.

McGray whispered in my ear. 'Ye were right; we shouldnae have left him alone with them. Half an hour and they've turned him into a bloody Frey!'

All the family were gathered there. Mrs Koloman looked quite at ease on one of the velvet sofas, admiring her nephew with proud eyes. And the twins, both seated on the piano stool, were clad in light dresses cut from the exact same pattern, only one was of a slightly lighter olive green than the other. From that distance I could not tell who was who – but apparently I'd made that same mistake before.

I cleared my throat. 'Is this a special occasion?'

Mr Koloman passed me a full glass. 'It doesn't need to be! Benjamin yielded to my insistence and agreed to be dressed and groomed like an aristocrat. I simply thought we should all match his effort.'

'It elevates one's mood,' said Veronika from the piano, with a radiant smile that concealed any trace of illness. 'Don't you think so?'

'I only wish we could have Dominik join us,' said Mrs Koloman, looking wistfully at her husband.

He in turn looked at me. 'Inspectors, I don't suppose you could, just for this evening –'

'Aye,' McGray replied, 'ye suppose well.' And he helped himself to the excellent red wine. He seemed to be developing a taste for it.

I thought there'd been a soft knock at the door but was not entirely sure until I heard it again, half lost under the Kolomans' sanguine conversation. The family only became aware of it because I went to open the door.

To my utter surprise, it was the plump, nervous Helena, fidgeting with a handkerchief and looking decidedly pale. She had also changed into a more elegant, albeit old-fashioned, turquoise gown. It was a model from the fifties or forties – something my grandmothers would have worn – but it somehow resembled the twins' almost Grecian gowns.

'You look so beautiful!' Mrs Koloman cried, rising to meet the girl and take her by the hand. The woman was nearly moved to tears. 'That was my mother's first party dress. It's perfect on you.'

Helena blushed, but very much like Benjamin she seemed to appreciate the attention. I doubted anyone had ever praised her looks. Maybe not even her mother.

'It's . . . it's very pretty, ma'am,' she mumbled.

'Oh, you can take it with you if you like it.'

Veronika approached her. 'Or you can come here and wear it whenever you wish. You wouldn't want it to get soiled or torn by goats.'

Helena's head was bowed, hardly daring to look at the beautiful twins. 'I don't think my mother would like that,' she said in a barely audible voice.

'Don't worry about that right now,' Natalja intervened, taking Helena's hand. 'Enjoy the moment. Come, I bet you'll love our music.'

Natalja cast me a furtive, testing look. I felt butterflies in my stomach as our eyes met, a hundred questions swarming in my mind. I was eager to bring up last night's scheme there and then, but I did not know how her parents might react. I had, after all, been nude in the presence of one of their daughters and stepped into the bedroom of the other without their consent. They seemed very progressive people, but last night's happenings might prove too much even for *them*.

All these thoughts came to me in an instant, and Natalja surely noticed my inner conflict. Whatever she read in my face she did not like, for she moved away swiftly. So did her sister, pulling Helena by the other hand, and the three girls gathered around the piano.

As Veronika played a lively mazurka, Helena looked in awe at the thick rugs, the bookshelves, the domed ceiling and the lavish furnishings.

'A "brave new world",' McGray whispered with a hint of sadness. He was surely thinking of Helena's disappointment when she had to return to the hardships of Juniper Island, with a sick mother, a barely sane father and – it seemed ever more likely – a convict brother.

'Do *not* quote Shakespeare,' I grumbled. 'I've had enough of him for a lifetime.'

Veronika's music was as accomplished as Natalja's, but it also had a certain brightness, an eagerness I had not heard in her sister's. I allowed myself a sideways smile; the girl now seemed fit enough for direct interrogation, and I'd see that it happened as soon as possible.

Natalja went to Benjamin and pulled him into their circle.

The twins' high spirits were so infectious that even the wary Helena was smiling, gently rocking her head to the rhythm of the tune.

'Ah, the pleasures of youth,' said Mr Koloman with a sigh, inviting us to sit with him and his wife.

'We should have Helena here more often,' she said. 'She is the most darling thing. Imagine what some manners and education could do for her. Perhaps now that Lazarus . . .' She looked down, hesitating.

'The mother would not allow it,' Mr Koloman explained to us. 'She thinks we are vain and our ideas far too liberal for her kin.'

I could see her point; the twins' scandalous clothes were the most immediate example (let alone the immodest attitudes I'd witnessed the night before).

'Would you look after Helena?' I asked. 'If need be, I mean.'

Mrs Koloman brought a hand to her chest. 'Of course we would! And not just out of charity. Look at her. She'd be so happy with my girls.'

As I looked, Veronika was inviting Helena to play the keyboard, the plump girl shaking her head coyly. Until then I had not really seen the beauty in her features, the pointy nose or the full lips. Cheerfulness is indeed the best of tonics. As I sipped my wine I wondered whether her brother's downfall and her mother's illness might in fact be blessings in disguise.

The boeuf en croûte was rather disappointing. The pastry was buttery and perfectly golden but the meat itself was far too rare for my taste, spurting scarlet juices whenever I pressed it with my knife.

McGray seemed delighted though, helping himself to huge mouthfuls and smacking his lips rowdily – I could not expect less from a man who dribbles over haggis. Veronika, to my utter surprise, seemed to like it just as much, eating with an appetite her ladylike manners could barely conceal. She seemed as though . . . nothing had happened.

Natalja sat next to me, and noticed how I stared at her sister.

'You are not blinking, Mr Frey,' she whispered, hiding her lips behind her glass of wine.

I pretended to reach for the salt cellar and whispered as low as I could: 'I know what you did last night.'

She dropped her glass, splattering wine all over the table. All the other conversations stopped.

'Nat, what happened?' Mrs Koloman asked, as Boyde ran over and began mopping up the red drink.

Natalja blushed intensely. 'I . . . I am *so* sorry –'

'There, there,' I said. 'It was just an accident . . . was it not?' I felt so much delight in those words that some guilt instantly invaded me. I steered the conversation away from the spilled wine, looking quite the gentleman. 'Thank you for sharing your excellent table with us yet one more night. I hope we will not have to intrude in your home for much longer.'

'The constables are certainly taking their time,' Mr Koloman said then, attempting – very poorly – to sound pleasant.

'Indeed,' I said. 'If they are not here by mid-morning tomorrow, I will ask my uncle to take a note to the nearest town with a decent constabulary.'

'The nearest proper town would be Inverness,' Veronika

said. 'That is sixty miles away. It is a full day's journey each way.'

McGray's full mouth did not hinder his reply. 'Indeedy, but we cannae wait any longer.'

'If it comes to that,' said Mr Koloman, 'I will accompany him. It is my son's freedom that's at stake.' He took a sip of wine. 'In fact, I will ask Smeaton to ready the carriage first thing in the morning. Just in case.' He nodded at Boyde, who bowed and left the dining room to pass on the instructions. 'If Dominik and Calcraft were not imprisoned, we could have used their steamer; it would take us just as long to sail to Thurso.'

The recrimination was still there, barely contained. Mrs Koloman changed the subject swiftly.

'You have hardly touched your beef,' she said to Helena. I'd already noticed the girl had been pushing the thick slice around her plate. 'If you don't like it, we can prepare something else for you. Anything, dear.'

She timidly shook her head and, like me, took only a mouthful of pastry.

'Are you worried about your father?' Benjamin asked in the gentlest of tones; something he might have picked up from the late priest.

Despite his kindness, poor Helena lost all her composure. She dropped her cutlery and covered her face with both hands, weeping so miserably I felt a lump in my throat.

Mrs Koloman jumped up and comforted the girl with a motherly embrace. Helena nestled her head on the lady's shoulder, almost as if nobody had consoled her in her entire life.

'He must be so . . . so frightened!' the girl said between sobs.

'Your father?'

Helena nodded. 'Lazarus goes to Isle Maree every evening

to talk to him and give him food. He didn't go yesterday. If nobody attends him tonight, I'm afraid my father –'

She could say no more.

'Can we help at all?' McGray asked. 'We have the two wee boats at the pier – the inn's and Lazarus's. We could send him food.'

Helena's eyes filled with hope. 'Oh, could you?'

'Indeedy,' McGray replied. 'I'll go myself if need be.'

I chuckled. 'With your seasickness, Nine-Nails? So that you can gag and vomit in the middle of the loch?'

He opened his mouth, closed it, reopened it as he pointed his knife at me . . . and closed it again. 'Och, ye win again!' But he had the perfect revenge. 'Looks like ye'll have to go yerself, Percy!'

Half the sky had cleared, promising – without the need of Mr Koloman's extravagant instruments – that a bright day would follow. As McGray and I stood by the pier, however, the only light we could see came from the stars and that indigo strip just above the horizon. The air was quite cool but still rather pleasant, and the tranquillity of the place invaded me once more. It was almost as if its waters were a magnet that soaked up all the noise and worries in the world.

Neither of us spoke for a while; we simply watched how Miss Fletcher jumped into the Nellyses' scruffy boat, carrying two baskets full of unperishable food and a few flagons of wine. As Helena had pointed out, we simply did not know when anyone would be able to go there again, and Mr Koloman had instructed Mrs Plunket to provide any articles the girl requested for her father.

Mr Koloman came out from the manor, bringing a nervous Helena with him. The girl carried a large lantern, shedding its golden light all around us.

'Keep a good eye on them,' I muttered to McGray before they reached us.

'I think I can manage, Frey. *Yer* the one who should be careful.'

I could not argue, for Helena and Mr Koloman were now by our side.

'Go to the boat, child,' he told her with an encouraging smile. When the girl was out of earshot he spoke in a worried whisper: 'Inspectors, this will strike you as utterly unusual . . .'

'*Ha!* Try us,' said Nine-Nails.

The man bit his lip. 'Well . . . Benjamin has insisted we take him to see his father's grave.'

McGray snorted. 'He's *what*?'

'As you heard. He is adamant, I'm afraid. He wants to see it now.'

'Now?' I repeated.

'Indeed. Since there will be a boat going there —' He shook his head. 'Sorry, I should have mentioned this before. We buried my brother on Isle Maree.'

I covered my brow. 'Oh Lord, *just* what we needed.'

Only then did I notice that Miss Fletcher had heard what Mr Koloman was proposing. She went so pale her face almost glowed in the dim light, and before I could say anything the woman turned on her heel and rushed back to the boat.

'I thought the boy —' I was about to say *despised* but reworded my sentence in time. 'I thought he had troubles coming to terms with his father's character.'

'Natalja and I talked to him this morning. We've told him

of the more redeemable qualities of my late brother. Benjamin is curious, which is only natural.'

My patience was wearing thin. 'Mr Koloman, that sad-looking boat will not take more than three –'

I turned to point at it, only to find that Miss Fletcher was already rowing with all her might, the boat and Helena's light quickly drifting away from the shore.

I ran to the pier, calling her back, but she ignored me.

McGray followed me and spoke in my ear. 'That poor woman keeps running away from her son.'

'We still have the inn's boat,' said Mr Koloman, nodding at it. 'And I assure you that Isle Maree is as safe as –'

McGray had to raise both hands and bid him to shut up.

'Och, I am so sick o' yer whining! Very well, the dandy here will take the boy.'

'McGray!'

Benjamin arrived just then and McGray pointed a finger at him. 'But youse will only stay there for a few minutes, and ye *must* stay where the flimsy English flower can see ye. D'ye understand? No wandering off, and if I hear that ye've but whispered, "Oh, one more minute, *please, sir* . . ."'

I would have argued further but I knew it would be to no avail. The decision had been made.

While they fetched Boyde I peered into the deep darkness ahead, hoping that we'd not just signed somebody's death sentence.

I wish I'd known then that the true tragedy was about to begin.

PART 3

'Take from my hand this cup of the wine of wrath ...

*They shall drink and stagger and be crazed because of the
sword that I am sending among them.'*

Jeremiah 25:15–16

35

What an eerie procession we were. Four stooped men in a silent boat, all looking grim, all carrying lanterns whose feeble light only heightened the immensity of the loch. The waning moon offered little help: it was but a silver line in the sky, and tomorrow it would not be visible at all. Boyde was staring at it, his lantern between his legs, projecting eerie shadows on his face as he rowed. I noticed the almost black rings under his eyes, as though he'd not slept in days.

Benjamin sat between his uncle and me, still wearing the very elegant black suit and white bowtie. He clenched his bull's-eye lantern with both hands, his bony fingers fidgeting on the rusty steel. Both Mr Koloman and I looked nervously in all directions, and I kept my hand on my breast pocket, ready to draw my gun.

Once more I felt as if we were drifting into another world, as if Boyde were the Grim Reaper and this boat were taking us into the thick shadows of purgatory. I shook my head at those thoughts. I would achieve nothing by alarming myself.

Again we rounded Juniper Island, and then I spotted a speck of light coming from Isle Maree. At first I thought it was Helena's lantern, and that Miss Fletcher must be taking her back to the manor before we could reach them. As we drew closer I realized it was not one but two sparks.

'They've lit that blasted skull again,' Mr Koloman grunted.

I instantly recalled the deer skull nailed to the tree.

'Who are *they*?' I asked. 'The witchcraft people Miss Fletcher told me about?'

'Yes.'

'What do you know about them?'

'Very little. Only that they come and go as they please. And they always leave that ghastly thing as you see it.'

I watched the sinuous shape of the antlers emerge very slowly, the pale bone reflecting the glow from those eerily wide eye sockets.

Boyde jumped out and pulled the boat ashore. As I disembarked I could see the candle stubs and their dancing flames, looking like the vertical pupils of a serpent, guarding against our arrival.

I pulled Benjamin closer to me. 'As I said, we will only stay here for a few minutes.'

'Shall I pull that down?' asked Boyde, his smudged eyes staring anxiously at the skull.

'What for?' replied Mr Koloman. 'They'll only put it back again.'

'It looks like it has been burning for hours,' I said, walking closer and inspecting the candle stumps, which were almost completely burned away. I looked around, peering through the twisted branches of oak and holly. Beyond I could see the graves, some of them reflecting the light from our lanterns, but the best part of the island was still swathed in darkness. 'I hope they made their ritual and left.' Indeed, I hoped that skull had been placed there by mere madwags; I did not wish to encounter the more vicious variety of witchcraft practitioners.

I gave Benjamin a gentle push, and then unsheathed my gun and raised my lantern to light the terrain ahead. The sooner we visited the blasted grave the sooner we could leave.

We ascended the gentle slope, pushing branches and leaves aside, and the first graves we stumbled upon were the three little tombstones that had unnerved Uncle Maurice so much. I remembered his sad face and his confession, and felt so sorry for him. I would spend a couple of weeks with him in Gloucestershire, as soon as we'd left this case in the hands of the local police – whether McGray liked it or not.

'Those are the graves of the Nellyses' first children,' said Mr Koloman, standing right behind me. 'None survived more than a few months.'

Benjamin frowned. 'Why? What happened to them?'

'He can tell us later,' I said, though I felt as curious as the boy. 'I do not want to linger here. Mr Koloman, where is your brother's grave?'

He walked solemnly amongst the tombs and pointed to a black granite stone, its edges carved to simulate natural rock. 'Here.'

There was a small oak sapling planted right next to it, so that, as it grew, its trunk and roots would fuse with the stone, where leaves and acorns were sculpted. We might all be long dead before that tree became the haunting, living memorial originally intended. Just as well; Maximilian Koloman now had an eternity to wait.

At first Benjamin stood still, simply staring at the grave and its Gothic engraving. He took a cautious step forward, as if he were looking at an intimidating, much alive tyrant. And then he knelt down, moving his lips in a silent prayer. I could only wonder what he might be pleading for – mercy for his father's sins, perhaps.

The scene made me think of my own deceased ones: my dear mother, first of all. She now lay in the family crypt in Gloucestershire, in a quiet corner of my uncle's estate, where

I myself hoped to rest when my time came. I thought I'd pay her a visit too.

Benjamin's trembling voice seemed to echo my thoughts. 'And where does my mother –'

A horrendous scream tore the air, chilling our blood. It was a male voice, soon followed by the most desolate female whimpers. Benjamin rose at once, and I pointed my gun towards the source. I saw a faint gleam coming from the other side of the island, from where old Mr Nellys lived.

'Stay here!' I barked, though I knew they'd ignore me, and ran across the graveyard, jumping over tombstones and dodging roots and rocks, my lantern projecting maddened shadows all around.

I ran around the shack and found its door ajar. Helena's lantern lay lonely on the ground, the leaves around it starting to catch fire. I kicked the door open and found the girl utterly distraught. She was curled up on the floor, covering her mouth with both hands, and crying and moaning in the most unnerving way. Miss Fletcher stood next to her, leaning over a shapeless bundle of blankets. I knew it was Mr Nellys only because another awful scream came from beneath the manky shroud.

'What happened?' I asked, but did not wait for an answer. I knelt by the man and uncovered his face. He looked so pale, blemished and ravaged by ill health my heart jumped. He was clenching his brown teeth, his face distorted by searing pain.

I pulled away the blankets and saw his hands were pressed tightly to his ribcage. His fingers were stained dark red. I tried to pull them away and inspect whatever lay underneath, but he looked pleadingly at me, silently beseeching me to leave him alone.

The pain overwhelmed him and he had to let out another

howl. I took the chance to pull his hands away and tear aside the ancient, stinking shirt he wore.

Helena let out a sharp whimper, and Miss Fletcher and I gasped. Mr Nellys's abdomen was covered in wounds, dozens of perforations all over his skin, some of them scarred, but many of them still open, the skin around them raw, oozing blood and some of them pus. The entire shack reeked of infection.

'How did this happen?' I demanded. 'Who did this to you?' I remembered McGray's words. 'Bites?' I mumbled, rather to myself, but Mr Nellys nodded as he growled in pain again. The wounds themselves were not fatal, but my instinct still told me this man would not live for much longer.

Miss Fletcher was embracing Helena, whispering soothingly in her ear, and then the flapping door was opened by Mr Koloman. Behind him came Boyde ... and ...

'Benjamin,' Miss Fletcher let out, looking straight into the boy's eyes. Though her voice was low everyone went quiet, as if time had stopped. Even Mr Nellys ceased his grunting.

Miss Fletcher's chest swelled, her eyes burning with a swirl of uncontainable emotions. I read shock, confusion, shame – even a brief flicker of joy.

I looked at Benjamin. The boy was giving her a confused stare, but his expression already showed a shadow of understanding.

Was he seeing what we all saw, what to our eyes was so glaringly obvious? Though Benjamin shared the Kolomans' blond hair and fine jaw, he and Miss Fletcher were of the same height; their eyes were of the same colour and shape; they even had the same freckled face and ungainly shoulders.

The boy quivered ever so slightly, and in that movement his eyes caught a glint from the fire. A mere twinkle, but for

Miss Fletcher it was enough to betray sixteen years of sworn silence.

'My father's eyes,' she said, unable to contain herself. 'You have –'

She covered her mouth at once, looking now at the enraged Mr Koloman, and then a lonely tear rolled down her cheek – something I would have never thought possible.

Mr Koloman let out a hissing breath, his face as red as a demon's, and what little joy might have been in Miss Fletcher's eyes gave way to sheer terror.

Benjamin gulped painfully. 'It's you,' he whispered, with misty eyes and oblivious to his uncle's fury. 'Why didn't . . . why . . . ?'

He could say no more. He cried copiously, unable to move, and we all stood around in awkward silence, not knowing what to say or do.

It was Helena who reacted first. She nudged Miss Fletcher, gave her a reassuring little smile and pulled the giant woman closer to her long-lost son.

But before they managed to say a word, or to touch hands, Mr Koloman made his voice heard.

'Fletcher, take that man to the house! Minerva will know what to do.'

For a moment it was as though he'd spoken in another language. Miss Fletcher started, turning her face to her master but seemingly unable to take in his words.

Mr Koloman turned red. '*Fletcher*, do as I say, dammit!'

What happened next was rather disturbing. Benjamin turned to face him very, very slowly, clenching his fists as he moved. There was fire in his stare, a murderous expression I had seen in only a handful of people. He planted himself between his uncle and his mother, shuddering with wrath.

The skinny, meek boy was being replaced by a blazing fiend. He mopped his tears with his sleeve, and when he spoke his incensed voice still trembled with self-doubt.

'She . . . she is not a servant.'

His uncle's jaw had dropped. 'Benjamin, please let me deal with –'

'*She's not a servant!*' Benjamin roared. We all jumped and Mr Nellys let out a pained groan. 'She is my mother! And you'll treat her with respect. You and everyone in the manor!'

Mr Koloman's eyes opened so wide I pictured his eyeballs falling out and rolling to the ground. He too made a fist, slowly raising it, and bared his teeth. Until then I had not realized how pale the man truly was. I thought he'd give Benjamin a mighty punch, and was preparing myself to break up the skirmish – Miss Fletcher was not someone who'd take that gladly – but then Mr Koloman's pupils flickered in my direction. He took a deep breath, shaking with ire.

He turned to Boyde. 'Take me back to the manor. We'll go in the small boat.' And he stormed out of the hut. Boyde bowed nervously and then ran after his master.

The shack remained silent for a moment, everyone stunned by what had just happened, by what might happen now. Benjamin turned to face his mother, but for a while that was his only movement.

How contradictory love can be. They were both desperate to embrace each other, yet neither managed to take the first step. Another tear rolled down Miss Fletcher's cheek, just as she managed to speak.

'I'm sorry,' she stuttered, bending her knees and ready to beg forgiveness, but Benjamin reached out and held her with unexpected strength. The first time they had touched.

'No, *no*,' Benjamin mumbled as he pulled her up, and then cradled her face in his hands.

'I'm sorry for everything,' she insisted, now crying unabatedly.

Benjamin made her rest her forehead on his shoulder, the son consoling the mother.

'You did what you had to,' he murmured. 'There's nothing to forgive.'

Miss Fletcher lifted a faltering hand, eventually bringing it to the back of her son's neck, while she cried out a lifetime of guilt.

The reunion could have lasted much longer, but Mr Nellys let out a growl of pain. He had managed to contain his groans, grinding his teeth as the emotional scene developed, but it had proven too much.

'I am afraid we need to take you to the manor,' I said. 'I can treat your wounds there.'

The man remonstrated as much as his wife had, until Miss Fletcher came over and lifted him as if he were a bundle of feathers. Mr Nellys then burst into tears too, one hand covering his ashamed face, the other his punctured stomach. He already smelled of death.

36

McGray stood for a long while by the drawing-room window, expecting to see a light appear. He did not expect Frey to dawdle on that island; he could almost hear the foppish Percy rushing everyone, nagging Benjamin to stay close at all times.

Helena and Miss Fletcher would be an entirely different story. The girl would want to stay with her father for as long as possible, and Miss Fletcher would probably have to drag the poor creature back to the mainland.

McGray sighed, feeling a pang of compassion for the Nellyses, and decided to make his way to the pantry. He thought he'd pay Lazarus a quick visit, tell him that Helena and Miss Fletcher were checking on his father. The young man might see this as a friendly gesture. He might even open up and finally say something to help his case – *if*, of course, there was anything to say.

The corridor to the storeroom was winding, dark and damp, and as McGray approached he heard the rustle of clothes. He turned the last corner and there he found Mrs Glenister, on her knees and about to slide a small piece of paper under the pantry door.

She didn't notice McGray's presence until he stamped his boot on the piece of paper. The middle-aged woman let out a squeal and instantly jumped to her feet. Even in the dim light McGray could see how flushed she was – Frey was right: Glenister did look like a sour governess.

'What's this, missus?' McGray asked, his foot firmly on the note. 'Desperate to talk to Lazarus?'

Mrs Glenister interlaced her fingers, her chin high. 'That is personal!'

'I wouldnae call it personal when yer trying to pass notes to a murder suspect.'

She didn't reply. She simply bent down to retrieve the paper. McGray let her pick it up but his voice was unwavering. 'Hand me that.'

Mrs Glenister pulled it away, but she only managed to tear it in half before McGray snatched it.

'Don't go anywhere,' he told her as he unfolded the pieces and put them together.

His eyebrows rose as he read the smudged lines. He was expecting to see a threatening message from the Kolomans, or a desperate note from Mrs Nellys . . . It was nothing of the sort.

McGray looked up, dumbfounded.

'Are ye . . . his mother?'

Mrs Glenister snorted. 'Of course I'm not! Do you see any resemblance at all?'

'Then why are ye telling him all this? Yer telling him to be brave, calling him yer child . . . This reads like a mother's letter. And I remember ye crying yer eyes out when I brought him here.'

Mrs Glenister smoothed out the folds of her skirts, the governess regaining control. 'Pray, come to the kitchen and let me pour you a cup of tea. I'll explain everything.'

McGray sighed. 'Very well, missus, but make it a glass o' wine instead.'

Something rather foul-smelling was simmering on the fire-place, the lid popping softly from time to time. The scullery maid was seated nearby, industriously scrubbing her master's glass distillation set with a soapy sponge.

'Leave us, Ellie,' Mrs Glenister snapped, and the girl ran as if doing so for dear life. The woman reached for a decanter and poured McGray a generous measure. She made herself tea – taking her time – and they both sat at the large table. Mrs Glenister wrapped her cup with both hands, and for a while she stared at the wooden surface, eroded and scratched after hosting years of servants' meals.

'I . . . was his wet nurse.'

McGray took a long drink. He didn't speak until Mrs Glenister lifted her face and shot him a testing glance. 'I see. How so?'

She lifted the cup, but it was as though the drink suddenly repulsed her. 'Mrs Nellys was sickly. She's always been a wreck, I'm afraid, and her babies kept dying. The first one lasted only a few weeks; the second one, a little girl, merely days. I've been told that the third child survived a couple of months, but then died just as they thought the worst was behind them.'

'That's very sad,' said McGray. 'Did they come asking for yer help?'

'You might say so. When Lazarus was born Mrs Nellys brought him here, as broken as we saw her today, with the dying child in her arms and begging for help. Her s–' She covered her eyes with a hand. 'Sorry, this is all too much.'

'Take yer time.'

Mrs Glenister shook her head. 'My masters of course couldn't refuse to help. They turned to me . . . I had just lost a child myself, you see.'

'I'm sorry.'

She shrugged. 'Losing a newborn child is common enough these days, yet still so tragic whenever it happens. I already had two daughters – they are happily married now – but I still . . . I still imagine my only son . . . He would be Lazarus's age, of course. The Nellyses' baby was a blessing. I would have died of sorrow had I not had him. To rock him in my arms, to see him grow big and strong . . . He soon came back to life; that's why they named him Lazarus.'

'I see. Does he ken ye –'

'Of course he knows. Just as Helena knows Miss Fletcher did the same for her.'

McGray nodded, recalling his visit to Juniper Island. Miss Fletcher had treated young Helena with the tenderness of a true mother, entirely at odds with her hard demeanour.

'We bonded with the children,' Mrs Glenister went on. 'It's impossible not to. If you were a woman –'

'Missus, I don't need to be a woman to understand sorrow. It must've been bloody heartbreaking to give 'em back to their mother.'

She nodded. 'Yes, though not as hard as watching them grow from afar, going through all sorts of hardships on those godforsaken islands while their silly, stubborn mother refused any help from my masters. The selfish woman just won't see that –' She brought a hand to her mouth. 'Sorry, it is not for me to judge, even if I find it so terribly unfair. Lazarus has worked so hard all his life.'

'Do ye see him often?'

She nodded. 'He is the one who brings us all the produce – the meat, the cheese, the gin. I usually receive him, though it should really be Mrs Plunket's duty.'

'Would ye say youse are good friends?'

The bitter, overwrought face softened with the slightest trace of a smile. 'Yes, I'd say we are.'

McGray knew there wouldn't be a better chance to ask this question.

'D'ye think he's capable of murdering someone?'

Mrs Glenister had surely expected it, for her answer sounded well-rehearsed.

'Lazarus is a good man. Why should he have to pay because the world lost a useless leech like that constable? He was one of those people who only spread misery. Nobody will miss him or visit his grave, yet there he is' – she nodded in the direction of the cellar door – 'well dead and rotting away, and still muddling us all.'

McGray breathed out, frustrated. 'Is that all yer telling me?'

And her face turned sour again. 'That's all I *can* tell you.'

Before McGray could say another word the young scullery maid burst in, yelling at the top of her voice. 'They're coming back! They're –'

The girl froze when she saw McGray, but he did not enquire further. He downed the rest of the wine and went straight to the pier.

He could already make out the silhouette of the Nellyses' boat, its flaky paint reflecting the glow of a lantern. And the other boat was on its way, though at the moment it was but a tiny spark floating on the waters.

'They are returning very soon,' said Mrs Koloman, coming out of the manor wrapped in a thick overcoat.

'Just as well. We didnae want yer nephew –'

McGray noticed something strange. He blinked a few times, though he knew his eyes were not mistaken.

'What is it?' asked Mrs Koloman.

'That's yer husband. Only they've swapped boats. He's coming in the Nellyses' shabby wreck.'

'Are you certain? He'd never willingly set foot into such a dilapidated –' she squinted. 'Oh, you are right. What could have happened?'

They would not have to wait long to find out. They saw it was Boyde rowing, the strong man dripping sweat from his temples.

As soon as the boat touched the pier Mr Koloman jumped out. His face was red and he snorted like a bull as he strode to the manor. His eyes met McGray's for an instant but he passed him without saying a word.

His wife went to him. 'Konrad, what happened?'

'Ask your nephew!' he barked over his shoulder.

McGray looked back at the waters. The second, larger boat would take a while to reach them, and no wonder. As it came nearer he saw the outlines of everyone else on board: Miss Fletcher and Frey, each handling an oar (Frey was pulling one of his shite-sniffing faces), Helena, carrying a lantern in each hand, and Benjamin at the back . . . cradling a pale, slight figure that from a distance looked like a corpse.

37

'This man needs help!' I cried well before we reached the shore. Boyde was still at the pier, and McGray and Mrs Koloman reached forward, the lady covering her mouth with both hands.

'What happened?' they asked at once. Apparently neither Mr Koloman nor Boyde had explained the mishap. Miss Fletcher threw Boyde the rope and he pulled us closer.

I tossed the damned oar to the pier, my hands already raw with blisters. 'Mr Nellys is injured. And his wounds are badly infected.'

'Dear Lord!' cried Mrs Koloman.

Miss Fletcher lifted Mr Nellys with utmost delicacy – the man already resembled a skeleton in her arms – and she went into the house with huge strides.

I helped Helena and then Benjamin to disembark. As we made our sorry way to the entrance I looked up to the manor's windows. Once more I saw Mrs Nellys staring at us.

'She is not going to handle this well,' I whispered.

Then I asked Mrs Glenister (who for some reason was terribly flushed) to look after Helena and Benjamin, and as McGray and I rushed upstairs I told him quickly what had happened.

He whistled. 'The laddie stood up to Mr Koloman? I wish I'd seen it! The man was fuming like a kettle.'

We reached the corridor to the guest room recently vacated by Uncle Maurice. The door was wide open so I pulled McGray to a halt.

'I saw the man's wounds,' I whispered.

'The bites?'

'I cannot tell for sure those *are* bites. They are not like the scratches on your arm. His are punctures, like tiny pinpricks.'

'But ye saw the wee beast's fangs,' Nine-Nails said. 'They *would* leave tiny puncture marks, if they had the time to bite at leisure. The auld man's wounds look like that.'

'That I can grant you, but also . . . I think they have been tampered with.'

McGray frowned. 'What d'ye mean?'

'I may not have seen bat bites before, but I have seen self-harm injuries, and I can tell you —' I took a quick step aside to let Tamlyn pass with a bundle of towels, and I lowered my voice further. 'Either this man scratched those open "bites" to oblivion . . . or he has been piercing himself.'

McGray's eyes widened, partly in surprise and partly in disgust. 'Himself? Ye really think so?'

'Indeed.' I nodded at his arm. 'Your wound has healed now.'

He frowned. 'Aye. Ye saw I even took the bandage off.'

'Precisely, and that also makes me think this man's wounds are *not* bites. Miss Natalja's book says that the bats administer some substance that prevents clotting. Now look at your wound: the effect is not long-lasting. In Mr Nellys's case, even with his poor health, those small punctures would heal very quickly, before there was any chance for them to become as badly infected as they are. If we were able to take this man to Edinburgh, I am almost sure Dr Clouston would corroborate the old man is harming himself.' I watched McGray mull over my words. 'He might not be as sane as he seems,' I concluded. 'I am sorry. I know what that implies for you. And for your sister.'

He shook his head. 'Can ye look at him more closely? Or is there a way to tell beyond doubt that –'

'McGray, look!'

From the other end of the corridor, dressed in a lavish dressing gown borrowed from Mrs Koloman, came Mrs Nellys. She was supporting herself on the wall, struggling to catch her breath.

'Where is he?' she asked. 'Where is my husband?'

There was an eerie determination to her stare, an unbreakable resolve that pulled her forward in spite of her body's weakness.

She saw the open door, the light coming from there, and before we could reach her she stormed into the chamber.

'*Leave my husband alone!*' she shrieked.

When we stepped in we found Miss Fletcher holding Mr Nellys firmly in place, while Mrs Koloman pressed a brass syringe against the man's bony forearm.

Mr Nellys was barely conscious, but he managed to turn his head to his wife, an exhausted, agonized look in his eyes.

'Minerva, what are you doing to him?' Mrs Nellys demanded. 'You're poisoning him!'

She darted forward, but McGray seized her by the shoulder. 'There, there, missus. She's just trying to help.'

Mrs Koloman finished administering the medicine, pulled out the needle and cleaned the wound with cotton wool. Only then did she look up.

'I am only giving him laudanum, Sabina.'

Mrs Nellys growled. 'Laudanum! Is that your answer to everything?'

But her husband was already letting out a long breath, his chest and his face relaxing as he fell into a deep slumber.

'See?' Mrs Koloman said. 'He already feels better.'

Mrs Nellys shook her head. 'She is poisoning him,' she told us, not with madness or despair but with a resignation I found unnerving.

'Madam, we are CID inspectors. I doubt this lady would be foolish enough to poison your husband right before our eyes.' I said those words staring directly at Mrs Koloman, who cast me a defiant look.

'All I've ever done is help them,' she said, 'even though many times I simply wanted them to go away. Even after my husband's countless objections.' She reached for a bottle of iodine and began dabbing Mr Nellys's wounds with dexterous hands.

'Your husband will be well cared for,' I told Mrs Nellys, gently pulling her arm. She resisted at first, but then allowed us to shepherd her back into her room. Helena waited there, muffling her sobs with a crumpled handkerchief. Miss Fletcher came right behind us, hugged the girl and whispered in her ear.

There was little we could do but assure them Mr Nellys would be kept comfortable. Mrs Glenister brought them food and drink, but something told me they would not eat.

McGray pulled the set of keys from his breast pocket and was about to lock the door, but then he shook his head and turned on his heel.

He looked tired, sickened even.

That night there was nothing but misery in the manor. You could feel it in the air, in the profound hush that had crept all around.

I swirled the wine in my glass – the *one* thing I would miss from this place – as I stared at the quiet loch from my room's window.

No wonder I felt that oppression in my chest. Under this roof, miles and miles into the Scottish wilderness, were a dying man, a decaying corpse, three murder suspects, a handful of distraught women and men, and two wary CID inspectors who were simply waiting for somebody else to come and take charge. I'd be only too happy to leave.

I finished the wine and went to bed, but I tossed and turned for a long while. I could not stop picturing that strange skull and its refulgent eye sockets. *Witchcraft*, I thought with a chill, thinking of Miss Fletcher's words. Could there be something else on those islands? Something we were yet to meet?

I shook my head at the idea, but an ominous feeling crept through my body, clutching at my heart like an invisible claw. A foreboding I can explain only in hindsight.

38

The following morning was sunny beyond any expectations.
Loch Maree reflected the pale-blue sky, the wet stones of the
mountains glimmered like mirrors and the pine trees of
the islands showed sumptuous shades of green.

The manor, however, felt as quiet and cold as a grave.
Nobody went to the breakfast room (not even McGray) and
I had my toast and coffee in a rush, as if that silence were
chivvying me. There was still no sign of any constables
arriving (and the anxious Tamlyn was less than helpful when
I asked for an update), so I walked along the corridors looking for any of the Kolomans. It was time we took the
situation into our own hands. We'd probably have to take
McEwan's body away, and the sooner the better. That was
not a trip I was looking forward to.

I heard voices coming from the Shadows Room – the
twins, apparently in the middle of a heated argument. I went
in without knocking, and nearly tripped over the edge of a
rug, for the place was, as usual, in the deepest darkness. The
girls were not even projecting their light spectrums.

'Who's there?' Veronika demanded from behind the Chinese screen.

Natalja, whom I recognized by her voice, came up to me,
holding a small oil lamp.

'Oh, it is you,' she said most insolently. 'Would you mind
leaving? We're discussing private matters.'

I knew that was the perfect time. 'I will leave as soon as you tell me why you two swapped places the other night.'

Veronika dropped the box she'd been holding and crystal prisms rolled across the thick carpet. Miraculously, none shattered. Her sister hardly showed any emotion, staring at me with cold eyes. She'd surely been preparing herself for this moment.

'What on earth are you talking about?' asked Veronika.

I took a step forward. 'Were you truly bitten by some-thing, Miss Veronika? Do you have scars you did not want me to see?' The girl could not have looked any paler, though a menacing anger was brewing in her eyes. 'I'd rather you told me now, so that I do not have to reveal the entire affair to your parents.'

Veronika's chest swelled, but Natalja simply gave a wry smile. 'Would you dare tell them . . . *exactly* what happened?'

She managed to make me blush. 'If need be,' I said nonetheless.

Natalja's smile widened but I could tell she was worried. The tendons of her neck were tense, and she sported the faint-est of frowns. She took a deep breath and looked sternly at her sister. Her voice came out hoarse. 'I think it is time he knows.'

I did not expect her sister's reaction. Veronika jumped up, kicking the prisms away as she approached her sister to grasp her by the arm. '*No!* No, Natty, you cannot tell him! You can't possibly –'

'It is the only way, dear.'

And all of a sudden Veronika was crying, tears rolling down her snow-white skin in streams. No wonder they were so pale, locked in this darkened room on the sunniest of days. 'But . . .'

'It's all right,' Natalja said in an affectionate tone, squeezing Veronika's hand and attempting a reassuring smile. 'It will all be all right. Trust me.'

Veronika looked at me with her sodden eyes, sobbing and struggling to swallow. I felt like her executioner . . . but I *had* to know.

Natalja kissed her sister's forehead and caressed her cheek. 'You don't have to be here, Vee. *I* will confess. You should go and have a rest. Ask Mrs Glenister to bring you some green tea.'

Veronika covered her mouth, muffling her voice. 'Green tea,' she repeated, and then let her sister guide her out. She threw me one last desperate stare as Natalja shut the door.

Suddenly we were in darkness again, lit only by her lamp and by the silver lines of daylight that filtered through the edges of a poorly drawn curtain.

'Shall I open that?' I snapped. 'I cannot stand this pointless darkness.'

'No,' she said firmly. 'It took me a long time to set up the room for today's experiment. Miss Fletcher does it every morning, but not today. I imagine she fancies herself lady of the house already.'

'She is your cousin's mother,' I said, to which she had no answer.

'Have a seat,' she offered, and we sat between the screens, face to face. Natalja placed the lamp on the low table, and the amber flame somehow made me think of the sun, floating in the black void of the universe.

I did not speak, simply waited until she gathered courage. It would not take long.

'Yes,' she said, palms together and staring into the light, as though she were about to pray, 'we swapped places. How did you know? We took care of every detail. I gave her my nightgown, even though we wear identical garments; I even wetted her hair with lavender water, recalling it had spilled on me from your bath.'

I sighed. 'She was very convincing. Quite frankly, I am not sure what made me suspect. There is something . . . in your air . . . in the way each of you moves. I cannot pinpoint what, but the difference is there. Your voices are the one thing I can instantly tell apart, but you, or rather, your sister, did not say a word in the corridor that night. I suppose your visit to my chambers was –'

She immediately raised both hands. 'Don't mention that again, please. Yes, it was a ruse. The only way I could think of to make you uneasy so you wouldn't notice our trick. That would justify my sister avoiding looking you in the eye. The embarrassment of –'

'Do move on, miss,' I said, feeling the embarrassment myself. 'We have agreed there was deception. To what end?'

She sighed deeply. 'I . . . I had better explain it from the very start.' She looked away. 'I believe you saw the scullery maid, Ellie, lurking around the spot where Constable McEwan died.'

I felt my eyebrow arching into my most quizzical look. 'I did. How did you –'

'I sent her.'

My jaw dropped. 'You did *what*?'

She stood up and went to one of the bookcases, finding her way in the darkness with surprising ease.

'I sent her there,' she repeated as she came back. 'I needed her to retrieve this.'

She extended her palm to hand me a small silver case, engraved with graceful vines and grapes. It looked like a cigarette case, but I had an inkling as to its true contents.

I opened it and found, nestled in purple velvet lining, a shiny syringe. Things began to take shape in my mind.

'I have seen these before,' I mumbled, and looked up at once, 'years ago, in the raid of an opium house in London! Does that mean –'

'Yes,' Natalja rather snapped, then she could not look me in the eye as she whispered, 'My sister is addicted to laudanum. She has been for a few years.'

I remained silent for a while, staring down at the lavish syringe, engraved with matching vines to those on the case. I had seen extravagant items like that, custom-made for the more affluent patrons of the opium trade.

'How did that come to be?'

'She spent a couple of winters in London and Paris. Uncle Maximilian was the only family member to chaperone her. He indulged her, took her to parties no lady should attend. When she came back from her second trip she was already addicted.'

I nodded. 'Is that the reason your mother loathes the late Maximilian?'

'Do you blame her? Mama felt so guilty when she found out. Veronika used to inject herself secretly.' Natalja covered her face, suddenly trembling with shame. 'In her belly, so our parents would not notice. That's what Tamlyn saw.'

My eyebrow was still arched. 'Are you telling me the truth?'

She laughed. 'You did not really believe that something had *bitten* her, did you?' I did not reply. 'Tamlyn is our most recent employee; she came here when Veronika was already recovering, so we didn't think she need know. All our other servants have been with us for years or decades. They are very loyal to us; they would not reveal my sister's secret, no matter what you told them.' She looked into my eyes, for my face was still distorted in astonishment. 'Does it shock you that a refined upper-class girl could hide something like that?'

I blew out my cheeks. 'Miss, I have seen the upper classes do far worse than this.'

She gave a bitter smile. 'That I believe.'

'What astonishes me is that . . . that she looks so healthy!'

'Of course she does. My mother may not have had university instruction but she is an excellent physician – far better than many preening graduates.' If that remark was directed at me, I pretended not to take the hint. 'Mama believes the best way to bring the addiction to an end is to do it gradually. If Veronika is disciplined, of course.'

I instantly recalled Mrs Koloman's words to the girl: *Discipline, my dear. That has always been your downfall.*

'My mother takes good care of her,' Natalja added. 'Hence my sister's regime of exercise and good food . . . And to appease her mind, dressmaking, science, languages, evening walks . . .'

I nodded. That was a treatment even the erudite Dr Clouston would have approved of.

It all rang true: the evidence, the twins' embarrassment, the very syringe in my hand. Still, there was something that felt out of place.

Whilst I thought, I ran my fingers over the case's soft velvet lining. It contained only the syringe, but there was room for several vials. My finger caught something. In between the folds I saw a tiny purple crystal, like a coloured grain of sugar.

'Your mother uses opiates far too liberally,' was the first thing that came into my head. 'She should not have applied it when your sister had that fit of pain.'

'As I told you, she believes in a gradual reduction of the doses.'

I lifted the case. 'Yet your sister carries this with her, presumably with her *reduced* dose?'

'Do you want me to say it a third time? *Yes*, she still injects laudanum! But not even nearly as much as she used to.'

I closed the case with a soft click. 'And that fit of pain your sister had?'

Natalja did not reply straight away. She bit her lip and rubbed her hands together. 'We . . . we don't know. She . . . well, she's had those episodes every now and then, ever since Uncle Maximilian brought her back. We don't know what causes them, but only laudanum seems to settle her.'

My first thought was that the girl must be faking those fits. If her mother ran to her with a laudanum syringe every time she showed pain . . . That would explain the absence of any other symptoms. It would not be the first time I had seen such behaviour, but I preferred not to mention it so bluntly. Natalja was already having a hard time confessing this.

'I could put you in touch with people who have treated this type of ailment. I also told . . .' I was about to say I'd made the same offer to Lazarus, for his family's skin condition, but could not bring myself to finish the sentence.

'Thank you,' Natalja retorted, 'but Mama has already looked for help elsewhere. She has found all the advice she needs.'

'Are you certain?'

Natalja leaned towards me and grasped my hand. I recognized the softness of her skin, but there was nothing left of that night's touch, and her cold fingers sent a shiver across my body.

'Please, do not tell my mother you know. She'd die of shame!'

'Miss Koloman –'

'Veronika is very healthy; you said it yourself. Why torment us all?'

The girl was desperate, and I had already intruded far more than I would have ever intended, so I did not insist. However, Veronika's condition would remain in my mind. I might even tell Uncle Maurice to try to talk to her, charm her into admitting she'd been enacting those seizures.

'Very well, miss. I will not trouble you further.'

As I stood up I shoved the case in my pocket.

'Can I have that back?' Natalja asked, stretching out her hand.

'I shall keep it for the time being, if you don't mind.'

Her face went stern. 'I *do* mind.'

I half smiled. 'And I only said *if you don't mind* out of good manners.'

She growled in frustration. 'Very well.'

I went to the door but halted before my hand touched the handle. There was a burning question that no amount of prudery or good upbringing could repress. I looked back. 'Miss Natalja . . . What . . . what would you have done if I'd given in? That night, I mean.'

She cackled. 'Do not think yourself so lucky. I had planned to burst into tears and feign a sudden bout of remorse. That would have been better for our plan; it would have made you feel even *more* guilt.' She gave me a sardonic smile. 'Quite frankly, we never expected you'd refuse . . . so categorically.'

I was already sorry I'd asked, so I opened the door swiftly.

'If it helps,' she said, for once with a hint of shyness, 'I respect you a little more after that.'

39

'Do ye believe them?' McGray asked as we walked along the path through the rhododendrons. I did not want anybody to hear us as I recounted Natalja's confession.

'Everything makes sense,' I said, 'everything except that abdominal pain.'

'Which ye said she might be faking.'

'It is possible. Addicts are known for being crafty. Then again, if it is a genuine condition . . .'

'Don't fret too much over it, Frey. Ye've offered help. If they refuse it, it's their own sodding problem.'

I looked at the manor, recalling how grand and beautiful I'd thought it was when I first saw it. It had been only three days ago, but it already felt like another era. How could I have guessed that such a sumptuous place would hold those terrible secrets?

And we were about to learn much more.

'What a bleeding useless bunch of prats!' Dominik cried, sucking on a cigarette with unsettling anxiety. We had just told him the constables had not come yet. 'And when those halfwits do arrive they'll only ask the same damn stupid questions you already have, and this bloody charade will never end!'

'Just eat yer damn food,' McGray grumbled as young Ellie cleared away last night's tray.

'*I want my freedom!*' Dominik shouted, and then smashed the cigarette on the table, grinding tobacco into polished mahogany with his bare hand – even the ignited tip. He dropped into his armchair, quivering.

I checked my pocket watch. 'Your father asked that Smeaton chap to ready the carriage for us. The man, unfortunately, is taking his bloody time. As soon as we can set off and take the corpse –'

'You have to let me out!' Dominik interrupted. It was not a request but a statement. He snorted and pulled at his hair. 'Even if just for a stroll. Five minutes will do. It's been *three bloody days!* This damned room is stifling me!'

McGray let out a loud cackle. 'Awww, yer bloody huge manor is stifling ye? Ye have yer soddin' goose-down pillows, yer unlimited supply o' wine and fancy food . . . ye even have fuckin' indoor plumbing in yer room! I bet even fat Queen Vicky still has to squat over a potty every now 'n' then.'

'You don't understand. I need air.'

McGray pointed his chin at the drawn curtains. 'Then crack the damned window open,' and he turned to the door as Dominik shouted to our backs.

'I'm sick of staring at that bloody loch! *You have to let me out!*' He protested further, but we were too tired to pay attention. We made our way through the door and were about to shut it when Dominik finally gave in.

'I will speak!'

McGray and I froze. We turned back to him, puzzled.

'If that's what it takes to escape from this cell, I will speak! Do you want to know why Calcraft and I went out that night?'

'The whole truth?' Nine-Nails asked. 'And nothing but the truth?'

Dominik's mouth was dry, his bare chest moving like bellows. 'Yes.'

We stepped back in. McGray looked at the young maid. 'Leave us, lassie.' And he closed the door behind her. He and I sat in the plush armchairs, and McGray pressed his fingertips together. 'We're listening.'

Dominik was trembling. He tore a page from his little Bible – from the book of Revelation, how fitting – and began to roll a cigarette. His eyes were glinting as if he were about to cry.

'There is a reason I travel all the time,' he began, making a mess of tobacco on the table. 'There is a reason I spend most of my time jumping from country to country ... with –' He only managed to drop uneven clumps of tobacco on the paper, but he rolled it up nonetheless. He could not bring himself to finish the sentence until he'd lit the twisted cigarette. 'With Calcraft.'

His trembling tone said everything I needed to know. I saw McGray's lips part, taking in a short, surprised breath. He too had guessed what Dominik was about to say, but we needed to hear it from his own lips. 'Continue.'

Dominik took anxious puffs, exhaling the smoke noisily. 'I . . . I believe the legal term is . . . gross indecency?'

He pronounced the words with mockery, wrinkling his nose as he smoked. Then he poured himself a good measure of wine and downed it in two long gulps. We did not speak until he put the glass down.

'Have you told anybody else?' I asked.

Dominik shook his head. 'Nobody. But my parents must suspect. My mother *loathes* Calcraft. He did ridicule Miss Fletcher at the time of her predicament, but a few lewd comments cannot justify her utter aversion.'

'And yer dad?' McGray said.

'My dad,' Dominik echoed, his voice oozing bitterness. 'Why do you think he is so keen to welcome Benjamin? He won't see the family name die so easily.' He crushed the end of his cigarette. '*Benjamin Koloman* sounds revolting.'

I sighed, my exhalation gradually turning into a tired moan. Things were not getting simpler. 'Dominik, you have just confessed to illicit behaviour. Those acts are banned by law.'

'Better to be prosecuted for gross indecency than for murder.' Dominik smirked. 'Besides, I trust you two won't mention this at the inquest.'

McGray crossed his arms. 'Do ye?'

'Yes. My confession is helping your investigations. Lazarus is now your only suspect.'

I raised a hand. 'Wait, Dominik, you are assuming too much.'

'Assuming?'

'Yes. Difficult as this must have been to reveal, it still does not prove you or Calcraft are innocent.'

And we were yet to hear from the constable in Thurso. His investigations into the priest's death must still be ongoing. For all I knew, he might already have evidence incriminating Dominik. However, I saw no need to mention that just then; Dominik could not have looked more enraged.

'What the hell are you saying?' he spat. 'I have just confessed what was going on at the time! If you tell Calcraft I've confessed, he will corroborate everything I've just said!'

'We appreciate yer honesty,' said Nine-Nails, for once with some embarrassment. 'But Frey here is right. Yer statement proves nothing.'

Dominik's breathing became more and more agitated. He sounded like a hissing steam engine.

'Rest assured we won't spread the word,' said McGray, 'but trust me, ye'll be better off mentioning none o' this at the inquest. Ye've a better chance simply relying on yer family's reputation, and Lazarus refusing to –'

Dominik pointed at the door. 'Get out!'

'Hey!' McGray protested. 'I was tryin' to help ye.'

'*Get out!*' Dominik howled, throwing the pewter carafe at the wall. It was nearly empty, but the splatter was huge nonetheless.

We did so at once, and just as I shut the door I heard the knock and splash of a dish being hurled at us.

Before I could even take a breath a soft, dreamy yet chilling voice spoke from behind me. 'Are you completely soulless?'

I was glad there were streams of daylight flooding the corridor; I would have screamed had I heard that in the middle of the night. It was Veronika.

She was crouching like a scared child, her back pressed against a corner of the hall, wrapping herself tightly in her dressing gown. Her beautiful eyes were glassy, as if she were about to burst into tears.

'Would you let me walk with him, sirs? He is so distressed . . . Just a little fresh air would do him good.'

I took a careful step closer. I cannot tell quite what, but there was something in her stare, something primeval that made me fear she'd attack me. 'Miss, are you feeling well?'

'Just five minutes,' she begged. 'Let me walk with him for just five minutes. Even if it's just from here to the hall! You can even guard us if you want.'

'Miss –'

'Do you not see the state he is in?' she hissed. 'He is my brother! Why do you have to torture him like that?'

McGray and I exchanged suspicious looks. He was about

to say something comforting, but then Mrs Glenister rushed up, clutching a blanket.

'Inspectors!' she cried, almost out of breath. 'You have to go to the cellar! Right away. I'll take care of Miss Veronika.'

'Why?' McGray asked. 'What's happened?'

'You can smell the stench all the way to the dining room. It's worse than a slaughterhouse's waste pit.'

I brought a hand to my brow. 'Oh, dear Lord . . .'

McGray cast Veronika an anxious look. It took him a moment to make up his mind. 'We'll go 'n' check, but ye make sure the lassie gets back to her room. Give her tea or somethin' to calm her down. *Nae* weird injections.'

They both looked up with panic in their eyes, and Mrs Glenister let out a throaty gasp. The woman clearly had not been told that we knew about the addiction. Even I was shocked by how casually McGray had referred to the matter, but we had no time to appease them. As we walked away I looked over my shoulder and saw Mrs Glenister wrapping Veronika in the thick blanket.

'Are they all suddenly going insane?' I grumbled, and McGray voiced what I already feared.

'Maybe they always have been.'

40

As soon as McGray opened the door the foul smell of death struck us.

'*Fuck!* This stinks like all the orifices of Satan!'

I must have turned greener than McGray on a boat, and had to cover the greater part of my face with my handkerchief. It took more than braveness to step into that darkened storeroom.

McEwan's body was still there, but his skin had turned a sickly grey and a nauseating, yellowish liquid dripped from the table. The trickle came from beneath the torso.

'It is already decomposing,' I said, pressing the handkerchief tightly against my mouth. The smell was so intense the inside of my nose actually hurt – something that had not happened even in the foulest sewers of Edinburgh.

Even McGray had to bring a hand to his nose. 'Ye don't fuckin' say, Percy.'

'I . . . I do not understand. This should not have happened so quickly!' Feeling sick beyond words, my eyes watering, I forced myself to lean over the body and carefully pulled aside the man's collar. 'I was not expecting him to last for long, but this room is fresh enough. Only a little warmer than the London morgue.'

'Can we wrap him and take him on the carriage? Perhaps on the roof.'

I shook my head. 'I am afraid –' and then I felt the contents of my stomach rise at full speed. I had to turn round, bend down and breathe. I barely managed to repress a wave of vomit. 'I'm afraid not,' I whimpered. 'And it is not only the bloody hellish reek' – which, to me, was good enough reason. 'This is a source of infection. Everyone in the carriage would be at risk. We need to inter him right away.'

'We are not burying that man in our grounds!' Mrs Koloman said at once.

All the curtains in the drawing room were drawn, the woman prostrated on the velvet sofa, pressing a damp cloth against her forehead. She dipped it in a saucer of water infused with sprigs of lavender, and then picked one up and held it to her nose. I realized the stench of the corpse had permeated into our clothes. Mr Koloman was behind her, making copious notes in a hefty meteorological log. He seemed slightly on edge.

'I concur,' he said, quite distracted, staring at his barometers and the weathervane display above the mantelpiece.

'I assumed as much,' I said. 'We thought we could put him on Isle Maree. It is consecrated –'

'That is out of the question!' Mrs Koloman snapped. 'That land is sacred. He doesn't deserve such an honour.'

'West-north-west,' Mr Koloman mumbled, mesmerized by the clock-like hand that marked the wind direction.

'*Oi!*' Nine-Nails yelped, waving his hand in front of the man's face. 'Are ye listening?'

Mr Koloman glared at him. 'I am, you little chap, do not insult my faculties. My Natalja is far more intelligent than either of you – and *I* taught her everything she knows.' He completed his notes before calmly saying, 'You can take the body to Juniper Island. The marshy grassland should be easy to dig into.'

Mrs Koloman sat up, mortified. 'How can you suggest that, Konrad? The Nellyses have their house there. Do you really want them living within yards of that corpse? Reminding them every day why Lazarus is in prison?'

It was not yet certain that Lazarus would be convicted, but it was not the time for petty corrections.

Mr Koloman let out an impatient breath. 'Very well. I suppose you can take him to Rory Island. Nobody ever goes there, that we know of.'

'Where's that?' McGray asked.

Mr Koloman went to his bookshelves and retrieved a hefty atlas bound in green leather. The maps looked faded but were drawn in exquisite detail. On closer inspection I realized they were all original watercolours.

'This is a gem of a book,' I whispered, but nobody paid any attention to my awe. Mr Koloman went through the pages until he found a perfect depiction of Loch Maree. The names of all the islands appeared both in English and in Gaelic – the latter in beautiful Gothic calligraphy. Juniper Island was in fact called Eilean Sùbhainn.

'This is Rory Island,' Mr Koloman said, pointing at the one furthest west. There were tiny pine trees drawn all over it. 'The woodland is very thick there, not very good for shooting. That's why we never go there.'

'At least it will be a quick trip,' I remarked, for it was the closest island to the manor.

I perused the map for a moment longer, admiring the delicate brushstrokes, some lines as fine as a single hair. Jarring amongst that painstaking work was an X drawn in dark ink. It marked a spot on the loch's northern shore, right above Juniper Island.

'What does that cross mark?' I asked.

Mr Koloman shrugged. 'God only knows. My late father bought this in an auction many years ago. It was already old back then.'

'I don't want to seem rude,' said Mrs Koloman from the sofa, 'but I've not had a headache as bad as this in years. Would you mind?'

Mr Koloman went to her, sat on the armrest and stroked his wife's head. 'It's the strain, my dear,' he said soothingly. 'You need but rest.'

And he looked at us as he said that, nodding at the door.

Preparing the body was an absolute torment.

We first wrapped it tightly with old bandages and rags, as I did not want any part of him to drop off on the way. My day was bad enough already.

I'd taken off my jacket and rolled up my sleeves, thinking I'd never wear those garments again. To protect us from the smell McGray and I tied damp cloths around our faces, which made the task only just endurable. As we worked our way upwards I thought my hands would surely stink for days.

It was downright impossible to feel any compassion: here was a man nobody had liked very much, whose inaction had caused more grief than many actual crimes, and who was now decomposing beyond recognition.

I felt a retch as we wrapped his slit neck. The flesh there had gone green, astonishingly similar to a joint of beef left out to rot.

'There goes the only piece of material evidence,' I muttered.

'Cannae believe nobody came,' said McGray. 'Ye sure yer uncle –'

'He might be a little self-indulgent and reckless, but he would not fail to do something so crucial . . .' *I hope*, I completed in my head.

'Well, they won't get the pleasure o' looking at this beauty now,' McGray said, tying up the last rags around McEwan's head. We took a step back to assess our work: a stinking mummy, crudely wrapped, which would have flour sacks for a sarcophagus.

'They say how ye live is how ye die.' McGray sighed. 'All righty, let's get rid o' him.'

And we carried the flaccid bundle away. There was a small service door close to the kitchen, so we did not need to further disgrace the main hall and corridors with that smell.

Boyde was already by the boat, carrying a pair of shovels and shading his eyes with a hand, for the sun was extremely bright.

'Are you ready, sirs?'

As I expected, nobody from the household was around. They'd all despised McEwan for one reason or other. Mr Koloman might have come, but he must be busy tending to his wife's migraine – astonishing how for centuries all refined ladies have developed headaches whenever there is something they do not wish to undergo.

We placed the body in the Nellyses' shabby boat – there was no need for the larger, heavier one. I was about to jump in but McGray held me back.

'It's *me* who should go, Percy. I cannae see ye digging a grave. That'll be a real man's job.'

324

I chuckled. 'Are you certain? With your biliousness and a rotting body by your side?'

McGray took a stubborn step forward, but then the wind brought us a fiendishly pungent waft of decay.

'Fuck, I hate it when yer right! And it's been too bloody often lately. Very well. But when youse come back we'll go and fetch those sodding constables from the nearest town. I'll make sure the carriage is ready. Now that there won't be a corpse we can take the suspect boys with us.'

I nodded, and then looked up at the windows, expecting to see a good number of faces watching our every move. There was not a single one. In fact, all the curtains were drawn. Somehow I did not like it.

'Keep an eye on them,' I whispered. 'You will be on your own again. If they wanted to try something stupid – like, you know, letting Dominik flee – they would do so now. And as you well said, they might all be going insane.'

Nine-Nails opened his overcoat to show the charged gun in his breast pocket. 'I think I can handle them,' he said, quite self-assured. But once I was in the boat and Boyde began to row north, he added, 'Don't linger there, Percy.'

I sighed as I watched him standing there, somehow dwarfed under the solid stone of the grand country house. I do not believe in omens, yet somehow, at that moment, I already knew my life would never be the same again.

41

McGray went straight to the drawing room, but Mr and Mrs Koloman were no longer there. Perhaps the lady had decided to nurse her headache in her room.

The darkness felt like an almost physical oppression, so McGray rushed to open the nearest curtain and golden sunshine immediately filled the room. It was sad that the glorious weather – maybe the last sunny day before the Scottish autumn began to creep in – had to be spent in such gloomy circumstances. It was almost impossible to believe that just four days earlier the entire Koloman family had gathered in that very room, laughing and opening presents as if it were Christmas morning.

He shoved an idle hand into his coat's side pocket and felt a piece of paper. It was Mrs Glenister's note for Lazarus – it had been in his pocket since he'd caught the woman trying to slide it under the door. McGray gave it a more careful look and noticed that some of the paper was rippled, as if it had got wet and then been left to dry. There was a slight scent of lemon . . .

Somebody opened the door rather brusquely. It was the girl Tamlyn, bringing in a porcelain basin and some towels.

'Here, sir,' she said, a little tremble in her voice. 'I thought you'd want to wash your hands after . . . handling *that*.'

McGray welcomed the prospect; the lingering odour of the corpse was too much, even for his toughened nose.

'Lemon?' he asked as he plunged his hands into the warm, scented water.

'Yes. Lemon and salt. They get rid of the worst smells. It's lucky Mrs Plunket and Mrs Glenister were making the curd last night; there were some rinds left.'

McGray nodded. Mrs Glenister must have jotted the note in between slicing lemons.

Tamlyn handed him a towel. She was shaking as if the room were ice-cold, her eyes reddened.

'Are ye all right, lassie?'

She nodded . . . and then shook her head. 'I've just told the mistress I'm leaving. I can't stay in this house another day.'

McGray frowned. 'Because o' the murder?'

The girl tensed her lips and frowned, suddenly looking ten years older. 'There's no one to ask for help,' she said. 'What if something were to happen to me once you sirs are gone?'

McGray leaned closer. 'Has someone threatened ye?'

'No,' she said at once. 'Mrs Koloman has been very understanding. She'll give me a good recommendation and some money to live on while I find my way. She knows I can't stay here. The good missus . . . she'll send me to Inverness. I'll leave next time Boyde goes to Kinlochewe, take a coach from there. I shall be glad to leave.' Saying no more, the girl picked up the basin and rushed away.

McGray did not like that at all. That was the girl who'd led them to their discovery of Veronika's addiction. It was more likely she'd been dismissed and bribed handsomely. What other secrets might she know?

McGray decided to go after her, but when he reached the corridor he found only Natalja, carrying a bundle of sheet music. Like everyone else, she looked pale, gloomy – and very tense.

'Inspector!' she cried, clutching the papers to her chest. 'You frightened me!'

'Aye. I'm that bleeding ugly.'

She laughed nervously, trying to be her most charming. 'No, nothing . . . nothing of the sort. I didn't know you were in the drawing room. Do you mind if I play the piano in there? Feel free to join me if you want.'

He let out a loud *Ha!* 'To give ye chance to play yer lying games on me?'

The girl stepped back. 'How dare you talk to me like that? I was simply –'

But McGray did not wait to listen. He made his way below stairs as the low, poignant notes of Natalja's playing began to flow throughout the manor.

The music could be heard all the way to the kitchen, where Mrs Plunket was fervently stirring a large pot on the stove. The girl Ellie was washing a large set of tiny bottles.

'Caustic soda and lemon rinds. We'll have to scrub all the walls and floors with this to get rid of that blasted smell!' the distressingly wide cook remonstrated as McGray peeped into the pot. The basin he'd just used was on the table, the towels thrown down carelessly next to it.

'Where's the lass Tamlyn?' he asked.

'God knows,' was the cook's perfunctory reply. 'She won't care any more what she does here, now that she's leaving. Happens like that with all the new girls; they get a wee bit of experience and they feel the world is theirs. If only they knew how hard it is to find good masters!'

McGray exhaled, suddenly feeling restless. He was tempted to ask for some of that tasty wine but decided against it; he wanted to keep his senses sharp.

Out of mere apprehension he decided to check all the locked doors. As he knocked and heard the doleful voices behind them, he felt as if a relentless misery had infected them all, like an invisible shroud wrapping the house ever more tightly. Natalja's mournful music did not help; in fact, it crept into him like a cold hand, making him feel like a broken orderly doing the rounds in Edinburgh's asylum – though even that place did not feel as gloomy as the manor.

Thankfully it would all be over soon, he thought as he went upstairs. As soon as Frey returned they'd take the suspects to the local authorities, and hopefully leave right away. They might even be on their way back to Edinburgh that very evening. He simply needed to keep himself sane until then.

McGray decided to see how Mr Nellys was faring, if only to keep his mind occupied. The old man's room was two doors from Dominik's. To his surprise, the door was slightly open.

McGray knocked softly. 'Mr Nellys? Ye all right?'

There was no reply. McGray walked in quickly, but to his utter relief the frail man lay peacefully on the bed. Alone. His curtains were drawn too, only a thin line of light falling diagonally over the richly embroidered bedding.

The man turned his head to McGray, and despite his weakness he smiled.

McGray walked closer, conscious of a sudden, inexplicable nervousness. 'Are . . . are they treating ye well? Ye look pale.' *Even more than before*, he decided not to say.

'I'm not in pain, my son, if that's what you mean. Come, have a seat. I shall like some company.'

McGray sat on the bed, somehow reminded of the old priest. The mere memory of the bloody mess that had become of that old man made him shudder.

Like Frey had said, it did not look like Mr Nellys was going to live for much longer. *We can always see it*, he thought, *even if our minds refuse to accept it.*

Mr Nellys let out a prolonged, tired sigh. 'I had a horrible dream last night. The islands were on fire: Maree and Juniper. The sky was full of flames and smoke, and I couldn't breathe.' He stared at the thread of light between the curtains, and he squinted, but not because of the glimmer. 'My children were screaming but I couldn't see them. My Lazarus and my poor Helena . . . The ashes were burning my eyes – and I couldn't move. I couldn't do anything to help them. Like always!'

Natalja suddenly played with renewed intensity. McGray wished she would stop.

'Just a dream,' he whispered.

'No . . . I don't think so,' Mr Nellys said, biting his thumbnail. 'We've got too close to the fire. And now we'll burn.'

McGray felt the man's pain as if it were his own. For a moment they even breathed in unison, as if facing the very same threat.

'Mr Nellys . . .' McGray said, leaning closer to him, 'what's troubling ye? Maybe I can help.'

Again the man smiled, showing his crooked teeth, his dry skin wrinkling like parchment. 'We are beyond help now. I only wish my poor children hadn't been dragged into this . . .' His eyes were watery yet burning with remorse, bitterness . . . and dread. 'I wish they didn't love me like they do.' He placed an icy, bony hand on McGray's and squeezed it with what little strength he had. 'Love is a burden, my son. I'm sure you know that by now.'

McGray felt a cold prickling at the back of his neck, almost like a physical presence building up from thin air.

Mr Nellys's eyes widened. 'I must confess something. My son . . . I hope you can forgive me.'

The man squeezed McGray's hand a little harder.

'Confess?' McGray repeated, his mouth suddenly dry.

The ghostly presence felt stronger. 'Did ye do it? Was it *ye*? Was it ye who killed the constable?'

Mr Nellys half smiled. 'We know your name ... your *other* name, Mr Nine-Nails.' He stared at the gap where McGray's missing finger would have been. 'We know what you investigate ... Millie read about you, about your interest in banshees and witchcraft and demons. You might understand as soon as I tell you this ...'

'Understand?'

The man's veiny eyes locked on McGray's, disturbing and penetrating.

'You do need a certain frame of mind to understand about demons ...'

The piano came to a halt, almost as if that word had stolen the music from the air. Then it resumed in sharp, staccato notes, like the pricking of needles. Mr Nellys put a weary hand to his belly. 'You've read plenty about demons, I imagine.'

'Ah – Aye, I have, but ...'

The man grasped McGray's forearm, startling him, pressing the still aching wound. 'Yet you fail to recognize one when you see him.'

There was a flash of madness in those eyes, the hint of a creeping smile, and the hand suddenly felt like an animal's claw around McGray's arm. He had to pull it away, disgusted by its touch, yet fearing he might snap those old bones.

'Don't say something ye might regret later. Ye better rest, Mr Nellys.'

The music resumed, low and funereal, and the old man's eyes filled with malice.

'Our family name isn't Nellys, my son. That's a contraction my grandfather made up so we wouldn't sound so foreign.'

The man looked sideways, listening intently to the music for an unnervingly long time. When he finally spoke again his voice sounded much lower, as if to come in tune with the dark serenade from downstairs.

'Our full name is – was . . .' he drew in air with a repulsive, throttling sound, 'Nelapsi.'

McGray rose to his feet, jumping back as if stricken by fire.

Mr Nelapsi finally allowed himself to grin wickedly. He no longer looked like a feeble, dying, sweet old man; he now looked like a desiccated corpse, freshly risen from the ground to torment the living.

'So you know the meaning,' he hissed with manic pleasure.

McGray nodded. 'Slavic folklore. It's an ancient name for –'

Mr Nelapsi cackled, and spat out his words as if stabbing the air. 'Monsters. Undead. Blood-drinkers.'

And just as McGray thought he understood it all, the presence he'd felt behind him became real, and a mighty blow fell on the back of his head. As he stumbled to the floor, searing pain darting through his skull, he had a fleeting vision of Mrs Nelapsi and her daughter.

And Benjamin.

42

Boyde smelled of lemon juice and garlic, which, combined with his perspiration and the reek of the corpse, made my face turn green: I caught my reflection in the water as he rowed swiftly towards the island. I tried to focus my attention on the slight breeze, the bright greenery and the imposing mountains all around us. Even at that moment, the loch instilled calm, a majestic mirror beneath the blue sky.

It took us just under half an hour to reach the island, the Koloman manor always visible behind us.

As we approached I had a better view of the shore. The pines rose abruptly from the very edge of the island, their trunks thin and perfectly straight, like the columns of a cathedral, and behind them the island was nothing but deep shadow.

The shore was not a beach but a rocky edge, sharp and unforgiving. Boyde had to tangle the rope around his waist and then clamber clumsily over a round rock, wet and slippery, before he could tie the boat to the nearest tree.

Getting the corpse ashore was a thousand times harder than I expected. Boyde jumped back into the boat and lifted McEwan's upper body, and only then did we realize our conundrum. I could carry the man's feet, but there was nobody on the rocks, level with my chest, to receive the load.

'I will go up there,' I said, climbing precariously up the wet stone. I knelt down, stretched out my arms and strived to take hold of the body, whilst Boyde did his best to bring it within my reach. He grunted and jerked, trying to heave that head and shoulders towards my hands, but he nearly fell over the gunwale. 'Try handing me the feet,' I said, and Boyde lifted McEwan's legs, dragging the man's head along the bottom of the boat, and again he tried to toss the body in my direction.

I wished we hadn't wrapped the corpse like a mummy, so I could have pulled his arm or leg, but then I had the ghastly image of a decaying limb coming off.

'Oh, this is a disaster,' I grunted, seeing the streaks of sweat on Boyde's temples. 'Prop him against the rock. I might be able to . . .'

Boyde again lifted the torso, and after nearly falling he managed to slam it against the granite. The spattering sound it made was repulsive.

Boyde sandwiched the corpse between the rock and his own body, pressing hard so it did not slide into the water.

I had to lean down so far I feared I'd plunge into the loch face first, but I managed to grab some folds of the flour sacks. I tried to pull up, but I did not have a good enough grip.

'*Push!*' I growled, feeling the jute tear, my fingers suddenly coming into contact with the body's actual skin.

Boyde snorted, squatted and thrust the body upwards with his last ounce of strength. I saw the wrapped head projecting up like a dart, and managed to seize the bundle and drag it so that it rested on the very edge of the rock. McEwan's torso, at least, was now firmly on the island, his legs hanging slackly above the water.

Boyde and I let out simultaneous sighs of relief. He joined me on steady ground, bringing the two shovels, and we both carried McEwan to a less precarious position.

I could finally take a look at the terrain before us. The

island was dark and ominous. Clearly the sun never reached the soil, for nothing grew underneath the majestic pines, their dead needles left there to dry and accumulate over the years.

'No need to bury him very far in,' I said, my mind set on getting back as soon as possible. 'Any spot will do.'

'Here?' asked Boyde, pointing with the shovel at a nearby clearing. It looked like the gap left by a tree fallen years ago.

I headed there, feeling the bumpy ground underneath the bed of needles and nearly losing my footing a couple of times. I glanced around with absolute weariness, cursing my luck at having to perform, with my bare hands, the last rituals for a lazy, irresponsible, misogynistic and insolent piece of rustic dung. Not that I would do a terribly solemn job . . .

Digging was not as difficult as carrying the corpse ashore but a soul-destroying task nonetheless. The bed of dry pine needles, even in that clearing, was almost a foot thick and below it the soil was hard and gritty.

By the time we'd dug deep enough I had blisters on my fingers, my arms and back and waist ached mightily, and I was dripping sweat like a coal miner – fittingly, for I was just as soiled.

Exhausted though we were, we managed to drag the body to the makeshift grave, doing our best not to breathe its offensive fumes, and then, without even thinking of saying something Christian, we rolled it over the edge. The corpse fell into the hole in the most ungracious manner, bouncing and then landing on its side.

Boyde wiped sweat from his forehead. 'Shall we position him properly?'

I looked at the curled up legs and the head, bent slightly upwards against the pit's wall. That poor body had been abused, mishandled and disrespected in every way imaginable.

'Would you care to?' I sighed.

Boyde shrugged, and we immediately began shovelling soil and stones back into the hole.

We were soon past caring, sweeping grit and kicking pebbles with our boots. Somehow, when we were finished, there was still a huge pile of rubble sitting next to the grave – far more than McEwan's body would have displaced.

I marked the place with a smooth, particularly dark stone, and rubbed the dust off my hands. We both sat in silence for a few minutes, not out of respect but simply catching our breath and resting our weary limbs. I looked at my now grubby watch; nearly three hours had passed since we left the manor. McGray would be sorely impatient by now.

Boyde saw me check the time and stood before I said a word. He picked up the shovels and started back to the boat, looking up at the fragments of blue sky visible through the canopy. I noticed a protrusion on the ground, right in front of him, and opened my mouth to warn him. But before I could speak Boyde tripped and fell flat on his face, the shovels rolling on the ground. I nearly laughed, but then he looked back at the object, the thick carpet of needles disturbed by his boot. And he squealed in panic.

'What is it?' I asked, jumping forward. Instead of replying, Boyde crawled away in an almost comical manner and ran for the boat.

I advanced cautiously, not knowing what to expect, until I spotted something white nestling in the dead foliage. Gingerly, as if it were a poisonous animal, I kicked the clumps of needles aside. I felt a chill, and I gasped.

It was a human skull, eroded and bleached by the elements. Its dark, empty sockets seemed to stare right back at me. Its jaw, almost toothless, had fallen open, locked in what looked like an everlasting cackle.

I gulped, giving myself a moment to recover from the first impression. After a few deep breaths I squatted down and carefully removed more dead needles. I uncovered a broken breastbone, surrounded by only a few remaining ribs.

'Dear Lord . . .' I muttered, peering at the sardonic-looking skull. It was completely dry, cracked in places, without a shred of flesh left on it. That body had lain there for years.

'Let's go, sir!' Boyde whimpered from the shoreline.

'Oh, come back, you silly brute! I need help here.'

I rose, thinking that this would open an entirely new line of investigation. I'd have to inspect the surroundings thoroughly, so that when the constables arrived I could give a comprehensive statement – and I would have only the help of this smelly young man.

'Why do these things always happen to me, while McGray is away having a bloody good time?' I grumbled, picturing him standing by a window with a large glass of wine.

Boyde approached, covering his mouth with his fists in a most childish way.

'Let's leave it here, sir. I don't want to –'

'Boyde,' I interrupted, trying very hard to sound comforting – not my greatest skill. 'There is nothing to be afraid of. This person has been dead for a good while. Now, help me uncover it. I need to see what lies here before we can go back.'

He bent down reluctantly, and began shifting foliage with quivering hands, almost one needle at a time, avoiding at all costs touching the skeleton.

'Boyde, you have just handled a cadaver that leaked and reeked, yet this – Oh, move aside!'

I sighed in resignation, not understanding this sudden change in him. I knew only that I would have to do most of the work myself.

Then, almost as if I were stepping out of my body, as if someone else had put the thought in my head, I said aloud, 'What are the chances you'd simply stumble across a dead body? This is a square-mile island.'

Just as I said that, Boyde again jumped backward, shrieking like a child.

'Oh, what now?'

He was looking away, covering his face, his voice muffled by his hands. 'That . . . that sod has three hands!'

'Boyde, do *not* be ridiculous. How could there be –'

I prodded into the carpet of needles with my shoe, and again I caught my breath. Boyde was right. On top of the breastbone there were the bones of two hands, resting like those of a body in a coffin. And then, right under them, I saw another set of phalanges. I uncovered two, three, four fingers. I dug further and followed the thin bones of a small forearm.

Then my boot rested on another bump. I stepped back and tossed aside handfuls of needles. There I found a ribcage . . . only it lay too far away to belong to either of the first two bodies.

I stood up at once, nearly tripping over another 'rock'. I dug: another skull. I dug a couple of feet to my right: two sets of femurs. I ran ten yards away, panting, and found another lump on the ground: a wide pelvic bone.

It became hard to breathe, and with my mind overwhelmed I turned in circles, staring at the myriad lumps in the ground that were still untouched.

I understood the enormity of what I was seeing, and my chest suddenly felt cold and hollow. I fell backward from the shock, dragging myself over the uneven terrain, knowing that each bump underneath my feet might be another skull or ribcage.

'God . . .' was all I could get out, a plea rather than a mere exclamation. And, to my own utter horror, I laughed.

Rory Island was a vast boneyard. A dumping ground for discarded bodies, left there to rot under the shade of that thick canopy.

43

McGray felt the rough rug pressing against his face, heard the rattle behind him, and then was perfectly conscious of someone tossing the blankets aside to pull Mr Nelapsi out of the bed. Downstairs the music stopped with a strident chord, followed instantly by Natalja's screaming. McGray could picture the scene in his mind, and his imagination went wild when he heard furniture breaking, shelfloads of books being hurled and brass instruments rolling about.

Yet, for a horrible moment, he could not move. He had to summon all his willpower to get his palms to the rug and then drag himself forward. The room spun around him madly as he grasped the edge of the bed to help himself up.

'I thought I'd knocked him down!' Mrs Nelapsi cried, and McGray saw Benjamin rush towards him, brandishing one of Mr Koloman's rifles.

It fell on McGray like a bludgeon, but just before it could crack his skull he raised his arm instinctively and pushed the rifle aside.

'Yer not that strong, laddie,' McGray panted, managing to stand on unsteady legs.

Benjamin retreated a few steps, pointing the rifle directly at McGray's chest. 'It doesn't take much strength to pull a trigger.'

McGray was about to tell the boy he would not dare, but Benjamin's expression told otherwise. His face was unsettling, stripped of every emotion but the purest hatred.

McGray raised his palms. 'Don't do something ye might regret.'

The rifle was shaking in Benjamin's puny arms, but he was standing so close it was impossible he'd miss McGray's heart. 'I'd say the same to you.'

McGray moved his eyes sideways and saw Helena and her mother wrapping Mr Nelapsi in a thick coat.

'Konrad's best,' said Mrs Nelapsi with a sneer. 'A new beginning.'

Miss Fletcher came in then, carrying a gun and checking that the cylinder was fully charged.

'I am sorry, Mr McGray,' she said. 'We must do this.' She nodded at Benjamin, who walked backward towards the door.

'How can ye go with *them*?' McGray cried. 'Half this is legally yers. Yer family is here.'

Benjamin let out a scornful laugh. '*Family!* They only brought me here to carry on their name. And Helena too. They want us to breed for them as if we were bloody goats, since my cousin is a damned pillow-biter.'

Miss Fletcher picked up the frail Mr Nelapsi and cradled him in her arms like a small child. She muttered, 'Don't judge him so harshly for that . . .'

McGray stuttered, watching the Nelapsi women scuttling away.

'And the threat against yer life?' he asked.

'I don't think there ever *was* a threat. At least, not to my life . . .'

He was about to say more, but Miss Fletcher was already at the threshold. 'Benjamin, we're wasting time.' Her blue eyes were fixed on McGray's, both determined and ashamed.

Benjamin went to his mother, the rifle ever pointing at

McGray. 'I'd love to stay here and chat, Mr Nine-Nails, but we have to go.'

McGray followed him with stealthy movements. 'Benjamin, there's still time to –'

'The master key?' Benjamin snapped, and Helena produced it swiftly.

'Master key? Where the hell did youse –'

In one swift movement Benjamin kicked the door to shut it, but McGray hurled himself against it with all his might, moving the door just enough to avoid the latch clicking.

'*Push!*' Benjamin howled from the other side, perhaps to Helena and her mother.

McGray moved his feet back, the better to shove forward, growling. The door creaked, giving way under his pressure, but only millimetre by painful millimetre.

'*The gun!*' Benjamin shouted. 'In Millie's pocket!'

But right then the door yielded and McGray's momentum carried him onward. His face nearly crashed against the opposite window, his hands slamming against the glass. He dashed towards the staircase, unsheathing his gun as he spotted Benjamin and Helena running away.

Just as he planted a boot on the steps he heard a gunshot. The bullet ricocheted off the granite walls and he had to pull back, instinctively raising an arm to cover his face.

'Och, respect yer elders, ye freshly weaned sod!'

McGray took a deep breath, his heart pounding, and stepped forward with his gun at the ready. He rushed down the stairs and saw that the bullet had hit one of the rich tapestries. Then he heard a cacophony of screams coming from the main hall.

There he found Mr and Mrs Koloman, bravely standing firm by the back door, blocking the Nelapsis' way. Benjamin was just raising the rifle to point at his uncle.

McGray half raised his gun, but he didn't have time to aim.

'Stop right there!' Lazarus snarled, coming from the opposite wing and holding one of Mr Koloman's guns – the polished brass and ivory grip could not have belonged to anybody else. He was aiming at McGray's face.

Lazarus must have been freed with that same master key, and then helped himself to the locked-up weapons, for he also carried two rifles and a sack of ammunition strapped to his back. He held a second gun in his other hand, and under that arm he carried a thick, dusty book.

Natalja ran in, armed with nothing but a pathetic letter opener. Her cheek was swollen and there was a trickle of blood at the corner of her mouth. She was about to strike Lazarus but halted when he pointed the other gun at her. The book slid from under his arm and dropped on to the floor, wide open. Helena rushed to retrieve it, closing it with anxious hands, and all McGray could see was that its pages were filled with tight handwriting.

'You got it,' Natalja muttered.

'Let us through!' Benjamin shouted at his uncle.

Mr Koloman actually smiled. 'Benjamin, *do* put that down. You could really injure someone.' His voice was all condescension. He still thought he was talking to a docile child.

'Don't upset the laddie,' McGray said, descending the last few steps as slowly as his legs allowed. He could see Benjamin's finger trembling on the trigger.

'Let us through,' Benjamin repeated.

'You are not going with them,' said Mr Koloman, the gravity of the moment slowly creeping over his face. 'I don't know what they might have told you, or how they made you take part in this preposterous scene, but you know nothing about them. *Nothing!*'

'That's what you think. It's *you* I knew nothing about.'

Mr Koloman looked at the ravaged faces of Mr and Mrs Nelapsi, one being carried like a child, the other cowering fearfully behind Miss Fletcher.

'What lies have you told him?' he barked at them, and then let out a mocking laugh. 'Whatever it was, you can't have told him the entire –'

'*Move!*' Benjamin roared, startling everyone. Even McGray.

Konrad ground his teeth. 'Why, you little –'

Mrs Koloman pulled her husband's arm, her voice breaking. 'Benjamin, look out there. You can't leave. You can't possibly –'

'I'd rather take my chances out there, Aunt. I'd rather sleep in the wild with *them* than in here with you.'

Nobody could answer that.

'We're wasting time,' said Lazarus, glaring alternately at Natalja and McGray.

'And my patience is wearing out,' Mr Koloman said, stretching out his hand. 'You *will* give me that.'

Benjamin held his ground. McGray even saw a drop of sweat fall from the boy's hand, his finger still wrapped around the trigger.

Mr Koloman shook his head, grunted and walked forward. 'You'll give me that! You little –'

At once Benjamin lowered the rifle and shot. Mr Koloman roared in pain and fell forward, curled up on the floor. His fine shoe was now an explosion of blood.

Not even Lazarus had expected that, for he half lowered both guns, and amidst the shouting and wailing McGray seized the chance to hurl himself on to him.

Lazarus growled, McGray grasped his wrist and then saw Natalja jump into the fray too. The three locked themselves in a fierce struggle, Natalja throwing clumsy stabs at Lazarus's face, McGray clutching the man's wrist, thinking he'd not yield until he felt those bones snap under his grip.

He felt an excruciating blow to his ribs and lost his balance, and Lazarus raised a foot high enough to kick him in the stomach. As McGray fell on his back he had a fleeting vision of Mrs Nelapsi, Helena and Miss Fletcher running to their freedom, dodging the squirming body of Mr Koloman.

'Let him go!' Benjamin commanded, for Natalja was still attacking Lazarus. McGray felt a chill when Benjamin hit her in her ribs with the butt of the rifle.

Natalja fell right next to McGray, grunting and crying.

'Cousin, *please*, don't do this!' she shrieked. 'We love you!'

Benjamin cast her a strange look, at once sad and enraged. 'I'm so sorry . . . but even *you* are full of lies.'

Natalja tried to say something but Lazarus pulled Benjamin away by the arm. The boy did not take his eyes off his wounded cousin until they reached the door and disappeared.

McGray crawled clumsily, a hand against his temple, the other feeling on the floor for his gun.

'Ye all right?' he asked Natalja. She barely managed to nod. McGray found his weapon, stood up and staggered forward. Mrs Koloman was kneeling by her husband, holding his hand and crying like a magdalen.

'He all right?'

But McGray could not wait for a reply. He heard a throaty scream coming from the kitchen.

'Where are the blasphemous bastards?'

It was Mrs Plunket, her fat fingers grasping a shiny meat cleaver. Her young maid followed, armed with a carving fork.

McGray pointed to the back door, and the cook pushed him ahead, her strength as vast as her hips.

They ran across the lawn as the Nelapsis took the boat from the pier, all of them crammed in there. Miss Fletcher was rowing and Benjamin stood straight as a lance, pointing the rifle at them. Everyone else was ducking down, covering their faces with their hands or their coats. McGray heard Mrs Nelapsi whimpering in despair.

'*Stop!*' Nine-Nails shouted, running recklessly to the edge of the pier. Still dizzy, he nearly fell into the water, but Mrs Plunket pulled him back. She threw her cleaver at the boat, and McGray watched it catch the strong sunlight as it flew through the air. Just as the blade hit the stern gunwale Benjamin shot into the sky, and then pointed the rifle back at them.

'Leave us alone!' he shouted.

McGray raised his gun, aimed and even squeezed the trigger a little, but then thought better of it. His head was still spinning and his vision was blurry from the blow he'd received. He felt a wave of burning rage, and roared and stamped his boots on the wooden pier so hard the old logs cracked.

He stared out across the water, barely blinking, but by the time his senses were somewhat back to normal, the boat was but a tiny dot in the distance.

'They win for now, sir,' said Mrs Plunket, 'but I'm sure you'll think o' something.'

McGray and Mrs Plunket had to carry Mr Koloman upstairs. His own room was the nearest, and they deposited the groaning man on the bed.

Mrs Koloman rushed in, sat by her husband and began

carefully removing the blood-soaked shoe. Ellie arrived seconds later, carrying her mistress's instrument case. At once Minerva pulled out bandages and iodine.

The twins also arrived, squeezing each other's hands. Veronika had not witnessed the commotion, but she looked as scared as everybody else.

'Everyone all right?' McGray asked, still pressing the side of his head. 'First time some soddin' bastard hit me like that 'n' got away with it!'

Mr Koloman nodded, biting on a handkerchief.

'Lassie?' McGray asked Natalja.

'I will live,' she said bitterly, a hand on her ribs.

McGray turned back to the parents. 'What the fuck was that?' The maid gasped at his language.

Mr Koloman spat the cloth from his mouth. 'That's what I'd like to know! How did Benjamin manage to free Lazarus? How did they get those hunting rifles? You locked those blasted rooms yourself, and I've heard the damn keys jingling in your breast pocket all this time!'

'They mentioned they had a master key,' McGray snapped. 'A fucking master key I'm sure youse kent about! Why didnae –'

'*We didn't know!*' retorted Mrs Koloman. 'If you want me to speculate –'

'I don't have time to bloody speculate! I need to catch them! They were going to their island. If I make haste –'

'They're not going there,' Mr Koloman interrupted. 'I think I know where they'll go first.'

Everyone looked at him in surprise, Mrs Koloman much more than the others, the bottle of iodine slowly slipping from her hand. McGray snatched it before it dropped and gave it to the maid.

'Ye sure?' he asked Mr Koloman.

347

'Not entirely sure,' he said, wincing in pain. 'But I have good reason to believe –'

'Tell me.'

Mr Koloman took short, laboured breaths. 'I lied before,' he finally said. 'That map I showed to you and your colleague this morning . . . do you remember?'

'Aye, I remember.'

'Do you remember the cross on the northern shore?'

'Aye.'

'That marks –'

'*Don't!*' his wife shrieked. 'You cannot tell him!'

Mr Koloman bared his teeth. '*Look at me, woman!* Look at your daughter! Don't you think your damned Nellyses have gone too far this time?'

Mrs Koloman jumped to her feet and turned her back on them, burying her face in her hands as she burst into desolate wails. Veronika left her sister's side to take her mother in her arms.

On the bed Mr Koloman trembled, half from the pain, half from what he was about to say. 'That cross, Mr McGray, marks an ancient cave, the Nellyses' lair. That's where they commit all sorts of atrocities. That's where I'm almost sure they'll go first.'

'Atrocities?' McGray echoed. 'What d'ye mean?'

Mr Koloman shook his head. 'It will take me a while to explain. If they go there, it will be only briefly. After that they may even disappear into the wilderness. If you really want to catch them, you must go there as soon as possible.'

McGray snorted. He could not wait for Frey to return; only God knew how long it would take the dainty Londoner to dig a grave. Boyde, who might have been of help, was over there too, and Mr Koloman was in no state to walk. To make matters worse, the Nelapsis had taken the last boat.

'That mad Maurice,' McGray whispered. He turned to Mr Koloman. 'They have spare boats at the inn, don't they?'

'I . . . I think so.'

'Yes,' Mrs Koloman confirmed, between sobs. 'They keep a couple for guests and one for their own use.'

'Good. I'll have to go on my own. Ye treat yer husband's foot, missus.'

Veronika jumped in. 'Dominik is a good shot. He can help you!'

Her mother grasped the girl's hand so tightly she let out a screech. 'No, he can't!' Mrs Koloman hissed.

McGray looked intently at them. Did he still have reason to suspect Dominik? The Nelapsis were fleeing, and the old man had uttered the words 'blood-drinkers'. McGray recalled McEwan's body hanging upside down, barely a drop left in him.

Then again . . .

'Yer mother's right,' he found himself saying. Somehow he didn't want Dominik armed and by his side at such a pressing moment. 'It's not safe,' he added as a good excuse. 'Nobody leave the house, youse understand?'

He headed to the door with huge strides, feeling as if the darkness of that cave were already upon him.

44

How could everything have spiralled like this? A simple, unofficial case, which I had even regarded as a chance to take a relaxed holiday, had become one of the darkest, direst episodes of my life. The repercussions of that boneyard were unimaginable; years and years of murders must have taken place in this seemingly peaceful area, human remains dumped like chicken bones . . . and I still had no idea what was behind it all. I wished we'd never come to this blasted loch, and I pictured Uncle Maurice and me in my parlour, drinking and smoking without a care in the world. I sighed. There was no point in torturing myself with what ifs; I had to concentrate on the situation ahead.

As the boat moved slowly south I watched the manor grow gradually, its grey stones reflecting the still bright sunlight. Little did I know that the place had just been shaken to its very core.

We approached the pier and I noticed that both sides were vacant. I instantly knew something was wrong.

'Where is the other boat?' I asked, looking in every direction, but Loch Maree was like a smooth, desolate mirror. 'Nobody was supposed to leave the house.'

Boyde, now drained from the digging and rowing – not to mention the shock of finding countless carcasses – barely shrugged.

I looked at the windows. All the curtains were still drawn and the place was in silence, but even from outside there was a different quality to it. I could not pinpoint what.

Then I saw that the thick back door was wide open.

'Hurry, please,' I told Boyde, who was taking his time to cover the last few yards. Even before he tied the boat up I jumped on to the pier, my hand already inside my jacket, my fingers on my weapon.

As soon as I walked in my eyes were drawn to a smear of blood on the polished floor. I immediately unsheathed the gun.

'Boyde, come here!' I called, taking cautious steps forward. 'McGray? Mr Koloman?'

The only answer I received was the echo of my own voice.

'Oh Jesus!' Boyde burst out when he saw the blood. He dropped one of the shovels and raised the other, as if ready to strike.

We moved towards the stain. I bent one knee and patted it. The edges of the smear were already dry. That blood must have been spilled a while ago.

I looked up, at the staircase and the enormous empty space above our heads. The grand house suddenly felt deathly cold, like a giant mausoleum. And there was still a persistent smell of death in the air.

There was a crimson trail, but it stopped only a few feet away. Whoever had been injured, they had probably been carried from there on.

'It looks like they went either upstairs or to the drawing room,' I muttered, and made my way to the latter. That door was also wide open, revealing a horrible sight: there were books strewn all over the floor; the decanters were shattered, the fine Persian rugs stained dark purple; the telescope lay bent on the floor, its lenses in smithereens; and the clock-like display of the weathervane had been ripped from the wall, the cogs now bare.

But there was nobody around.

'Mr Koloman!' I shouted again, and Boyde began calling the names of all his fellow servants.

'There might be someone upstairs,' I said. 'Dominik must still be locked up there – hopefully.'

As we went out I noticed Mr Koloman's thick weather log lying open on the floor. What first caught my eye were the tiny drops of blood on the pages, but when I knelt down for a closer look, the dates and times, recorded in bright-red ink, made me gasp.

'The twentieth of August,' I whispered, remembering my first day at Loch Maree. 'They were here. They were here all the time . . .'

'What is it, sir?'

I shook my head and stood up. 'Never mind. Let's look upstairs.'

There we went, and found that all the doors in the main corridor were open. Even Dominik's.

'Oh, I hate this . . .' I said, noticing a key still inserted in the lock. 'Where did they –'

I took the key and put it in my pocket as I stepped inside. The room was in relative order, except for a trunk in the middle of the room, open and half filled with clothes, shoes and several glinting pieces of gold – cufflinks, rings, a large watch on a thick chain . . .

'He was packing,' I said, 'ready to flee, but for some rea-son he stopped . . .'

I looked around, looking for more clues, but then we heard the murmur of voices.

'Next door?' Boyde asked. I nodded, realizing that the whispers had indeed come from McGray's room.

We moved back into the corridor, the sound of a woman

speaking now unquestionable. I kicked the door open to not one but two female cries.

Inside I found Veronika, lying on the bed, her mother sitting by her side. Mrs Koloman had raised a small derringer, but when she saw me she sighed in relief.

'Thank goodness, I thought they had come back!' She stood up and came to me, ready to take my hand. I lifted my palm immediately to keep her at bay.

A torrent of questions swirled through my mind. I saw there was blood on the bed.

'Where is McGray?'

'Oh, your colleague is fine,' Mrs Koloman said promptly. She peered at the blood too. 'My husband was shot in the foot.' She gulped. 'By Benjamin.'

'Benjamin?' I squealed.

'Yes,' Veronika took over, for her mother was crying now. 'He helped Lazarus escape. They took my father's guns and ran away with Helena and her parents – and Miss Fletcher.'

I frowned, utterly confused. 'Ma'am, would you give me that gun?'

Mrs Koloman's fingers closed more tightly on the small weapon. She made to say something, but then handed it to me.

'Where is everybody?' I asked, shoving the derringer in my pocket. 'Again, where is Inspector McGray?'

Mrs Koloman went back to her daughter. 'He went to the inn to borrow their boat and chase the Nellyses. He mentioned something about getting help from Mr Plantard.'

Veronika looked away when that was said.

I realized that Boyde was still wielding the shovel. 'Put that down,' I told him, but he only did so when his mistress spoke.

'Do as he says,' she snapped. 'And bring him some water. He'll want to wash his hands after digging a grave.'

Boyde bowed and left. Mrs Koloman was probably expecting my gratitude, but she'd be disappointed.

'Your son is gone too, ma'am,' I said.

'We had to let him out,' said Mrs Koloman. 'Konrad insisted on going to Poolewe to get help. Your colleague can't face the Nellyses on his own. Konrad was adamant he'd take the carriage, and Dominik wanted to help.'

I raised my hand in a movement calculated to make my gun visible. I wanted them to see I was armed but not to threaten them yet. 'It looks as though your son was about to flee . . .'

Mother and daughter bit their lips in perfect synchrony.

'The idea did cross his mind when we unlocked his room,' Mrs Koloman mumbled. 'We talked him out of it, not without struggle. But he understood there is no need for him to run, not now that the truth is evident.'

What truth? I thought. For all I knew they might have shot McGray whilst he lay in bed and the men were out there now, perhaps adding his body to the pile of bones on Rory Island. What on earth was going on?

'How did you unlock the door?' I asked. 'McGray had all the keys.'

Mrs Glenister came in then, bringing a tea service. There was a large patch of blackened blood over the right-hand side of her head, highlighted by her grey hair. She nearly dropped the tray when she saw me.

Veronika's voice became ominous. 'Benjamin seized a master key from *her*. He used that to free Lazarus and to get my father's weapons. Lazarus dropped it in the library,

354

where he attacked my sister – she is fine, Inspector. We found the key there and used it to free Dominik when Papa insisted on leaving.'

Mrs Glenister continued in, hunched, and put the tray on a little table.

'You had a master key we knew nothing about?' I shrilled. 'Why would you not –' I turned to Mrs Koloman. 'Did you know of that key? You *must* have.'

She shook her head fervently. 'No, I swear! I mean, we had a master key but it went missing a couple of years ago. Or at least we *thought* it had. We seldom lock our rooms so never came to replace it.'

Veronika sat up then, her eyes stern. 'Mrs Glenister, you gave them the key, did you not? You gave it to Benjamin!'

The old woman's silence was eloquent enough.

Mrs Koloman stood up slowly, her pale skin turning red. 'You gave it to them? You kept it hidden all this time and now you gave it to them? You treacherous old hag!'

I had to stand between the two women.

Mrs Glenister was glaring at her mistress. 'You can't move us all about like pawns, Mrs Koloman! You can't give me a child, ask me to nurture him right after my own baby died, and then take him from me and expect me to forget about him, as if nothing had happened. I still love him as if he were my own son.'

Mrs Koloman was open-mouthed. 'How dare you talk to me like that? We've done nothing but help you. When your husband died we kept you here. When your daughters married I gave them money to settle away, just as you wanted!'

'Yes, ma'am. I wanted them away. And you know why!'

Mrs Koloman raised her chin, suddenly looking terrified.

'And you should be glad I helped the Nellyses,' Mrs Glenister added. 'I told them to be kind to you and your family.'

'Kind? My husband took a bullet! Lazarus battered Natalja's face!'

'You should be thankful the young miss is alive at all. You have no idea how much Lazarus despises your family.'

Nobody spoke after that, I least of all – I still did not know whose words I should believe. Everyone seemed to have lied to me at one point or another, and I could not picture freckly young Benjamin lifting a weapon against anybody. What should I do next?

'Mr Frey!' someone said behind me. It was Natalja coming in from the corridor, her cheek swollen and beginning to bruise. I felt a pang of compassion for her.

'Are you all right?' I asked, but she would not answer the question.

'Look,' she said instead, handing me a few sheets of paper. 'I just found these in Benjamin's room. It seems he's been in touch with the Nellyses all along!'

'Let me see those,' and I took the sheets from her. They were scraps of crumpled wrapping paper, and gave off a strong smell of lemon and vinegar. The scribbles on them – in three different sets of handwriting – did not look like ink but rather dark singes, and the corners of more than one sheet were partially burned.

'I have seen this before,' I mumbled. 'If you write with vinegar, or lemon or orange juice, instead of ink, and leave it to dry, the words will be invisible and only appear when you bring the paper close to a flame.'

Mrs Koloman came over for a closer look. 'That's wrapping paper from Mr Newington, our most trusted merchant in Poolewe! I'd recognize it anywhere. Why would he –'

'Not him, Mama,' Natalja jumped in. 'Miss Fletcher takes parcels to Juniper Island all the time, the food and provisions you send them. And Miss Fletcher also wraps our own parcels and takes them to Poolewe or Kinlochewe for shipping. We send and receive correspondence at least once a week. They have been reusing the wrapping paper, or hiding their messages in the parcels' wrappings.'

Mrs Koloman covered her mouth. 'Good Lord, and we always keep fresh lemons!'

I looked at the door, thinking of Boyde's swift exit. I recalled he'd smelled of lemons before the rowing and the digging had made him break sweat – and I raised an eyebrow.

I looked alternately at the papers and at Natalja. 'So . . . you are saying that Miss Fletcher has been the go-between, passing notes from the Nellyses to Benjamin and vice versa?'

'That is what it seems,' said Natalja, pointing at the writings.

'Why would she do that?'

'She clearly didn't want Benjamin to live with us. Perhaps she still hates my mother for sending him away. But do read. From the notes I think they had this escape planned all along.'

I tried to read them, but my mind was a whirling mess. Natalja had to point out the relevant lines:

Benjamin,

The day we've feared so much has finally come. The Kolomans will send for you.

Be prepared.
Love, H. N.

The next note read:

Benjamin,

You'll have to do the deed as planned. That which we can't speak of.
I'm so sorry, but there is no other way. I know it will be so hard
for you, but we will be at your side. It's all been arranged.

You know we love you so!
S. N. & H. N.

And the next sheet, its edge burned dangerously close to
the message:

Benjamin,

We'll be looking from the island. Leave a light in your window so we
know you have arrived. I'll be looking just after sunset every night.
Excellent view from Rory Island. Code in another message.

All our love,
L. N.

After that the sheets were a collection of ciphers, a sort of
simplified Morse code with series of dots and lines to mean
things like '*I am here*', '*They are nice to me*', and then much
darker ones, like '*Help!*', '*Don't approach!*', '*They are coming for
you*' or '*Death is near*'.

'The lamp!' I spluttered, rushing out. Natalja followed
closely and we stormed into Benjamin's room. I went straight
to the window, where I'd seen his oil lamp every time I came
to leave his meals. There it was, in the exact same spot, and
next to it, wide open on the window seat, a thick book. I
picked it up.

'Its pages are all singed,' said Natalja. 'He must have used this as a –'

'As a screen to block the light at intervals,' I interrupted. 'He sent Morse code messages with this lamp.'

Mrs Koloman and Veronika had followed us, and they'd heard it all. They stood there, pale and open-mouthed.

'Benjamin was in here when the constable was murdered,' I said. 'Unless he managed to climb down . . .' I was about to draw the curtains aside to look, but Natalja held my arm.

'You are thinking what I'm thinking, are you not?' she said, grasping my sleeve. 'Benjamin killed Constable McEwan. Maybe Benjamin killed the priest too.'

45

McGray covered the distance to the inn at full gallop, spurring one of the carriage horses with frantic shouts.

He let out a victorious cry when the brown stones of the inn appeared in the distance. The lace curtains and the quaint flowerpots were still there, looking prim and pretty, annoying reminders that nobody else in the world knew what had just happened at the manor.

McGray reined in and jumped to the ground. The snorting, panting horse was drooling in exhaustion.

'Och, I'm nae that heavy!' muttered McGray, and then he hollered, '*Mr Dailey!*'

McGray strode swiftly to the main door. The place, as usual, wasn't locked, and he stormed in, calling for the owners again and again. A very alarmed Mrs Dailey came out from the kitchen, her chubby hands smothered in flour and dough.

'What is –'

'I need yer boat. And where's yer husband? He might be of help.'

'Why? What's happen–'

'*Where is he?*'

The woman's lip trembled. She pointed east, splattering drops of dough on to the carpet. 'He . . . he went to Kinlochewe to get some supplies. He won't be back 'til the evening.'

McGray cursed. 'And where's that soddin' fake Froggie?'

'Mr Plantard? Well, he's in the sitting room, but I don't think ye –'

McGray was already rushing there, and as soon as he opened the door a pungent wave of a fruity bouquet hit him like a fist.

Maurice was lounging in one of the armchairs, an empty glass in his hand and a rosy blush across his face. He looked as if he'd been slowly sliding down the seat, his body as slack as softened butter.

'Och, what the fuck!'

The man grinned at McGray, his words slurring. 'Why, Mr Nine-Stumps! I'm trying to drown a few bad remini . . . reminisce . . . some bad memories. The Kolomans were so kind as to send me away with a cask o' their wine . . .' And he waved his glass in the direction of a little barrel that stood almost proudly at the centre of a nearby table. 'Oh, do sshoin me! You look like you have your share of tribulee . . . treeba . . . troubles.'

'Nae, thanks. I once tried to drown my sorrows in whisky. The bastards just learned how to swim.'

And McGray went to him and picked him up by the lapels.

Maurice dropped his glass and flapped his hand about, trying to retrieve it. 'Oh, what are you – You, my rustic Scotch, are no sschentleman!'

McGray cackled. 'Aye, and yer about to see how fucking *ungentlemanlike* I can get!'

McGray felt indescribably exhilarated when he pushed Maurice's head into the loch. The drunken man jerked and kicked about in despair as McGray held him firmly in place from the edge of the pier.

It took three long – long – plunges for the man to sober up, not completely, but just enough to understand McGray's instructions. He pulled Maurice's limp body back on to the pier, where Mrs Dailey waited with a towel at hand, and a mug of steaming coffee.

'Did ye need to be so harsh, sir?' she asked, gently wrapping Maurice's shoulders. The man was coughing and spitting.

'"Need" can be open to interpretation, hen,' said McGray, patting Maurice's cheeks a little too vigorously. 'Can ye hear me now?'

'Oh, *stop it*, you bloody bundle of bestiality!'

'Ye fit enough to row?'

Maurice took a long sip of coffee. 'Are you fit enough to sit in the boat without turning green?'

'I'll take that as an aye.' McGray turned to Mrs Dailey. 'We cannae waste more time, missus. I need ye to go to the Kolomans' and wait for Inspector Frey. As soon as he arrives back at the house, tell him I'm all right, and that the Kolomans are speaking the truth. He might doubt their word, especially since I'm nae there.'

'Truth?' she repeated. 'What are ye talking about, sir? What's happened?'

McGray snorted. He had no time to explain that the Nelapsis had just confessed to being blood-drinkers or that Mr Koloman had been shot.

'Ye'll see when ye get there. Just tell Inspector Frey exactly what I've said.'

McGray made the woman repeat the message twice, and then made her fetch any weapons her husband might have. She came back with a light shotgun Mr Dailey maybe used to shoot pigeons, and a little pouch full of bullets. McGray weighed the weapon in his hand; it was the kind of thing one would hand to upper-class ladies (or Frey) to keep them entertained during a hunt.

'Better than nothing,' he grumbled.

'It's the Nellyses youse are after, right?' Mrs Dailey asked, unable to contain a small smile of relief.

McGray didn't answer, though he knew his silence was confirmation enough.

'Get in there,' he told Maurice, who threw him a killing stare before crawling inelegantly into the boat.

'Your turn, young chap. I'm looking forward to watching this.'

McGray took a deep breath. He felt nauseous already, just from looking at the sway of the boat.

He took a faltering step forward. He did not fear the cave nearly as much as he did the trip there.

46

I looked at the messages, reading the lines again and again, Natalja's words spinning in my mind.

'So Lazarus didn't kill the constable . . .' Mrs Koloman whispered, sinking on to the bed. She reached for Natalja's hand. 'But it was Benjamin?'

'It makes sense, Mama,' the girl insisted, and then looked me in the eye. 'Benjamin was not locked in here the first night. He told me so himself.'

She seemed far too keen to convince me. Perhaps because she was defending her brother, but what if there was . . . another reason? I felt as though my head was about to explode.

'Why would Benjamin be in touch with the Nellyses?' I said. 'I can see why he might murder the constable, but then why the priest? And why would he and Miss Fletcher want to go with them? It makes absolutely no sense.'

Mrs Koloman trembled and lost all self-control. 'And now Helena will become like them . . . sickly and burned and –'

She halted, her eyes instantly flicking in my direction. She tried to say something else, but it was too late.

I took a step closer to her. 'Madam, I can see, as clear as day, there is something you have not yet told me.'

Mrs Koloman grasped Natalja's hand, looking as scared as a cornered cat. Veronika sat next to her mother and took her other hand.

'It is no use,' Mrs Koloman mumbled, inexplicable defeat in her eyes. 'I'll just –'

'You must tell us all, Mama,' Natalja prompted. 'Start by –
Before Inspector McGray left, Papa mentioned something
about . . . the atrocities the Nellyses commit . . . He mentioned a cave.'

'Indeed,' Veronika jumped in, 'and he said that a cross on
the map of the loch showed its location. How could he know
that? You and Papa have been hiding something from us,
have you not? Something about the Nellyses?'

Mrs Koloman cried silent tears. I waited for her next words,
not pressing her but holding my breath, as if I were stalking a
nervous doe and the slightest sound might scare her.

The woman stood up and reached for the side table, where
there was a carafe of wine. Benjamin had not touched it, for
it was still full to the brim. Mrs Koloman poured herself a
full glass, drank long sips, and before the initial effect of the
alcohol receded she spat out the words: 'Sabina Nelapsi is
my sister.'

'I knew it,' Natalja mumbled, looking down, as if a sea of
unconnected pieces suddenly began to fit together in her mind.
'That's why you help them all the time . . . That's why you
wanted Helena to move in here so badly. She is your niece!'

I went to Mrs Koloman, for neither daughter attempted
to move. There was something odd, some strange expression on their faces I could not read. Were they appalled at
their own mother? Were they disgusted by this new information? I took the glass from the woman's hand and put it
aside. Only then, knowing the truth, did I see the resemblance between her and Mrs Nelapsi. The same cheekbones,
the same lips . . . but Mrs Koloman's skin was smooth and

unblemished, and her eyes, not as pale as her sister's, had a resolution, an energy the other woman seemed to have lost long ago.

She smiled bitterly, perhaps reading my stare. 'We are twins too, would you believe it? Fraternal, not identical . . . but we still looked so much alike.' She covered her face. 'God, I still love her! Even after all that's happened.'

'Go on,' I said softly. 'Did you grow up together?'

'Yes. We were brought up between Norway and Germany, but we travelled all the time. On one of those trips my sister met that hideous Nelapsi man – that is his actual name, Mr Frey: Silas Nelapsi. Sabina was madly in love with him from the very start; that was our first real fight. I never liked the man, not one bit.'

'Why was that?'

Her lips trembled. 'When . . . when we met him he already looked as he does now. And I think he was already losing his mind; he would say the strangest things about blood, and the nature of cruelty . . . once, at the dinner table, he simply stood up for no reason and began reciting the works of some twisted philosophers. My mother opposed the marriage, of course. I was already engaged to Konrad; he and his father didn't like Silas either, and they confronted him. That very night Sabina eloped, taking my mother's jewels and my father's gold. We didn't hear of them for years – until they came to our door one winter, begging for our help.'

Mrs Koloman shed tears, one, two, and then a torrent. 'I could barely recognize her! She had already become what you see now, in only a few short years! By then Silas had gone completely insane and Sabina had squandered all her money looking for a cure, travelling across Europe and consulting the worst type of charlatan. What could I do but help her?'

'What sort of help did they want?' I asked. 'More money?'

'No,' said Mrs Koloman 'She had heard the legends about that miraculous well on Isle Maree . . . and other horrid tales of witchcraft. They wanted us to help them settle on the island, which we did. Konrad sent men to help them build their house. I sent them food, money – but every time I helped them they seemed to resent us more and more. They needed our help but it did no good to their pride. And then . . . to everybody's surprise . . . Silas became better! Nobody knows how.'

I raised my chin. 'So . . . Miss Fletcher told us the truth about that?'

'Yes, and it was then that they attempted to have children.' Mrs Koloman had to cover her face. 'I watched her little ones die one after the other. The graves of her poor babies are lined up on Isle Maree . . . Until I talked some sense into her . . .'

'And you sent Miss Fletcher and Mrs Glenister as wet nurses,' I completed, for she'd fallen silent.

'Yes. And like Glenister said, I watched them become attached to the children. *I* became attached to them. They are also my blood!'

She bit her lip, regretting she'd uttered that word.

I spoke as gently as I could. 'We seem to have come to the point, madam. Do you know of –' I cleared my throat. There was no way to soften my words. 'Do you know anything of blood baths . . . and rituals involving blood?'

Natalja gasped and covered her mouth. It took Veronika another moment to react, and then she mirrored her sister.

Mrs Koloman looked at her daughters with a strange, eerie grimace, and then pulled her hair, a hint of madness in her face. For an instant her attitude reminded me of

Veronika, crouching and pleading in a dark corner of the corridor.

Natalja took her sister's hand, as if to gather courage. 'Mama, is that the reason the Nellyses keep those bats?' Her mother merely grunted in assent.

'How can they keep them alive in winter?' I asked. 'Those are tropical beasts.'

'The cave,' Mrs Koloman said, nodding at Veronika. 'They keep them warm and fed in a cave. Do you remember my husband's maps? That cross on the north shore Veronika just mentioned?' She did not wait for my answer. 'The fishermen from Kinlochewe told us every autumn they see the bats swarming around a cave there. And then they see them emerge in the spring, always from the same crack in the rocks. That cross marks the spot.'

'Why?' I asked yet again. 'Why would they want to breed bats that ruin their livestock?'

Natalja's eyes flickered, her mind apparently working at full speed. 'Leeches,' she said, looking at me. 'Do you remember that book I gave you, Mr Frey? They must use them to keep the goats' wounds open . . .' She shuddered. 'Mama, do they really . . . Are the tales from the villagers true? Do they really drink their goats' blood? And . . . oh, dear Lord . . .'

Mrs Koloman did not need to answer. We were all thinking of McEwan's slit throat. We all had seen him, the dregs of his blood still dripping. And I had another, much darker image in my head: the piles of human bones strewn all over Rory Island.

'Why?' I prompted. 'Why would anybody do something like that? Is it a ritual? Do they think it is a cure for something, like the well? Does it have to do with their skin –'

A nasty chill invaded me and I could not finish the sentence. Mr Koloman's weather log, lying on the drawing-room floor, had come into my mind. Also the crystal prisms and the light experiments.

Now I understood . . . Not what they had told me, but rather something that they purposely hadn't.

Mrs Koloman went back to the bed, staggering a little, and sat down. 'Something must happen to them when they drink the blood. You can tell they do so from their skins. There must be a physical . . . a chemical explanation – but I believe it is evil itself that makes them that way. It has to be their own wickedness taking hold of their minds and bodies, turning them into such wrecks. That makes me think that Helena can still be saved; she still has innocence in her eyes.'

I looked at the creased notes, still in my hand. My fingers had gone numb and I barely managed to repress a slight tremble. Of course, Benjamin and Miss Fletcher had fled with that lot . . . It all made sense! I usually felt exhilarated when I got to the bottom of a case. Now I just felt deathly cold.

'Would you . . .' I breathed in, choosing my words very carefully. 'Ma'am, you seem quite upset. Shall I open the window to allow you some fresh air?'

There was an awkward silence, soon broken by Natalja. 'Oh, don't worry about us right now, Mr Frey. Glenister will see to us. You should go to the inn now. See if you can help Mr McGray and Mr Plantard. Your colleague said he'd go straight to the cave.'

She sounded far too keen again. I seemed to have touched a nerve.

I took a very small step towards the door. 'Yes . . . yes indeed. I should go.' I looked around, feeling the tension build up in my muscles, my legs and arms stiffening, just like the lips of the three women.

'Miss Natalja . . .' I began, 'I . . . I might instead wait for the return of your father. He is bringing help, after all.'

'Wait?' she repeated, looking at me with sudden hatred. There was no turning back now.

'Yes,' I mumbled. 'There is one thing I want to ask him. Would you . . .' I looked at the curtains, still drawn. 'Would you mind guiding me to the gardens? You might even join me for a little walk?'

'A *walk*?' she screeched. 'Right now?'

I took another little step to the door. I was but a couple of feet from the threshold. 'Indeed,' I said. 'It would help my . . . mood.'

Silence. The air around us seemed to have congealed into an oppressive, icy mass. I said no more, and waited patiently for a reply.

Then, with the speed of a wildcat, Natalja rose to her feet and leaped forward, but just in time I reached the door and slammed it closed.

I clumsily hunted for the key in my pocket, my other hand gripping the doorknob to keep it in place. I felt the women attempting to turn it with a surprising combined strength.

'What are you doing?' Natalja shrieked from the other side, and I heard fists banging on the door.

I felt my grip slipping and I growled as I pulled the key from my pocket, barely able to hold the door in place. My hand trembled, I missed the keyhole twice, the women shouting all manner of insults, but I finally managed to lock it.

Sweating, I took a step back. The door was being battered, the knob jerking madly as they all screamed and tried to open it.

'Why are you doing this?' Mrs Koloman moaned amongst the racket.

'We are not the bloody villains!' Natalja shrieked, bashing the door between each sentence. 'The Nellyses will kill you! You and the idiotic inspector! And then they'll come for us!'

Doubt crept into my mind, but what was done was done. If these women had not concealed the crucial detail I thought they had, I'd be able to come back and explain later. I turned on my heel, thinking what my next move should be.

'What have you done, sir?'

Boyde stood in front of me, holding a ewer and basin. His eyes were wide. 'Did you just lock the mistresses in there?'

Mrs Koloman and her daughters were still shouting.

I raised a palm, slowly bringing a hand to my breast pocket, where I'd put my gun whilst inspecting Benjamin's room.

'Erm . . . I might have. But I *can* explain –'

From behind the door came a chorus of desperate cries: 'Help us, Boyde!' and 'He's trapped us!'

'Oh, ladies, would you *please* –' I'd turned my face to the door just a fraction but Boyde took the chance to throw the hot water at me, and then the basin, which I barely managed to block with my forearm. And before the china had shattered on the floor he was already upon me, his thick, sweaty arms pushing me against the door. I threw a few punches at him, but he soon grabbed my neck and squeezed it.

'Oh, you . . . damned brute!' I gagged, my limbs flailing about as the man strangled me. I saw stars and felt a chill spreading from my fingertips to the rest of my body. The women were shouting but I could no longer understand their words. The world had reduced to that unyielding pressure on my throat and my futile attempts to draw air in, witnessing how my vision began to blur.

I gagged, making one last attempt to breathe, but then everything around me went black and I fell limply to the floor. And then came a miracle: air rushed into my lungs and Boyde's body fell right in front of me. I pressed my forehead on the carpet, taking in noisy, guttural breaths, my mouth opened as wide as possible.

A hand squeezed my shoulder and helped me up. I saw Mrs Glenister's stern face and a silver candlestick in her hand, now stained with Boyde's blood. She'd just saved my life, but there was no trace of emotion on her lined face.

'You'll understand I have to run now,' she said, and before I could reply she strode down the corridor, the girl Tamlyn by her side. They reached the staircase, and I never saw them again.

47

McGray nearly fell out of the boat as he leaned over to vomit. Again.

Maurice was not faring much better. He was feeling the worst effects of the hangover now, his head beating, and the Scot's continual gagging made everything worse.

'Have you not yet managed to spit out your spleen?'

'*Och, fuck o–*' Another noisy spurt of vomit.

Maurice focused his eyes on the beauty of the lake. The sky was beginning to turn pink, and the canopies of the pines . . . No, he could not. The sound of retching was too much. 'I am so sorry I did not try the salmon here. Mr Dailey said it was top quality, but now that you have so graciously emptied yourself in these waters I will have to wait for at least a lustrum before –'

'*Will ye ever shut up?*'

Maurice smirked. 'Not very nice, is it? Being on the receiving end?'

McGray turned his head to him, wiping his mouth with his sleeve, and unsheathed his gun. 'One . . . more . . . fucking word . . .'

Maurice did close his mouth, but began rowing in a more erratic way.

'I imagine you have some sort of plan,' he said as they crossed the winding strait between Juniper and Rough Island.

'Aye,' said McGray. 'Raid that cave. Seize the bastards and then escort them to the nearest police station.'

Maurice chuckled. 'Why, so very simple!'

McGray shook his head. 'Och, yer worse than yer sodding nephew. Yer probably more inbred too, did ye ken that?'

'Oh, do excuse me . . . Did who *what*?'

'Sod off.'

They crossed the north side of the loch without speaking. McGray took in deep breaths, sounding as if he were in labour. He saw the craggy rocks that delimited Loch Maree: ancient granite, dark and eroded after centuries of rain and wind, and the bushy oaks that grew beyond. The mountains rose behind the trees, imposing and unassailable.

'I will try to keep to the shoreline,' said Maurice. 'If we follow it closely it might be longer before they see us.'

'Aye,' answered McGray, but he was only half aware of what had been said.

Maurice rowed straight to the jagged rocks. When they reached them he spun the boat, and then used an oar to push against the stone and propel the boat forward.

'What does the cave look like?' he asked, peering intently at the rocks.

'Just look for a bloody crack,' McGray said – or rather moaned.

They rounded a promontory and they saw it.

'I assume that is the spot,' said Maurice, pointing to a boat moored ahead of them. It had been tied to a weather-beaten, algae-covered pole, perhaps the only remnant of a very old pier. The boat was empty, rocking gently and from time to time tapping a wet stone by its side. It was a natural formation, but it looked as though someone had built a small, flat step. Unlike the pole, that step was not covered in algae but was caked with layers and layers of a repugnant whitish matter, like the bottom of a birdcage that had not been cleaned in years.

'Guano,' said Maurice, grimacing.

McGray retched. 'I hate that word. What's wrong with "bat shite"?'

That rocky step led upwards to a thin sliver in the rocks, its edges dotted with splatters of the same substance.

'That's the entrance,' said McGray. It was little more than a foot wide (the Kolomans' cook would not fit through) but ample enough for either of them. Just as he said it a dark form came fluttering across the sky: a bat looking for shelter.

Maurice brought the boat closer and tied it to the pole. There was not much room to manoeuvre, so they had to jump into the other boat and then on to the stone step. McGray went first, his boots skidding on the slimy guano. Awkwardly but effectively, he planted himself on the rock and squatted down, thanking heaven for the firm, still surface. He pinched his septum and closed his eyes. *Breathe*, he thought. *Just sodding breathe!*

'Not that I want to make you feel worse, but remember we still have to go back,' said Maurice, standing up in the boat as he looked west, where the sun was just setting between the mountains. It was an arresting, heavenly view, the fading light painting sky, water, leaves and stone in shades of gold. A soft breeze brought the sweet scents of moss and pines, and then another bat came by. Its meandering flight added to the serenity of the scene as the creature plunged into the shadows.

'Glorious world,' Maurice whispered, and then sighed. 'Have a good look at that, Mr McGray. It might be the last sunset we ever see.'

They'd need a place to roost, Frey had said. *A cave, perhaps.*

McGray remembered those words as soon as he set foot in the cavern. He felt his feet plunging into a milky mess, the layers thicker and fresher the deeper they went.

'Disgusting,' Maurice muttered behind him, but the bat excrement was the least of McGray's worries. He knew he was about to witness a monstrous thing – a series of them – and that certainty built up in his chest like an icy, clenching hand.

The rocky floor went from flat to a narrow V, and they had to place their feet at odd angles, pressing their hands against the walls to keep their balance.

'Oh, saintly mother of God . . .' Maurice moaned, for the rock was damp and sticky with a ghastly mixture of guano and the water that infiltrated through the ground. The place reeked of ammonia.

'Don't drop that shotgun,' McGray told him, his own weapon aimed forward, his eyes peering into the ever thicker darkness.

'We should have brought a lantern,' said Maurice, squinting. 'I do not –' Then a bat came in, its sharp squeaks filling the passage. In its rush it clashed against Maurice's shoulder, and he let out a repulsed cry.

The bat flapped about, screeching and bouncing between the rocks and the two men. McGray felt the leathery, furry wings against his face, and he shivered just as the animal found its way in.

'A johnny-come-lately,' he said, his heart pounding.

He took a few deep breaths, noticing how dark it had become. Then the passage bent, and as they took the turn they plunged into absolute blackness. They picked up faint noises ahead, like the rustle of feathers, intermingled with muffled squeaks.

There was not just a handful of animals inside. It sounded

like a multitude, like a colony of thousands. Could there be that many, or was it only the echoes bouncing and multiplying across the void?

McGray was looking for his lighter, but then he saw a faint glimmer ahead. The wet rocks caught a weak shine, and then he heard scratching on the rock. A pair of bats clung to the walls not a couple of feet from him, grooming each other. Their huge eyes were like flashing beacons, amplifying what dim light they reflected.

McGray heard Maurice's agitated breathing right behind him. He was going to say something to soothe him, but then they heard voices.

He moved on slowly, the guano now so thick it made a revolting squish when they stepped on it.

The light became slightly brighter, just as they came across another pair of bats, and then a cluster of five, and very soon the animals covered a good deal of the rock.

From then on McGray struggled to find a spot to rest his hand; wings and stubbly ears constantly brushed against his skin. He felt the urge to scratch himself.

Maurice could not repress a small whimper. McGray turned back to him, but then accidentally pressed his hand on the head of a bat. The animal screeched, baring its tiny fangs, its hairy muzzle smeared in crimson, and stretched its wings defiantly.

McGray took a deep breath and looked for another support.

A few feet ahead the floor became flatter again, and then, after another turn, the passage opened into what appeared to be a small gallery. From where he stood McGray could see only the opposite wall, and he had to gulp.

The entire rock seemed to move, its shape shifting like the

squirming insides of a living thing. He had to blink a few times to convince himself: it was a thick carpet of wings. Hundreds and hundreds. Bats huddled all over the cave's surface, their wings pressed against each other's. The cave was a black mass of coriaceous skin, matted fur and glowing little eyes, covering every square inch available.

McGray had to hold his gun with both hands to steady it, and took a careful step forward.

The gallery opened to his right, lit by a crackling fire, but McGray's eyes went to a bat that unhinged itself from the ceiling and glided down to perch on a nearby stone fountain. It was one of those ornaments for garden birds, only this one was not meant to hold water. McGray felt a shiver as the animal bent down to drink blood from it.

He had to repress a gasp, for the girl Helena stood beside the fountain, her back turned to them. She held her arm up high, a rather large bat clinging to her long sleeve, upside-down and wrapped in its own wings. The girl dipped a little glass into the fountain and fed the ghastly, viscous substance to the animal. The bat licked noisily, like a hungry cat.

McGray looked beyond her and saw the rest of the Nelapsi family gathered around a small hearth ensconced in the rock. None of them was looking at the entrance, their eyes and ears rapt on their distraught matriarch.

'How could you do it, Lazarus?' Mrs Nelapsi was screeching, her hands resembling claws. *'How could you?'*

'I did what I had to . . .' her son retorted. He was leaning towards his father, who lay on a bed of moth-eaten cushions close to the fire. Lazarus was offering him wine, which his mother knocked from his hand. The pewter goblet fell to the floor with a loud racket.

The woman stood up, covering her mouth in disgust. And then she saw McGray.

'*Don't move!*' he roared, his shout disturbing wings throughout the cave. He moved forward, making room for Maurice to step in and point the shotgun. The bats moved and squeaked nervously, the one under Helena's arm extending its wings and showing its teeth at the intruders.

All the Nelapsis turned to face them: Lazarus made to stand up; Miss Fletcher, who'd been leaning against the wall, started forward; Benjamin, seated on the opposite side of the hearth, jumped to his feet.

'I said, *don't fucking move!* Are youse deaf?'

Helena's bat flapped its wings madly. The girl whined and dropped the glass of blood, which smashed to pieces on the filthy floor.

Behind her McGray caught a slight movement: Benjamin was slowly stretching his arm towards a rifle that rested on the wall.

'Leave that there, laddie,' McGray told him, aiming his gun directly at the boy's head. He looked at Helena. 'Go to yer mother, lassie.'

Her chest heaving and her eyes pooling tears, the girl carefully deposited the bat on the edge of the fountain and then rushed to her mother's arms.

Both McGray and Maurice moved their aim from left to right, watching everyone's movements.

Miss Fletcher cautiously raised one of her large palms. 'I can explain –'

'Shut it, lass! *I'll* do the talking.'

He didn't do so immediately. First he had a good look around.

There were two long tables in the centre of the cave, crammed with all manner of artefacts, most of them splattered with guano. There were bat skeletons, the swirling tubes of distillation systems, all manner of knives, scalpels, saws and tweezers. And a multitude of jars of all shapes and heights fitted snugly into every spare space between: jars of urine, of black powders, of flakes of desiccated guano, of blood samples that ranged from the slightly crimson to the almost black. McGray sniffed, disgusted by the mixture of ammoniacal and sulphurous smells that the containers gave off.

'Youse drink blood!' McGray cried, his eyes drawn to the stone fountain.

Nobody answered him. The only sound, besides the incessant murmur of the bats, was Helena whimpering. Until Lazarus snorted.

'*Yes!* Yes, we do, just like you eat venison or blood-soaked steaks. What's the damn difference?'

McGray smiled wryly. 'I wish Frey were here to hear this. Why d'youse do that?'

'We are cursed,' said Mr Nelapsi, struggling to turn on the cushions. 'If we don't drink it, we die. My family has been cursed for centuries.'

Mrs Nelapsi hugged her daughter more tightly. In the light from the fire the blemishes on her skin were even more evident. 'So has been mine.'

McGray smiled. Things finally made *some* sense.

'I've read about that,' he said. 'Creatures in Hungary and Rumania that only come at night and feed on human blood.'

'We're not *creatures*,' Lazarus protested. 'It's a curse. Our ancestors committed horrible crimes and were cursed with madness and frail bodies.'

'Youse have been doing this for centuries?' McGray yelped.

'No!' Mrs Nelapsi wailed. 'Our families discovered only recently that blood helps.'

McGray looked at Lazarus. 'So ye killed McEwan and emptied him. Is that his blood?' He nodded at the fountain.

Lazarus laughed. 'Would you believe me now if I said I didn't kill him? If I told you it was the Kolomans, and that they killed Father Thomas too?'

McGray laughed in return. 'Aye, right. They did.'

'He's telling the truth!' cried Helena, the only one who still seemed to have some spirit left. Her face was drenched in tears. 'I swear! On my own life. The Kolomans have murdered hundreds of souls to feed themselves! That's why they look so strong and healthy. And when they're done with them they throw the bodies on Rory Island, the furthest one to the west. They don't even bury them. You'll find their bones just lying on the ground.'

McGray felt terribly sorry for the young girl, but he would not be fooled again.

'How convenient, lassie. D'ye expect me to go there now, in the dark, and verify yer telling the truth?'

'We no longer expect anyone to believe us,' said Lazarus, 'or help us. You're as gullible as the others.'

McGray breathed out. 'I almost drowned trying to catch ye. Why should I believe yer word now?'

'I don't give a damn whether you believe me or not.' Lazarus showed his teeth in a wicked grin. 'In a moment it will make very little difference.' His was a blood-curdling, twisted face, quivering shadows dancing on the sharp cheeks and the sunken eye sockets. He separated his incisors a little, and McGray thought the man was about to burst into laughter. Then Lazarus made to bite his lip, and just as McGray realized what was going to happen Lazarus let out the loudest, most piercing whistle.

The cave came to life, every single bat jumping into the air and filling it with their high-pitched shrills.

McGray raised both arms, trying to protect his face as he staggered amidst the mayhem. He felt the vile wings, the furry bodies and the sharp teeth all over him. Maurice screeched for help and the Nelapsis were all shouting, but McGray could see only the blurry blotches of dark creatures swirling all around him.

And then he heard shooting.

48

Boyde had fallen and the back of his head was bleeding, but he'd not been knocked out; he was growling and struggling to stand up. He stretched a hand in my direction and I desperately crawled away. I rose to my feet and ran to the staircase, still coughing and holding my tender throat. And without the faintest idea what to do next.

I felt a wave of panic and forced myself to think. I needed to get out of that house and soon, that much I knew, but I needed more than a gun and a tiny derringer. I had a last glimpse of Boyde, already on all fours, trickling blood on to the carpet.

I thought of the boats, and the cave, and how to find my way around the loch, so I went upstairs, to the astronomy room. I ripped the smallest brass telescope from its tripod and then went to the ground floor, not even daring to glance into the corridor where Boyde had been hit. I could still hear the Koloman women yelling for help.

That reminded me . . .

I rushed to the Shadows Room, threw the curtains open and rummaged through the drawers. I felt my heart racing and kept my gun at the ready, ever pointing at the door, expecting Boyde or Dominik, or even the exceptionally wide cook, to burst in any second. I looked for another syringe case – the one I'd taken from Natalja was in my bedroom, and I would not go back to that corridor. If my suspicions were correct, this could be crucial evidence.

Instead of a syringe I found a little glass tube full of tiny purple crystals. I pocketed it and then looked for more practical items. Inside the girls' black box I found a small oil lamp, its thick glass container full of fuel, and a box of matches. Just as I grabbed them I heard frantic footsteps upstairs, and I rushed to the hall and the back door. I felt a chill on the back of my neck, as if someone was running behind me, almost stepping on my toes. I did not dare look back; I simply ran until I reached the pier, threw my loot into the boat and jumped aboard.

I rowed until my arms burned, my eyes fixed on the doors and windows, expecting Boyde and the twins to come out at any moment, ready to shoot me with more weapons they'd never told me about.

My heart thumping, I focused on nothing but getting as far away as possible. I stopped rowing only when there were a good three hundred yards between me and the shore. I needed to hide, to find a spot where I could stop, calm down and ponder my options. As the momentum carried my boat onward, I tried to recall Mr Koloman's map. Rory Island was the nearest, but I would *not* go there again. Between it and Juniper there was another large, weirdly shaped island I remembered was called Rough, with many little bays and peninsulas. I thought I'd row there, and then find a good place to dock on the northern shore, out of sight of the manor.

I panted with each pull at the oars, the pain expanding from my arms into my chest and back, but I did not stop. I could not even think from the effort of rowing, my eyes focused on the little rocky islets that passed me by at an impossibly slow pace.

On my right I saw the tall pine trees of Rory Island pointing to the sky like an army of lancers, guarding the horror that lay beneath. After a seemingly endless time I turned eastwards, following the dramatic contours of Rough Island. North of it there was another, smaller island, on which I spotted a little sandy beach, ensconced in a narrow bay. I rowed there, the last few yards an excruciating ordeal, and as soon as the boat hit the shore I jumped out, dropping face up on the damp sand. I closed my eyes and I tried to catch my breath, my mind already working on my next move.

It would be dark soon – a new moon if I remembered right – and I'd be trapped in the middle of the loch with only a pathetic oil lamp and a few matches. I opened my eyes and saw the still light sky. I remembered we were so far north there would always be a thin strip of dusk on the horizon; I might not be able to make out any detail but at least I'd be able to tell north from south.

'Where to go now?' I asked out loud.

Juniper Island, to look for evidence that confirmed or refuted my suspicions? To the mysterious cave on the northern shore, which might not even exist? To the inn, to reunite with Uncle and run as far as we could? The Kolomans had said McGray had gone there . . . Only I no longer believed their word. Was McGray even still alive?

It all made sense now: the family connections; the syringes – which I was now sure had never contained laudanum; the books on blood transfusion I'd seen in the drawing room; the meteorological artefacts; even the crystal prisms and the Shadows Room . . . The more I thought about it, the more sense it made. All the pieces had been there, staring me in the face, and I had opened my eyes only when it was too late.

I groaned in despair and jumped to my feet, if only to make myself feel a little less overwhelmed.

'Think, Ian,' I said, again aloud. I had no plan, many possible destinations and hardly any certainties. 'What can you do now? What can you rule out?' I turned in circles, feeling I was about to go mad. I saw the little telescope on the boat, reflecting the dying daylight. The map instantly came into my mind. 'I can at least rule out the cave . . .'

I went to the boat, seized the telescope and then strode to the other side of the tiny island, not twenty yards away.

The sun was already projecting long shadows on the jagged rocks. In a matter of minutes I would not be able to make out a thing. I lifted the telescope, focused the lenses just enough to make out the main shapes, and scanned the northern shore swiftly but carefully.

Nothing. There was nothing that looked like the entrance to a cave, just crags of granite.

I did a second pass, this time moving the telescope more slowly. I could tell the shadows were already longer and darker. I'd probably not have a third chance.

I saw something, not on the rock but on the water. At first I thought it was just the shadow of the waves, but it was larger: something floating at the edge of the loch. Trembling, I twisted the telescope for better focus and watched the dark spot grow sharper.

At last I made out not one but two pointy ends. I was looking at two boats.

I let out a sigh of purest relief. There was a good chance McGray had galloped to the inn, borrowed a boat and rowed to the cave. And given his seasickness he'd probably asked for my uncle's help. I now knew where to go.

I looked for any feature that might guide me there in the growing darkness. The boats floated exactly in between two little waterfalls, mere trickles from tiny brooks, but at least

I'd be able to hear them, and they were only a few hundred yards apart.

I felt a wave of excitement but it would be only a fleeting triumph. I turned, ready to sprint back to the boat . . . and what I saw froze the blood in my veins.

The loch was ablaze with at least a dozen little lights, drifting in my direction from the west, their gleams reflected on the disturbed waters. I looked back at the spot where the cave would be, and out of the corner of my eye I caught sight of another set of trembling fires, these coming from the east. I did not need the telescope. They were flaming torches, lighting the way for a small armada on its swift way to that cave.

Powerless, I felt pricking needles all over my spine as I watched them approach.

49

McGray threw blows all around, felt his fist going through wings and crushing little bones, and then a hand gripped his shoulder. He turned on his heel and threw an aimless punch. He hit a torso and heard a female growl: he'd just punched Miss Fletcher, and through the mess of flapping wings he saw her wince.

'*Stop it!*' she shouted. 'Or they'll kill you!'

McGray hesitated for a split second, long enough for the woman to hit him right in the nose.

'Och, ye *bitch*!' He punched back but hit only air. A well-directed blow got him in the ribs; McGray bent and jerked about, feeling another pair of hands take hold of him and push him down.

He thrashed about, seeing bottles of ghastly things fall and shatter on the floor, Mrs Nelapsi running about, Maurice pinned against the wall, a rifle stabbing him in the chest and a trickle of blood coming from his upper lip.

McGray felt the barrel of a gun pressed hard against his temple.

'*Enough!*'

It was Benjamin's steely voice, and McGray could do nothing but surrender. Benjamin pulled McGray's gun from his hand, and then sent another piercing whistle across the cave.

The bats went slowly back to the walls and ceiling, and McGray at last had a chance to see how things stood.

Lazarus, despite a bullet having grazed his arm, was the one pointing a gun at Maurice, with bats perched on his shoulders like hellish parrots. The shotgun lay on the rock, not a yard from their feet. Helena bent down to pick it up and then went to her father, who was still by the fire, covering himself with trembling hands. McGray had a knee on the ground, Benjamin and Miss Fletcher holding him firmly in place – not that he'd move with a gun at his head.

Everyone remained silent for a moment, catching their breath. The bats were also unsettled, and even though most had perched themselves back in place their agitation would not subside. A few kept gliding from one side of the cave to the other.

'I say we kill them now,' Lazarus hissed, pressing the rifle harder against Maurice's chest.

'Because that's how you'd like to solve everything?' his mother snapped, picking up the few jars that had not shattered.

'You know we need to flee,' Lazarus went on, 'and we don't want them to follow. If we don't kill them, we'll have to leave them here tied up, and God knows how long it might be before someone finds them. It would be more humane just to shoot them and –'

'Let me explain them!' Miss Fletcher roared, banging a fist on the nearest table. Bloodstained instruments rattled and fell over. She forced herself to take a calming breath. 'I brought them here, after all.'

'Aye, ye did,' McGray said. 'Ye promised me a cure. Ye said yer brat was in danger –'

'I thought he *was*!' she cried.

'Do listen to her,' a struggling voice said from the back of the cave. Mr Nelapsi was sitting up, aided by his daughter.

'Millie is the most honourable person you could have found at the Kolomans' house.'

McGray laughed bitterly, and Miss Fletcher rushed to speak. 'I was a marionette, Inspector. I swear. The Kolomans have played me like a chess piece all my life and I didn't even know it.'

'Ye told Frey there was a threat to yer son's life.'

'I thought there was! The note and the brick did smash my window, but I must have been deceived. I don't think there ever was a real threat. The Kolomans must have done it. They knew that bastard McEwan would do nothing, like he did nothing when I –' She inhaled deeply. 'It was Mrs Koloman herself who suggested I contact you. As I told Mr Frey, she read about you just over a month ago, when the Edinburgh papers were raving about that Henry Irving scandal. She told me I should go and meet you, and then bring you here to investigate. She seemed to know everything about you, about your poor sister and how you've been looking for a cure for years.'

McGray laughed. 'Doesnae take much digging. Everyone in Edinburgh kens that story.'

'She also suggested I mentioned the healing waters. She said that would tempt you to come here and help me.'

'Was that a lie too?' McGray asked.

Mr Nelapsi leaned forward. 'Not exactly. We honestly thought the waters had worked for me. All of us except my son.'

Miss Fletcher raised a hand. 'I will explain that too, but first I want Mr McGray to understand why the Kolomans wanted him here so badly.'

McGray raised an eyebrow. 'Very well. Explain.'

'The Kolomans instigated your trip because they wanted

to incriminate Lazarus. They orchestrated to murder that damned constable while you and your colleague were here. When I appealed to you and Mr Frey I of course didn't know that the murder would take place.'

Lazarus looked terribly ashamed. 'They also manipulated me. Dominik asked me to meet him that night in the woods. He was supposed to give me . . . medicine for my father.'

'Medicine?' Maurice asked.

'Yes, but he never came. I walked to the very spot we'd agreed upon, and all I found was McEwan's body hanging from a tree. I heard the Koloman girls approach, so I hid. I thought Dominik might still come . . .'

'I saw you,' said Miss Fletcher. 'I didn't know what you were up to . . . I even suspected for a while you might have done it, so I kept quiet.' Then she looked at Mr and Mrs Nelapsi, an inexplicable sorrow in her eyes. 'I knew that Lazarus going to jail would leave you and Helena completely unprotected.' She looked back at McGray. 'I'm sorry, sir. I couldn't do that to them. I couldn't let them blame Lazarus for the death of a man I despised so much.'

McGray turned to Lazarus. 'And why did ye keep quiet? We could've confronted Dominik and –'

'I couldn't!' Lazarus roared. 'It was not the first time I met with Dominik.'

'Och, are ye also a sodo–'

'He gave me medicine for my father. I told you. It wasn't the well that improved his health. It was the Kolomans' medicine.'

McGray's jaw dropped. It took him a moment to realize all the implications of that statement. His trip there had been futile, merely a trap to incriminate an innocent man, set by a ruthless family taking advantage of his and Miss

Fletcher's despair. He ground his teeth, thinking how much he'd enjoy punching Mr Koloman's face to a pulp.

'I still believe the waters work . . .' Mr Nelapsi whispered, attempting an encouraging smile, but his words now seemed hollow.

And another question had crept into McGray's mind.

'Why would the Kolomans have a cure for yer . . . for yer curse?'

There was a moment of eerie silence, until Mrs Nelapsi spoke in a quivering whisper. 'Our curse is their curse.'

'What the – D'ye mean . . . ?'

The woman banged a jar on the table. 'Minerva Koloman is my sister. My parents, like their parents before them, spent much of their wealth looking for a way to rid us of this . . .' She stared at her blotched hands. 'This curse.

'My mother met a man, Konrad's father, who claimed he knew of a *cure*.' She sneered. 'Konrad and his father told my mother what the cure was . . . and . . . if I ever doubted this was a curse, I was convinced then, when they told her what they did. They said the only way to keep our symptoms at bay was to –' She covered her eyes, and Helena buried her face in her father's chest. 'I was so scared I eloped as soon as I met my dear Silas.'

McGray looked at their stern faces. 'What symptoms do ye mean? Yer skin condition?'

Miss Fletcher nodded. 'And fits of terrible pain . . . always in the stomach.'

McGray instantly thought of Veronika's unexplained seizure. As he tried to take in all that had been said, he looked at Helena. 'How come yer lassie's skin looks fine?'

'It's the sun that makes us blister,' said Lazarus. 'That's why the Kolomans never go out; that's why they spend their summers here, where the sun hardly ever shines, and on sunny days like today they keep all their curtains shut.'

'And that's why Mr Koloman is so interested in weather science,' Miss Fletcher added, 'to predict if they can go out or not. That's why he had instruments built with indoor displays.'

'We, sadly, can't afford those measures,' said Mrs Nelapsi. 'We have to go out and tend to our animals and plough our crops, whatever the weather. But we try to spare Helena as much of that as we can. She does indoor chores mainly.' She cast a longing stare at her daughter. 'Minerva has always thought my girl is very pretty. More than once she offered to take her in, to adopt her' – she let out a mocking laugh – 'and twist her like she's twisted her own children. She offered me the blasted medicine so many times – I only accepted it when I was pregnant. By then I'd seen three of my babies die in my arms . . .' Again she covered her face. 'I know it's a dreadful sin but I would do it again. I'd do anything for my children.'

'Again, wait,' said McGray. 'The human blood, this . . . *medicine* . . . do they need it all the time?'

'Yes,' said Lazarus. 'And at higher doses when they have fits of pain.'

'So how do they keep it?' McGray asked. 'I've nae seen them murdering folk every other –'

And then he knew, and shook his head in disgust.

Lazarus nodded. 'Yes, Mrs Glenister told me the truth. She said the Kolomans sent us human blood in wine.'

'*What!*' Maurice yelped. 'I have been drinking that bloody wine every day since I arrived!'

Lazarus raised an eyebrow. 'Full-bodied, is it not?'

'They fooled us with that wine for years,' Mr Nelapsi said.

'When we moved here, which we did after hearing of the healing well, Minerva insisted on aiding us. They sent us clothes and food . . . and their blasted wine. Sabina and I drank it unawares. For a while we even thought our families might reconcile, but then we discovered the truth and refused to keep accepting their *help*.' He looked at McGray with a gentle smile. 'Their wine repaired my body, but it was the waters from the well that cured my mind and my soul. Saint Rufus's waters did the miracle. I decided that was all I needed. That's why my body has been decaying lately.'

McGray remembered Mrs Koloman mentioning precisely that.

'You'd be far worse if I'd not intervened,' said Lazarus. He looked at McGray. 'My father's fits got worse and worse. I couldn't bear to see his pain. I nailed a deer skull to a tree and put candles in the eye sockets, like we knew the so-called witches used to do, years ago, on the island. I told my father to light the candles whenever he felt ill, so I could take him some gin, if only to dull the pain with alcohol. Sometimes I'd give him laudanum, if we had any at hand.'

'I was having a seizure when your colleague came,' said Mr Nelapsi. 'It was very fortunate Benjamin and Helena came by just then.'

'That's something I feared,' said Lazarus, 'that one day I might not be around to help you. Dominik came to me one day, when I was at Kinlochewe, not long after my father had had a particularly nasty seizure. Dominik saw how desperate I was. He offered me some of their wine – my mother had already told me all about it – and I accepted, even though I knew where it came from. I fed the wine to my father and I kept the secret even from my family. That's why I didn't say a word about where I was on the night of the constable's murder; I was as bad as an accomplice . . . and I couldn't face my parents' reaction.' He cast a guilty look towards his mother. 'If it helps, I did it only when Father seemed truly ill; I gave him just enough of that vile stuff to stave off excessive pain. That's why his body never fully recovered.'

His mother hugged herself, on the verge of tears but attempting to smile at her son. 'I knew you couldn't have done it. I knew you couldn't kill a man like that. But you *had* gone out that night and you refused to tell us where you'd been . . . I know I've been too harsh on you, but I would have understood, Lazarus. Believe me. I was so desperate I even went to that horrid house and begged that harpy to let you go.'

'So,' said McGray, 'Dominik planned to kill the constable and make it look like ye'd done it, while Frey and me were around to investigate . . . Why?'

'Lazarus in jail would have left us unprotected,' said Mr Nelapsi. 'They wanted Helena to move into the manor with them, and without my son around she would probably have been forced to do so.' He looked at his wife. 'And you too, Sabina. It doesn't matter how twisted Minerva is, she still cares for you.'

The woman clenched her fists. 'I would rather die than partake in their abominations.'

'And Konrad knows that,' her husband retorted. 'He might have fooled his wife into thinking you would yield to his foul ways, but I think he knows better. Not that it really matters; whether you surrendered or not, he would still have had Helena under his roof.'

Maurice cleared his throat. 'Do excuse me, but – delightful as your girl might be – it seems an awful lot of trouble to go to simply to –'

'They wanted us to marry,' Benjamin interrupted, 'to continue the family name. Natalja told me some stories of how proud her grandfather was of their lineage. She said he wanted to keep it *pure*.'

'And this is not an easy curse to keep secret,' said Mrs Nelapsi. 'Not many people would understand . . .' She looked longingly at her husband. 'Silas and I are first cousins. We loved each other very much, still do, and we knew nobody else in the world would understand us. Not quite.'

A deep hush fell on the cave. Even the bats seemed to have gone quiet. Only a single squeak was heard, coming from underneath the tables. Helena went there and picked up a little injured bat; its wing's fine skin had been torn, perhaps trampled on during the struggle. Helena cradled the creature in her arms as if it were a puppy, and then picked a bobbin and needle from the mess of jars. She sat by her father and began stitching the wound meticulously.

Maurice stared at her, and then turned his gaze to a couple of bats that were drinking from the fountain. He grimaced in disgust.

'We are very much like them,' said Mr Nelapsi, watching his daughter's dexterous work. 'Ugly . . . misunderstood.'

'What's with the bats?' McGray asked, and then pointed his chin at the instruments and bottles. 'And all this shite youse keep here.'

'We tried to replicate the cure,' said Lazarus. He nodded at the fountain. 'We tried animals' blood: pigs', goats' . . . We once even tried using a little vial of human blood I bought from a dubious doctor. I poured it into wine, but it wouldn't do.'

'The Kolomans do something to the blood . . .' Mrs Nelapsi said. 'They treat it somehow to make it work.'

'But of course they've never told us,' Lazarus added. 'They like to keep people in their grip.'

'They have all manner of chemicals and contraptions in the manor,' said Miss Fletcher, 'but they're very secretive about it. I think Calcraft knows a lot; Mrs Plunket too . . . and maybe Boyde.'

'We thought that Benjamin might be able to find out more,' said Lazarus. 'As the new heir he'd be free to roam around that damned house. That's why we contacted him a short while ago, as soon as we heard his father was dying. None of us could have had a better chance to discover the secret.'

'You should have told me,' said Miss Fletcher bitterly. 'I wouldn't have allowed my son to take part in such a dangerous –'

'And that is precisely why we didn't tell you,' Lazarus jumped in. 'If it helps, our plan worked wonderfully. Benjamin managed to find the Kolomans'. . . let's call it *recipe* book.'

McGray remembered the thick tome he'd seen them take from the manor. He looked around but could not see it amidst the cave's clutter.

'Though I nearly failed,' said Benjamin. 'That's why I made friends with Natalja. She seems to be the smartest one of the lot, but she grew suspicious when I asked too many questions. I had to start lurking around the manor at night. I managed to find the recipe, but I knew I couldn't just walk out with the book under my arm. We had to flee like we did.'

McGray glared at every member of the Nelapsi family. 'So are youse planning to drink human blood too? Is that why youse want the recipe?'

'Of course not!' cried Mr Nelapsi. 'But that book may hold vital information . . . something to help us find another cure. A more Christian one.'

'Now, we have answered enough of your questions,' Lazarus snapped. 'I have one for you. How on earth did you find this place?'

McGray knew his answer would shock them. 'The . . . the Kolomans have a map that marks this spot. They told me about it right after youse left.'

'That's impossible,' Mrs Nelapsi mumbled, her voice barely audible. 'How could they know?'

'It's not impossible,' Lazarus said. 'They have eyes everywhere. Everyone in the region owes them in one way or the other – their school, their loans, their custom. They know very well how to manipulate people and make them feel indebted.'

'Doesnae matter now,' said McGray. 'They showed me the spot on the map and sent me here to capture youse . . . Only . . .'

'They would have known these people might tell you the truth,' Maurice intervened. 'Why send you here if there was a chance you'd find out Dominik was the murderer?'

McGray rolled his eyes. 'They're nae stupid . . . Maybe . . . maybe they want to catch us all in one go . . .'

They all froze, their mouths open, their eyes fearful. Lazarus even lowered the rifle from Maurice's chest. 'They might even be on their way here.'

'We have to go now!' said Benjamin.

'What's that?' Helena cried, looking up. The bat in her arms was twisting itself free, and the ones across the cave began to stir and squeak, especially the ones close to the entrance.

Lazarus began to tremble, very much like the animals perched on his shoulders. His mother's chest was heaving.

'Give the men their guns,' she spluttered. 'Now!'

But there was no time. Their executioners had arrived.

50

I saw how the lights clustered around the cave, like glow-worms. Despite the distance and the darkness I crouched next to a thick pine, irrationally fearing I might be seen; I even found myself breathing as quietly as possible.

I heard shooting, and then saw a small ball of fire burst amidst the boats and ascend swiftly to the sky. Could they also have brought explosives? I gasped at the notion.

Even through the telescope I could barely make out what was happening: I could see the outlines of men lit by their torches, moving about, and I could hear them shouting unintelligibly. I realized that one of the boats had caught fire, and saw some splashes around it, but that was all I could distinguish.

There came a wave of cheering, the kind one hears in the direst tavern. Then the wind brought the echo of a female screech, anguished and guttural, and I even squinted in dread.

The glow-worms then got in motion again, clustering together more tightly as they navigated across the loch. They were moving towards me.

'It cannot be!' I muttered, not believing my eyes. How could anybody know where I'd gone? I waited for a couple of minutes, the telescope fixed on those lights, until I could not deny the fact any longer. They were coming in my direction.

I found myself panting, again not knowing what to do. I looked around, desperately searching for shelter. I crossed the narrow islet and looked west. I saw the outlines of Rory

399

Island cut sharply against the dusk, looking more like the mouth of a black cavern. There, floating almost perfectly still, was an isolated, silver beam of light – merely a few hundred yards away!

I dropped to my knees and crawled to hide behind the nearest tree, clutching the telescope. Very slowly, every muscle of my body painfully tense, I moved my head around the trunk, just enough to have a look. Again I saw the straight beam of light: a bull's-eye lantern, moving in slow circles like a lighthouse. I used the telescope and had a clear view of a lonely boat, and the entire Koloman family in it.

They were all as still as their boat, as if waiting for their armada to join them. Mr Koloman was standing in the bow, holding the lamp with a steady hand. Mrs Koloman was seated close by, a hand lifted towards her husband, in case he might stumble. It looked like he *had* been injured. Behind her sat Dominik, holding the oars and wearing what must be his most showy overcoat: purple velvet and black fur. The twins were next, also wrapped in thick coats and looking nervous.

Right at the back was Mrs Plunket, the immeasurably wide cook. She might have been a hilarious sight, tilting the entire boat under her weight, but she was armed with a broad cleaver that caught the light like a mirror. Her arms were almost as thick as my waist, and I realized that this woman might well be able to sever a man's head with a single stroke.

Then I saw my own boat on the sandy beach and my heart skipped a beat. It might be visible even *without* the light, let alone if Mr Koloman pointed his lantern in my direction.

I put the telescope down and followed the beam. Konrad was moving it from north-east to east, towards the beach and the boat, slowly but steadily. The light touched the northern edge of my island, illuminating the rocks and the pine trees like the brightest sun. I felt a bead of cold sweat run down my forehead as the light came closer and closer to my boat.

'Look!' Natalja said, and again my heart jumped.

Mr Koloman moved the lantern swiftly, but not towards me. He lit the waters beyond the islands, where the small flotilla was approaching.

The Kolomans waited patiently until the cluster of torches came closer. Then I heard Calcraft's voice.

'We have them all!'

I instantly looked through the telescope; the torches made it easier to make out what was happening. The first face I recognized was Mr Dailey's, rowing one of the leading boats.

'All the Nellyses?' Mr Koloman shouted.

'Yes, all the family. And the freak Millie and her bastard.'

'And both inspectors?'

'Just the Scot and the Plantard man.'

'Then you don't have them all!' Mrs Koloman barked in a harsh, commanding tone I'd not heard from her before.

I moved the telescope from left to right, looking for other familiar faces in the multitude of boats. I could see only Miss Fletcher, whose bright blond hair stood up well above the surrounding heads. I searched for McGray's garish tartan, or my uncle's square shoulders, but found neither. The boats were in constant motion, making their way swiftly to Rory Island. I did recognize a couple of men from my short stop at nearby Kinlochewe: villagers surely ready to serve the wealthy Kolomans at the snap of a finger.

'Start a fire as soon as you get there,' Mr Koloman commanded, followed by a female cry I thought was Helena's.

Her shout ended quite abruptly, and I pictured the poor girl being beaten with the butt of a gun.

I looked back at the Kolomans. Dominik was turning the boat away from me, and I could finally exhale. They were not coming for me after all. However, as they turned I had a perfect view of Natalja's face gazing directly at my hiding place. Again I held my breath, not daring to move a muscle. She seemed to stare for a moment, but then turned her head away. I cursed inwardly, unable to tell whether she'd seen me or not.

I saw how the boats gathered at a little bay, beyond a promontory that blocked most of my view. All I could see now was the glimmer of the torches, expanding through the thick woodland as the men spread out across the island.

What could I possibly do? I looked at my tools: a gun with only eight bullets, a ridiculous derringer and a pathetic boat. I could never face around thirty men on my own, but neither could I go and get help. The nearest settlements had come to aid the very people I was supposed to fight, and there were no more villages or towns for at least thirty miles in any direction.

I realized that our message had never been sent to the police. The telegrapher had probably just pretended. He would have needed but to unplug the wire and tap the instrument as Uncle Maurice watched. It would not surprise me if they had also accelerated the decay of McEwan's body, heating the cellar at night, perhaps. They would have wanted to get rid of any forensic evidence, or maybe they wanted me to find those corpses on Rory Island and blame those deaths too on Lazarus or his father.

None of that mattered now. We had been fooled and there was nothing I could do but sit there and hide. I could only imagine what terrible fate awaited McGray, Uncle and the Nellyses on that island. Would the Kolomans kill them? If so, would they do it swiftly? Would they torture them first? Why did they want a fire? Would they drain their blood like they had McEwan's?

I dropped both the telescope and my gun, pressed my back against the base of the tree and covered my face with both hands, ducking like a young child in the dark. The silence of the night had never felt so deadly.

51

I heard a growl.

It made my blood curdle. It was a painful, throaty noise, ebbing and flowing over the water. It reminded me of the unnerving sound that deer sometimes make when shot, only this repeated itself again and again, at intervals as regular as clockwork. Each time it was a little louder.

I risked peeping around the tree, but I saw only the darkness of the moonless night. I waited for the noise, not even blinking, but it did not come again. I listened out, holding my breath, and just as I thought the sound had gone for good, there it was. It coincided with a faint movement on the water – nothing but a shadow, barely lighter than the surroundings. It did not look much clearer through the telescope, but there was something familiar in those jerking movements, something I soon recognized.

'Dear Lord,' I whispered. 'Mr Nellys.'

And that realization made his growls all the more unnerving. The man was rowing himself, forcing his feeble limbs and bones, each stroke a wave of excruciating pain. My own arms were sore enough from the rowing; I could only imagine what the old man was going through.

I ran to my boat and pushed it back into the loch. I was tempted to light the little oil lamp, but decided not to. Though the Kolomans were already out of sight, I did not know who else might be watching.

It took me no time to cover the distance that separated us.

The man was so focused on his rowing that he heard me only when I was about ten yards away. I could see his frame more clearly; then the poor man stood up, his knees cracking, and lifted his one oar in the air.

'Leave me alone or kill me!' he barked, the oar shaking above his head.

'It's Inspector Frey!' I shouted back. 'I'm here to help you.' Though how, I did not know.

He did not reply but simply let himself drop on to the wooden boards. I rowed until our gunwales hit, and jumped into his boat. The man lay on his back, panting like men do on their death beds.

'Are you all right?'

He coughed horribly and spat into the water before answering. 'What a stupid question. Do I look all right? No, I look so wrecked they didn't even bother to carry me. They left me in the cave to die alone. They thought it was jolly good fun. I dragged myself out, found this boat . . .'

The old man was wrapped in a very thick coat, and as I helped him sit up I heard the rattle of bottles underneath the garment.

'What is it you carry –'

'We told your colleague everything,' he blurted out. 'The Kolomans drink blood and –'

'No, they do not,' I said firmly.

Mr Nellys seized my collar. '*Did you believe their lies?* How could you –'

'They inject it!' I snapped. I produced the little glass tube with the purple grains. 'This is it; they probably dissolve it right before they use it. They have been injecting you. Those marks on your stomach are not bat bites.'

The poor man stared at me without blinking. He had not

yet managed to catch his breath, so I gave him time. He slowly moved his eyes sideways. 'I knew it . . .' he whispered. 'I knew I wasn't losing my mind . . . But how did they do it without me . . .' He fell silent.

'You are guessing, just as I am. They must have put something – some narcotic – either in the water of that well, which you drink daily, or in the food they send you. I doubt even Miss Fletcher knew about it.'

'She couldn't have. She would've told us.' He looked up. 'How did you know?'

'I read about your family's condition several years ago, when I was studying in Oxford, but I only remembered it when Mrs Koloman told me you were all related. I realized both you and Miss Veronika had suffered terrible abdominal pains, and you both had wounds on your stomachs. They tried to conceal her marks, and then they tried to make me think the girl was addicted to laudanum.'

Mr Nellys touched his leathery forearm. 'And you saw our skins . . .'

'Yes. I realized I have never seen the Kolomans outside when the sun is strong. They refused to meet us at the inn the other day, when the sky was bright and clear – they told us they'd gone out on an errand, but I happened across an entry Mr Koloman had made in his weather log at precisely that day and hour, so he had been at home. And just today I tried to persuade Miss Natalja to go out for a walk; I might as well have asked her to walk on fire.'

There was a gleam of hope in his eyes. 'So you know of a cure? Have you read about that too?'

I sighed. 'No. I am sorry. As far as I know there is no recorded treatment. The Kolomans must have discovered it and have kept it to themselves.'

The poor man looked down, dejected. I wanted to say something reassuring, but my explanations had already taken far too long.

I pointed to Rory Island. 'They've taken your family there to –'

'Kill them and milk them dry,' was his crude reply. 'Konrad may have put up with us all these years, he even tried to help us, out of consideration to Minerva . . . but not any more. Not after we've rebelled against them like this. And they won't let you or your colleague get away, knowing all you do now. Their puppets from the nearby villages will help them see to that.'

Again I felt terribly cold, but the old man was not finished.

'I won't go without a fight. I brought this . . .' He unbuttoned his coat, and when he showed me what he carried under the inner lining I gasped.

'Is that . . . ?'

His smile was wicked. 'Yes. When you spend years breeding bats you learn a thing or two about guano.'

He handed me one of the many jars. It was full of dark granules, and a wick ran through the lid.

'Of course,' I said, recalling the ball of fire I'd seen through the telescope. 'The ancient Chinese harvested guano from bat caves to make gunpowder . . .'

'It's a nasty recipe, son.'

I could only smile. 'I know, but this gives us some hope!'

52

McGray could hardly hear a thing. They'd covered his head with a stinking cloth, and tied it so tightly around his neck he could scarcely breathe. Even so, it had taken three pairs of hands to guide him to a boat, where two pairs of boots had pinned him down, a hand ever pressing his head against the coarse wooden boards.

His only relief had come from hearing Calcraft's words. They didn't have Frey. Somehow Percy had managed to discover what they were up to – he'd managed to escape! McGray only hoped the Englishman had the good sense to run away; there was no need for another death.

He felt the boat hit the shore and men dragging him across what must be dense woodland. He could smell fragrant pines, feel the cushioned bed of needles as he trod over the irregular terrain, and then came a night breeze, fresh and gentle. Despite his fear, McGray tried to take in all those sensations, for he knew he'd soon be dead.

'Got the barrels?' somebody shouted in the distance, and McGray sighed. So that was what they had in store for him: he would be slaughtered like a pig, to feed a clan of perverse blood-drinkers.

He saw some light filter through the cloth and heard the crackle of a fire, just as someone kicked the back of his knees and pushed him forward. As soon as he fell on the ground one of the men ripped the cloth from his head.

There was a pile of logs and dead foliage right in front of

him, catching fire. Calcraft was pouring over spurts of oil, the flames bursting upwards with each load of fuel. The bonfire was at the centre of a small clearing, flanked by an almost perfect circle of trees.

There were human skulls and ribcages dotted all over the ground. So this was Rory Island, and Helena had told the truth. That meant that Frey had surely found those bones, but McGray could only wonder what he had done next.

Maurice was forced to kneel down right next to him, and then Miss Fletcher and Lazarus. The men were kinder, however, to Helena and Mrs Nelapsi: two rowdy-looking sailors held them by the arms but the frightened women were not thrown to the ground. McGray noticed that Helena was still cradling the wounded bat close to her chest and another two were perched on her shoulders.

'Barrels are ready,' said Boyde, who'd been piling them at a prudent distance from the fire. They were the size of large beer casks. Dominik was seated on one of them, one of his sleeves rolled up, and Mrs Koloman was injecting him with a silver syringe. The twins were standing by their mother, Natalja shaking a thin vial that contained a dark-purple substance.

When Lazarus saw that, he tried to stand up, but someone pushed him back down. 'You don't drink the blood!'

Mrs Koloman barked at him, 'Of course we don't drink it, you stupid fool!'

'It wouldn't get past the acid in your stomach,' said Natalja. 'You'd know as much if you had deigned to open a book in your life.'

Dominik looked at McGray. 'This is the reason I was so desperate to get out of my room. I needed my . . . we call it blood serum. I believe my good sister even begged you to let me out so I could have a little "walk" with her.'

Mr Koloman appeared from the midst of the forest, limping and supporting himself on a silver and ebony walking stick. His foot was wrapped in bulky bandages.

'My grandfather's cane,' he told McGray and Maurice, grinning. 'I knew it would become handy one day – not so soon, though.' He sighed deeply. 'The poor man died at the very young age of forty . . . and he looked even older than *your* father, Helena. He didn't know all that we do now, but he made progress. He already knew the problem was in our blood; he told my father so, and my father attempted blood transfusions. You might have seen some books on that subject on our shelves, Mr Nine-Nails?'

McGray had, but he did not bother answering.

Mr Koloman went to his daughters. 'Yes, my good grandfather would cry with joy if he could see my girls.' He caressed Veronika's alabaster skin. 'My dear Vee's condition is almost as severe as his, yet look at her! A little injection every day and she is one of the two jewels of the county.' He looked at Helena and could not repress a sneer. 'It's been hilarious to watch you breed bats and attempt to drink goats' blood. Whatever inspired you? The Bible?'

'You blasphemous wretch,' Mrs Nellys hissed.

But the woman's outrage only made Mr Koloman laugh. 'See, all you need to keep blood from clotting is this.' He pointed his cane at the barrels. Calcraft servilely took the lid off the nearest one, and a citrusy smell wafted across the clearing. 'We prepare this solution with lemon juice and caustic soda. It could *not* be simpler, but we do need an awful lot of lemons throughout the year. We had to make Mrs Plunket's lemon curd for the villagers so people wouldn't suspect.'

Dominik shot Lazarus a look as haughty as his father's. 'It was particularly ironic that the inspectors locked you in the pantry; the very room where we keep our sacks of caustic soda. You probably used them as cushions.'

'And then we separate the serum with centrifugal forces,' said Natalja. She looked at Helena's puzzled face. 'You spin it really fast and it settles down. Boyde uses a butter churn for that. Sadly, the serum doesn't keep well.' She passed her mother the small vial. 'Not as a solution, at least. We have to crystallize it – with Papa's distillation kits – and we dilute it only when we need it, otherwise it becomes very toxic.'

'That's what killed my poor brother,' said Mr Koloman. 'He was never constant; that was his main fault. That and not taking rejection very well.' Miss Fletcher stirred and Mr Koloman bowed to her. 'I am very sorry, Millie; I have said it countless times.'

'And it still doesn't make it all all right,' Miss Fletcher growled.

Maurice kept looking around. 'What did you do to Ian?'

Mrs Koloman seemed about to burst into tears. She finished injecting her son, wiped her hands and looked at Maurice. 'I am *so* sorry it had to come to this. We never intended to treat you this way . . .'

'You have only your nephew to blame,' said Natalja. 'We dropped all the hints we could, trying to incriminate the Nellyses – sorry, the Nelapsis. I gave him a couple of books on bats and leeches; we put Lazarus at the scene of the murder; we even made sure Mr Frey had to come here to bury the corpse so that he would see the bones . . . In one swift move we would get rid of the constable, whom we all hated, bring Helena into our family and also make sure all the bodies in this island were not blamed on us. It was a brilliant plan. My father came up with it, of course.'

'I would rather we had killed Lazarus,' Mr Koloman said,

'but my poor Minerva persuaded me not to.' Mrs Koloman looked away, her face flushed with repressed anger. Her husband went to her and squeezed her shoulder affectionately. 'I understand you, my dear. They're blood of your blood.' He sneered at the Nelapsis. 'To me they've only ever been the most uncomfortable in-laws.'

'But we underestimated Mr Frey's training in medicine,' Natalja went on. 'He probably connected Veronika's symptoms with those of our relatives. He must have read Schultz's papers.'

'Or the writings of Joseph Stokvis . . .' Veronika ventured.

'No, they haven't been translated from the Dutch. And Englishmen seldom bother learning any language other than useless Latin.'

'Very true, Sister.'

'But what really gave us away was the light,' said Natalja. 'We are very careful not to expose ourselves to the sun.'

'And these have been very unusual days,' said Mr Koloman, pointing up at the starry sky. 'I correctly predicted that it would be bloody sunny the afternoon we were supposed to first meet your colleague, so we had to lie and ask him to join us for dinner instead. Today, too, was very bright, which eventually gave my wife and girls away. Mr Frey was very lucky – he might not have ever discovered our secrets had it been raining.'

McGray nodded. 'That's why youse have that soddin' Shadows Room.'

'It is useful on sunny days,' Natalja answered, 'but that is not the main reason. I really am interested in light, and I do want to know why the sun affects us but things like these torches don't. I was attempting to develop a sort of glass that would protect us from daylight. Something we could put up in our windows, and the windows of our carriages.'

Veronika held her sister's hand fondly. 'My clever Nat! You also thought we might come up with something we could use on our skin – like we use make-up – so that one day we might even be able to go out and enjoy ourselves in the sun, like everybody else. I still wonder what Venice looks like in a searing summer!'

'A little far-fetched, that idea,' said Natalja, 'but possible in theory.'

'As you can see, Mr Nine-Nails,' said Mr Koloman, 'unlike this sorry lot we didn't just sit idle, waiting to be saved. Nobody in the land would understand us, so we worked, we studied – we *cured* ourselves.'

McGray chuckled. 'Aye, it's really fuckin' praiseworthy to lurk in the shadows harvesting fresh blood . . .'

'Oh, that is my speciality,' said Dominik. 'That is why Calcraft and I travel all the time. We never kill more than once a year in the same country.'

'Disgusting,' said Miss Fletcher.

'There, there, Millie,' said Mr Koloman. 'When we told you your son would end up like his wretched relatives you were only too keen to bring him here.'

Benjamin looked at his mother, appalled beyond words. '*Is that true?*'

Miss Fletcher shed only a single tear. A fit of distraught weeping, however, could not have shown more sorrow. 'They told me you'd never know . . . That they'd give you the medicine but would never tell you where it came from. I did what I thought was best for you.'

'If it makes things easier for you, my dear Ben,' Dominik went on, 'we look for people like that idiot McEwan, people nobody would ever miss . . . people the world is better without.'

Mrs Nelapsi raised her chin. 'What about my cousin Thomas?'

'Yer cousin?' McGray repeated. 'Father Thomas was yer cousin?'

'Once removed,' she mumbled.

Dominik buttoned up his showy coat as he approached McGray. 'As you very well guessed, Mr Nine-Nails, I paid him a visit the night before you and I first met. I did indeed leave my steamer just offshore and went to Thurso in a small boat – untraceable, impossible to prove *beyond reasonable doubt*, as we would have said in court, if it ever came to that. I even took the precaution of having one of those disgusting bats shipped to me from a Norwegian circus.'

'Why?' Benjamin asked, tears rolling down his face. The horror in his eyes was even worse than when McGray had found him cradling the bleeding neck of the dead priest. 'Why did you do that? He was like my father! What could he have done to you?'

Dominik pulled out his pocket Bible and began rolling up a cigarette. 'Believe me, cousin, I really didn't want to. I slid through his window to tell him you'd be all right, that you'd live a long, healthy life, unlike him.' He turned briefly to McGray. 'The man was forty-eight. Can you believe that?' Then, to Benjamin, 'He told me he intended to write to my mother, also his relative, and I volunteered to take the message. The good priest dictated to me a very, very harsh letter, in which he threatened to expose us – in his very words – as the *monsters* we truly are. He said he would do so if we insisted in luring Benjamin into our – again, his words – *dark arts*.' He chuckled. 'Poor man, he couldn't have been more Christian. I had to get rid of him even before he finished dictating that letter.' He paused as Calcraft lit his cigarette. 'I abhorred having to dispatch him in such a cruel manner, but I could not let him carry out his threats. I hope you understand, cousin. I was thinking of *your* future too.'

Benjamin roared, made to stand up, and when the men behind him grabbed his arms and torso he writhed like a wild animal. Someone had to smack him in the face with a gun, and as he fell face down on the ground Miss Fletcher let out a screech worthy of an eagle. She too had to be restrained, crying her eyes out as she watched her poor son struggling to push himself up.

'Well, we don't want this to drag on, do we?' said Mr Koloman. 'Mr Plantard, I must join my wife in her apologies. I had high hopes for you and my Veronika. If things had gone as planned . . .' He sighed. 'Well, what's the point of discussing that now? We are where we are. But I am not a monster, and you *have* been a proper gentleman, so I'll be kind to you. You shall be the first to die, so that you won't have to witness all of tonight's unavoidable gore.'

Maurice was hardly able to breathe. He was about to burst into tears. 'You are . . . a real gentleman!'

'*And* we shall do it quickly. Believe me, Lazarus and this nine-nailed man will wish I had such consideration for them.'

Mrs Koloman rushed to her husband and whispered in his ear. McGray only just managed to catch her words. 'Spare my sister and the girl, I beg you!'

Mr Koloman simply patted her shoulder and said something McGray could not hear.

One of the men pulled Maurice's arm, but he would have none of it. He rose in one swift, elegant move. 'Leave me my dignity, please.'

His breathing was choked, but he still managed to step

forward with a noble air, his chin high, as he mumbled, 'Christ receive my soul!' again and again.

Boyde and Calcraft guided him to the open barrel and held him in place, pushing his torso forward so that his neck was held right above the cask.

'It was a pleasure to meet you, sir,' said Mr Koloman. Maurice looked him straight in the eyes, halted his prayer but could say no more. Mr Koloman bowed and stepped back. 'Veronika, we need your touch. I don't want him to pass on all frightened like this.'

The girl hesitated for a moment, until her mother and sister gently pushed her.

She went to Maurice, smoothing out the folds of her dress, as if looking for something, and when she stood merely inches from his face she attempted a smile. For once, Veronika looked shy.

She ran her fingers through his dark hair. 'You have beautiful eyes, Mr Plantard. I've been meaning to tell you.'

He gulped, his eyes flickering from one blue pupil to the other. 'Yours . . . yours are the most beautiful I have ever seen.'

The girl finally managed a proper smile, but the gesture was full of sorrow, her lips trembling.

She stretched up to kiss his forehead. It was a long, gentle kiss, and she held his temples with both hands. It was clear she didn't want to let go, and when she did her eyes were misty. Slowly, with utter tenderness, she moved her hands over Maurice's face, caressing his cheekbones, his jaw, running a thumb over his lips.

He could not take his eyes from hers as she cradled his chin and then moved her small, soft hands to the sensitive skin of his neck.

'We would have had a long engagement,' she whispered. 'We would have spent an entire winter in London meeting all your relatives, and then the summer somewhere far north . . . And we'd probably have married . . .' She gulped. '. . . here, on one of the islands. It would have been a lovely midsummer ceremony at dusk. The forest would have been full of candles. And then we would have spent every Christmas in Gloucestershire; you hunting, as you told me you like to do, and I waiting for you at home with a glass of brandy – and a child or two, impatient for Daddy to come and play. Would you not have loved that?'

Maurice could not answer. He was bewitched by the girl's eyes. And it was as well that he did not even try, for Veronika had already cut his jugular open, and his blood was dripping into the cask, a crimson thread of liquid that barely made a sound.

53

A thunderous blast and a ball of fire shook the entire island.

All eyes turned to the light, the pines igniting as the flames rushed upwards. The second blast came from behind the Kolomans, and they all turned, bedazzled and scared. Some of their men were already running away, like ants from a disturbed nest.

Only then did I see my uncle. From where I stood, lurking behind the trees, it looked as if they'd tied a thin ribbon around his neck. It was only the glint in Veronika's hand, reflecting the fire, which made me realize what had just happened. It was a tiny scalpel – and Uncle Maurice was . . .

A monstrous roar filled the air – my own voice, as I charged against them, breaking into the small clearing like a wild beast. Someone grabbed my arm, someone else my leg, but I hurled myself onward so savagely I dragged them both with me. The entire clearing had become a mad skirmish, but I hardly noticed. They all seemed to move so slowly, their shouts reaching my ears only as muffled voices.

Mr Koloman looked at me with distraught eyes, paralysed. I shot directly at his face, but just then a third man grabbed me by the waist and my bullet missed him.

I jerked and struggled, *still* moving forward, and aimed my gun at Calcraft and Boyde. I shot again, catching Calcraft's shoulder, and he roared in pain and let go of my uncle's body. What a horrid sight: Uncle Maurice dropping on to the barrel, nearly knocking it over, and Veronika holding it in place – not before a splash of blood stained her dress red.

'*You bastard!*' I spat in a howl that made my throat sore. Boyde and the twins dragged the cask away, kicking Uncle's body aside to make way.

The third explosion came from one side, exactly where I'd left the jar of gunpowder, and men screamed in terror and ran away – so much for loyalty.

I heard a female roar: Mrs Plunket was running towards me, her mouth wide open, her cleaver glinting as she raised it in the air to strike me. Using all my strength, my muscles burning, I managed to free my hand and turn my gun in her direction. I shot without thinking and hit her chubby hand, blood splashing from her wrist as the blade fell. The woman squealed like a hog.

Mr Koloman was still staring at me in fright; I was still dragging the three men in my frenzy. He put a hand to his breast pocket, perhaps to draw a gun, but then I heard Miss Fletcher shout, 'He's *mine!*' She hurled herself on the man and they both fell to the ground, locked in an unrestrained fist fight.

The men finally managed to bring me down. I fell sideways, my face hitting the ground mere inches from the bonfire. From there I could see Dominik giving Benjamin a mighty beating. I could see no trace of Mrs Nellys and her daughter, or of Mc–

Just as I thought of him, Nine-Nails appeared and began throwing punch after punch at the men who held me.

As I rolled onto my back I caught a glimpse of Uncle's face, his cheek pressed against the floor, his dark blood seeping through the pine needles. His eyes were wide open, as if staring directly at me. Only . . .

There was no expression in them. I realized there was no turning back; I had lost him.

Someone stamped on my wrist, sending stabs of pain through my arm, and I lost grip of my gun. McGray and I punched and kicked in every direction, the image of my poor uncle imprinted in my eyes, and for God knows how long the world became a mess of pain and shouting.

'*Stop!*' a weak voice screamed, but nobody listened. It was Mr Nellys, who might well kill himself with the effort of shouting. He screamed again, and I saw from the corner of my eye that he stood not far from us, his flimsy knees shaking. He had Mrs Koloman's derringer.

He shot once, then again.

'That's my son!' Mr Koloman screeched, and we all came to a standstill.

Dominik, his knee still on Benjamin's chest, was pressing his belly. Blood trickled between his fingers.

'*You . . .*' he hissed, 'you old – with my mother's gun!'

I saw a slim shadow come from behind Mr Nellys, and before he could shoot again Calcraft had clasped him by the wrist. I heard the crack of bones as Calcraft twisted the old man around and punched him in the stomach. The blow threw Mr Nellys backward, just as Benjamin crawled into the darkness on all fours.

Miss Fletcher let go of Mr Koloman, and she too ran from the clearing, surely to go after her son.

'Break the bastard's neck,' Mr Koloman cried, Miss Fletcher's fist marks all over his face, as he moved closer to Dominik.

Calcraft, wounded shoulder and all, opened and closed his fists, readying himself to finish the poor old man off.

Mr Nellys only smiled, his teeth smeared with blood, and

then laughed scornfully as he produced a jar from his breast pocket. And my own lighter.

At once Dominik knew what was about to happen. He tried to crawl away, leaving a trail of blood. 'No –'

Someone tugged at my jacket and dragged me away, for I could not take my eyes from the horror. It took an instant, but I saw what happened in utmost detail: Dominik's body in front of Mr Nellys, then suddenly the explosion lifting him in the air and engulfing the clearing in fire. The blast hit me and for the longest second I felt I was flying, the searing heat burning my eyes and my face, and penetrating through my clothes.

My shoulder hit the ground first and my body rolled. Before I went completely still, before I could even reopen my eyes, I was hauled up again.

'Come on, Frey,' McGray cried, 'ye'll have to row for me.'

He put my arm around his shoulders and darted forward as my feet dragged on the ground, the cool breeze of the night a heavenly gift.

'Where's yer boat?' he asked. He had to repeat it before I could answer.

'South,' I mumbled. 'Little bay, just south . . .'

I vaguely pointed in the right direction, which apparently was enough, for I soon recognized the outline of the boat, lit by the fire that by now engulfed large sections of the island. I heard the voices of men all around us, screaming.

We staggered down to the pebbled shore, and just as I thought McGray would throw me into the boat he plunged us both into the icy waters. That felt more painful than the fire, like a thousand daggers stabbing me all at once. I could not even shout, drawing air in with a noisy gasp. McGray made a very similar sound, closely followed by his worst swearing.

I was about to say something, but then he plunged my entire head into the water.

'Yer hair was on fire!' he said as soon as I re-emerged.

But there was only one thing in my mind. 'My uncle!' I said between frantic pants. 'We . . . we cannot leave him.'

'Frey, if we go back –'

'*I cannot leave him there!*' I howled, wading back to the shore. A monumental pine tree, right in front of me, had caught fire and its entire canopy was ablaze. Hundreds of years old, I thought, yet consumed in an instant.

Right then McGray grabbed my arm. 'I'm *so* sorry, Frey. Really. But we have to go now. This is our best chance to get away . . . If we don't go now, we'll never go.'

I stood there motionless, mesmerized by the fire, my mind simply not functioning. I had just lost Uncle . . . It could not be. Life did not end like that. Life could not, *could not* be so damned fragile.

McGray tugged my arm gently. 'We have to go, Frey. Now.' For a moment I did not move, and he pulled at me again. 'He would have wanted you to live.'

A blazing branch fell from the tree, throwing sparks and ashes all around.

'There has to be something we can do,' I said, attempting to free myself. 'There *has* to be –'

Then I saw a shadow in the distance: a tall figure coming towards us, looking black beneath the burning trees.

'Miss Fletch–' McGray began. Indeed it was her, tottering in our direction.

She had my uncle in her arms. I tried to run to her but McGray held me firmly in place, and I felt my first tear run down my cheek.

'I am sorry, sir,' she said, not stopping but going straight to the boat, where she deposited my lifeless uncle with the greatest care. She had covered his face with a cloth, and I shuddered at the thought of his charred skin. Miss Fletcher picked up an oar and offered it to me. 'Now go!'

She was a woman of few words, but her expression told me everything I needed to know. There was such sorrow, such guilt in her eyes.

McGray had to pull me in her direction, take the oar and put it in my hand.

'I need ye to row. I'll look after Maurice.'

I had no will left to argue, and was barely conscious of McGray and Miss Fletcher helping me into the boat. My eyes were fixed on my dead uncle.

'D'ye have somewhere to go?' McGray asked her.

'Yes. My son is waiting for me on the east shore. We still have to retrieve the book; we left it in the cave.'

'The book I saw Lazarus –'

'Yes, sir. Benjamin thinks it contains the recipe for the serum.'

'Will youse –'

'*Go!*' Miss Fletcher barked. 'I'm losing precious time too.' She cast me a tortured look. 'I only brought your uncle because – well, I've done enough harm already.'

'We cannae –'

'*Go, dammit!*'

And she pushed McGray against the boat, turned on her heel and darted away, her powerful legs sending out huge splashes of water.

McGray jumped in, the boat swaying dangerously, and he had to grasp both gunwales. '*Fuck*, how I hate sailing!'

It took all his determination to bend down, pick up Uncle's torso and cradle him on his lap. McGray placed a gentle hand on the cloth, carefully keeping it on Uncle's face.

He nodded at me. 'I'll look after him. Let's go.'

I took hold of the oars and rowed, barely conscious of my burning joints, the prickling on my skin and my tear-filled eyes.

We heard another couple of gunshots, brought by the cool breeze, and saw a handful of torches dotted all across Loch Maree: men fleeing in their boats, too busy saving their own skins to pay attention to us.

Rory Island gradually dwarfed in the distance, a roaring beacon against the blue immensity of the night. As I rowed, I watched how the fire rose, swirling from the towering pines, as if hell itself were erupting through the dark loch.

Avoid this place like the poison of a snake.
Distrust even its rose shrubs, lush and divine,
with beautiful flowers but a thorny vine,
for their scent announces death and doom and ache.

And you're not a soul I'll easily forsake.
If you lose your path you'll see my candle shine;
I'll share with you my meal, my bread and my wine
and you'll forget the warning my verses make:

Though I'll seem to play an angel's mandolin,
with a voice as tender as a summer bud;
though I'll give you my best songs to make you grin,

I will sour your lips with vinegar and mud
and before you discover my deadly sin
I'll make you quench my thirst with your warm blood.

Attributed to Konrad Koloman

Epilogue

I studied myself in the mirror before I put on my shirt.

My neck and arms were still black and purple, and my face was speckled with marks from the last fire. Joan, my former housekeeper, had brought me a homemade unguent, and though it stank of camphor and old potatoes it had really helped my scalds and blisters. Still, I knew I would have yet another set of scars to show. I wondered what Uncle Maurice would have thought of that.

The arrangements for his funeral had been, fortunately, dealt with swiftly. Layton, my stiff valet, who had served my uncle for more than ten years before working for me, shed genuine tears when I gave him the news. He insisted on handling the entire affair by himself, and I was only too happy to oblige him. Uncle would be buried at the Plantard shrine in Gloucestershire, next to my mother and grandparents. Just as he had wanted.

My brother Elgie was already on his way there. He'd sent me the most affected letter, the ink smudged with his tears, his handwriting quivery. I could not wait to see him, for the rest of the Frey family appeared to be treating the tragedy with remarkable indifference. Father had replied a day after Elgie, telling me that my odious stepmother had a cold and could not travel at the moment. My two other brothers had not even sent a word.

I sighed as I adjusted my tie. This would be the first time I had stepped out of the house in four days; I had hidden indoors, pretexting that my body needed to recover.

It was not entirely a lie – I had pulled muscles I'd not even known existed, and only last night had I finally been able to lift a full glass of wine. After our escape I had rowed perhaps five miles east before we stopped – not because we deemed it safe but because I could endure no more. I took the boat to a small beach on the north shore, its light sand almost glowing in the night. We had crouched in the semi-darkness as I caught my breath, but the very early sunrise meant we had to keep moving.

McGray summoned up strength and helped me row from there. We reached the eastern end of Loch Maree, which then gave way to a meandering river. We were tempted to look for help there, but we had no idea how far the influence of the Kolomans would extend. We kept on moving at a sluggish pace until the sun was high in the sky. McGray then left me to look for help on foot. I told him he was mad to think we'd find a soul, but he went away nonetheless and a couple of hours later came back on a cart driven by a gentle farmer. I could not understand a single word the man uttered, but he was our saviour. He fed us, let us rest in his little house, and even put some of his clean clothes on Uncle Maurice. Ironic how the humblest of people are also the most generous.

He then took us to a 'nearby village' called Garve (it was by no means near, and to call it a village was a gross overstatement). Our journey back to civilization was much smoother from then on.

Indeed, my body still ached, and I wanted my blisters to subside a little before showing my face in public – but the truth is I had not gone out simply because I did not want to see or speak to anybody.

I am no stranger to death. My mother's passing taught me very early, very clearly, that our days are finite. Nevertheless, we always seem to forget it. Uncle Maurice, always cheerful, always carefree . . . how could anybody expect someone like him to die? To him tragedies were tiresome; tribulations were strictly reserved for others. Then again, that very philosophy had also been the root of his worst mistakes.

I walked away from the mirror, feeling terrible for blaming my dear uncle for his own demise . . . but he had been so wrong about Veronika and the Kolomans, letting them lure him with their charm and their pleasantries. He had conducted himself with the self-confidence and recklessness that is possible only in men who have nothing to look after. He had been hedonistic and vain, and had probably never quite understood the darker mechanics of life. He'd only come to grasp that a mere day before his death. The story about his dead child – I could still not come to terms with that. Indeed, Uncle Maurice had been so wrong about so many things . . . but I had loved him so much nonetheless.

He was – still is – dearer to me than my own father, who is as cold and lifeless as a teaspoon dropped in the snow. He was dearer to me than my own brothers, my only beloved relative until Elgie was born.

I put on my jacket, recalling Uncle Maurice himself had suggested I wore that cut and colour. That had been just over a year ago, yet the memory seemed so trivial, so distant now. As I stepped out of the house I remembered how delighted he'd been when I finally gave in and let him take me to the tailor. And he had ended up commissioning another three jackets for himself.

I smiled. He'd led a good, lucky life. He had enjoyed his

time, and he had made me and so many others very happy. I should be grateful for it.

As soon as I stepped into our basement office I felt the urge to retreat. The sight of McGray's cluttered artefacts, the smell – a mixture of old books and damp, the many articles still where I'd last left them . . . they all reminded me of what life had been merely two weeks ago. It was a sensation more than a memory per se. I took a deep breath. How could things change so dramatically in such a short period of time?

I ignored the clutter and went to my desk, which I found loaded with correspondence and pending documents.

We had told everyone in the police about the Kolomans' case and constables had been dispatched to investigate, but I still needed to file a comprehensive report, whose weight I could already feel. I had to detail the location and contents of the Kolomans' manor, where the constable's body had been buried, how we'd been led to believe Lazarus Nelapsi had committed the crime . . . I also realized I'd have to write a short description of the families' ailment. And I'd have to telegram my old friends in Oxford, who might be able to send me those old papers by Dr Schultz.

I saw McGray had left me a note. Apparently he had been in touch with Constable McLachlan, who was still investigating the death of Father Thomas in Thurso. The man had sent telegram after telegram to Poolewe giving updates of his progress, but these, unsurprisingly, had never reached us.

There was a report from the team of constables who had had to force their way into the manor, for all the entrances had been locked. They'd found very little, mostly discarded books (novels, that is), old clothes and the sort of bric-a-brac one would leave behind in a hasty move. No trace of any chemicals, scientific instruments, medical literature, documents such as property deeds or birth certificates, valuables, works of art ... even some of the plants had been uprooted, leaving but huge holes throughout the gardens. The Kolomans had acted swiftly, and if they had a tenth of the brains I thought they did, they'd never set foot in Britain again. A thorough investigation on the Continent, particularly around the Moravia region, where they said they had their vineyards, could be instigated, but such an enterprise might take years and vast resources and still not reach any conclusions. Besides, with the police force still lacking a leader, the whole affair did not seem to be anybody's priority.

McGray found me lounging in my chair, pondering all this. He also looked terrible – even worse than usual, with the back of his neck still blistered.

'Ye didnae have to come in today, I told ye.'

I sat up. 'I had to leave the house at some point.' I picked a letter from the pile of unread correspondence on my desk. 'That chap Stoker wrote again.'

McGray shoved the envelope in his pocket. 'Aye, he's becoming a nuisance. I see ye've read my notes.'

I shook my head. 'It is pretty much what I expected. Did they question the villagers?'

'Aye. Nobody wanted to tell a thing. They all said they'd had naught to do with the family, that they rarely came out to mingle with the paupers.'

'That could easily be proven false. Even if they were not aware of the Kolomans' dark deeds, I'd say all of them would have heard enough that night at the island.'

'Indeedy, but even if ye and me went back there and managed to find all the damned sods involved, we'd probably end up arresting two entire bloody villages, and I don't think that's goin' to happen right now.'

I sat back, interlacing my fingers. 'Indeed. I . . . I have been wondering . . . Who do you think survived? The constables found no corpses. Other than the piles of old bones, that is.'

Nine-Nails sat on his desk and lighted up a cigar. 'Who kens? I think we can safely assume that Dominik and Silas were blown to smithereens. Everyone else is in doubt.'

'The twins and Mrs Koloman were the first ones to disappear.'

McGray was kind enough not to joke about the girls. 'Aye. And Miss Fletcher said she was going with Benjamin.' He puffed at his cigar. 'I saw the book she talked about. A michty hefty tome, Frey, and it was crammed with hand-writing.'

I took a deep breath. 'Do you think the Nelapsis, if they survived, might . . . adopt the Kolomans' treatment?'

'Cannae tell. I'm not even sure they'd be able to make sense of it. Kind though they were, the Nelapsis were nae precisely highly literate.'

'True,' I said. 'Do you think the Kolomans will be able to continue? Having lost their book?'

McGray arched an eyebrow. 'I hadnae thought o' that. They might know the procedure by heart . . . then again . . .' He sighed. 'Nae use wondering now, is there?'

'No,' I mumbled. 'No use indeed.'

I remained silent for a good while, unaware of my sombreness until McGray spoke.

'I'm very sorry, Frey.'

I bit my lip. This was one of the reasons that had kept me at home. I did not want commiseration; I did not want to have to reassure people I was doing *all right*.

'Thank you,' I said. 'I know you are.' I broke the silence before McGray could say any more. 'I have been thinking of this disease. I read the study about it a while ago. Here is something you might be interested to hear.'

McGray leaned forward, biting his cigar and grasping his knees. 'Tell me.'

'I remember only the generalities, but this man, J. H. Schultz, described a patient who had fits of pain, skin sensitivity, an enlarged spleen and reddish urine. The man eventually lost his mind. Schultz called his ailment *pempigus leprosus*.'

'I doubt that name's the important bit,' said McGray.

'Well, Schultz suggested that the madness was not really a physical symptom, that it is the constant strain of the pain and seizures that disturbs the patients' minds. And if Mr Nelapsi found some physical relief from that blood serum, if his fits and pains became less frequent, it makes sense that his mind would improve. The waters might have had nothing to do with his recovery.'

McGray nodded. His answer was far too predictable. 'Aye. Ye said *might*.'

I sighed and looked away. I had no patience to argue, but this time I understood him like never before. What would I be willing to do, or believe, if I thought there was even a slight chance of bringing Uncle Maurice back?

'I sent a vial o' those waters to Doctor Clouston,' McGray admitted.

'You did what?'

'I collected a wee vial when I went to Isle Maree. I thought it'd be better if I didnae tell ye.'

I sighed again. 'McGray, if you believe in those legends, you should also believe that there was a curse on anyone who took *anything* off that island.'

'Aye, I ken. Too late. Clouston has it now, with my specific instructions to post it to Pansy as soon as he can. He should send me a report soon enough.'

I attempted to say something encouraging, but no words came out.

McGray put both hands on the desk, his missing finger somehow more noticeable than ever, and pushed himself up. He knew what I thought and, just like me, he had no energy left to argue, so he simply made his way to the door.

What I said next came out of nowhere, as if somebody else had put the words in my mouth.

'McGray, if you are not otherwise engaged, would you care to join me at Great King Street for a measure of whisky?'

He halted, turned very slowly and looked at me sternly. 'Frey, I ken yer hurting, but ye sound like yer losing yer mind.'

I smirked. 'No, that will be the day I offer you a glass of Bordeaux and expect you to appreciate it. In fact, it is your own bloody whisky I will be serving.'

'Och, aye! That ill-gotten whisky ye tricked out o' me!'

'Tricked? It was won most fairly. In fact, you should still be supplying me bottles, and you know it! But I should not expect any better; the bloody Scotches have no word, just like my father has always said . . .'

'All right, all right, I'll come to yer house and drink my

own bloody whisky. But only if ye promise ye won't talk too much. Ye ken I hate yer Soothron accent.'

Cassandra Smith, head nurse, brought a stack of files back to the superintendent's office, her back aching. It was nearly eleven, according to her little pocket watch, and the corridor windows showed that the skies were as dark as they could go.

She knocked, the good doctor answered promptly and she stepped in.

Dr Clouston was still seated at his desk, the fire behind him the only source of light. And he was still staring at the little sample.

'You've not turned your lamp on,' Cassandra said, leaving the files on the desk. 'Shall I do it for you?'

Clouston was lost in thought. It took him a moment to answer. 'No, no, Miss Smith. I was about to go home.'

Cassandra saw Mr McGray's letter on the desk, exactly where she'd seen it two hours ago. She interlaced her fingers and approached slowly. The vial caught a glimmer from the hearth, the ounce of spring water as clear as the purest glass.

She had to ask the question now.

'Have you . . . have you decided?'

Dr Clouston massaged his temples. 'Yes, I have. I am simply gathering the courage.'

Cassandra went to the threshold, made sure the hallway was deserted and shut the door. By the time she turned back Dr Clouston had already opened the vial, and before his determination waned again he poured its contents into the fire.

The flames flickered and the water hissed as it became nothing but vapour.

Clouston threw the vial into the hearth too, then turned away and buried his face in his trembling hands. Cassandra came over and, confident nobody was looking, placed a comforting hand on the doctor's shoulder.

'You're only doing what you must.'

He took a deep breath.

'I know. May God forgive me.'

Author's Note

The plot of this book relies on a physical impossibility: that in the 1880s the north of Scotland could see two sunny days within a single week. Everything else is based on strict scientific fact (and no, I am *not* going to tell you how to make explosives from guano).

Acute porphyrias are a group of rare genetic disorders, the sufferers of which produce abnormally high amounts of porphyrins, precursors of haemoglobin. The symptoms vary widely depending on the type of porphyria, but photosensitivity and attacks of acute abdominal pain are the most common. Madness, as mentioned by Frey, can occur in severe cases (George III is rumoured to have had the disease); however, this is triggered not by the porphyrin imbalance itself but by the anxiety and depression that the ailment can cause. The most severe varieties of porphyria, though very rare, can lead to harrowing manifestations like loss of hair, nails and ears, and eye abnormalities.

Because of these unique effects, porphyria sufferers have been unjustly associated with vampires in recent times. However, the only (somewhat) shared symptom between vampires and porphyria patients is photosensitivity, and this does not even feature in the original folklore tales. Bram Stoker was one of the first authors to state that vampires could be killed by sunlight, and the first one to mention them turning into bats. *Dracula* would not be published until 1897.

Treatment for porphyria is now available. Patients experiencing seizures are injected with human heme, the iron-containing part of the haemoglobin molecule, which stabilizes the blood through inhumanly complicated biochemistry I do not need to go into here.

The full process for heme synthesis remains proprietary knowledge; however, I can tell you that plenty of the medical research has relied on isolating heme from the blood of healthy human donors. This treatment was, of course, not known in Victorian times, and they would not have had the means to produce complex synthetic proteins. On the other hand, they *would* have been able to isolate heme from fresh human blood, and the method would have been surprisingly uncomplicated. It would be unethical to give away such a recipe, so I only kept in the first steps: isolating haemoglobin with a centrifuge (which Boyde is seen doing in the kitchen) and maintaining the blood liquid.

The anti-clotting properties of leeches and bat saliva have been known for centuries. Sodium citrate, despite the simplicity of its synthesis (it really can be made out of lemon juice and caustic soda), was not successfully applied as an anticoagulant until 1914 in Belgium. It is still used nowadays in blood banks and laboratories.

Light diffraction has been used to identify proteins since the mid nineteenth century, even if the mechanics behind it were poorly understood. Crystallization of proteins is an even older practice.

The rapid degradation of human heme into toxic compounds, mentioned in the story, was a real challenge, and it limited the efficiency of the treatment for many years (about half the heme decomposes as soon as it is dissolved with traditional methods, which would account for the high doses needed by Veronika). These issues have been addressed in recent decades and treatment with human heme is now safe. The medicament now has a much longer shelf life too.

I want to stress the fact that porphyrias are serious, painful disorders, often misdiagnosed even today, and I raise my glass to all the men and women who have worked for decades to make the treatment widely available.